THE SHARDS OF ETHERIOUS: ARISEN

COLIN J.D. CROOKS

Cover Art by DANIEL SCHMELLING

Edited by HOT TREE EDITING

Edited by HANNAH SULLIVAN

Proofreading by SHEILA L. HUTCHISON

Map by HANNAH RODGERS

COLIN J D CROOKS

For Sarah.
You are my dreams come true.

LYRIA

DUN
SKALL'VAN

DUN
JORGHEIM

OPPENFAULD

DUN
KARTHA

DUN
UNGOLITH

FALDARIS

SOVEREIGN GUARD
MOUNTAINS

DUN
OTHUND

DUN
AVARD

GLEN
CLEALEN

RAIDER'S
WATCH

DUN
AL'VERAN

DUN
ROTH'EIM

CRANN BRAGH

MOTHER TREE

MOTHER'S
VALE

ELLODRIN

N

W   E

S

ETHERIOUS
WORLD MAP

WYRMSBANE

LUN'OVAN

WYRM'S
WASTE

MIROVEAN
GREAT LAKE

ILLUVAND

MIR'EVE

FEENDVALL

CAR'UK
VOLL

PLAINS OF
FANGMAR

VAL'UND VALE

AL'VERAN

I RAISED A FIST. The tromp of boots and the clatter of weapons fell silent. I dismounted and stepped to the edge of the Willows Bridge. On the other side of the great river Al'veran sat the garden city of Ellodrin. It flickered with a fae light despite the early hour. The city was nestled under the great boughs of the Mother Tree and forever within her shadow. So the goddess had cultivated bio-luminescence into every leaf and flower. A blue-green light followed the citizens as they went about their lives, and from this vantage, the city looked as if one of the transcendent gods had reached into the night sky and stirred the stars. Five hundred thousand souls, and if all went according to plan, every last one of them would be dead by nightfall.

My gaze followed the trunk of the Mother Tree and up to her branches. They extended over the city and vanished over the horizon. Her immensity always made me feel insignificant. I hated it.

The exhilaration of imminent battle coursed through my veins. I couldn't let anticipation give me away. Decades of planning rested on the next few hours. Pulling in a breath, I took hold of my nerves.

Light blossomed a few hundred yards down the bridge as the Spriggan delegation made their way to greet us.

I turned and paced before my acolytes, examining their ranks. They stood at attention, heads held high, lacquered armor gleaming in the torchlight. These men and women were the best of the best, each of them a weapon, their hearts burning with true zeal.

"I will do everything in my power to prevent the contingency plan," I lied. "But should I fail, you know your orders. And should Strothheim beckon you to her walls, know I join you before the day is through." Fist to chest, I saluted.

A single uniform beat of gauntlet on breastplate replied. No rousing cheer, no voices raised in gladness at the glory to come. Just hard faces set to a grim purpose, the Fauldic way.

I made the sign of the sword, a blue tracer following my fingers. It hung in the air, pulsing with Khyber's radiance. His blessing washed over them, and conviction reflected in their faces. "Though shield shatter and blade lay broken."

"I will fight on," they responded with the ritual words.

"Though blade pierce me and I gasp my dying breath."

"I will fight on."

"For I am the blade in his hand, the shield that guards his realm." The emotion of the moment stuck in my throat. "And so long as one of us remains."

"This blade is not yet broken."

"Stand sure, my brothers and sisters."

"Stand sure."

"Avatar Wrath," said a snide voice from behind me.

"Chancellor Talmor'ook." I faced him, sweeping my cape out behind and giving the smallest bow propriety allowed. "Permission to enter the city."

His amber eyes scanned my acolytes. "The Mother Tree welcomes you to her sacred grove. But tell me, why have you brought so many warriors to a council meeting?"

I thrust a finger at the fool. "You reported arachnids encroaching from the south. They must be driven back before they can establish a colony."

"We sent an ambassador."

I shook my head in disbelief. "Then they're already dead."

"They will be reunited with the Mother Tree."

"Not if Eericas claims their soul."

"The arachnids are sentient beings and must be given the chance to break from Eericas's domination. All life upon Etherious, no matter how wretched"—the corners of his mouth curled into an almost imperceptible sneer as he eyed me—"can find redemption through the grace of the Mother Tree."

"You have a responsibility to protect your allies."

"We do. We just don't reach for steel as a first reaction."

As I gripped the pommel of my sword, the metal protested. I carefully relaxed before my augmented strength could deform it. *Patience.* "As you say." I bowed once more.

"Humility? It seems the years have taught you temperance."

A soldier shifted behind me. I raised a finger and they went still. "And they've made you complacent, but let's put these old arguments aside for the time. There are matters of state to discuss."

Chancellor Talmor'ook drew a complex rune in the air. The symbol of the Mother Tree blossomed as vibrant as a bouquet. "Your men may not enter the city so armed."

"I require but a single squad. The rest have orders to scout the causeways."

"The Mother Tree won't allow soldiers to traverse her boughs until diplomacy has failed."

My stomach clenched. "What about the judges? They carry no weapon but their faith. Allow them to inspect the outposts, maintain the imbued looking glasses."

Violet light pulsed from the rune. "The Mother agrees. Your judges may traverse her boughs." Chancellor Talmor'ook spread his arms, the petals of his skin sliding with the motion to reveal others beneath. His attendants bowed deeply, and the air filled with a blend of aromatic scents. Disgusting ritual, like being sprayed by a cat. No matter what their excretions smelled like, cinnamon, rose and half a hundred other things. Bloody vulgar.

"Vanyard," I said. A grizzled veteran strode from the ranks and took the reins of my charger. "Give the order."

"Fourth squad. Judges. Extinguish torches," Vanyard bellowed. "Forward march."

I fell in beside Chancellor Talmor'ook, and the curtain of vines serving as a gate parted of their own accord. We walked in silence, save for the hollow ring of steel-shod boots on the deck of the bridge. The length of it was a single piece of living hard wood, which glimmered with a luster no human varnish could match.

I'd once nearly lost myself in the alien beauty of this place. Even now, it threatened to cast a spell on my heart. So I soaked it in, felt the anxiety, the guilt and the awe — for nowhere else on Etherious had life such as the Spriggans been created. And owning my actions was the only form of penance I could offer these people.

On one of the many terraces growing from the side of the bridge, a family played on a soft lawn. The eldest turned to watch us. She reminded me of the belladonna flower, her head a dusky violet and a melancholy expression on her face. She returned to peering over the rail, her blue-black eyes tracking the churning water of the Al'veran fathoms below.

"You are awfully quiet. Not going to try to sway my vote?"

"We both know there's no point."

Chancellor Talmor'ook chuckled and turned that snide smile to me. "Then why call this meeting at all?"

"Because Oppenfauld has an obligation to warn her allies of the threat the Myi'eshans pose, even if you will turn a blind eye until it's too late."

Talmor'ook made a sound like wind rustling dried leaves, and a spicy scent filled the air. The human equivalent of a sigh. "I thought it would be something like that. Why must you always look for trouble? If you'd only give yourself permission, your life could be filled with joy."

"All of this"—I gestured to Ellodrin.—"the peace, the safety, it's an illusion. One that the Fauldic have paid for with blood and sorrow."

Talmor'ook's calm and measured response was blatantly false. "For millennia our lords have stood united and repelled all that would bring the Ascendancy War to our lands. We all sacrifice to keep our masters from harm's way, so why can't you leave well enough alone? Your predecessor was never like this."

"During his reign we saw three wars, all of which were fought on allied soil. For someone that is so long lived, how can you be so shortsighted?"

Beyond the bridge, the streets were clogged with Spriggans. Music and cheering finally overcame the roar of the great river. A fanfare, gathered to welcome their Mother's allies. Gods, how I hated this nonsense.

Talmor'ook stopped a few hundred feet away from the end of the bridge. I was forced to halt or look like a child throwing a fit. He smiled at me benevolently, his every line radiating the elder offering wisdom. It was a spectacle for the people and one he'd used to humiliate me before.

His voice was just loud enough to carry. "The Mother Tree's grace is undaunted by the intent of others. She created us." Talmor'ook opened his arms as if to embrace me. "To be her hand, extended in peace and love to all those with the bravery to take it." He held his hand out to me.

The last time he did this, I'd slapped it away, but I couldn't afford the luxury of honesty. I'd have to be the politician, no matter how much it stung. I released the visor on my helm. It decompressed with a hiss, and the metal lost its transparency.

I slid the faceplate up and raised my voice. "We, the people of the sword and shield, have gladly born the weight of peace." I threw all the earnestness I could into the speech. "We raise our shields in defense of the Mother's grace. Our swords are only used to protect the ones we love. Now and always the Fauldic will take your hand. We may have our differences, but we share a common purpose and that unites us as one people."

A cheer went up from the gathered Spriggans, and the acolytes hammered gauntlets against shields. I screwed on my best smile, took the chancellor's hand. He hid his surprise well, didn't want to lose face in front of his congregation. But I could see the resentment behind those inhuman eyes at having his barb turned against him.

He plastered over it with chaste gratitude and drew me into an embrace. It churned my stomach to acid, but I kept up the charade. I raised our joined hands to the sky, and the peasants roared.

As mindless as the common dirt-grubbing filth back home. Least they were human, or as close to it as any farmer got. My face cramped, and thankfully Talmor'ook was as eager as I was to pull away.

The chancellor drew the Mother's sign, blessing me and my men. I felt the taint of a goddess not my own settle upon my skin. I bowed my head, accepting the insult. He was pushing for a reaction, something to make me lose face. I waved like one of those foolish Mirvish hymnals after a performance and set off down the bridge. The chancellor quickened his pace and caught up.

"The years truly have taught you temperance," he said under his breath.

"Thank you." I smiled, and the contempt I felt for this fool must have shown, for the seam down the middle of his body began peeling back. He recovered quickly, hiding his nervous anger by turning to a Spriggan woman standing near the edge of the bridge. She proffered her squalling sapling, and the chancellor performed a benediction.

Damnation, I'd made him suspicious. Acted too out of character. Nothing to be done about it now.

I leaned over to Vanyard. "Have the judges sanctify each other. I want them cleansed before they reach the stair."

He snapped a salute. "Yes, Avatar, and thank you, sir."

"For what, Sergeant?"

"For trying, sir. It means a lot to the men."

I looked him in the eye and nodded solemnly. "Stand sure."

"Stand sure." Vanyard muttered my orders to the men, and more tactfully than I would have.

The judges filed off the bridge and past the fanfare, following the southern road that skirted the city. It was obvious to me how they labored under the weight of their pack, the straps pulling at their shoulders more than just replacement lenses and tool kits could account for. I tore my eyes away, certain that someone would notice how hard I was looking at them.

I drew the sign of the sword, and calm focus washed through me, all hint of frayed nerves gone. I smiled and took my place beside the chancellor.

THE PARADE WAS the usual affair: pretty lights, the locals making inane noises at the people who mattered. I raised my hand. Chancellor Talmor'ook waved, and the citizens cheered. Performers cartwheeled and backflipped. They stood on each other's shoulders and made starburst patterns with their bodies while a single Spriggan held the lot of them. Gods, how these people loved to rub their physical prowess in human faces.

The Mother Tree made less than subtle displays of her power. Flowers bloomed in a moment or turned to face us as we passed. Some shot seed pods into the air and exploded with a shower of bioluminescent pollen, which sparkled like dying embers. The civilians stared in fascination, strange for a people who had such a visceral aversion to flame.

Four times we passed a street that would have taken us to the parliament buildings. Every time, I felt Chancellor Talmor'ook self-satisfaction rise. I fixed my smile in place and waved all the harder. The son of a goat all but purred.

The buildings gave way to an open meadow surrounding an irregularly shaped lake. People of every race within the alliance milled about, drinking and laughing. Most were Spriggans. As a species they were as vibrant as a bouquet, making the blandness of the other races stand out.

Perhaps one out of every two hundred was human. Mirvish predominantly, the garish fools strutting like peacocks. Instruments in hand, vomiting out melodies of the common folk, heedless of how the lot of them combined into a discordant jumble. A few White Flame missionaries strolled about, shawls hiding all but their faces and an air of chased penitence about them.

A pack of Norven clustered on one of the lake's miniature islands. They'd positioned themselves in a defensive ring around their chieftain and had cordoned off half the island. A hymnal strolled off the bridge and wandered too close. One of the Norven lunged forward, all but goring the man on the horns of his war mask. The minstrel fell on his ass and vanished from sight. The Norven came on, brandishing his double-bladed war axe and thumping his chest. The hymnal reappeared and scurried back the way he'd come.

A hearty laugh drew my attention to a willow that had draped itself over the water. It took me a moment to spot the Ivory Elf. The browns and greens of his attire blended well with the foliage. He lifted his hood over knife-long ears that rose from silver hair to reveal a face the color and texture of aged bone. The elf watched the hymnal push his way through the crowd; then, without looking, he hooked his legs around a branch, tipped upside down out of the tree and scooped a drink from a passing server. As easily as walking a flight of stairs, the elf righted himself and lazed back, sipping his beverage.

"Is this necessary?" I gestured to the gathering.

"You have somewhere to be?" Chancellor Talmor'ook smirked.

"The matter I bring before the council is time sensitive," I said.

"It can keep a few hours. It took you a week to get here. Besides, if we hurry Sylvie away before she's refreshed herself, she'll only make things drag on."

"That's what we've come to? Lubricating each other just to get things done?"

"It's politics." Chancellor Talmor'ook laughed. "Take some time to enjoy the company of your peers."

"Amid the sea of peasants?"

A servant came by with a tray of drinks—fluted flowers brimming with a bubbling liquid. I scooped up the closest. Chancellor Talmor'ook did the same. "All people are equal," he said before melting into the crowd.

I turned to Vanyard. "Go to the council chamber and get the lay of the land. I don't want any surprises."

"At once, Avatar." Vanyard saluted.

"What a magnificent beast," a sultry voice said from behind. "Look at those lines. Excellent hocks."

"Hello, Sylvie."

"Rodrick Corwyn." Sylvie smiled impishly. Always a handsome woman, the years had been kind, but they'd robbed her of some inner light. It seemed she tried to compensate with her elegant navy-blue gown and jewelry. Necklace, hairnet, rings and a belt all silver and pearls. "You really must let me bring a mare or two for breeding." She stepped in, extending a hand for the horse to sniff.

The charger pinned back his ears, curling his lips away from his teeth.

"Careful, priestess," Vanyard said. "He'll nip off your fingers."

"Oh my." Sylvie retracted her hand and stepped into my shadow. "You only have to look at him to see he'd be a champion jumper. I'll have my staff send to Faldaris and make the arrangements. Enris will be so pleased. What's his name?"

"I don't name my tools," I said.

Sylvie pressed her lips into a line. Vanyard gave a stiff bow and led the horse away. The Spriggans shied from the pair like rabbits would from wolves.

"You're sporting new armor." Sylvie traced the outer rim of a pectoral muscle. "I recall a very impassioned speech the last time I asked you to remove your helm. All about an Avatar's sacred armor. How did you put it?" She touched a mocking finger to her lips. "Oh yes, your soul crafted in steel. So what, you just cast the old one aside? Or do you shed your soul like a snake does its skin?"

"Khyber forged it for the coming age. Who am I to deny his will?"

"The coming age. Very ominous." She gave a little giggle. "You sound as if the sundering is tomorrow."

I chuckled, a genuine smile blooming on my face. Excellent. I knew I could count on her to disregard anything I brought to the table. She froze, the glass's soft petals brushing her lips, a look on her face as if she'd just realized her best friend was an Arisen.

"Maybe not tomorrow but within a generation or four. However, the Ascendancy War is what brings me."

"Let them come. There isn't a demon or Ascendant that can break our combined might."

"Combined might?" I met her eye. At least she had the grace to turn away. "Does Enris share your faith in our unassailable strength?" I asked.

She recovered by taking a drink. "My lady flourishes in

times of peace. Her influence is spreading and has been for some time. She has the bit in her teeth, so to say. I advise as much as any mortal can, but words of caution are not well received."

"I see." I gestured to the various hymnals wondering about the event. "She can't expect to convert any of the Spriggans."

"Nay, though a few of the White Flames followers might be swayed."

"Seduced, more like it." My gut twisted in revulsion, and her impish smile returned.

"I don't see Anastasia." She took a step closer and rested a hand on my forearm, the motion exaggerating her cleavage.

"I am here as Avatar. Bringing the shrew would be inappropriate."

Sylvie purred, "I'm holding mass this evening. Perhaps after?" Her fingers explored the contours of my breastplate.

I gripped her wrist just hard enough to elicit a gasp of painful pleasure. "Perhaps," I growled.

She bit her lip and batted her eyelashes. Lust and contempt welled within me, and I forced her to take a step back.

"I preferred the old set. Not as showy." She curtsied. "Avatar Wrath."

"High Priestess." I bowed as she swept her dress out behind her, making for the closest server with a drink tray.

I gazed over the crowd. The mention of my wife brought her pinched, angry face to mind. I dispelled the image and found myself idly fingering my belt pouch, eyes fixed on Chieftain Volovodov. I chided myself for my carelessness. Do that too often and Talmor'ook would notice. He'd sense the mordrem blossom, and there'd be no denying I had ill intentions. I subtly checked the vial—still there. I gripped my pommel and took a sip from my drink.

Bubbles assaulted me, salty, with the tang of minerals. Spriggans, those non-humans, had revolting tastes. Probably spiked with euphorics. I looked about, but Vanyard had gone. Pity. The whiskey in my saddlebags would have gone down nicely... if it hadn't been poisoned.

My eyes drifted back to the Norvish chieftain. With all the people about, this was my best chance to get to him. I wove through the crowd. These Spriggans didn't know their place. Commoners milling about at a function of state. Bloody disgraceful, another layer of insult engineered by Talmor'ook.

A hymnal was blurting out some fisherman's lament. He pumped the bellows on an accordion. The whole affair sounded more like murdering a donkey than music.

"Put me out of my misery," said a voice from above. The elf lounged in the tree, his all-black eyes narrowed against the musical assault.

"Give me a dark alley, and I'll teach him to sing."

The elf grunted. "A generous offer, though it'd be more fun to show him the view from atop Wyrm's Bane." The elf mimed someone jumping off a cliff with a hand, quietly screaming down a long drop with a sudden silence.

"That's a performance I'd pay to see."

"You and me both." He sat up, swung his legs over the edge. "I don't believe we've met. Gilundan of Illuvand, Glyodrin's newly appointed ambassador."

I took the proffered hand. "Avatar Wrath, high priest of Kydaism. Tell me, Gilundan, how fairs the Wyrm's Bane?"

"Cut right to the quick, don't you." He jumped down from the branches, landing without spilling a drop. "On the record or off?"

"I've read the official reports. I want to know what's not being said."

Gilundan lowered his voice so it wouldn't carry over the accordion. "Wyrm's tactics have changed."

"Disturbing. Has he done that before?" I asked.

"Not since Glyodrin created the great wall."

"But before that?"

Gilundan's eyes got a faraway look. "We both know the answer."

I'd read the history of the meteor fall, yet this elf clearly remembered it firsthand. "So what changed?"

"All we have are assumptions. The Wyrm spawn are coming in waves, and it takes every hand that can hold a bow to keep them back, even down to our younglings." Gilundan polished off his drink. "We're seeing more humanoids, which means Wyrm has conquered somewhere in the Far East. Also the spore count is up. Our sanctification protocols are holding... for now. However, we're pushed to capacity, and it has affected export in everything from lumber to fabric to fruit. Between you and me, it hasn't been this bad for thirty years."

"And the scorpions Khyber sent?"

"Powerful but ineffective. They take too long to reload."

"Even with the new crank?"

"They take three to operate, and that many could bring down two dozen in the time it takes to get off a single shot."

"Damn, and Glyodrin still won't accept reinforcements."

Gilundan's expressionless face managed to give me a wry twist. "Forgive me, Avatar, but what did you expect after the way Khyber reacted to the last time we called for Fauldic support?"

My mind's eye replayed the retreat order and my men's

faces as we pulled back and allowed Eericas to escape. "Those were hard times."

"And bitter." Gilundan spun the empty flower in between his hands.

"It's Khyber's deepest hope we can put those harsh words behind us. If Glyodrin could find it in his heart to—"

Gilundan raised a hand, forestalling me. "That is between our lords. I am but a mouthpiece here. My words hold no more weight than the wind that carries them."

"This news saddens my heart, on both accounts."

With a shrug, he emitted a faint sound like sandpaper on pottery. "What it is to be mortal." He waved dismissively.

"Not for all of us," I said. "Khyber has need for those with strength and honor."

His black eyes stared through me. He chuffed, then touched his forehead, heart, then lips and cast it toward the sky. "I am glad to have met you, Avatar Wrath."

"And I you, Gilundan. Remember Khyber is always there if you need. All you need do is pray."

He laughed. "High priest indeed."

We clasped forearms, a strange sensation even through the gauntlet. Like shaking hands with my daughter's porcelain doll.

The accordion stopped. The crowd cheered, but Gilundan jeered, sending me into a belly laugh. With a wink, he sprang back up the tree. I glanced after him. A pity I'd have to kill him.

3

SPRIGGAN SAPLINGS JUMPED off the bridge's rails. A plume of water sprayed the watching adults. The surface slowly returned to gentle ripples. What I took for the young ones' parents drank and gossiped unperturbed when their children sank straight to the bottom. Suddenly, the water churned and bubbled as the pack of young ones wrestled, each trying to force the others to break the surface. The adults egged them on.

I turned my attention to the clansmen. They occupied most of the available space on the miniature island. The Norvish warriors had arrayed themselves in a defensive semicircle around their chieftain. They'd pressed the civilians into a single lane of traffic running between bridges.

When I stepped off the bridge, the clansmen fixed me with challenging stares. The closest thumped his chest, brandishing a fallen tree he used as a club. A display of dominance. All I had to do was hold my ground and they'd let me pass.

The clansman spread his arms aggressively and strutted up to me. I hooked a foot around his ankle and redirected his momentum. Six hundred pounds of solid muscle caromed into his fellows. All the way down the line, they toppled into each other and crashed into the water. The other half of the clansmen roared, putting themselves in between me and their chieftain. They muttered Zenos's mantras, an eerie calm falling over them as the heightenings took hold.

Frightened civilians pushed to exit the island by way of the bridges, and a few more wound up in the water. I lowered my visor. Opening myself to Khyber's divinity, power flooded me, and my holy armor responded. I raised my fists. They came at me with a deathly calm.

I caught a kick. Drove my fist into the Norven's abdomen with enough force to rupture a human's organs, yet it simply knocked the wind from him. I pulled him off balance and struck an elbow into his inner thigh. He went down.

A punch came at my face. I ducked. Countered, he stumbled back, clutching his mouth. I swept the legs out from the next, booting him in the ribs on the way down. My armor rang with a flurry of blows to the back of my head. I trapped the Norven's arm, twisted it behind his back and drove my fist into the base of his skull. With a groan, he slumped face-first into the grass.

Volovodov slapped a palm over the other fist. "Avatar Wrath, we meet again."

"The Bloodied Spear clan is honored by your restraint, Volovodov." I returned the gesture.

"The duality is a cruel way of life," Volovodov snarled.

"Perhaps you should take up the sword and shield instead."

"Never!" He tossed his head, the curled horns of his mask looping menacingly through the air. "What makes you shame my men, Avatar?"

"I craved something stronger than laced mineral water, and a warrior to share it with," I said.

"Then you have belittled my clansmen in vain. We are guests of Talmor'ook and will not insult him by accepting things outside of his hospitality."

"And if I challenge you to a duel?"

"To the death?"

"No, sparring only—but to what would be a killing blow."

"And the prize?"

"The drink of choice of the winner."

Volovodov bared his stained fangs. "Agreed." His warriors roared their ascent.

I stepped to the center and drew both my blades. They sang as they left the sheaths, filling the island with Khyber's glory.

Volovodov held out his hand, and a clansman passed him a polearm, a combination between a billhook and a halberd. A twelve-foot shaft with a curved crescent moon axe blade. An exaggerated hook stuck out the back, and from the top jutted a spear.

He spun his weapon with a practiced ease, maneuvering through a few warm-ups. The air whistled with its passage until he stilled. An eerie calm stole over him as his breathing slowed. He shimmered like heat above a fire. The fine fur covering him was lifted by an unseen charge, drifting as if in an invisible current.

I made the sign of the sword, more to demonstrate Khyber's presence than for any need. My lord didn't require any of these mind tricks from his followers. His strength was freely given to those with enough devotion.

I dropped into a forward stance, all but inviting Volovodov to take my head. His serenity contradicted the grief etched into his war mask. The noise of the party diminished as the guests turned to watch.

The halberd launched at my head. I sidestepped, guiding the strike with my right-hand blade and lunged to disembowel him. Volovodov glided out of the way and nearly hooked my blade. I disengaged, struck at his throat, groin and ankle.

Volovodov deflected each blow using his polearm like a quarterstaff. I was now on the defensive. He rained blows upon me, stabbing inside my guard, spinning the haft. Nearly got my arm with the hook. I sprang to the side, my armor's speed the only thing that saved me.

The stalemate stretched on. And he seemed all too happy to wait for me to make a mistake. Once more, I stuck my head out. The halberd jabbed. I slid under. Stabbed. Volovodov pushed off, sliding a dozen feet back. I was after him, second blade going for the axilla. Fabric ripped, and something tugged on my cape. Volovodov spun away, his axe hacking at my legs.

I accelerated to the full extent of my armor and leaped over his strike. Slashed at his neck, his fingers, drove the point at his ribs. Each blow was met, all with unnatural calm. His skill was breathtaking. He was a blur of tawny hide flashing in the blue-green light.

My sword parted the furs covering his torso. Vibrations skittered up the blade as if I'd drawn it across stone. A touch, and I'd overextended myself. The halberd's haft rang against my forearm. We parted, and with a bow, I drove my left-hand blade into the turf, tucking that arm behind my back.

Volovodov readied his weapon. I took an aggressive stance, and once more he took the bait. He went for my head. I slid under his guard, but I'd used this trick one too many times. The haft came up, nearly ripping the blade from my hand. He advanced, forcing me to retreat. Off balance from switching my footing, I barely caught the steel-capped butt before it cracked my temple. The crescent moon whistled toward my neck. I darted in, taking the haft on the pauldron and halting the point of my sword just before it would have punched through his ribs.

"Well done," Volovodov said. With a twitch, the hook on his spear tugged on the back of my neck.

I laughed. "Well done indeed." I sheathed my blade. "A tie, then."

"You're a good fighter, Avatar. Pity we never face each other in true battle. I would gain much honor in killing you."

"You'll have to be satisfied with drinking me under the table."

The chieftain threw back his head with laughter. "Good. I drink your whiskey, but you"—he placed a massive paw on my shoulder—"must have Grundstrad unkova."

My stomach churned in remembered trauma. The fermented milk was the foulest drink on Etherious, and the Norven lapped it up as if it were cream. "Excellent," I said.

"Seems our fun is over." Volovodov tipped his chin.

Talmor'ook hustled over the bridge, his face puckered in disapproval.

"By all appearances, we'll both need a drink after this tongue lashing." But he wasn't listening. The charge about Volovodov faded as he reversed his way through the meditations.

Talmor'ook came onto the island. "Quite the spectacle, gentlemen."

"We offended with our sport." Volovodov regarded the distant shoreline, and I followed his gaze. The press of bodies had diminished. Most of the remaining people were human. The few Spriggans wore dour expressions.

"Nonsense," Talmor'ook said sarcastically. "I've simply accelerated our timetable."

Volovodov planted the blade of his halberd, and with a ritualistic motion, he knelt, pulling a dagger from his belt. "I have failed in my duty, shaming us all." He extended the knife to Talmor'ook. "I beseech your forgiveness."

Talmor'ook shot me a dirty look, clearly accusing me for the situation he found himself in. He accepted the blade, and Volovodov exposed his throat.

Talmor'ook sliced open Volovodov's furs, baring the fine tan fur that covered his hide. A thin line ran across his chest, a mild scrape the only mark my sword had left. Talmor'ook placed the blade on Volovodov's sternum and drew the blade across his breast, down diagonally to the middle of the sternum, then up to the original incision. Blood thick as syrup flowed from the wound, but it was Talmor'ook who appeared to be in pain. Talmor'ook pinched the skin and delicately filleted the section free.

He brandished his bloody trophy to the sky, Norvish blood dribbling down his forearm. The clansmen slapped their fists into their palms, took a knee and exposed their own throats. As one, they asked Talmor'ook to forgive them as well.

"Your chieftain has repaid all. Rise, honored warriors, and stand with pride." Talmor'ook drew a rune in the air. It pulsed a vibrant green. With the grace of a dancer, he guided the symbol to touch the earth. A thornbush sprang from the ground while Talmor'ook's fingers darted as if weaving a tapestry. The bush followed his movements, growing into an oval with a thick central stem surrounded by angry barbs. The runic light faded, and he picked it up.

He speared the bloody hunk of hide and placed the crown of thorns upon his head.

"Let all see your shame has been washed clean."

The Norven raised their fists and howled like the damned come to steal the marrow from living bones.

"You honor the Bloodied Spear clan." Volovodov bowed, his men following suit.

Talmor'ook held his mask of serenity though his eyes gave away the disgust he felt. "No more than you honor me with your friendship and commitment to our alliance. Come, we have matters of state to address."

I caught his elbow. "I too wish to apologize." The opportunity to bait him was far too rare to pass up. "It was never my intention to offend the delicate sensibilities of your people. I thought it might be a comfort to see the skill of those who have sacrificed so much to ensure their way of life."

"Apology accepted," Chancellor Talmor'ook said flatly. He turned and glided over the bridge, head held high and hands folded over his abdomen, for all the world completely oblivious to the clotted blood dripping on his brow.

"Humans," Volovodov said with a rueful shake of his head. "You think simply asking for forgiveness is enough. Without redress, resentment festers. You would do well to remember."

The Norvish delegation followed Talmor'ook over the bridge. I snatched my sword from the ground and fell in behind.

4

ELLODRIN HAD RETURNED to its natural rhythms now that the splendor of welcoming foreign dignitaries was over. The city was eerily quiet. The loudest was the Norven's breathing as they marched up the street. No hawkers cried their wares. No voices raised in argument, no clink of mug to mug after a hard day's labor. No industry at all. The entire population was idle, lazing about day after day without purpose. This was their vaunted peace.

I'd rather be cast into the Void than be condemned to a life such as this.

The street wound in the twisted way of roots, it's craggy bark free of wheel rut or any sign of hard use. The structures to either side held more the feel of a woodland glade than true buildings, though I had no doubt they'd been sculpted.

The closer we came to the Mother Tree, the wider the streets became. The nature of the buildings changed as well. Not so full of leaf and vine, more interlocking trunks flowing into one another. The Mother Tree loomed above, as unfathomable as a hurricane.

The parliament buildings were thick columns of hoary old-growth as one tree grew into the next, lovers locked in an eternal embrace. The doors opened of their own accord as Chancellor Talmor'ook strode in, a king in his palace. A warmth settled about me as I crossed the threshold. This was sanctified ground, one of the Mother Tree's holy places of power.

Vaulted ceilings rose in a complex tangle of woven branches. Knots contorted in ways no craftsman could hope to replicate. Flowers bloomed high above, like glittering blue-green gems.

Vanyard and his squad of hard-faced acolytes stood at attention in the foyer. Two rows of five, they saluted in the formal martial fashion, left fist to chest, right hand on pommel, left leg extending behind, allowing them to bow without ever taking their eyes from the passing dignitaries.

I flagged Vanyard over, and he trotted up as the honor guards for the Mirvish and Norven guards filed through the door behind me. He handed me my ceremonial shield and whispered, "Only the one exit to the council chamber. There's a back door, if the main entrance gets blocked."

"Well done. Should you feel Khyber's sign..." I held his eye.

"Yes, sir, but it won't come to that." His craggy face showed no sign of the hope in his voice.

I nodded. "Get my saddlebag."

"Wilcons," Vanyard barked.

An acolyte came running up, holding the bag. I pulled out the bottle of whiskey, a pewter sifter and the document roll. "Stand sure."

The squad returned my salute.

I strode into the council chamber, and the doors closed behind me. A five-sided table grew out of the floor. I popped the cork, filling the cup as I went. With a smile, I placed both before Volovodov, clapped him on the shoulder and took my customary position.

He raised the sifter. The thing was a child's toy in his hand. Before he could take a drink, Talmor'ook coughed, his eyes cold as ice. The son of a goat didn't even have lungs. With a sheepish grin, Volovodov put the glass back on the table.

Talmor'ook stood and addressed the room. "The Fauldic representative called this gathering of the allies. Apparently, the matter could not wait for our regularly scheduled meeting next month. Out of respect for your time, I will pass the floor to Avatar Wrath."

"Thank you, Chancellor. I know many of you have traveled a long way, for which I am grateful. I am sorry to say the issue I bring should have been resolved thirty years ago."

"You speak of the Frostbite Wars?" Sylvie said.

"I do."

"That chapter is closed." Talmor'ook's lip curled.

"So long as a single Myi'eshan still breathes, the threat from Lyria will never end, only pass to future generations." I opened the document tube and handed around the briefing. "Here is a full accounting of our findings. To sum it up, Lyr'eris has used her divinity to manipulate the Myi'eshans' physiology. Giving birth to twins and even triplets has become the norm."

"How they pup is no concern of ours," said Volovodov, running a finger around the rim of his glass.

"It will be for our children," I said. "In a single generation, they've replenished their losses from the Frostbite Wars. Look at the graph. See how their population grows exponentially? Every generation, it doubles. In thirty years, their population will outnumber all five of our nations. In sixty they'll have two hundred fifty percent of our numbers. Those demon worshipers will come for us in a tide that cannot be held back no matter how high Oppenfauld's walls. Norvish strength, Elvish guile, Mirvish spirit and Spriggan diplomacy will be no match for their bloodlust.

"We've experienced a period of unprecedented peace. You forget outside our borders the Ascendancy War still rages. Eericas, Lyr'eris, Wyrm or some other unknown demon or Ascendant will come for us. Eventually, we will fight on allied soil. Do not delude yourselves by thinking this period of peace will last. We have a duty to protect our gods and their subjects. We must strike preemptively and eradicate the Myi'eshan people."

"Genocide!?" Talmor'ook hammered a fist on the table. "To what end? Lyr'eris has transcended. We have no hope of killing her."

"They've done nothing to provoke us." Gilundan absently traced the wood grain of the table. "There hasn't been a raid in decades."

Sylvie gave a nervous titter. "And once we're done, you'll want us to march on the Ethereal Battle."

"This life is the training ground for the next, and if we can't stop Lyr'eris in the mortal plane, what hope do we have in the afterlife?"

An uncomfortable silence settled about the room.

"If we march on Lyria, the Myi'eshan will take to the sea," Volovodov said.

"So we'll attack from the north. We take the next five years and build ships. In your briefing, you will find designs for a state-of-the-art trireme. It's more maneuverable than our current model and impossible for a man in a canoe to board."

"Cut them off from the ocean?" Volovodov scratched his chin. "Nearly inconceivable, yet it could work." He picked up the cup and smelled the liquor.

Damnation. If I'd swayed him, and he drank... "Yes," I said, feeling a rush, like betting everything at the card table. "We drive them south and east. They'll break upon Oppenfauld's walls or run straight into the open arms of the Mirvish."

"And those who don't"—Gilundan sat a little straighter, an eager light in his black eyes—"will have nowhere to flee but into Wyrm's waist."

Talmor'ook brought his fingers to his temples though dropped them before touching his crown of thorns. "I will not sanction a genocide."

"Not just sanction, Talmor'ook. I'll not have another Arachnid War. We need a joint task force. Mirvish, Spriggan, Norven, Elvish and Fauldic. All of us need to take the field or this will fail."

"Mir'eve's role has always been support. Our people are not fighters."

"Neither are the Spriggans." Talmor'ook nodded gratefully at Sylvie. "We will defend our home. We will never attack."

"It is time for change," I said. "You have relied upon the three of us for too long. We need you to take up this burden and stand by our side, or else the net will be too thin to catch them all. And all we'll have done is kick the problem farther down the road."

"Do we need to do more than that?" Sylvie asked with a look of longing at the whiskey. "If the sundering is only three or four generations away, why go through all this effort?"

"So we have the resources to reinforce Wyrm's Bane,"

Gilundan said.

"Precisely," I agreed.

"It's murder," Talmor'ook said angrily.

"Its preemptive self-defense," I snapped back.

"They are primitives with bone clubs." Talmor'ook pounded a fist on the table, and the vibration reverberated through the chamber.

"They're demon-worshiping cannibals whose goddess has become powerful enough to change them on a structural level. What will she be capable of next?"

"What you ask is an abomination." Talmor'ook rose from his seat, stabbing an angry finger at me. "It's anathema to the Mother's aspect. She gives life, she does not take it.

"Yes, what I propose is an atrocity. But put your emotions aside and weigh the facts."

"This decision is not ours," Gilundan said. "Let us confer with our lords."

Each delegate made their respective holy symbol, bowed their heads and silently consulted with their god. I took a moment to watch their faces. Gilundan was as unreadable as any elf, though he had seemed eager. Volovodov had the air of a restrained stallion. Sylvie had a slight greenish ting about her jowls. And Talmor'ook had given up hiding behind his false benevolence.

I made the sign of the sword, and Khyber filled my soul. *"My son,"* Khyber's voice resonated within me with a power that threatened to rip my soul from my flesh.

"I fear I may have spoken too well, my lord. The Elvin and Norvish representatives appear to have been swayed," I responded within my mind.

"If you have, then my deepest desire will be fulfilled, and you will come home a true hero."

"And if they vote as we suspect?" I kept my face impassive.

"Slaughter them all. Without their high priests, the others will be crippled."

"As you command, my master."

"The other Avatars are in position to construct the weapon. Move quickly. No one else can do this but you."

"I will not fail. By this evening you will transcend."

"Do this, Rodrick, and I will place you at my right hand for all eternity. I will make you High King in Strothhiem and commander of my forces within the Ethereal Battle."

"The Mother Tree's soul will be yours."

"Stand sure, my son."

"Your will, my hands."

The emblems died out as the gods finished commanding to their servants.

"Are we prepared?" Talmor'ook glanced into each face, holding their eyes. "All in favor of invading Lyria and massacring every man, woman and child."

I was the only delegate to raise my hand. Sylvie glanced about the room with unease. Gilundan refused to meet my eye. Volovodov pouted like a sullen child, staring into the pewter cup. So Zenos had chosen a solidarity vote rather than commit to what needed to be done.

I made the sign of the sword to confirm Khyber's will. A blue tracer followed my fingers. It hung in the air, radiating a sense of strength and confidence.

"Those in favor of allowing the peace we have enjoyed for the past twenty years to endure." Chancellor Talmor'ook's face remained impassive, though smug satisfaction rolled off him like a bad perfume.

Sylvie raised a hand, then Gilundan, Chancellor Talmor'ook and, with an irritated snarl, Volovodov.

An unexpected pang of regret rang my heart. I'd been disappointed by these people so many times I was surprised to find it still hurt. Though I'd known it would turn out this way, this meant the end of so many things. Each of them drew their lord's holy symbol, and in doing so signed their own death warrant.

"Oppenfauld's request for troops is denied," Chancellor Talmor'ook said with a cheery smile.

I rose, placing a hand over my heart, and bowed, then made for the door.

"Nothing to say, Avatar?" Talmor'ook taunted. "No outraged speech?"

I peeked my head out the door. Vanyard and his squad stood to one side, their faces full of hope. I crushed it with a shake of my head. "Hold the door, Sergeant."

"Yes, Avatar." Vanyard and his squad took a defensive position on the other side of the door. I closed it as the clansmen barked a challenge.

"Time and time again, Khyber's warmongering is brought before this council," Talmor'ook went on, his voice growing sharp as I ignored him. "I warn you, Avatar Wrath, the Mother Tree's patience grows thin."

I took the shield from my back and wedged it between the handles. A distant boom sounded, and the earth groaned in response. Talmor'ook clutched his chest and cried out in pain, pure horror filling his face.

"Rodrick?" Sylvie's voice rose in alarm. "What was that?"

I slipped a dagger into each hand, and in one fluid motion flung one at Volovodov, the other at Gilundan. They struck home. The elf fell off his chair, the sound of breaking pottery filling the room. Volovodov looked down at the blade in his meaty neck, the pewter sifter poised upon his lips. I turned and made the sign of the sword over the shield. The imbuement spread to barricade the doorway in a shimmering barrier of translucent energy.

Volovodov fingered the blood flowing over his collarbone. Rage took him. He flung the cup and reached for his halberd. I drew a rune in the air. Red lightning arced across the room, striking him. It launched him into the back wall. Where he lay motionless, the air filled with the scent of cooked meat and burnt hair.

Sylvie screamed, staring from me to the two dead men. With the greatest threat taken care of, I went for Talmor'ook, who gripped the table and tore it free. He swung it as if it were no more than a pillow. Though I dodged, the thing was massive, and it clipped me. I tumbled across the room and crashed into the wall.

Khyber filled my senses, warning me of danger. I kicked off the wall, slid across the floor. The table crashed into the spot I'd just vacated. I slid past Talmor'ook. He picked up his chair and smashed it into my legs. I spun, the world lost in vertigo. Then came a bone-jarring crunch as I hit something. Khyber flowed through me. He stopped the world from spinning and numbed the pain in my leg.

I rolled to my feet. Talmor'ook was halfway through the transformation. He rattled, deep and ominous as a snake. The petals down his midline peeled back. I drew a quick rune. More lightning arced out, and Talmor'ook screamed like tortured wood.

I charged. Blows struck me from the side, my armor protesting with each impact. I drew a shield rune, and a shimmering barrier sprang up between Sylvie and me. She drew runes with both hands, launching razor-sharp shards of crystal. They exploded in a shower of glass, filling the air with a sparkling cloud.

"Rodrick, what by all the gods are you doing?" Sylvie's voice trembled. "We've been friends for years!"

Danger! I brought my sword round, blocked. Honed as

the steel was, it only scored Talmor'ook's forearm. Damn it, the other blade had been imbued to kill Spriggans. He grabbed the blade, squeezed, and the metal deformed as if it were putty. I dropped it, reached for the other.

Talmor'ook attacked. The skill he lacked, he made up for with ferocity. "Traitor," he snarled, petals retracting into a stiff red crest along his spine. "The Fauldic will pay for this. I'll see they starve." His talons raked for my face. I sidestepped, drew my blade and, with an almost casual strike, cleaved his head from his shoulders. His neck gave no more resistance than a stalk of grass.

"Crystal Lady, save me. Crystal Lady, save me." Sylvie opened her mouth and sang, a long sharp note that twisted through my skill.

I inscribed a lightning rune. She went up an octave. My vision swan and my hand trembled. Incomplete, the rune dissolved.

Sylvie's voice broke, and the note cut off. I gritted my teeth against the lingering pain and advanced. She gave up her attacks and backed away. "Rodrick, please. We're lovers." She sobbed. "Please don't."

Volovodov sat up, muttering the heightenings. His mask hung askew, torso covered in burns. He pushed himself to his feet, halberd at the ready, a deathly calm about him. Sylvie's eyes flicked between the two of us, and then she ran to the door and began barraging the barricade with crystal shards.

I drew another rune, and lightning collided with Volovodov. His flesh rippled as if blown by a strong wind. A burn the size of my fist bloomed at the impact site, though he remained unfazed.

As he twirled his halberd in a display of prowess, I leaned forward, inviting him to go for my head. I tucked my left hand behind my back and fumbled with my belt pouch. He attacked, assuming I'd duck under the blow. He drove the butt of his weapon to where my face should have been. I retreated, pulled the mordrem blossom from my belt pouch, crushed its wax covering and flung it into his face.

His face contorted to match his mask, the halberd clattering to the floor. He clutched at his throat, unable to scream. Blood poured from his eyes, rivulets streaming from his nostrils. His skin bubbled and cracked. He toppled to the ground in a choking, twitching mass.

The barrier holding the doors shattered, bursting into hundreds of motes that fluttered to the ground like cherry blossoms in the wind. Sylvie wrenched my shield from the handles, threw them wide and ran straight into a Fauldic spear. It took her in the throat, a second under the arm, the third straight through the chest.

I gave Volovodov a wide berth. It pained me not to give him a swift death, but if I came within six feet, I'd be the one whose airways were melting. I knelt down and dabbled my fingers in a half-spilled water jug.

Gilundan was murmuring softly. He'd dragged himself halfway across the floor before his strength gave out. He lay in a pool of his own blood, head propped on an arm, and was likely communing with Glyodrin. I drove my boot through his skull before he could further warn his lord, and the emblem winked out.

The squad was buckling under the constant assault from the Norvish heavy weapons. A fracture line spread across the barrier, but it could hold for another minute or two.

I knelt over Talmor'ook's corpse, picked up the head and placed it where it could watch, then set to work removing the core. "You're the worst kind of hypocrite. You send my people to die while yours refused to lift a finger. The Mother

Tree's peace isn't freedom, it's tyranny. You forged chains of hope and shackled us to a lie. My only regret is you won't be here to watch when I cut her down." I grunted with effort, and the central stem cracked open. "Between you and me, I'd have killed you anyway, no matter which way the vote went." With a pop, the core came free.

"Avatar?" The tone caught my attention, something jagged and raw that spoke of a gut wound. Vanyard stood in the doorway, expression as hard as a paving stone, but he appeared to be sound.

"Sergeant?"

"Our barrier's almost spent." His eyes drifted to Talmor'ook's remains. "Then we're down to a few planks of wood between us and those heavy weapons."

"On my way." I stood, tucking the core into my belt. "I hope we meet in the Ethereal Battle," I said to the Spriggan's severed head. "I'd love to do this again." I strode to the door, scooping up my shield from the ground. Vanyard's eyes flicked behind me, a bead of perspiration rolling down his cheek... no, a tear. "Is there a problem, Sergeant?"

"No, sir." His face never changed, yet I sensed the barely restrained fury.

"They chose this. Remember that."

For a moment I thought he'd strike me. Then he made the sign of the sword. The blue tracer sank into his chest, and he relaxed.

"I will."

"See that you do. Give the order."

"Center. Make a hole," Vanyard yelled.

Two acolytes in the middle of the shield wall took a single step back and behind the soldier to either side. I rushed forward using my increased speed and rammed into the clansmen. Bones should have shattered, ribs should have caved in, but I did no more than knock a few from their feet.

The clansmen glowed with the heightenings. The eerie calm left their faces slack, making their horrific war masks all the more intimidating. I laid about with my sword. None had the skill of Volovodov, and my blade bit flesh.

I drove the pommel of my sword into the closest Norven's teeth. The force of the blow sent him reeling, but he got back up with no more than a bloody lip. I hacked a forearm, my blade sinking in an inch. He swung a double-bladed axe. I twisted, stabbed, took him through the eye. The next came at me, a massive club hammering into my shield.

This was taking too long. I dropped my blade and drew a rune. Khyber's anger flowed through me, and red lightning erupted. I poured my faith into it. Lightning arced from Norven to Norven. I held on as the smell of roast mutton filled the room. Smoke rose from my gauntlet. My hand blistered. Nevertheless I held. The heightenings winked out one at a time as the Norven warriors succumbed.

I flexed my hand, feeling the skin crack. As I wouldn't need my hand much longer, I saw no point in treating the wound. The sign of the sword eased the pain, and with the squad at my back, we exited the parliament building.

A concussion echoed over the city. The earth screamed in response. Buildings shook, and I barely kept my feet. High above, munitions flashed. A second later came the sharp crack of the explosion. The judges, hard at work, had blasted a crater in the lowest of the Mother Tree's limbs. Before long, they would bring it down.

More flashes, and I figured they must be under siege. An ember fell from their position, a tail of flame coiling in its wake. It sparkled, became ten, sparkled, became a hundred glowing embers drifting lazily onto the city. Everywhere they landed, flames sprang up.

"Acolytes, double-time."

"My lord, the horse?" Vanyard gestured round the corner.

"Leave it. We move as one."

Jogging, we tried to stay out of sight, though with the accursed light following our every movement, stealth was useless. We approached a bucket line, where Spriggans were desperately dousing the flames. As if guided by some external mind, they turned, shrieking a single word —"Wraaattthhh!"—and rushed us with startling speed.

Petals peeled back from their midlines, revealing the grotesque thing hiding beneath their beautiful shell. They came rattling like wheat in the thresher. We locked shields and braced. Their strength put the Norven to shame. Two blows and the barrier fractured. They were unprepared for our weapons. Crafted by a god for this exact purpose, they cut through their wooden bodies far easier than the sharpest axe. In a matter of moments, the Spriggans lay in a ruined heap.

"Set a marker. We'll come back for the cores. To the bridge," I commanded.

Sounds of battle echoed down the street. I could just make out a double-rowed shield wall holding the base of the bridge in a V formation. Hundreds of Spriggans assaulted the acolytes. Moving as fast as my squad could, we ran to their aid.

The Spriggans had finally adopted some tactics. They walked into the river and sank below its surface, returning with arms full of stone. They lined up and hurled a volley of rocks the size of my head at the blockade. So far, the barrier held, and the stones ricocheted into the distance.

Immediately after the volley, they rushed in and attacked the fracture lines. Imbued spears wounded every Spriggan within reach. One threw itself at the barrier, heedless of impalement, its final act to take down two shields' worth with a mighty punch.

As stones sailed into the breach, the unfortunate acolytes folded around the projectiles and were flung behind the lines. The Spriggans charged, and the defenders would have been overwhelmed if not for Avatar Might stepping into the opening. He laid about him with his massive hammer, reducing the Spriggans to kindling. A judge stepped up behind and threw a little clay ball, a tail of flame in its wake.

The Spriggans shrieked, the ones in the front suddenly retreating, those behind pressed to attack. The munition detonated in a cone of liquid fire. The sight was magnificent. Flames clung to them as they tried to escape. Those on fire desperately climbed over others who hadn't been in the blast radius, setting them alight. Panic sent them in every direction, some straight into the inferno, others into Fauldic steel.

"Strothheim beckons," I roared. The squad at my heels, I hammered into the Spriggans. Shields knocked them aside while swords felled them like wheat at the reaping. I made the sign of the sword, and Avatar Might's eyes fixed on me through the press of bodies. He raised his hammer, and the first row advanced. Their feet drummed the rhythm of war, thump, thump; spears delivered death. Thump, thump, death. Thump, thump, death.

The shield wall opened, and we were behind the lines. We made a controlled retreat, but the fight had gone out of the Spriggans, and those who hadn't fled lingered, crying out as the remains of their fellows turned to ash.

"Avatar Wrath." Might clapped a fist to his chest as he took a knee. "We've begun to assemble the weapon on the ridge." He pointed to the cliff-side overlooking the Al'veran. "Justice, Mercy and Compassion are overseeing the judges. Last report stated they were on schedule. You have about twenty minutes."

I gazed out over the river and up to the ridge, noting the blue glint of imbued torches at work. Spriggans were scaling the cliff, and the flash of barriers under attack lit the darkness.

Another explosion echoed over the city. Flames

bloomed from high in her branches. The sound of splintering wood was deafening. One, perhaps two more blasts and the limb would fall. The distraction had done its job, for the Spriggans scaling the cliff jumped into the river, hurrying to defend their Mother.

"Permission to assault the city, my lord?" Avatar Might held my eyes. His holy visage wore an expression of longing.

"Denied," I said. Might's faceplate snarled, the metal shifting to match the expression underneath. So real, so life-like. This was his true face—not the one he'd been born with but the one Khyber had crafted for him. "You're needed to siphon."

"Yes, my lord." Sadness crept over his face. "It's been an honor, sir."

"Do not mourn me, my young friend." I raised my voice so all could hear. "Strothheim beckons. I must answer its call."

Might rose. "May we stand upon her battlements one day."

"One day." Below, the Spriggans had regrouped. They lurked at the edge of the fire, their numbers growing with every passing second. "Khyber will need you in the days to come. Do not be too eager to join me."

Blue-green light blazed in the streets just beyond the battleground. Spriggans in their thousands clogged the streets. A few in the front rank wielded entire trees. Uprooted and limbless, their weapons were heavy enough to turn a man into a red stain. Others bore boulders that must have outweighed the Spriggan carrying it two dozen times.

Might hefted his hammer and strode forwards. I caught his arm.

"Your duty is on the ridge."

"Without me, they'll be overwhelmed in moments."

"Moments may be the difference between victory and defeat."

Might's shoulders slumped. "Hold the bridge," he ordered.

"Strothheim beckons," the acolytes boomed, surging forward like pit dogs straining at the leash.

"Stand sure." Might made the sign of the sword, blessing them, then turned his back on his men.

"Vanyard."

He saluted.

"Care to see this through to the end?" After the debacle of the Arachnid Wars, I owed it to this man.

"Yes, sir." He saluted again, in the formal fashion.

We ran up the bridge. Toward my destiny, my glory, the moment I'd been working for. Nothing could stand in the way. Khyber would transcend, and Strothheim would take its place in the Ethereal Battle.

Behind us, a battle cry went up from the Spriggans. Distorted by rage, the promise for vengeance was unmistakable. "Wraaattthhh!"

A hollow thunk as the Spriggans slammed into the imbued battier. The desperate cries of men struggling to survive.

"Run," I bellowed, but Vanyard and his squad had already abandoned their packs and, with no more than sword and shield, sprinted as if an Arisen was on their heels.

We exited the bridge, and I took the path along the cliff edge. A burst of light made me glance back. The barrier went down, and the Spriggans rolled over the defenders like a tidal wave.

Ellodrin was in flames, though it looked as if the Spriggans had contained the spread. The bioluminescent light betrayed their movements. The majority of them were heading for the bridge. The rest were moving towards the other Fauldic engagement points. If the branch didn't come down within the next two minutes, the Spriggans would overwhelm us by sheer weight of numbers.

I reached the top of the cliff, and five centuries clogged the clearing. The shield wall opened to admit me. Spriggans boiled up the path. The acolytes closed the gap just in time. With a flash of white light, the mass of bodies slammed into the shield wall.

Pride filled my heart. *Let them come. They'll break like waves upon the rocks. And their corpses can light my funeral pyre.*

My life's work was nearly complete.

6

SPRIGGANS LAY DYING all around me, their long lives ebbing like spilled wine through the floorboards. Imbued weapons rose and fell, cleaving through their wooden flesh as smoothly as a spade through tilled earth.

"Hold the line!" I shouted. The sound of breaking glass echoed across the clifftop as one of the shield's kinetic imbuements failed. Too slowly, the acolytes disengaged. The shield wall exploded inward. A half-dozen soldiers careened through the air as a Spriggan barreled through the ranks.

Rushing forward, I drew my sword. The Spriggan raised a talon, aiming for a fallen acolyte. I took it off mid-forearm. The Spriggan darted back, rattling like a barrel of snakes. With its remaining hand, it grabbed a soldier by the ankle and swung him. Nothing could be done. I dodged, and he slammed into the earth. Ignoring the hideous crunch, I lunged, slashing upward, careful to miss the Spriggan's core. Two halves fell to the dirt, each taking its own time in dying.

"Fill the gap," I shouted needlessly. These people knew their profession.

I turned to the fallen acolyte and rolled him over. His

face was unrecognizable. I made the sign of the sword over the corpse. "May Khyber's light lead you to Strothheim, my brother."

Sergeant Hilstrad sat up, coughing and holding her ribs.

"Easy, soldier. Anything broken?" I asked, placing a hand on her shoulder.

"Just winded, sir." She failed to hide a wince.

"Take a breather till one of the physics looks at you."

"Sir, no, Avatar, sir." She hefted her shield, testing the weight. "Fight's not over."

I clapped a fist to my chest. "Stand sure, Hilstrad."

"Stand sure." She saluted. "Avatar Wrath." She fell back in line.

The fourth and largest detonation sounded over the garden city of Ellodrin. The limb finally broke free, seeming to fall for an eternity. The impact crushed the mid-west of the city and miles of forest beyond. Debris hurtled through the air.

Swords cut down the stunned Spriggans as they stared at the ruination of their sacred grove.

"Shields!" I commanded.

The acolytes closed ranks, forming a tortoise.

"Judges, complete the ritual circle," Avatar Justice barked.

The four robed priests continued chanting. Sparks flew as their imbued torches melded the final pieces together. The circle closed. The judges jumped back as red lightning crackled from rune to rune, activating the various nodes. It was perfect, the precision needed to bring the facilities online at the exact moment the judges completed. My heart swelled with pride. Today, a generation's worth of work paid off.

"Huntsman, bring the sacrifices," I said.

Melcor rose from where he'd been crouching, his every movement punctuated by the grating of chains. He hefted his gigantic sword onto his shoulder as if it were no more than a willow switch and collected the prisoners.

Debris from the city peppered the shield wall. "Brace for impact!" Avatar Might yelled. The acolytes shouted defiantly as a two-story section of building hurtled toward us.

"Hold! Khyber will protect us." Avatar Shelter's voice rang over the din. She added her shield to the apex of the wall. "Lord, lend us your strength." Shelter's armor flared with blue light, which rippled across the shield wall. The broken building hit, and the soldiers cried out. Cracks spread across the shield's imbuement. The building bounced, then spun end over end, over the edge of the cliff. A collective sigh of relief escaped the acolytes. Then it caught the underside of the precipice. The bank gave way, and two ranks fell with it.

"Hold the line!" I commanded. My acolytes adjusted, grim faced as some held against the Spriggans while others searched the sky. Not one paid attention to the cliff. They all knew the risk and what we stood to gain.

The huntsman yanked on the chain. The Norven's shear mass pulled most of the bedraggled prisoners from their feet. The filthy beast exposed its canines, its muzzle the only part of its face not covered by its war mask. A shame this abomination had to be present. If Melcor had been a mere Norven, a mortal, the insult could be borne, but a demon...

The prisoners huddled together as if safety dwelled in each other's arms. Except for the Spiral's high priestess. Her face twisted in disgust as she studied the ritual circle.

"This will throw the Spiral into chaos," she raged.

"Don't be ridiculous," I sneered.

"The Neather Realms reflect the mortal," she said.

"I'll believe my senses over conjecture. The Ethereal Battle has raged since the dawn of time. Gods and demons slay each other every minute. What happens here is a single spark compared to a forest fire," I said, voice laced with scorn.

"A spark that may cause the whole world to burn." Her anger faded. "Please." She reached for me with grubby peasant hands. "Violence will further tip the scales. You aid the Void."

I allowed her to paw my leg. "You're wrong. This will bring order."

"These are our allies. We have stood side by side with the Spriggans for centuries. Khyber is sworn to protect the Mother Tree."

"Do you have any clue what waits outside our borders?"

"The alliance has kept Oppenfauld safe."

"You have it backward."

"Since when does Khyber practice blood magic?" the priestess spat. "How long has he sacrificed his own?" The other prisoners cried in horror as they realized their purpose. "Or has he always been a demon?"

I raised a gauntleted fist. The priestess flinched. No, striking the heathen would teach her nothing. "You're not Fauldic. You turned your back on the king to worship a gravitational phenomenon."

"I have lived my whole life in Oppenfauld!" the priestess said, her manacled hands held defensively.

"You spit in the face of your rightful lord."

I lowered my arm, and she pushed a few strands of graying hair out of her face.

"I worship the fabric of existence, something your god is a part of."

"There's no underlying consciousness to the universe.

You turn your back on a god you can touch to whisper empty words into the night."

"You tempt fate. Even transcendent gods don't fully understand the inner workings of the Spiral."

"We make our own fate," I replied coldly.

Dejectedly, she stared at her bloody wrists.

I softened my voice. "Your good works have not gone unnoticed. Renounce your worship of the Spiral. Accept Khyber as the one true god and I will spare your life." I extended my hand. "Together we can save our people."

Her jaw worked, tears suddenly flowing. "All's written in the fabric of the Spiral. What will be will be." Her followers echoed her words. I shook my head. She was too indoctrinated to see reason. In death, she'd serve king and country.

I put the hand that offered her salvation into my belt. Power rolled off the vial in tingling waves. I said a silent prayer of gratitude. To be trusted with my lord's very essence... For the first time in years, I allowed myself the luxury of a single tear.

"Don't do this!" The priestess grabbed my arm. Melcor yanked her away. The vial went flying, bounced, and rolled. I stumbled after it. It landed beside his boot.

He pinned the priestess to the ground and rested the jagged end of his blade upon her abdomen. Pools of crimson welled through her mud-caked robe. Though she squirmed and pleaded, she had as much hope of wriggling her way out from under a portcullis. The freakishly large blade probably weighed thrice as much as she did.

The Arisen stooped, collecting the glass vessel.

"The vial." I held out a hand.

Melcor gave a mocking half bow, the chains binding him snapping as they rolled over each other. He handed it to me. "Avatar Wrath." His words resonated hollowly within his mask. The grotesque thing was the final bit of Norvish culture he retained.

I took the vial with care, inspecting it for damage. Triumph welled within me. Within the hour, I'd be walking the halls of Strothheim. If I ever saw this demon again, I'd be able to feed it steel.

I stepped into the ritual circle and opened my connection to my lord, blue light spilling from my armor as Khyber took possession of me. Crimson bolts danced from the runes, coursing through my body. I bore down, controlling the pain. Laughter brimmed with defiant glory burst from me. I'd spent years training for this, the moment I bought my lord his place amongst the heavens.

I unstopped the vial. Khyber's blood defied gravity, flowing out at its own accord, down my armor and into the central rune. Blood coursed from rune to rune, staining the silvered steel a deep crimson. The judges' chanting rose in intensity as the spell gained momentum.

I stood at the focal point of the spell. I lifted my sword high above my head. Red lightning arced, coursing up my body and to my blade. The steel glowed as red as the setting sun, then shattered. The fragments spun through the air, each taking up an orbit around the circumference of the circle. All was ready. I assumed the posture of the sword. Energies converged, lifting me into the air.

"Now, Melcor!" I cried.

He drove his imbued sword through the priestess, severing her body in two. The other sacrifices cried out in horror. Melcor bared his fangs and circled them. Like frightened sheep, they shied away, backing to the edge of the circle. Two strokes of Melcor's massive blade and their pathetic cries ceased.

"Don't waste the blood!" I barked.

Sergeant Vanyard picked up the priestess's upper body. He held it so her blood would drain within the ritual circle. Somehow she was still alive. She clutched at Vanyard's wrist and whispered something to him. He pulled a dagger and rammed it through her eye. By Strothheim, it had been an honor to lead these soldiers.

Vanyard saw me watching and saluted, a silver chain dangling from his fist. Then he bent to clear the remains from the circle. Let him keep whatever it was. Khyber knew little to no spoils would come from this mission.

All thoughts were driven from me as the pain doubled. My armor was overheating, the imbuements failing. I had to focus and leave my subordinates to their tasks.

Smoke filled the inside of my visor. I released the faceplate, lest I die of smoke inhalation. I had reached the limit of my training. This was the point of no return. I bore down as the will of my god ripped through me.

Someone said something I didn't catch. Grudging the distraction, I spared a glance. Avatar Justice stood at attention. The softhearted fool had abandoned her post. Her faceplate was up, and tears streamed down her cheeks. She mouthed, "Goodbye."

How dare she make this about her?

The world erupted as a column of crimson lightning burst from me. Khyber unleashed his killing blow. I was the eye of the storm, the weapon in his hand. A deafening crack rent the air as the lightning lance struck the Mother Tree. She split down the middle, and every remaining Spriggan screamed before falling dead, their bodies limp as kelp tossed up by the surf.

I was beyond my mortal limits, but I had succeeded. *"Thank you, Lord,"* I prayed silently. *"This death is all I ever wanted."*

The six other Avatars opened themselves to Khyber. Justice turned away, hurt raw upon her face. Damnation, I had said nothing to her for days. No wonder she'd made such a display.

There would be time in Strothheim.

The only thing keeping me conscious was Khyber's possession. He held me back from death so I could witness his victory.

The Avatars flanked me, Khyber's spiritual projection encasing each of them. Six replicas of the lord of sword and shield stood three to a side of the lightning lance, his shoulder-length hair whipping in a neathereal wind, his armor glinting in the harsh light.

Khyber was safe behind the walls of Faldaris. My fellow Avatars and I insisted he not risk coming in person. The ritual had been designed to conduct the Mother Tree's soul straight to him. His projections were merely a precaution.

My lord would finally transcend, and Strothheim would take its rightful place amongst the Ethereal Battle. My country, my people, would survive the sundering. I could die at peace, ready to carve us a place amongst the stars.

Through the vision granted by Khyber, I watched the Veil tear. The goddess's soul rose toward the Neather Realms.

Something was wrong with the spell. The weapon kept firing. Something was inhibiting the secondary function from starting. If the Mother Tree passed through the Veil before Khyber could establish a foothold within her realm, we would lose all.

No, I had tested the spell. It had worked perfectly.

Something sparked at my feet. Another presence appeared.

"Break the circle!" I yelled, but all that came out was an unintelligible bellow.

Another divine was interfering. It couldn't be allowed a direct connection to Khyber's realm. A transcendent god could scour Oppenfauld from the face of Etherious.

A vortex opened beneath me, and a section of the ritual circle contorted into a spiral. Suddenly, my connection to Khyber was severed. The Mother Tree's spirit was drawn from the Veil. She fought like a swimmer being pulled under by a riptide, helpless against the current. Green and golden light slammed into me.

"Traitor!" Melcor bellowed, cutting down the closest judge in his haste to break the circle. That should have been it. I should have dropped to the dirt, yet I remained in the air. The unknown divine had me in its grip. I was helpless to stop, to pull away, as I was force-fed my lord's prize.

Pain, so much exquisite pain. My screams stuck in my throat like a lost lamb in a tar pit. Time became irrelevant. I was filled with souls. I felt their passions, their heartache, each distinct and precious. It all moved so fast. The lives of thousands strobed past. Elves, Men, Norven, Spriggan.

All at once, the visions ended, leaving my soul scorched.

I lay in the dirt, staring up at the vibrant green of the canopy. Green quickly fading to a sickly yellow, then brown. Disorientated, I tried to blink, but my lids were fused open.

Six voices spoke as one, filled with rage. "Traitor!" They surrounded me. The Avatar's armor mirrored the soul within. All were predatory, fearsome to behold. Animated not only by the person within, but the metal itself shifted as if infused with life. Khyber's merciless visage overlay each Avatar. A spectral projection promising retribution.

I tried to speak, to deny, to explain. A wheezing mash barely resembling speech was all I could muster.

"You? My highest servant." The Avatars spoke in unison, each voice resonating with an unearthly majesty. "The one I trusted most!" His anger hit me, a force that drove me inches into the earth, bending the metal of the circle.

Again, I tried to deny his accusations. Again, my body wouldn't respond. Cruel hands ripped the visor from my helm. Justice's catlike armor snarled with rage. She hurled my holy visage over the precipice.

The others wrenched the rest of my plate armor from me. Seams snapped and metal squealed as it peeled away. Strips of flesh went with it, though I felt little more than a sickening pull. I was thrown, acolytes scattering out of the way. Their faces held everything from shock to murder. Some stared, others jeered. Didn't they know me better?

"I damn you, Rodrick Corwyn!" Khyber, the King Ascended, said through his Avatars. "I named you son. I made you an extension of my will. I set you above all other men, and you, you betrayed me. You who know the price of treason better than anyone."

Icy fear gripped my insides at the memories of what I had done in my lord's name. He'd go after my family first, for he knew that would hurt the most. No, he had held Mara on his knee. He taught Eric the sword, he danced with Anastasia at our wedding, and surely Dianna was safe. Yes, Justice would protect them. I looked into his eyes, and six times over I saw the promise of pain. He would break them —mind, body and spirit—before casting them into Damnation.

With a wavering hand, I made the sign of the sword over my breast. *Please understand, it wasn't me.* Avatar Compassion stepped forward and booted me in the ribs.

"Blasphemy!" they roared.

I skidded to a stop with one arm and my head dangling

over the edge of the cliff. The great river Al'veran churned at the base of the cliff. A leaf the size of a blanket fluttered to the water hundreds of feet below.

"Begin the ritual again. I will have what I paid for," Khyber said

"My lord, we've used all the sacrifices," Judge Warwick said.

"Fourth file, step forward and remove your breastplates," Khyber replied.

Without a second's hesitation, the fourth file stepped forward and began disrobing. Pride swelled within me at their valor.

I rolled, the Veil opening to embrace me. There wasn't time to repair the ritual circle. Any moment I would pass beyond the Veil. I reached out a pleading hand. Justice turned away. How had this all gone to shit so quickly?

My fingers found the jagged end of a broken blade. This was fate. Damn the Spiral's priestess and her quaint notions. This was a sign. My lord would win this day and the wars ahead. His holy symbol would send him my soul.

The looks of disgust and hatred from my fellow Avatars were too much. Leaves fell like ash from a volcano, already burying the world in the colors of summer's death. However, Khyber's anger was so great that the leaves were charred to ash as they entered his aura.

I'd prove my loyalty, save my family and protect my country from the war this day would start. I clutched the blade to my heart. If the Avatars wouldn't send me to Damnation in time, I'd ramming do it myself. Khyber would have my soul, and I'd make him see the truth.

A deafening scream of tortured wood rent the air. The weight of miles upon miles of branches was too much for the Mother Tree's split trunk. The earth bucked and heaved as the remains leaned, and the cliff beneath me crumbled.

"Noooo!" Khyber screamed through his mortal instruments. As one they moved to catch me, their armor lending them unnatural speed, but it was far too late.

I fell, tumbling through the air. The blade slipped from my ruined hand. I glimpsed the Avatars helping each other back onto the ledge. My last sight was the Al'veran rushing up to meet me.

7

I PLUNGED into a sea of night as death claimed me. My spirit rose toward the Neather Realms. I had no fear. I knew where my soul would reside. Khyber would find me. Stars streaked past, yet I was the one moving.

Except for him. Khyber hurtled towards me, a blue comet that arced with crimson lightning. The look on his face chilled me to the core. This was my chance to prove myself. I must weather the torment and regain my honor.

I marveled at how his spirit looked the same as it did in mortal flesh. Strong, vibrant, regal, full of purpose and drive, yet honestly imperfect as all men were.

I strained against the pull of the Neather Realms. Everything had gone so horribly wrong. Everything would be all right the moment Khyber claimed me. I'd take my rightful place at his side. Together, we would hunt the traitors and make their deaths last years. I reached out; he was so close. Soldiers would already be kicking in Anastasia's door. I'd not let this lie stain my legacy. I was Avatar Wrath. Acolytes were supposed to venerate my deeds for centuries.

I was yanked away, our fingers almost brushing. Khyber

had drawn the attention of the transcendent gods. Khyber was batted aside, as if he were a midge. The soul he had been so determined to claim—stolen.

Vast and terrible, malformed or perfect, all had survived the sundering of their home worlds. Grown in power as they cannibalized each other, feasting on the remains of the fallen. I was a scrap of meat fought over by mastiffs. They tore me apart. Memories ripped out, swallowed, or thrown aside like dross, to be snapped up by smaller fish.

One of them gained the upper hand. With a blow that could destroy planets, she banished the others and made off with her prize. Lyr'eris held me with all the gentleness an iceberg shows a ship. Terror-stricken, I looked up into the face of pure malice. She cast me into her realm. I fell through a blood-red sky. I crashed into cold gray stone, smooth as polished marble.

The impact would have killed me had I not already been dead. My body regained its shape. The laws of mortal flesh meant nothing here. Long bones set back into place. My skull became spherical once more. As painful as it was, it was a relief from the savaging I received within the Veil.

A three-fingered hand hauled my broken body from the impact crater. An eyeless wormlike head smiled down at me, showing row upon row of hooked fangs. It said something in a demon dialect. When I didn't react, it backhanded me. Before I recovered, it shoved crude weapons of some cold chiseled stone into my hands. One a spike, the other a club. My palms adhered to the surface, and a rime of ice crept up my arms.

The worm dragged me to the edge of the plateau. A barrier of shimmering light rose in the distance. The place where realms collided.

Below me stretched the endless war of the gods. I knew

my theology, but to see the Ethereal Battle with my own eyes... The pervasive stink of spilled viscera blasted its way through the shock. I was a warrior who had slaughtered more sentient lives than I could count, but this made my stomach heave. This single field of engagement held more combatants than the entire population of the five allied nations.

My instincts told me to run, to flee. What was wrong with me? I had never felt such revulsion. I reveled in war, but this... carnage stretched from horizon to horizon. Butchery without pause since the dawn of time.

A command hit my mind. My will, my sense of self, blew away like the last autumn leaf in a winter gale. Ice snaked up my neck and down my back, encasing me. I'd become a prisoner within my body.

The demon pulled out a blade from a roll of fat. It carved a hunk of flesh from my flank, threw its head back and choked down its meal. It raised a stump of a leg and kicked me over the edge.

I landed amid a press of bodies. Somehow, I remained conscious. My broken arm moved of its own volition. The club hammered into a man's skull. Muscle and sinew tore against splintered bone. Heedless of the pain, the club rose and fell. I could not grunt even to voice my agony. My arm finally stopped. Lyr'eris commanded me to rise. My arms buckled. I splashed face-first into the puddle I had made.

Gods, ram it. Anastasia was right. The cold bitch. I deserved this. I could just see her smug expression as she learned of my disgrace.

Lyr'eris must have sensed my anger, my despair. Her spirit filled me with an all-consuming need to kill everything in sight. A silver stag ran past, aiming to gore a demon to my left. I threw myself on its tines, frantically stabbing at the base of its neck. It went down.

I rolled, came up. Facing an ivory elf. Her eyes narrowed. Fluids spilled from the gaping hole in my belly. I charged, though my legs could barely hold my weight. She raised a bow, drew the string. I deflected the first shot. The second took me through the chest. Lyr'eris's primal rage pushed me on. The third pierced my neck. I swung and the club shattered the elf's bony shell. Her face collapsed, spilling black blood and what looked like bits of broken porcelain.

I fell. Peace lasted only a heartbeat. Battle raged. A Norven's foot flashed before my eyes, the heel connecting with my temple. Blackness.

I awoke, my body frozen to the cold stone. Lyr'eris bid me rise. I broke free from the permafrost. Somehow, I had come to the barrier. Lyr'eris willed me through. Soft black soil squished between my toes. A hint of lilacs and blackberries rode the wind. Birds sang amongst the lush greenery. Lyr'eris's hatred of this place suffused me. She commanded me to the middle of a meadow. She raised my arm and drove the spike into the earth.

A wave of death spread out from me—grass, trees, flowers withered and died. Fertile soil was replaced with cold, hard, unnaturally smooth stone. An anguished cry came from the land, the air, as this wholesome place was razed.

Anger, revulsion welled within me at what Lyr'eris had forced me to do. Lyr'eris's gloating laughter echoed through my mind. It reminded me of all those times I watched my father beat my mother. I had tried to be everything he wasn't. How had I wound up hurting so many people?

The gods clashed overhead. Sheet lightning crackled across the sky; winds threatened to fling me into the air.

Lyr'eris's grip on me slackened. I was in control again. I pulled the spike from the ground. The world stopped shifting to cold stone, but it didn't revert to lush forests.

I sprinted for the trees, the leaves whipping at my face. The grappling winds faded. I braced the weapons with my foot. I wrenched my hands free, leaving behind the skin of my palms.

Cradling my hands, I fled into the forest, desperate to get away. Suddenly, Lyr'eris lost her hold on me. I dropped to my knees, breathing in the warm, sweet air. Ice fell from me in sheets.

"Look at me, man-child," said a voice from the branches. I saw nothing till she moved. I wasn't sure what I was looking at. A Spriggan, a young girl, some kind of hunting cat? One second, she was slinking through the foliage. The next, she was right on top of me, a slender hand gripping my throat.

"What luck," she purred. "I fought so hard to claim your soul, and you stumble into my realm of your own accord. And the others say the Spiral has no justice."

I tried to speak, but roots had stitched my lips closed.

"Thanks to you," the goddess continued, "I have all but lost my hold on Etherious."

I panicked. Of all the realms to blunder into, why did it have to be Cypress?

"Can you even comprehend the loss of life your actions have caused—will cause? All but one of my mortal children are dead because of you."

I struggled to break her grip. Khyber warned me we'd directly oppose some of the transcendent gods. I never thought I'd have to face them without him.

Cypress crooked a finger and roots entangled me. "Can your tainted soul even conceive of the magnitude of your crimes?" Roots forced their way into my mouth, down my throat. "You'll never atone for the suffering you've caused."

Soil covered my face. Immobilized with all the weight of the forest bearing down upon me, pushing me deeper, I couldn't breathe, couldn't see. Her laughter filled my mind. The world became nothing but pressure.

Each moment an eternity of agony. I fought, I struggled, the pain going on without end. Amping, ebbing, flowing. I retreated, seeking refuge in memory. She must have been waiting for me to do just that. One at a time, Cypress wrenched my memories from me, removing the pieces that made me, me. I descended into madness. She brought me back to sanity, leaving me nowhere to run.

I fought her at every moment. When I moved a toe, she'd drive splinters under the nails. I'd gasp for breath, and my lungs would fill with earth. I struggled to hold myself together, but that inevitably summoned the images I was trying to hide. Then she'd rip them from me, the spirit one with the flesh. Memories carved off as if I were a pig on a spit.

Khyber help me, I prayed. I had been so free in dealing out torment. This was what it felt like under my knife? Helpless. At least they had the escape of death. *Khyber, please don't do this to my children.*

Days, weeks, years? I couldn't tell. All I had left of my life were a few memories. Holding my three infants. My wife sitting on a swing, her auburn hair ablaze in the evening sun. Sharing a whiskey with my king, our heads thrown back in raucous laughter. The rest was all blood and screams and steel biting flesh.

Desperately I grappled to keep the fragments of who I was. My only hope was to wait for her attention to falter as it had done with Lyr'eris.

Cypress toyed with me like a cat with an injured spar-row. Time passed. I discovered Lyr'eris had left a stain upon me. Lust, rage, ferocity seemed to be anathema to Cypress. That part of me she refused to touch, leaving a hole in her attack.

I picked away. At any moment she could catch me. I couldn't shake the inkling we had done this dance before. She'd allow me to taste hope, to break the surface only to drag me under while she laughed.

My actions had placed me here. That made the torment easier to bear, but I had condemned my family. The injus-tice was a silent lash that drove me to escape. I had scorned the weak willed as they broke. Now I understood.

At last it happened. Cypress shuddered in pain, the full measure of her attention relaxing. I threw my will into the crack of hatred. The final sliver chipped away. I didn't care what was on the other side; I had to get out.

Corruption billowed forth, burning like acid, annihi-lating everything it touched. Black tentacles coiled about me. Root and soil dissolved.

Gods, no! I had burrowed my way into the Void.

Cypress shrieked in pain; her realm shook. The Void spewed from the hole. I had brought death beyond the after-life, to the goddess of all that was green and good. I strug-gled to cling to her. Let roots crawl through my bones forever. Gods, please, anything but this.

I sank through blackness as thick as tar, catching a single glimpse of light before the Void dragged me under. I floundered, lost in emptiness. No gravity, sound or atmosphere. The spark that was me fading into eternal nothingness.

Abruptly it held me up for examination. Something pressed its way through the writhing mass of tentacles. An eye that drank in the darkness, brimming with alien intelligence, more terrifying then anything I could conceive. The Void communicated with me, though there were no words spoken, no images within my mind. What passed between left me feeling violated in ways I never thought were possible. It liked what it saw.

"Damn you! End me!" I screamed, unable to hear my voice within the Void.

This creature of pure hatred and malice found kinship with me. It had read my soul and approved of the deeds that led me to this moment. And it made me long for true death.

It struck. Dark, horrible things filled the empty spaces of my spirit, like seawater will a drowning man. Inexplicably, a rift opened. The Void flung me into brilliant light. Dripping with corruption, thousands of tarry black tendrils groped at this unknown world.

No, I would not be destruction's tool.

I willed the tentacles to stop. They constricted as if to smother the life from me. I didn't relent, drawing each one into myself. I would pay this price; I would follow Khyber's teachings and own this burden. They grew tighter and tighter, finally sinking into my skin.

I knelt and tried to breathe past the clot of root trapped in my windpipe. I pulled it from my mouth, retching, gasping, wishing I could expel the Void as easily.

"Shh now, shh" came a soft voice. "You're safe."

A soul approached me, innocent and full of love. She glowed with white fire, reached out a hand to comfort me. I cringed back in fear of what might happen.

"It's all right. Here you shall heal and be lov—" She brushed my cheek, and the scream that escaped her broke my heart. She fell clawing at her arm as if to rip it free. Black filaments spread up her arm, dissolving her spirit flesh as it climbed.

I punched the ground in frustration. Inky fissures spread, contaminating this paradise. I scrabbled away, looking for somewhere to escape.

A brilliant flash and the White Flame loomed over me. His aura eased my pain. The Void retreated, burrowing deep within me. My soul was torn and ragged, used beyond its ability to repair. I hid my face, ashamed to have such majesty look upon my wretched state.

The White Flame scooped up the innocent. He held her in the palm of his hand and deftly drew the corruption from her. A ball of evil that undulated like mating snakes. Fire consumed it. I turned my back, unable to bear the heat or the hope that swelled within my breast.

The White Flame cradled her in comforting arms, kissed her brow. He said something that made her laugh, then sent her into the light beyond my view.

Eyes flickering with righteous indignation fixed on me. He gestured, and flames engulfed me. The Void fought back, corruption spilling from every pore, protecting its host. Light and dark dueled, consuming fire against annihilation. The White Flame proved the stronger by sheer volume and forced its way into me.

In that introspection, watching myself burn from the inside out, I found a residue. A shard of Cypress and Lyr'eris embedded within my soul, struggling for domination. Also, a connection from me to the source.

I was slipping away. The White Flame meant to kill my soul. Death beyond death, no different from the blackness of the Void. A voice inside me echoed the words that had governed my life. *Stand sure.* My body may lie rotting, food for worms in the Mortal Realm. My spirit battered beyond repair. Yet this blade was not yet broken. I struck back. A pitiful effort but enough to give the White Flame pause.

"I will not suffer another Ascendant to join the war. You end now," he bellowed and drew power from his realm, collecting the heat of a thousand suns in his palm.

I mimicked him, violently yanking on those connections. Reclaiming the missing pieces of my soul. They tore from transcendent gods, half digested, barely recognizable. The lesser beings I had encountered came in their entirety.

The innocent spirit that had tried to help me screamed for her lord as I absorbed her soul. Then a cascade of demons and spirits piled into me. The land where my blood had spilled, the trees that had drank it. Filled me. Changed me.

The White Flame sent a torrent of liquid fire. I moved fast as thought but barely dodged. Nearly falling into his second attack, I was hopelessly outmatched. I tore a rift in his realm. Instantly I was weaker, slower.

Water took me from my feet, saving me from the gout of flame. I had lashed out at random. *Fool! You could have opened a rift to the Void.*

I landed on my back, gazing up at the sky. The perspective was the opposite from the Mortal Realm. I was at the center, looking out at endless constellations, gradually being drawn inwards.

That was it, the Veil. Thin as lace, yet a distance that would take millions of years to travel. My way back to Khyber. To escape the afterlife, prove my innocence, save my family. If there was anyone left of them to save.

The fabric of space tore. I fell upwards. The White Flame bellowed like a forge fire. He pursued me, wings unfolding, a spear forming in his hand. Screams made him hesitate. Water was extinguishing his world. He flung the spear and turned back to close the rift.

Using what felt like the last of my strength, I twisted, just enough to miss being skewered, though the heat scorched me.

Wreathed in flames, I fell. The horror of the Ethereal Battle became no more than pretty lights, save for the Void, a great emptiness that devoured all it touched.

Around me, millions of souls traveled in the other direction. Sorrow filled me. Life was pain and suffering, but what lay beyond it was worse.

A distant blue orb suddenly grew huge, such was the speed of my descent. Etherious rushed up to meet me. My soul slammed back into my body.

8

Consciousness returned, I felt as if I gazed from the bottom of a silty pond. My joints were locked, and a blessed numbness cradled me. Muffled voices broke through the haze that clouded my mind.

"Sister, it's happening," said an old woman, her voice breathy.

"I told you this one would be worth our while. Feel the power rolling off him." The second ancient had a rasp to her words. "Not a sack of bloat flies now, eh?"

"Ya, ya," Breathy said through labored breaths. "Once we're young again, gloat all you like." My head bumped over a stone. The women each held a leg and dragged me through a tunnel.

"Bloody heavy," Breathy said, kicking a loose rock from her path.

"All that river water," Raspy said.

"Aye. Some men sure can hold their drink." They broke into laughter.

"I'll have hair again," Breathy said with longing.

"Yes sister, I recall. Silken, black as coal," Raspy said.

"And yours, living fire. Skin pale as milk."

"It's been so long I can barely remember."

"Nonsense. I've seen you sizing up that farm boy over at Marrypole. Not just for a liver pie, I'll wager." Breathy all but giggled.

"Mmm. Guilty." Raspy laughed. "It's been too long since I've seduced a man without a glamour."

"Don't get greedy now."

"Come, sister. You know we share everything. I'll even let you have the first bite of pie once I'm done with him." They cackled. Something was happening. A warmth bubbled inside my chest.

One of them tripped. I rolled, stiff as a training dummy. Torchlight reflected off an underground lake, the opposite shore lost in darkness. I toppled onto my front, my face dangling over the water.

My reflection was hideous. I'd been dead for some time. My lips were peeled back, skin dank and moldering, pocked with insect holes.

"Mirvish slattern," Breathy hissed.

"Norven sow," Raspy wheezed.

"Shut your filthy hole before I die from the reek. Help me up."

Raspy laughed. "Quit your flailing. You look like a beetle."

"And that toothless grin of yours makes your mouth look like an ass crack."

Raspy muttered angrily and dragged me by the ankles, my forehead bumping over the stone path.

"Get back here! We don't have time for this. Sister? Eleanor?" Breathy yelled.

"Slave!" roared Raspy. "Take our snack to her pen. We're having something more substantial for supper."

"This is too important for games."

The tunnel opened into a good-sized cavern. I passed a dining table situated near the edge of the lake. A pair of armchairs faced a crackling fire in a soot-stained hearth. She dumped me like a cord of wood in-between the hearth and a stone ledge. Deep brown stains ran over the rim and down to the floor. I mistook it for a copper vein, but I'd seen how blood seeps into the very matrix of all it touches.

"Slave!" bellowed Breathy. "Get me up, now." There was the sound of a latch closing, then slow uncaring footsteps.

"Wipe that smirk off your gods damn face or I'll chop you up for perfume," Breathy said, her voice skipping across the lake. "Ho yes, sigh away. You've got it so rough. Slave to those terrible bog hags. Ha, well, if it weren't for us, you'd be firewood with the rest of your kin. So show a little gratitude."

Raspy opened a hardwood box atop the mantel and retrieved a dagger. "Sister, the blade's hungry."

"The Void always is," Breathy wheezed as she came into the chamber.

"If we could harness just one of these waves, we'd live for decades untouched by time," Raspy said, her voice dreamy.

"I'm more than happy with what our percentage should net us. We will have a century. Each!" They cackled like gaudy mummers.

"We'll hunt again," Raspy said.

"Arisen are thick as wheat these days, easy pickings," Breathy said.

"Never easy."

"Too right. I misspoke."

Warmth spread down my limbs. I might have been able to roll over, but that would have given me away. Raspy flashed a curved knife before my eyes, tentacles entwining to form runes down the blade. I kept still, praying they'd keep gloating.

A Spriggan stood off to the side looking bored. Guilt, anger, fear flooded me. *Cypress can't get me here. This was merely a coincidence. I make my fate. Calm your mind, focus.*

My vision was clearing. I needed to assess my options, but my gaze locked onto the Spriggan. There was something else about her, something other than the physical. A virulent purple energy encircled her. An infection? It pulsed through her organs—or at least what passed for organs in her kind. It extended in some sort of umbilical cord that connected her to the witches.

"But worth the payoff," Raspy finished, licking her lips. They grunted, heaving me onto the ledge. "Gor, he's gotten heavier."

"It'll be a close thing if we wait too much longer," Breathy replied.

"The potential. He's an ocean stuffed into a rain barrel. Just a little longer and we may get two hundred years." Raspy's jowls quivered with excitement.

"A bird in the hand."

"Always so practical, together."

"Together." They clasped hands, fingers locking around the hilt.

This was happening too fast. I frantically reached for something, anything. They said I had power. For Khyber's sake, what did that mean? I couldn't move my arms to draw a rune. Besides, I'd been excommunicated. Khyber wouldn't answer.

"Now, sister!" Raspy cried.

They raised the knife. I wouldn't go back. I yanked as I had done when I reformed my soul. Nothing happened. I slashed, attempting to open a rift. Nothing happened. Gods damn it. Why wasn't this working?

I screamed in defiance, but only a puff escaped my lungs. The knife plunged. I rolled, shifting only a few inches. The point scored my chest rather than punching through my sternum. The witches shrieked, losing their balance. One fell and dragged the other down with her.

"Slave, help us up," Raspy hissed.

Pain flared across my ribs. No... This was not physical pain. It extended beyond my body to the puddle of blood leaking from the cut.

The Spriggan glided over, helping Breathy to her feet, the petals of her skin wrinkling in disgust as she touched the old woman.

"Naughty, naughty little dumpling." Breathy's voice dropped an octave. The pain in my side grew, a raking as if hooked barbs were tearing something vital.

Raspy leaned against the ledge. "You broke my leg," she said through gritted teeth. "One good turn deserves another. Don't you think, sister?"

"It certainly does," Breathy agreed. "But let's end him before he gives us any more trouble."

They gripped the dagger once more. The tearing was at a breaking point. Every instinct was telling me to resist. I had to do something. Gods, this felt as stupid as putting my hand into an open flame.

"He's crying." Breathy laughed.

"No! The blood," Raspy said, grabbing at her sister, pulling her away.

I pushed. Something ruptured, and an essential force

left me. Roots shot from the pool of blood, finger thick with the speed of a bolt. The witches hung like marionettes on a peg. They twitched and gurgled, and three heartbeats later, the only sound was blood pattering to the cavern floor.

9

TIME LURCHED to a halt as the Veil parted. The witches' souls rose like poisonous gas. Their shades were grotesque, twisted by a lifetime of cruel depravity. Something in me salivated at the sight of souls freed from mortal flesh.

Darkness reached through the Veil, and a smothering blanket of terror fell. The witches quailed, desperately clinging to their bodies. Blind tendrils searched. Desire overwhelmed my impulse to cover my eyes and hide. Revolted yet powerless to stop, I reached out and snatched the shades from the Void, devouring their wretched souls like a child gobbling an overripe strawberry.

Approving laughter assaulted me as tentacles slithered back through the Veil. Time resumed.

My limbs tingled as life flooded through me. Whatever sustenance the souls imparted worked fast. Edges and colors crisped. The film that coated my eyes lifted. The chill of bare skin upon rough stone broke through the numbness. Disquiet wriggled in my belly. No point dwelling on what was done. The use of blood magic was one more sin to lie at Khyber's feet.

I pushed the implications out of my mind. Muscles protesting, I sat, legs dangling off the ledge. I eyed the roots that sprang from my blood. I touched a finger to the stone. It came away dry.

A scent, an undertone, beckoned from underneath the moldering rot. I flexed and tested. Thin and weak, a shadow of my former self. Skin hung off my bones. I looked weak, barely strong enough to wield a fork, let alone a sword. I leveraged myself to my feet. *What is that smell?*

Three tunnels led from this chamber. Up the one on the left, someone was doing a poor job of holding back tears of frustration. I'd already seen the path along the lake's shore. I had no interest in finding out what else the witches kept down there. The last was opposite the lake, nearly lost in shadow. Cooler air wafted from that direction.

A sound similar to burning parchment. The roots that affixed the corpses in midair were disintegrating, like ash taken by an evening breeze. With a muffled thud, the witches crumpled to the ground.

My knees buckled as a wave of dizziness hit me, causing my heart to hammer in my ears. A hunger rose, cramping my guts. I hit the floor. That delicious smell. I pulled myself towards it. My muscles knotted. I couldn't get to it.

I breathed in, but not with my lungs. It was akin to consuming the souls but visceral, something of the flesh. Blood flowed, running along the floor like beaded mercury. Crimson pearls defied gravity and traveled up my arms, over my cheeks. Warm and metallic, it poured down my throat.

The flow ceased. I crouched within a circle two arm spans in diameter, sucked clean of blood. I frantically scrabbled over to the closest body and sank my teeth in. Thick with clots, it filled spaces within me I didn't know existed.

I drank until she ran dry. I rubbed my mouth, disturbed,

profoundly shaken. Unable to stop, I bit into the other. Deep primal satisfaction purred at my core. All else faded.

I came back to myself holding a dried husk to my lips, shriveled and stinking of urine. I stood, breathing heavily. The pervasive ache that steeped my body ebbed away. I stumbled to the lake, fell to my knees. Slurped a mouth full of water, gargled, spat. The exquisite aftertaste was wholly unwelcome.

I rested on my haunches, watching the ripples spread. Accusations screamed within my mind. *Arisen, Arisen, Arisen.* Eventually the lake grew glassy. Nothing would calm my mind but action.

I leaned forward. My reflection was not what I had expected. A ragged beard hugged my chin while my scalp was shaved smooth. I ran a hand over three faded scars that went from the back of my skull to over my left ear. Startled, I examined my hand. It had filled out. My entire body had. I wasn't layered with muscle, but I no longer looked like a plague victim.

A lattice of scars crisscrossed my arms and torso. I couldn't recall where I'd gotten them. Most were barely visible. Still, you'd think I'd remember at least one. I massaged my shoulder. I vividly recalled the skin coming away as Mercy ripped off my pauldron.

My reflection held the stern deep green eyes of a familiar stranger. "Your name is Rodrick Corwyn." Even my voice sounded wrong.

A rustle from behind brought me into a fighting stance. It came from the far tunnel, the one I suspected was the way out. Cautiously, I made my way over. The Spriggan slumped against the wall, feebly twitching in a death spasm.

She was an amazingly beautiful creature. She resembled a young girl, if girls were made of interlocking layers of leaves and flower petals. Her skin had grown to resemble clothing, a skintight corset that left her shoulders and arms bare. Her legs implied a dancer's leotard with a skirt around the midriff.

The Spriggan was sick, wilting before my eyes. The last of her kind, and I was responsible. There had to be some way to help. This entity wasn't even a mammal. Anything I tried might only make it worse. I'd get some water. Plants liked water.

Out of the corner of my eye, I saw the virulent purple cord. It had been severed and was slowly receding into the Spriggan. The shorter it got, the closer she came to death.

Damn it, how could I save her? A brief sense of vertigo, and for a split second, I was somewhere else. In a reflection of this cave. The witches knelt before me, and their knowledge became mine. I blinked as I stood over the Spriggan.

An enslavement spell. Void runes had been engraved upon her, binding her life force to the master's will. With the bond broken, the Spriggan should be able to get up and walk away. Instead, she was dying, her soul eroding.

"I think I can help you," I said.

"I don't want your help, human," the Spriggan replied, voice filled with contempt.

"It appears to be an easy fix," I muttered.

She gave a bitter laugh. "Go away. Let me join the rest of my kind."

Red lightning, explosions, Spriggans dropping dead. I blinked the image away. "I can't sit here and let you die," I said.

"Blight and burn you, human. Let me pass in peace." Her amber eyes were slivers of pain.

I distorted my vision, allowing me to see the dark energies. If I dispelled the runes engraved on the Spriggan, that should set her free.

I fetched a piece of charcoal from the hearth, knelt over the Spriggan and drew a rune on her abdomen.

"Stop!" she slurred, batting at my hand. Kittens had more strength.

"Let me work." I drew the second. The flow of energy changed. The cord grew agitated. It shrank at an alarming rate. She groaned like timber under pressure. It echoed through the cave. The Spriggan curled in on herself. I quickly rubbed out the runes.

The cord grew still. The enslavement spell was the only thing keeping her alive. If I had finished, I would have killed her.

"Just go," she choked. "Leave me what peace I can find."

She was right. My religion demanded I respect her wishes. If I did, her species would go extinct, and it would be my fault. No, I had been an instrument of Khyber's divine will. To help her would be sacrilege.

I studied the runes. It was just as I'd feared. The Void would never let her go. If her soul survived the strange degradation, it would be claimed by the Void. The only way to save her was to take command of her bondage. She wouldn't thank me. No, quite the opposite, but she'd live. At least for a few more weeks, till I surrendered to Khyber. Yes, that was the only moral course of action. Let Khyber decide both our fates.

I focused on the severed connection. It flopped about like some headless eel. It wouldn't take much, a single rune inscribed on my chest. The Spriggan's eyes fluttered, losing consciousness. She'd be dead in minutes if I didn't act.

I drew the rune on my chest, bent over the cord. Nothing

happened. Confused, I traced the rune again. I had drawn it correctly.

The answer came to me—I needed to pay for the power. Khyber's mercy. How could something so basic slip my mind?

I picked up the sacrificial knife from the floor. A chill crept up my arm. I dropped it. Not worth it. I found a fork, pricked my finger. The blood refused to cooperate. It was as if I had barely any to spare. I had to press the prong into the meat of my palm to get a droplet. The tiny drop that formed was shy as a child hiding behind their mother's skirt.

I pressed the droplet to the rune. Icy numbness ran its length. The cord snapped into place like a magnet to a blacksmith's anvil. Instantly, she was in the back of my mind. The virulent purple suddenly pulsed with green veins. I could see her growing stronger and her pain ease.

Replaced with unbridled hatred, the Spriggan rattled, halfway between threshing wheat and a hive of angry bees. Petals peeled away from her mid-line, a wholly alien snarl. Her beauty was a mask for something hard and dark.

She kicked, trying to lacerate me with the thorn at her heel. I stopped her with a thought. Her strike arrested abruptly.

"You're all the same, you humans. Nice words until you see something you want, then you take it no matter the cost."

"I just—" She threw up a hand, silencing me mid-sentence, then climbed to her feet and stumbled up the tunnel.

I let out an angry breath, raking one hand through my beard. It came away greasy. I looked down at my britches, bug-eaten and crusted with mud. I inspected my chest. No visible sign of the rune. When I unfocused my eyes, it stood out, violet as a bruise. I traced a finger over the cut along my ribs. There wasn't a mark. I looked closer. A line of unblemished skin passed through the existing scars.

Frustrated weeping echoed through the cavern. I took a torch from the wall and followed the third tunnel. It opened into a grotto, its beauty still evident despite the ill use. Two four-poster beds with rumpled sheets and torn hangings were hunched at opposite ends of the cavern. I wound around a few stalagmites to the rear. In the back corner was a cage. A slender arm was prying at a join in the bars.

I stepped closer. Whoever was inside scrabbled away. A useless gesture. The cage was waist high and barely as long.

"Don't be afraid," I said softly. "I'll get you out." The cage was poorly crafted. Bars were misaligned, fastened with some kind of leather.

"The people that put you in there aren't going to hurt you anymore," I said.

Silence. A bar set into a groove in the floor held up the folding door to the cage. I undid the latch that affixed the bar to the floor. Nausea roiled; the latch was a human mandible. Then I saw it, bones lashed together with hide.

I freed the bar. The door folded forwards. Huddled in the corner, peering at me over scraped knees, was a woman, her dress so stained the original color was impossible to tell. The hem had frayed and hung haphazardly.

I knelt beside the door. The state of her filled me with cold anger. I did my best to smile warmly. In reply she snarled like a cornered dog, balling her fists. At least she had spirit.

I held up my hands. "Name's Rodrick. What's yours?"

Blue eyes calculated an escape route. Damp hair dangled in front of her face. Finger marks marred her upper arm.

"They're dead?" she whispered.

"Yes."

"Back away," she said bluntly.

I did as commanded, retreating to the limit of the torch-light. She climbed out, attempting to hide how stiff she was. She was tall and too slender for her frame. Younger than I had originally thought, but there was nothing young about the suspicion in her eyes.

"I need to find a change of clothes," I said.

"There's a room behind that tapestry," she said, pointing to a wall behind me. "They go in there with bundles of things and leave them there."

"The one with the cook fire. Oh, that's morbid." I pushed aside the graveyard scene. "I don't want to leave you in the dark." I offered her the torch. She darted in, all but snatching the light.

I stepped into the dark room. Something crunched. The young woman followed me in. I shifted my weight and found a pair of wood-rimmed spectacles. A year's wages for a laborer crushed underfoot. What a waste.

This part of the cave had a much higher ceiling, yet the piles of personal effects made it feel claustrophobic. The ragged girl went around lighting wall sconces. The chamber filled with warm light.

I rummaged in the closest heap, found a thick cotton shirt, sweat-stained and too big but better than my skin. With some perseverance, I found a sturdy pair of leather boots. An excellent green coat with a purse in an inner pocket, a hunting knife and thick woolen trousers with leather suspenders.

The girl examined something under a sconce. She saw me looking, clenched it in her fist and scrubbed away a tear.

"This was Shannon O'Donnell's," she blurted out. "She

went missing on Penance Day, seven years ago. She could climb a tree better than anyone. Shannon was always so kind, full of joy." Her lip quivered.

"I prayed every day I was in that cage. Never truly believing I'd—" She gestured with the thing in her hand. "No one's ever come back after they went missing. Mam always said it was an Arisen praying on the careless... " Her lip quivered, and she put her face in her hands. And I thought I heard her ask someone named Dunlop for forgiveness. "Lyr'eris, give me strength. Take my weakness, my stupidity, and shatter it with your frozen fire!" She forcefully exhaled, regaining her composure.

I felt my stomach clench at Lyr'eris's invocation. "You worship Lyr'eris?" I asked.

"I do," she snapped.

"Alright, didn't mean anything by it. Just you don't seem like a good match."

"What's that supposed to mean? A woman is supposed to follow the Crystal Lady, wear pretty dresses, bat her eyelashes and worship on her knees, is that it?"

I was taken aback. "I didn't mean that. I'm a Kydaist. It's just hard to understand why anyone would worship a goddess that cruel."

"Right, Khyber's such a flexible an' forgiving lord. Lyr'eris is harsh cuz she's trying to teach you to find that cold hard place within. That place where you can survive anything life throws at you. Most Fauldic hate her cause of the Myi'eshans. Believe me, Lyr'eris is no more cruel than Khyber."

"Khyber is nothing like Lyr'eris," I replied.

"That's right, lord of the broken sword, king of men and god of war has nothing in common with the fangs of winter, goddess of survival."

I shook my head, holding up a hand. "Arguing theology won't get us out of here, so let's agree to disagree."

"Fine." She glared at me.

I gave a half bow, pulled the tapestry aside.

"Cassy," she said. "My name's Cassy Forester."

"Well met, Cassy." I left her to her search, relieved to leave the irritating slip behind.

I filled a large copper pot with water from the lake and hung it over the fire. The armchair was surprisingly comfortable, but the shriveled corpses wouldn't let me rest. I tossed their remains halfway down the path that ran along the lake.

When I returned, the water was barely tepid. I didn't have the patience to wait. I piled my clothes on the dining table and stepped into the lake. The water was an invigorating shock, and I scrubbed the worst of the grime off as quickly as I could.

I climbed out and checked on the cauldron, then poured half into a pail.

"Cassy," I called as I lugged the water up the hall.

"Just a moment," she called through the tapestry.

"It's fine, just left you some wash water." I placed the pail on the ground.

The hunting knife was dull, but it scraped that manky thing off my face. A little hot water soothed the rawness.

I'd just finished dressing when Cassy emerged from the hallway. She wore a coat and britches, her brown hair tucked up under a wide-brimmed straw hat.

"Find any food?" she asked.

"I'd rather trust to luck than eat anything kept in this filthy place. Even a wrinkled winter apple," I said.

"I'd eat damn near anything," she replied, warming her hands over the fire.

"There's dried meat."

Her face grew pale. "I'm not that hungry."

"Me either. Let's get out of here."

"I found these tucked in a corner," Cassy said, handing me an old root fashioned into a club and a pack.

I peeked inside. A change of clothes, a hat and a pair of gloves. "Thank you," I said with genuine surprise. Consideration was the last thing I'd expected from a demon worshiper. I hung the club from my belt and shouldered the pack.

Cassy blushed, fighting to maintain her stern expression.

"The hags aren't the only danger in the swamps. Mam says dead is dead, by spell, fang or knife." Her shoulders drooped.

"We'll get you home, don't worry."

She stood to her full height and looked down her nose at me. "I'll meet you outside," she said and left me behind.

Cold sweat covered me at the sight of her exposed neck. "I'll be right there." She was already gone.

Thirst stirred within me. I took a deep breath and tried to steady my shaking hand. My mind's eye kept replaying the moment I drank the witch's blood, the satisfaction near ecstasy.

Spasms wrung me like a dish rag, and I retched up the remains of the Al'veran. Gods, I'd consumed pints and pints of blood. Where'd it go?

The thirst grew. It would be so easy to slake. If I killed that innocent girl, I'd be no better than the cannibals who had kept her in that cage. What if taking in the witches' souls had cursed me with their dark needs?

Another spasm hit me. I had to eat. The need was taking control. I shuffled after Cassy. Gods help me, I was going to kill her. I forced myself to stop. Thirst shredding my insides, I punched the wall.

Pain forced the hunger to recede. Knuckles met stone, bringing me a little more awareness. The need surged like a rogue wave. I hit the wall repeatedly, blood staining the rock. The tingling pressure started. I punched again, felt something crack, and the thirst fled.

"Khyber, help me," I prayed, tension building. "Please." The pressure escalated far beyond the broken bone. I fought against that pressure, afraid of what might happen should I release it. The pressure became agony. My entire hand felt as if it would burst.

I rested against the wall, inadvertently moving closer to the spilled blood. The closest drops sped over my hand and back into the cut. The pressure eased. I breathed in, pulling against the pressure. The remaining droplets bounced along the vertical stone and reabsorbed into the wound.

I flexed my fingers. *Yep, still broken.* I'd look like a bloody maniac if I ever had to do that in front of people. Better than letting the hunger win. I took the gloves from my pack, hid the cuts and bruises, plastered on a false sense of confident ease and strode up the tunnel.

❦ 10 ❧

THE EARLY MORNING light was gray and cold. Wisps of fog obscured the swamp that surrounded the cave mouth. Cassy looked at the sun, calculating the angle with her arms. To my great relief, the thirst didn't return.

"Raider's Watch is that way." Cassy pointed through a patch of willow lilies. "If we keep the sun to our right, we should get there."

"Are you sure?" I asked.

She adjusted her hat. "My dah harvests peat from this swamp. Best peat in the kingdom, he says, as if you could really tell the difference. I've been in and out of this bog since I was still in nappies."

I held my hand out. "Lead the way, then."

She set off along a well-worn trail. The short turf was soft and squelching, the path a meandering knot that skirted pools. We kept a good pace for an hour.

The Spriggan's presence crouched in my mind, a cold ball of fury that railed against her servitude. She watched us pass. I swear I looked straight at her and couldn't make her out amongst the foliage.

"May I ask a question?" Cassy asked.

"Go ahead," I said.

"How'd you end up in there?"

"I got separated from my squad, fell, blacked out. When I woke, the witches had me." The improvised half-truth came out smooth. "And yourself?"

"Ran an errand for my mam, and I ... I ..." Cassy stuttered.

"Sorry. Put it out of your mind. It's just with so many missing, you'd think the local judge would patrol the roads better."

"Raider's Watch is safe enough. 'Sides, the Garrison's more focused on river traffic and the Kings Highway than the comings and goings of farm folk." She sighed. "'Sides it was my fault An eclipse was falling and—"

"What was so important it couldn't wait until the next day?" I asked.

"Lyr'eris needed an offering. How else were we supposed to survive?" she started. "Look at those." She pointed to a pair of footprints in the soft earth.

"We've walked in a circle," I puzzled. "But we kept the sun on our right."

"Good, I thought I was going crazy."

"Let's carry on and just pay more attention."

The sun was at the correct angle. Perhaps a quarter of an hour later, we came to the edge of a marsh. The footprints we'd followed disappeared into the water.

Cassy paced back and forth, hands knotted over her stomach. "What in the ... ?" She looked from the sun to the prints.

"It's a warren in here. We'll backtrack and try another path."

We came to an intersection, where multiple sets of footprints covered the trails.

"This is bad," Cassy said.

I examined the deep heel strikes. They were my prints.

"Those hags cast some kind of hex on this swamp," Cassy added.

"Follow me." I picked a path barren of any mark. A fine misting rain trickled from the overcast sky. The trail ended on the bank of a small lake. We backtracked again and found ourselves on the grassy shore of the lake. We followed it, quickly coming on more of our footprints pressed into the mud. We were on a small island.

"That's impossible," I whispered.

"Lyr'eris, give me strength, take my weakness, my fear. Fill me with your frozen fire!"

I said a silent prayer. The words rang in the empty spaces of my mind. The lack of a response was all the answer I needed.

"Something's moving under the water," Cassy gasped, quickly putting herself behind me.

We stepped away from the shore. Two long silver antennae broke the surface.

I raised the club. Cassy grabbed my forearm. "A shrimp!" She all but dragged me away.

Two bulbous eyes swiveled, focusing on us. It heaved itself onto shore using long scythe-like claws.

"No, no, no!" Fear made her voice shrill.

We skidded to a halt just before careening into hip-deep water. Behind us something huge crashed through the reeds.

"This way!" I yelled.

"It can't be an island ... We walked here." Cassy threw a stone. A tree cracked and toppled.

I searched the far bank for a way to get across. The Spriggan smiled maliciously, leaning forward, eager for a show.

The shrimp burst through the reeds, stabbed with a claw. I sidestepped. Fumbled for the knife, but I couldn't close my fingers around the handle. Cassy screamed, jumped into the water. The creature swiped. I danced back.

"WWAAAHHHOO, go, monster! Kill him!" the Spriggan cheered.

I swung, aiming for an eye stem. The claw was already coming back around. *Gods, that thing is fast.* I blocked, tripped on a hidden root. Landed hard. Brought my weapon up. The head of the club dangled by a few splinters. Frenzied splashing drew the shrimp's attention. Cassy had made it a quarter of the way across the lake. Her pack and clothing made every stroke worth ten.

Whatever mind lay behind those bug eyes preferred the odds of catching its dinner in the water. It lugged its vast abdomen with its powerful forelegs.

Cassy screamed as the shrimp came for her. "Take my fear, give me strength," she panted.

I threw the broken club at its head. I may as well have thrown dandelion fluff for all the effect it had. I drew the knife with my good hand and ran up its tail. Slipped halfway up. Fine barbs lacerated my knees. I drove the hunting knife down, trying to wedge it under the folds in its chitins. The blade sank in. A spiderweb of cracks shot out. The shrimp gave a warbling cry.

Blood poured from a half hundred cuts, and tingling pain escalated as my blood covered the shrimps back. The shrimp bucked. The knife broke. I flew forward and crushed one of its antennae. The monster reared, flinging its head back. I had too much forward momentum, and I kept rolling. Landed with a heavy thud right on my ass, in-between its raised claws.

I'd be impaled before I could move. My blood had saved me once before. I pushed, feeling as if my veins were being pulled out. A deep chill crept down my legs and burst from me. The shrimp squealed, stumbled, its claw plowing the earth by my head. I crawled for all I was worth. The shrimp's warbling echoed over the lake as it swiped a great claw at its back.

Icicles pierced the shrimp's carapace. It gurgled, listed to one side, toppling another tree. I kept my distance while it finished its death throes.

Time froze. The Veil parted. On the other side was a primordial world. Steam rose from festering swamps. Strange hopping lizards snatched bugs from the air. The shrimp's soul would be at peace.

A hunger awoke within me. Different from the violence of the thirst, a gaping emptiness that couldn't be resisted. I'd been able to fight the thirst but not this. I opened myself and devoured the soul.

Time resumed. Blood pulled itself from my trousers and sank into a wound, itching fiercely as the lacerations closed. The broken bone in my hand knitted back together, and my strength started to return.

Splashing drew my attention. Cassy laboriously pulled herself from the lake. Her head hung and she gasped for breath. The Spriggan's features shifted from disbelief to murderous rage.

"Damn you rat-breeding humans!" she yelled, petals peeling down her midline. Her hatred turned upon Cassy. The scrawny girl screamed and fled, stumbling into the muddy shallows.

"I'll kill every last one of you." The Spriggan tore a

boulder the size of my chest from the earth. She raised it above her head. I fumbled at the bundle of sensation in my mind. I ceased her, forcing her to stop. For half a heartbeat, I held her. Then the intensity of her rage overpowered my control.

"Cassy, run!" I yelled.

Cassy tried to get to her feet, floundered in black mud. The Spriggan gave a wordless roar as she overcame my control. Cassy threw up a hand. "Dah, help."

The Spriggan threw the boulder. It sailed over Cassy and into the lake, sending a fountain of water into the air. She stood, her chest heaving. "Did they cry out for mercy?" The Spriggan balled her fists and yelled at the sky. "They're gone. Everyone I ever loved, burned in the fire of human treachery!"

Cassy crawled through the muck and back onto dry ground. She gave the Spriggan a wide berth. I took a firm grip on the Spriggan, locking her inside her body.

I fumbled around for my pack. It lay on the far side of the swamp monster. I stepped over the shrimp's outstretched claw. It would make a formidable long sword with a proper haft.

I put the heel of my boot through the shrimp's forelimb. It snapped with a juicy pop. I picked it up and gave it an experimental swing. It almost took my head off. The joint had too much mobility. I'd have to core out the joint and drive something up the center to wield it.

Cassy leaned against a small tree, shivering while she wrung out her hair, all the while keeping an eye on the Spriggan. The Spriggan, however, had given into the mental restraints and stood motionless.

I had to get out of this swamp before I met another shrimp. I loathed the thought of facing one without a real weapon. If I took the time to make something, we would spend the night here. Blood magic had defeated this thing, so that was my best defense. No matter how distasteful.

I dropped the claw, sniffed my hands. Gods, I hoped that stink would come off. I picked something that looked like wild parsley, used it to scrub my hands and rinsed them in the lake.

A quick look about confirmed this really was an island. I'd have to swim. I stuffed my clothes into the pack and waded into the lake. It was bitingly cold, and my nethers shriveled before I was up to my knee. I swam with one arm, holding my boots and pack above the water.

Cassy was washing her trousers as I emerged. Her face went radish red, and her eyes darted nervous glances at my manhood. I sighed at the backwater sensibilities of civilians. Spend some time on the front lines and your sensitivity to a little bare skin quickly vanishes.

I put the pack on a dry rock and scraped the water off. My clothes were as welcome as a dip in a hot spring.

"Here," Cassy said.

I looked up from my boot laces. She wouldn't meet my eye. Gods, I really had upset her. "Take it," she spat, thrusting the club into my hand. "It's not as if I'll put it to any use."

"What?" I asked, confused.

"I ran." She rubbed her eyes. "I've damned myself. Lyr'eris, set me free to prove myself, and I fled again."

"You're alive. That's what matters," I said.

"It's my soul that matters," Cassy replied. "See the ice? She smote that creature in mockery of my fear."

My jaw worked for a moment before any words came out. "But you survived."

"I fled from battle. Proven myself unworthy and condemned my soul to be chattel in the afterlife."

"Everyone that's ever faced a battle has had to confront and master their fears. It isn't cowardice to retreat when you know you're facing certain death, it's common sense," I told her, handing her back her club.

She made an incredulous noise and pointed at the corpse of the shrimp. "That thing was the size of a horse, and you didn't run," Cassy said.

I shook my head. "I got lucky... damned lucky."

"I left you to die," Cassy said, tears welling in her eyes.

"If she damns you for following her tenets, then she's a hypocrite."

I stepped around Cassy and approached the Spriggan. "Are you going to be civil?"

"If I must," she replied.

"Would you prefer I leave you here?"

"I'd prefer to be dead." Livid hatred billowed from her, somehow making her colors more vibrant. Greens shot with red, yellow swirls wrapped in blue, hints of indigo around her amber eyes. In form, she was as stirring as a pretty young maid. But her beauty was only a veneer.

"I'm sorry for your loss," I said.

"That's more than I ever expected to hear from a slaver."

I took a deep breath and remained calm. I opened my mouth, and she interrupted me.

"Slaver was perhaps too kind. Rapist would be more accurate."

"I did nothing of the sort," I gasped, offended. Cassy came up beside me, shooting me an uncomfortable look.

"Every moment you hold that bond, you rape my soul."

"I saved your life. Without this bond, you'd die."

"And that gives you the right to control my body? Rob me of my free will?"

"It damn well does if you're about to murder someone," I growled.

"Your king committed genocide!" she yelled.

"You survived. Perhaps there are others?" I offered, guilt twisting a cold blade through my guts.

"No. Our lives are tied to the Mother Tree. When she died, we all did." Her voice went numb. "I am the last."

I pulled a piece of grass from the soil to have something to do with my hands. The Spriggan looked at me as though I'd just spit in her soup.

I dropped it. "What's your name?"

"Humans are incapable of—" She swirled her hands as she searched for the words. "—pronouncing my name. Your species lack the correct organs."

"I can't keep calling you 'Spriggan.' Tell me. I'd like to try." The scent of rose, pine and a spicy heat filled my senses. I looked at her questioningly. "What was that?"

"My name," she said flatly.

"Your name is a smell?" I said.

"Just because you have such a limited form of communication doesn't mean that the rest of creation is restricted to your sliver of sensation."

"So..." I gritted my teeth. "What would you like me to call you?"

"I don't care."

"Are those Rowan berries you're wearing?"

She reached up and touched her ear.

"That's what I'll call you."

Rowan's face went dark. "I can't tell if you intended to insult me in the most hurtful way possible or if you are trying to show respect." She sniffed the air. "Ha, confusion!" She threw up her hands. "Why would I expect anything else other than ignorance from a human?"

"Look," I said, irritation strangling the guilt, "we're lost. You've lived here. Would you please help us get out of this swamp?" She stared at me for a long moment. "Let's work together and get that young girl back to her mother."

"You're trying to manipulate me." She crossed her arms defiantly.

"So, you don't care if she never sees her mother again? When you could so easily reunite them?"

"No. I don't."

"Liar."

Sharp eyes fixed on me. "Burn you," Rowan said. "Root and stem."

"I'll take that as a yes," I said.

Her facial petals started peeling back. I raised my hands, fending off her anger.

"We don't need her help," Cassy interrupted. "Leave her here. She'll be right at home amongst the weeds."

"She's as much a victim of those hags as you were," I told her.

"She was my jailer," Cassy protested.

"Yes, well. She was under a dark spell and not in control of herself."

"Was?" Rowan said.

Cassy sniffed, brushing wet hair back over her shoulder. "How could you know that?"

"He stole my bond for himself using the same dark magic as the witches," Rowan said maliciously.

"I have ears, and I use them to understand... words." Cassy wiggled her fingers as if she was conjuring her ears. "Did he lie when he said you'd die without it?"

Rowan crossed her arms. "No, he stole that from me too. The peace of the afterlife."

"There is no peace in the afterlife," I said.

"There is for me," Rowan replied.

"Don't trust her, Rodrick," Cassy said, glaring at Rowan. "We'd be better off on our own."

"For the first while."

"What does that mean?" I asked.

"You killed this region's Pleocyemata illusory arthropod. Its net is down," Rowan said.

"Illusory arthropod? We were caught in an illusion?" I asked.

Rowan rolled her eyes.

"Leo Cy what pod?" Cassy said.

"Giant shrimp thing," I said.

"Why didn't she just call it that?" Cassy asked.

"To prove that she's smarter than us, I suspect. Don't let it bug you. I expect we'll have to suffer more of her petty barbs."

Rowan growled, "As I was saying, you have killed this region's"—her voice became laced with sarcasm—"*giant shrimp thing,* so the net covering its territory has been dispelled. However, once you enter the next *giant shrimp thing's* territory—" She looked to the sky shaking her head. "—you'll be caught in the net and lured straight to its lair."

"You can lead us out?" I asked.

"I can," Rowan said.

"Will you?" Cassy asked.

Rowan smiled broadly, with a hint of mischief. "She's smarter than you."

Cassy and I shared a meaning-filled glance, and I had the distinct impression that Cassy had just saved us a world of trouble.

"I will. But only because Cassy asked," Rowan said. "This way, Master." She started walking away.

Cassy hastily grabbed her pack, and we caught up to Rowan just before she melted into the greens and browns of the swamp.

11

"Keep up, Master."

"We need a rest, Rowan," I said.

"Blessed Mother, how did fleshlings ever defeat us?" Rowan mumbled. "Do you want to be there before nightfall, or would you prefer to be some creature's dinner?" She touched a finger to her lip. "On second thought, take all the time you need."

I sat down on a log and pulled off my boots. Cassy stumbled up beside me. I fingered a sore spot at the back of my heel. Blisters would cripple a man as surely as an arrow through the knee.

"The things that hunt Cran Bragh at night can see body heat," Rowan explained. "That would make a wonderful experiment. Two hapless humans at night in the heart of Crann Bragh. How many more predators would the fire attract? I would need a minimum of twelve humans, three rounds with a control."

I silenced her.

Cassy slumped down beside me. Her lips were a pale lilac, and she shivered weakly.

"Cassy, why didn't you say anything?" She stared at me blankly. I touched her forehead—cold and clammy. Her jacket was sodden. Her slender frame hadn't generated enough heat to dry her clothes.

Cassy's pack was heavier than mine. I expected to find a change of clothes, but it was full of odds and ends. Barrettes, ribbons, a stone, a small painted placard, nothing of use. I dug into my own pack, pulling out my change of clothes.

I stripped her out of the wet things and wrapped her in my coat while I rubbed life back into her, evoking groans of gratitude. I stuffed her into a dry shirt and pants, dried her boots with my handkerchief, then massaged the chill from her feet before rewrapping them.

Her teeth chattered. "You're a good man, Rodrick."

"What were you thinking?" I scolded. "You could have caught an evil humor."

Cassy smiled, and her face regained some color. "I'm all right now."

"Damnation you are. You're still half frozen."

"I can walk," Cassy said.

"Good, you need the body warmth," I replied, "but you're ready to collapse from exhaustion. Climb on my back, and you can rest."

"I'm fine," Cassy insisted.

"How long were you in that cage?" I sat down to rewrap my feet.

"A week, maybe more."

"That's a long time," I said. "No wonder you're not at your best. We need to keep up our pace, so let me carry you for a bit."

"Yes, Father," Cassy sneered. "Thank you, Father."

"You can be as indignant as you like, young lady," I

replied, sounding like the stern father figure she was mocking, "so long as you get home in one piece."

"Young lady. That's rich coming from you." I frowned at her. "Talking as if you're old enough to be my father." Cassy scoffed, "You're what, twenty, twenty-one at most? That would make you a couple of years older than me." She tossed her hair over her shoulder, snatched back her pack. "Make sure you keep up, Grandpa."

I released Rowan. The Spriggan shot me an ugly look and stalked off down the path, Cassy close behind.

Twenty-one just felt wrong. An image of my wife rose to my mind's eye. Her porcelain skin, hair aglow in the fiery evening light. She laughed as I pushed her on a swing. The echo of her kindled a longing so profound it hurt. It hurt in all the ways a man was never supposed to show. Was she grieving for me? Was she cursing my name from Damnation?

My children. I hadn't been there for them. My sweet burbling babes, too young to understand why they were being hurt. *Please, Khyber, spare them. Let my children grow up. Climb trees and learn the sword. Let them stand at your right hand, as I did.*

Whoever tampered with the spell had sentenced my family to unending torment. In life or death, I'd find the traitor and make them pay threefold for the damage done to me and mine. After experiencing the extremity of what could be done to spirit flesh, I'd show the fool why I'd been named Wrath.

How they'd tampered with the ritual eluded me. The runes established a direct connection between a god and his priesthood. There should have been no way for another deity to interfere.

What happened was impossible. Unless a flaw had been

engineered into the runes. If that was the case, Khyber wouldn't have answered. An impurity in the steel may have caused the explosion, but the components would have to have been severely contaminated.

I designed those runes. I had overseen the smelting and formation of each link. Gods, I was the only logical suspect. I'd supervised every aspect of its conception through to execution. So what was it I'd missed?

The true traitor must have had the means, motive and opportunity. But that didn't add up. Those with the motive hadn't interacted with the spell until it was too late. Melcor, I could get to. The high priestess was beyond the Veil. She was the only one who could have cast a counterspell, but the Spiral was inert and couldn't grant its priesthood magics.

I had to look at those with the means and opportunity. All the judges who came on the mission would have to have been in collusion. The acolytes were on a need-to-know basis, and only the officers had been given the details.

A chill ran down my spine. What if the traitor was an Avatar? Khyber had possessed them. The king would have looked into their souls, seen their intentions. If that was so, why did he think I was the traitor?

I'd intended to surrender at the first Fauld I came to. An Avatar would be summoned. If the traitor was an Avatar, they'd make sure I never left that cell. The local judge wouldn't question an Avatar. Khyber would never know. My family would continue to suffer.

Was there anyone trustworthy? I could gather evidence, see what happened at the spell.

No, the other Avatars would have already done that. If one of them was the traitor, they'd have wiped away any trace.

That left getting to Khyber and pleading my case. I tried

to visualize a map, but I couldn't shake the image of the spell, the lightning lance. Mentally flogging myself was doing no good. I had to get out of this bog. So I concentrated on putting one foot in front of the other.

12

"HOW ARE we going to cross that?" I asked. "Is there a bridge nearby?"

"None that connects the south bank to the north," Cassy replied. "We'll have to swim."

"No," I said. "That river's at least ten miles wide, and it looks to have strong currents. We'll never make it."

"I've swum in the Al'veran my whole life!"

I looked out at the swirling currents. A branch floated past. I'd have to jog to keep pace with it.

"You can't tell me you've swum across this before."

"Well, no, but I've played in it since I was little," Cassy admitted.

"The farther out we are, the stronger the current will be. You could do it if you condition yourself, but we're tired and hungry. To swim that right now would be a terrible idea."

"Here," Rowan said, coming out of the bushes with a canoe in her arms. It was crafted from a single piece of wood. Pictographs were carved into its sides.

"Where did you find that?" Cassy asked.

"Someone murdered a grove of poplar. I found this in

the structure they'd built with their corpses," Rowan replied, her voice laced with scorn.

"That's a Myi'eshan war canoe. Gods, what's it doing here?" Cassy said.

"The Al'veran is the main waterway into Oppenfauld," Rowan said. "They were most likely scouting or raiding."

"The Myi'eshans haven't raided here in a generation. Lyr'reis, protect me."

"You share the same goddess. Why would you have anything to fear from the Myi'eshans?"

"They're extremists."

Rowan chuckled to herself and set down the canoe. "Look, child. This is Lyr'eris's religion."

The craftsmanship was astounding but the content unsettling. A sequence of scenes ran from stern to prow. They told of bare-chested men paddling upriver, slaughtering farm folk, raping, pillaging and feasting on the flesh of the fallen. The last scene: a man rising from a pile of severed heads, his body rimed in ice. The Myi'eshans kneeling before an Arisen.

"As I said, they take it too far."

"Which part?" Rowan asked. "The cannibalism? Or that they all wish to return from the Ethereal Battle?"

"Not all Arisen come back as monsters," Cassy said.

"So, you figured it out." Rowan smiled wickedly.

She frowned. "Figured what?"

"That he"—Rowan jabbed at me—"is an Arisen."

Cassy looked at me horrified, putting a shaky hand to her weapon.

"I pulled his desiccated corpse from the witches' meat locker." Rowan smiled cruelly. "He rose from the dead and slaughtered them and drank their blood."

I felt my face grow hot with anger and embarrassment. "That was self-defense."

"He is a monster, Cassy. It's only a matter of time before he steals your soul. You saw what he did to—" Rowan rolled her eyes. "—*the giant shrimp thing*. His true nature is hidden, but give him time, and you'll see what lies beneath."

I held out a hand. "I won't deny what she says. Take the canoe and go home. May the lord shield you."

"All Arisen start this way, but eventually they turn. You don't want to be around when he loses himself to the darkness."

"It's you I don't trust." Cassy turned on Rowan. "Look at how much you're enjoying this. All you do is cause trouble." She put her club back into her belt. "Rodrick has saved my life twice. He has been nothing but a gentleman. He's earned the benefit of the doubt."

"Remember my words as he's sinking his teeth into your neck."

"Rowan is right, Cassy. I'll make my own way. I'd never willingly harm you, but—"

"No," Cassy said. "Come home with me. The least I can do is give you a warm bath and a hot meal."

Rowan laughed. "Blood's hot."

"Shut up," Cassy snapped.

"This canoe isn't old," I said. "It's been stashed here because they're coming back for it."

"Get in," Cassy said. "Once we're on the other side, it'll be the judge's problem." She pointed to the distant keep, sitting atop a cliff.

"I have to warn them," I said, pushing the canoe to the river.

Cassy climbed in the front and picked up a paddle. I waved for Rowan to get in. She crossed her arms and turned up her nose, but her legs moved in accordance with my will. The Spriggan sat in the middle, glaring at me. I pushed off, regretting that I didn't leave the poisonous flower behind.

We stowed the boat in a thicket. I ensured it couldn't be seen from the water. The last thing I wanted was to tell the local judge that I had evidence of an enemy raiding party and then not be able to produce said evidence.

Cassy fidgeted with the buckles of her pack. "I can't believe I'm almost home."

I put the last branch in place. "That's great." I examined my work for flaws.

Cassy grunted.

"I'll walk you home, then go to the Fauld. I'll tell them what we found."

"I'm sure that it hasn't occurred to either of you," Rowan said, "but I can't enter this village without putting myself in danger."

"With your attitude, I'm surprised you've survived this long," I replied.

"I don't think the villagers would do anything. Most of us haven't seen a Spriggan before," Cassy said. "You'll be the talk of the town for a generation."

"How wonderful... I could be a one-Spriggan grotesquerie." Rowan struck a pose. "From this day forward, my life's purpose will be to entertain the pig-face simians of Oppenfauld." Her bright tone curdled. "No, child. I would be hacked to pieces by the keep's garrison, and as much as I desire release from this farce, I refuse to die at the hands of Fauldic swine."

"Go, then," I told her coldly. "Take your venom with you.

If I never see you again, it'll be too soon."

"Alas, if only I could, but you hold my leash, and I can only roam so far. I'll see you when you aren't around so many other humans." She paused, some of her hostility melting away. "Farewell, Cassy. I am sorry for my part in your captivity." Rowan walked downstream. "No one should be a slave." She looked pointedly at me as she disappeared amongst the reeds.

"I wasn't a slave, I was cattle." Cassy frowned after her. "This way." She led me to a well-used path. At the top of the bank was a grove of old oaks, leaves burning with late evening light. The path led to a cart track bordered on one side by a rough-hewn fence.

The land opened into cultivated patches of corn, rye, potatoes and the myriad of things that peasants grow. Homesteads dotted the field, and a few miles beyond lay the modest village of Raider's Watch. It sat at the base of a hill, and atop it was the Fauld.

The limestone glowed in the setting sun. Its towers dominated the skyline, and the battlements radiated strength. It was a sight of rare beauty. It told me I was home.

"I'd often wondered why the king would build a Fauld here," Cassy said. "There's nothing but a few farms and wilderness between Dun Avard and Dun Al'veran. This place always seemed to be the ass end of nowhere. Most of the river traffic doesn't even stop, but after finding that canoe..." She shook her head.

"How long has it been since Raider's Watch has seen the Myi'ehsans?" I asked.

"My father tells stories of raids from when he was a child. There hasn't been a sighting in my lifetime," Cassy said. "The Frostbite Wars have always been a distant thing, just words in a history book."

I grunted, thinking back. Events were muddy, a haze of red, roots burrowing, the Mother Tree broken and listing.

"Gods, it's as though we're suddenly at war with the whole world," Cassy continued. "The Myi'eshans to the northeast, Arachnids to the south, Wyrm, the White Flame and now our allies turning on us."

"Hold on," I said. "Our allies turned on us? Have they attacked?"

"All I know is Judge Connell called a muster over a month ago."

I put a hand to my forehead. Of course they'd spin the story. They couldn't tell the citizens we struck first.

"Are you all right?" she asked, taking a cautious step back.

"I'm fine. I hit my head when I got separated from my squad. My memory's still a little fuzzy." I smiled, and the tension left her face.

"My house is just around the corner. Let's have a meal before we go up to the keep."

I contemplated finding a tavern. The coins in my pocket would buy me a meal and some rations, but it wouldn't get me to Faldaris.

"I'd be grateful for a bite. But there's no need for you to come. I can warn them."

"I'm coming with you, Rodrick," Cassy said, putting her hands on her hips. "I'm local and known to the guard. You're not. Judge Connell will revel in making you wait."

I nodded, not wanting to argue. If Cassy came with me and they recognized me, she'd be arrested for harboring a traitor. I wouldn't let her put her neck in a noose. I'd have to insist she stay with her parents. "A chance to wash up would be lovely," I said.

13

As we approached a modest single-room cottage, raised voices could be heard from the road. Cassy came to a stop at the lane and began muttering to herself.

"Go on," I said. "You're coming back from certain death. They'll be ecstatic to see you."

Cassy shot me an offended look. "Is that supposed to be funny?"

"Sorry."

"Rodrick, don't imply that either of us came back from the dead. It's... it's, well... rude and dangerous."

"I spoke without thinking. Won't happen again."

Something shattered against the door. Cassy scrubbed at her face. "Lyr'eris, give me strength."

"It'll be fine. The pain of losing you must be eating at them." I put an arm around Cassy and led her down the lane.

"Fine, then just abandon your family" came a shrill voice from the cabin.

"Family," scoffed a man. "All our children are dead, Molly. There's no family left."

"And me? What of your vows?"

"Don't you dare! You love rubbing my nose in your cuck-oldry. Our marriage ended the first time I caught you."

"Are you going to cry?" Throaty laughter rolled from the house.

Cassy's face was blank and pale. The look of someone who's seen this all before.

"You're pathetic. If you'd give yourself to Lyr'eris, you might actually satisfy."

"For years I said nothing while you mucked up our children with your devotion to that demon but—"

There was a loud smack. "How dare you speak such of my lady? Look at you. You don't even have the balls to hit me back. You're a sorry excuse of a man."

"It's not weakness that stays my hand." The final word was so loud I could feel the vibration through the stoop's handrail.

"Ha ha ha. So, yes, my noble farmer, the great provider. All Khyber's tenets do is make you waste your life." A dish broke. "There's your honor, your ideas. There's your religion."

"I can't believe you just did that. If anyone from the garrison saw, you'd hang."

"So go snitch. It's what I'd expect from a coward."

"I'm done, Molly. I know it was you. I can't prove anything, or I'd have had the Avatar here after Evan died."

"You think I...?" Molly screamed.

I knocked on the door.

"Lyr'eris smite you where you stand." There was another crash as something else was thrown across the room.

"Save your false outrage. I know you too well. I'm going to press charges. Though I hardly need it with the look on your face. My religion is the only reason I'm giving you fair warning."

I knocked again.

The door opened, and a short thickly muscled man peered out. "Good eve, friend. Now is not the best—"

A plump flushed face peeked around the door. "Get off my land, vagabond! Gods, I can smell you from here." The door slammed with all her weight behind it. It bounced back open, and I saw the man waving a hand, trying to shake away the pain. He made a fist, and his eyes flashed with bottled fury.

Cassy sat on the stoop, her face in her hands. Yelling resumed. I sat beside her, not knowing what to say. Another dish broke.

"There won't be any dishes left if she keeps it up," I mumbled.

Cassy half-heartedly chuckled. "Mam's a potter."

The door swung open. Cassy jumped to her feet.

"Say what you like. You can't hurt me anymore. We're done. I'll be back, and the truth will come out. We both know it, and you'll answer to the Avatars."

"Dah, Mam," Cassy said into the brief silence.

The man dropped his pack and bedroll, shocked.

"Cassy! Broken blade. You're alive!" Cassy's father ran forward and swept her into a hug. "My daughter, you're home. You're safe. Thank Khyber."

Cassy gave a little coo, then patted his arm.

Molly horked and spat on the porch. They both looked at the pear-shaped shadow that took up the doorframe. Their mirth curdled like vinegar added to milk.

"Come here, child." Molly pointed to the space in front of her. Cassy tore away from her father and stood where her mother was pointing.

"You survived," Molly said.

"Yes, Mam," Cassy replied.

"Then her frozen fire finally came to you. I am so proud." She gave her daughter an awkward hug while keeping malice-filled eyes on her husband.

"I was right, you lying sow. You sent her out during an eclipse as some test." The man kicked the porch railing, and the banister clattered to the ground. "You're sick, Molly."

Cassy's father pulled her out of Molly's grip. "Come, Cassy. Bring your friend."

"But—" Cassy protested.

"For once, do as I ask. Your mother sent you out during the astral eclipse. You're not safe with her."

"Don't listen to him, sweetheart," Molly told her. "This is your home, and I couldn't be prouder. Come in, and I'll get you something to eat."

"No." Cassy's voice was small.

"What did you say?" Molly's voice grew sharper with every word.

"I was taken by a pair of witches." Cassy's fear ignited to anger. "They kept me in a cage! They debated on the different ways to cook me. Joking about what part of me they'd savor most."

"But they didn't. You escaped and are stronger for it," Molly said.

Cassy took something from her pocket and held it up for Molly to see. Molly took an involuntary step back and clutched at something that hung from her neck. Cassy pulled an identical pendant from her shirt. An icicle carved from bone.

"I found these in the cave. The witches taunted me with them. Saying how happy they were to complete the set," Cassy said, her voice still quiet and small.

Her father came up onto the porch. "Come away," he said gently.

"Mind grabbing my pack, friend?" I did and followed as he led us away.

"Cassy, get back here—NOW!" Molly yelled.

Cassy curled in on herself but let her father guide her away, still clutching the necklaces in her hand. We reached the road and headed towards town.

The night was clear and chill. The stars were bright, and the moon bathed the land with a silvery light. For the first time since returning, I saw the night sky and the beauty of the Ethereal Battle. Reds and greens, yellows and white winked in a great dense band across the sky. They danced like revelers packed into the streets. Below the band of stars sat the Void, a darkness so empty it swallowed the light.

"Name's William Forester," Cassy's father said, extending his left hand, his right around his daughter. I awkwardly shook it.

"Rodrick," I replied.

"You helped my girl home?" William asked. "I can't tell you how grateful I am. I was certain that—" He coughed, turning his face away.

"Rodrick saved my life," Cassy told him.

William stopped and embraced his child. He grasped my shoulder with a hand that could crush walnuts, his voice hoarse. "Thank you. By Khyber's mercy, thank you."

Cassy tentatively hugged him back.

"Come, let's go to your aunt's."

"Mam says I'm not allowed."

"The Void take your mother. You're more terrified of her than you were of an astral eclipse." William took his daughter's chin and made her look into his eyes. "That creature is not your mother. She is cruel and soulless. I was too beaten down to protect you. No more. We'll start fresh, you and me. We'll move away from here and leave this nightmare behind. Come on."

We jumped a fence, picking our way through orderly rows of vegetables. The farmhouse was much larger than the Forester cottage. It boasted two full stories and glass in the windows.

William knocked. The laughter and clinking of dishes continued without interruption. A tall, thin man, clean-shaven, stood at the door, his bald spot reflecting the candlelight.

"William," he said, smiling and reaching out a hand. "Reconsidered enlisting—" He stumbled back, clutching his chest. "Good lord!"

"Bill, what's the matter?"

"Maggie, it's your brother," Bill said.

"What did that witch do?" Short, dark and as thick as her brother, Maggie stormed up to the door.

"Cassy!" Maggie exclaimed. "By the Avatars, we searched for days. Come in, come in." Maggie pulled Cassy into a hug. The girl uncomfortably patted her aunt's back.

Bill pulled his wife away, his face darkening. "William, have you tested her yet?"

"It's Cassy," William said defensively.

"The tenets of Kydaism," Bill replied, his voice hard. "Do not suffer an Arisen to walk amongst the flock. And you bring her to my home, untested. My children and grandchildren are here." Bill shook his head angrily and called inside, "Mark."

"Ya, Dah."

"Fetch my knife, and the sword and shield from the mantle."

"Bill, I know my daughter," William protested.

"And if it were my sons, you'd do the same."

"He's right, Dah," Cassy said. "We'll wait by the barn." She hooked her arm in mine and led me off the porch.

"Cassy, I can't pass."

"If you run, they'll have the whole village after you. You saved me. Let me repay the favor."

"I don't want to risk—"

Bill blustered up, berating his brother-in-law. "Damnation, William, you know the undead act just like the people they were in life. How could you be so stupid?"

"I know I was, it just... I thought she was gone. Like Evan and Francis. Then she... I just..." William said, shaking his head.

Bill's sons jogged up. The older had a knife and a couple of pitchforks. The younger bore a statue. Khyber's holy symbol—a sword driven into the ground with a shield resting against it.

Bill took the statue and set it on the ground. He handed a pitchfork to William and his youngest. The two boys held their makeshift spears at the ready. Both had the easy grace of long hours of practice with polearms. William looked uncertainly from Cassy to Bill, then shifted his weight into a fighter's stance.

Cassy stepped forward and held out her hand. Bill nodded in appreciation. He pricked Cassy's finger, careful to not touch the blood. Cassy dripped a few drops onto the figurine. Nothing happened. The droplets ran down the shield.

Bill looked up with a wide grin across his face, and he scooped his niece into his arms. Cassy's cousins joined in, laughing. She gave a grudging smile and made soft sounds of protest.

"Glad to have you back, Cass," said the older one.

"Thanks, Lucas," Cassy said, pushing them away. "Uncle Bill, this is my friend Rodrick. He saved my life."

Bill smiled. "Thank you." He reached to shake my hand with his left. Odd. Perhaps it was the custom in these parts.

Quick as lightning, Bill slashed. I sidestepped, using his momentum, and sent him stumbling forward. Lucas lunged. I kicked the pitchforks, tangling the tines with his brother's.

"Stop!" Cassy shouted. "They just want to see if you're an Arisen."

I did my best to keep the anger from my face. "Then why not ask?" I knew full well that my blood defied the laws of nature.

"You had a nervous air about you," Bill said, dusting himself off.

"Rodrick," Cassy said, meeting my eye, "trust me."

She took the knife. I'd only known this girl for an afternoon. Why was she so eager to protect me? Why in Damnation was she willing to put her family at risk? I gave her my hand. She slipped the knife between my fingers and into her own.

"Cassy! Don't touch the blood!" William cried, reaching for his daughter. She made a show of squeezing. The blood dripped through her fingers and onto the statue. Nothing happened. Three heartbeats passed, and the younger lad gave a nervous laugh. The smell seemed to crawl inside my brain. My pulse quickened.

William handed Cassy a handkerchief, and Bill gave me his. I accepted reluctantly. The thing was filthy and as stiff as if it had been starched.

"Maggie," Bill called to the woman standing on the porch. "All's well."

"Ho, thank the blessed lord," she said, wiping her brow.

"That was needlessly stupid," William growled.

"Its fine, Dah." Cassy patted him on the shoulder.

"Lord, save me from headstrong women," William said to the sky. "You don't touch fire or go out in the snow without a jacket. You don't stand in front of a stampeding horse, and you do not touch a stranger's blood."

"Sorry about the knife, friend," Bill said, shaking my hand softly this time. "Bill Harris. Let me make it up to you with some supper."

"Thank you. I honestly can't remember the last time I ate."

"Well, we can fix that," Bill said, picking up the sword and shield. He clapped his younger son on the shoulder and led us back to the house.

"Maggie," Bill said, "this is Rodrick. Apparently, he saved Cassy's life."

"A pleasure."

The thirst was amping. I pretended to trip on a loose stone and rammed my shin into the bottom step.

"Strothheim, are you all right?" Maggie asked.

"Yes, thank you." The pain drove away the thirst.

William reached down and helped me up.

"My boots are a size too big for me," I explained.

Maggie's eyes flickered over my mud-crusted clothes. "Please come in."

"Thank you, but I've trekked through a bog today and would hate to track muck all over your floors." I laughed inwardly as the tension left her shoulders.

"Leave those troublesome boots out here. I'll fix you a bath. Had the water on for the babes anyway."

"That's very kind," I said.

"Hold a moment. Let's have a drink in the evening air," Bill said. "Tea, ale, or something stronger?"

"I'll take that something stronger,"

Bill gave a jaunty grin, revealing a set of hideous teeth. "Lad after my own heart. Lucas, would you mind?"

"What year?" Lucas asked.

"He brought Cassy home. You know the one."

"Come on, Cassy. You can have the tub first," Maggie said. William followed, unwilling to let his daughter out of his sight for any longer than necessary.

"Come, sit." Bill motioned to two chairs. A pair of rocking chairs sat at the far end of the porch. The view of the night sky was stunning. "Gods, it's so beautifully terrifying."

"Terrifying," I murmured in agreement.

"Did you study astrological theology in school?"

"I did."

"It was my favorite," Bill told me. "Show me another place in the world a simple farmer can have a lord's education for free."

"Then why not become an acolyte?"

"Children at fifteen," Bill said. "There!" His finger shot towards a flash of light with sparks spraying from it. "If only we had one of the university's imbued looking glasses. I've always wanted to see the shards being absorbed into the Neather Realms. One day that'll be us. Fooshhh." He flicked his fingers. "Our world torn asunder. Every day, we draw closer to the end." He swallowed, and his egg-sized Adam's apple bobbed up and down. "Not in my lifetime, but my children's? Hm, definitely my grandchildren's."

"You getting all philosophical on our guest, Dah?" Lucas asked, handing me a simple clay cup. I sniffed at the contents and found it anything but simple. Bill and Lucas watching me avidly, I raised my cup, and they did the same.

"A night with Enris!" I declared. Bill's eyes danced. I took another sip. "Slightly spicy at first. Then a smokiness rolls in, followed by a toasted biscuit. By the gods, a caramel apple finish."

"Boy knows his whiskeys, I'll give him that," Bill said, topping up my glass.

"Where'd you get this?"

"Made it ourselves," Lucas replied, his chest swelling with pride. Hopefully he'd grow into his frame, but by the look of his father, he'd be all arms and legs for life. "Grew everything right here, the wheat, barley, corn. Even harvested the peat from Crann Bragh."

A child shrieked and ran through the front door. His very pregnant mother snapped him up before he could run out into open air. "Lucas, can you take him? I have to sit down."

"Of course, love." Lucas smiled, handed me the towel he'd tucked under his arm and took his son.

"Tub's off the front hall, last door on the left," Bill said. "I'm feeling hungry for babies."

The boy shrieked, squirming in his father's arms. Lucas ran through the door with Bill close behind making a truly hideous face at the little man. Joyous laughter rang through the house and out over the fields.

Thirst hit me like a slaver's lash. I was on my feet and took a step after them. I clutched the banister. It would be too easy to go in there and take them all. Bill had shown skill with the knife. But with this fury boiling inside, it'd take more than a knife to stop me. I'd kill the men first, take my time with...

I found myself leaning against the doorframe.

No. I breathed deeply, trying to gain control. Another laugh cut me. My instincts screamed for me to hunt, to feed. I bit my knuckle, and warm blood filled my mouth. I was nearly swallowed by insanity. I opened my eyes, and the statue of the sword and shield sat on the banister before me. The holy symbol of Khyber. I lurched towards it.

"Help me, Lord, please." I reached for the figurine. Red light emanated from the statue, stinging my eyes and filling my mind with a tooth-rattling hum. I pulled my hand back as though it had been seared. It had. The tips of my left hand were red as though scalded.

The thirst retreated like an eel darting back into its cave. "Thank you, Lord. You saved them. You saved me."

"Rodrick?" Cassy stood in the doorway drying her hair with a towel. "The bath's ready."

"Thank you. I just need a moment to finish praying."

She hesitated before going back inside.

14

"I couldn't eat another bite," I said.

"Come now, a strapping lad like you," Maggie said conspiratorially.

"I've eaten enough for two men. It truly is the best trifle I've ever had."

Maggie plopped a third helping on my plate. "It has to be gone by morn." Her eyes sparkled with pride. "I'm not leaving this dish behind. Cassy dear, would you like some?"

Cassy sat stiff-backed, her hands folded in her lap. "No. Thank you, Auntie."

"But you barely touched your food," Maggie protested.

"Mum says I have to watch my weight."

"Watch your weight!" Maggie said with a huff. "How many meals did you miss while you were gone?"

William touched his sister's elbow. Everyone met each other's eyes with looks that were thick with unspoken meaning.

"You are traveling somewhere?" I asked.

"Dun Al'veran," Mark said.

"By the look of those chests in the other room, you aren't going on a holiday."

The room went silent.

"Put your foot in that one," Mark snickered.

"Mark, no need to be rude to our guest," Bill chided the boy.

"Where are you from, Rodrick?" Lucas asked. "You have the accent of the North."

I opened my mouth to reply, but the answer died on my tongue. "Faldaris?"

"He hit his head," Cassy said, looking at me through a curtain of hair.

"You were taken by the same witches that took our Cassy?" Maggie blurted, her eyes brimming with tears.

"I was separated from my squad. Fell off a cliff, and when I woke—"

"You poor dear." Maggie wiped her eyes with her apron.

"An acolyte?" Bill asked.

I smiled around a mouthful of strawberry and let them come to their own conclusion. "I believe I'm presumed dead. I have to report in, if nothing else than to ease the suffering of my wife and children."

Cassy looked up sharply.

"I'm sorry," William said.

"Go see the Avatar. She'll get you home," Lucas said.

"No, lad, not anymore," William added. "More likely he'd be back on the front lines before he's had a chance to fully recover. Did you even pay attention to the new proclamations?"

"Ya, war is coming. All Kydaists are to evacuate their homes and go to the closest Dun. What do you think I'm doin' here?" Lucas snapped. "My child would rather be asleep in his bed, but we're ready to fight."

"Least you got the parts that affect you right," William said, blowing out his mustache.

"Lucas," a girl called from the other room, "come kiss James goodnight."

Lucas got up and stomped out of the room.

Maggie returned from the kitchen with a plate mounded with two pieces of pie, the remains of the trifle, canned peaches and pears, all of which was laden with fresh whipping cream. She placed it in front of Cassy as if she were setting the pin on a bear trap and fled the room.

Cassy glared after her aunt, then down at her plate. She crossed her arms and tossed her hair behind her like a frisky mare.

"She's likely in there baking you a pan of cookies," Bill jibed. "You'd better eat something, or you'll be buried in cakes and tarts by morning."

Cassy refused to look at her uncle or the plate of offending desserts.

Lucas returned, hand in hand with his wife. They both gave off an aura of contentment.

"Susan, you're the best thing that ever happened to him," William said.

"I know." Susan gave her husband a kiss.

Cassy rolled her eyes.

"What did this proclamation say, William?" I asked.

"Martial law has been declared due to the breakdown of the alliance. Those that worship the King Ascended are ordered to retreat to the major cities." William said. "An attack is less likely here in the west, but all across the country, Kydaists are being moved behind walls. It is a dangerous time for us all."

"How is that any different from what I just said?" Lucas asked, his hackles rising again.

"It's what's not said that's important," William said. "Martial law suspends civil rights and religious freedoms. Only those that worship Khyber are being evacuated. Foreigners and followers of other deities will be given no shelter in the war to come."

"Mam and me," Cassy said, sitting up. "What are we supposed to do when the war comes?"

"Your *mother* will have to fend for herself, for the first time in her life," William said darkly. "Children are exempt."

"I'm no child." Cassy snorted. "I've been of age for four years."

"But you never did your civilian service," William told her.

"So?"

"So, you are still legally a child."

"I'm seventeen."

"Long past time for you to prove your commitment to Oppenfauld. Mark is nine, and he's already done. It'd be different if you were married," William said, gesturing at Susan. "But your mother chased off every suitor." Cassy's face went blank. "I know it rankles, but this is a blessing in disguise. Come to Dun Al'veran, do your two years, and see where life takes you."

Cassy stared at her lap, refusing to acknowledge what her father had said.

"Look at me, Cassy. The alliance is broken. Religious freedom is gone. The peace and prosperity our country has known is over. For the first time in thirty years, the Ascendancy War will be fought on our soil."

"But it doesn't make any sense," Cassy whined. "Why would the allies turn on us and slay the Mother Tree?"

"No mortal can understand the will of the gods," Bill said. "All we can do is defend our land and lord."

"Stand sure," I said.

"Stand sure." Everyone except Cassy made the sign of the sword over their breast.

"Please, Cassy," William went on, "think about it. The world has just gotten a lot scarier."

"And what of my integrity?" she asked, her head held high.

"Lyr'eris isn't worth dying for." William scrubbed at his beard, then stood. "Anyone else for another cup of tea?" He pointed to Cassy's plate. "You should eat that. It may be the last time you ever get to enjoy your aunt's cooking." When no one replied, he picked up the teapot and went into the kitchen.

Cassy glared at the closing door. She picked up her spoon and prodded a piece of pie.

"SORRY, Rodrick, there's just no more beds in the house," Bill apologized for the fourth time.

"Bill, I'm fed, bathed with clean clothes on my back, and you're giving me a place to rest for no more than a handshake. Honestly, the barn is wonderful. Besides, I should go straight to the keep. The garrison needs to be warned."

"Judge Connell will make you wait till morning anyway. Get some rest. Trust me. That hoary old goat won't thank you for waking him. Besides, there are things that prowl the night. Even with the witches dead... Just keep a wall between you and the night."

He led me across the farmyard and into the barn. Horses whinnied and sheep bleated as we entered. Bill lit a lamp, hung it on the wall. I was led past two fully loaded wagons and to the back of the barn.

"There's a bunk in the tack room. It smells of leather and horse, but it'll keep you safe," he added. Saddles, halters and bridles were hung from every space you could have a hook, but sure enough, there was a bed.

"I can't thank you enough." I held the blankets in one arm and shook his hand.

"We're leaving at dawn. I'll send Mark to wake you for breakfast," he said as he closed the door.

I lay down and was asleep before I pulled the blankets up to my neck.

15

I STARTED out of bed at the sound of splintering wood. "Arisen!" yelled a harsh female voice. "You killed my child?" was followed by a chorus of angry voices.

I hurriedly tugged on my boots and coat. I blindly felt my way across the tack room. Screams and cries of anger came from the house. Torchlight flickered through the planks in the walls. I bumped into a table, sending tools clattering to the ground. I peeked through a crack, praying no one had noticed my blunder.

Bill and his family were dragged from their home. Maggie was pulled along by her hair. Bill had his arm twisted behind his back and a knife to his throat. Cassy fought like a cat about to be given a bath, and Mark was thrown to the dirt, cradling his arm.

"Here's the Arisen!" Molly screamed, storming up to Cassy. "Demon! Release my daughter's soul!"

"Mam, it's me, you kno—" The slap cut though the yelling.

"Hold your tongue, creature."

A round matronly woman hurried through the front

door, red faced, with tears glistening on her cheeks. In one hand she held a doll, in the other Cassy's backpack. She waved the doll at the man who held the knife to Bill's throat. Sobbing wordlessly, she buried her face in his shoulder. Shock passed over the man's face as he took the doll from the woman. The crowd grew quiet.

Molly took the pack from the woman and rummaged inside. She brushed blond hair back over her ear to keep it out of her eyes. "Proof." Molly held up the pack. "Trophies of those it took."

"Burn it."

"Hang 'em. There won't be any blood!"

"Arisen."

"Jack was only four."

Molly held up a hand for order, but no one was paying attention now that vengeance had them in its grip. A rope was produced, one end flung over a tree limb.

I got the oil lamp, flint, and steel that Bill had left me. There was a clatter as someone entered the barn. I peeked out the door. The double doors had been flung open. Animals danced as men swooped in. They rolled the wagon out and around the corner.

"Hang the rest, but the Arisen must be sacrificed to Lyr'eris!" Molly yelled over the crowd.

I found the oil lamp and struck a spark. I frantically searched and found a baling knife. It'd be little use against a mob, especially if their blood was up. But most people were cowards, and the sight of steel would buy me a few moments.

The barn was empty. I slipped into the closest stall. The horse whinnied and stomped. A soft word and a soothing touch allowed me to push past it and out the paddock door.

I could repeat what I'd done to the witches, but if I did,

the mob would know for certain that there was an Arisen. They'd turn on me, and Bill's family would most likely join them. No. Whatever tricks lay in my blood, they were better off staying hidden.

I peeked around the corner. Lucas's limp body was being carried by a muscular youth, while Susan and James were driven like cattle by a fat woman with a switch.

Bill was hoisted onto the back of the wagon. He said something to the man with the knife. The reply was a punch to the kidney.

I had wasted enough time. I picked up the lamp and walked around the rear of the barn. All eyes were fixed on Bill. A loop was fastened around his neck, the slack taken up, pulling him to his toes.

"The king proclaims"—Molly's voice carried over the angry crowd—"we are no longer Fauldic, so I say his laws no longer apply to us." The mob cheered. "Let's show what decent gods-fearing folk do to those who harbor demons."

Lucas was dropped like a side of beef. His mother quickly put a hand to his forehead. It came away bloody.

"This is our town!" someone yelled.

"Ya, hang the bastards!" screamed a brunette no older than Susan. A grandmother cackled, pointing at the tears staining Maggie's cheeks.

"I dedicate these deaths to Lyr'eris. May her frozen fire blacken their souls," Molly shouted, and the crowd cheered. She pulled out a crude cleaver, just a piece of hammered metal with an edge. The jagged symbols carved into its sides steamed in the night air and glowed with a chill light.

Two men hauled Cassy to the front of the crowd and forced her over a chopping block. I had a perfect view. Her mother's eyes glittered with triumph as she raised her cleaver.

I pushed past a burly man with a soot-stained face. He grabbed me by the collar and spun me around. "Got him, Molly," he yelled over the din. He raised a meaty fist. I drove the knife into his armpit. He crumpled around the wound. Someone else thrust steel at my chest. Some reflex made me shift my weight, avoiding the strike. I retaliated, and the woman fell back, hand clutched to her ruined face. The world erupted in screams, and the mob parted like minnows scattered by a pebble. I danced back, fleeing the scent of blood.

I smashed the lamp on the ground. The mob recoiled from the flames. I spun just in time to see a bearded face and a fist. I took the blow on the chin and stumbled back. Heat flashed up my leg. I blinked away the stars. A boot drove at my chest. I knocked it aside and kicked my attacker in the groin. He bellowed like an ox. My oil-soaked boot connected with a burst of flames. The bearded ox threw me, panic granting him startling strength. I skidded, and dust and gravel sprayed.

William came out of the dark, brandishing a table leg. He sent the man holding Cassy flying, blood spraying from the hole that used to be his nose. Bloody Nose fell into Bill, knocking him off the wagon. Molly hacked at William. The cleaver left a line of crimson on his shoulder. William caught Molly's wrist and twisted, while Maggie and Susan rushed to lift Bill back onto the wagon bed.

"Maggie!" I yelled and tossed her my knife. It landed in the dirt. She gave no sign of having noticed.

The bearded ox hauled me to my feet. A fist the size of a Clydesdale's hoof rocked my head back, and I was back on the ground.

Time stopped. The Veil tore, and a rift opened into the emptiness of the Void. Tentacles curled around the opening as if trying to force it wider. A soul screamed as more tentacles reached through, coiling about the man I'd stabbed. Pure animalistic terror shot through me, an uncontrollable need to hide. The soot-stained man was pulled into the Void. The Veil closed, and time resumed.

The ox rammed his heel into my gut, taking the breath out of me. I wrapped around the blow and pulled him off balance. He fell, I kicked, his beard ignited. I rolled away while he thrashed at the flames.

I scuffed dirt over my foot, extinguishing the flames. The pain of the burns suddenly hit me.

Bill fell to the ground. Susan stood atop the wagon, the baling knife in one hand, the severed rope in the other. The mob roared. Maggie loosened the noose around Bill's neck. Mark darted out from behind the wagon, dragging his bawling nephew behind him.

"What are you going to do, coward?" Molly taunted as William held her in an arm lock. He glanced at Cassy, then to the cleaver still clutched in her mother's hand.

"You were going to kill my child." Her forearm snapped, and she screamed as though she were giving birth. The cleaver spun to the dirt. "With this hand! You were going to kill your own daughter!" He pushed her face-first into the dirt. Two more snaps much louder than the first, and her arm bent in ways it was never meant to. "MY CHILD!" He brought the table leg up, poised to bash her skull in.

"Dah." Cassy touched William's shoulder. He looked between his wife, daughter and the table leg. He bottled his fury and released his grip on Molly.

"Pathetic," Molly choked. "Both of you."

Cassy winced. William took in the mob. The braver ones crept around the fire. Bill was on his feet, stout Maggie supporting his weight. William jogged over to me and helped me up.

The adrenaline was wearing off, and the full extent of the burns were making themselves known. It wouldn't be long before the oil fire died. By the look of the mob, they wanted blood.

I tested my leg. I wouldn't be able to go far or fast. "Give me that. I'll hold them as long as I can."

"What? No!" Cassy protested.

William met my eye and handed me the table leg. "Stand sure, brother."

"Stand sure. Now save your family."

William strode over to Lucas and picked him up. Something inside him must have severed. Time slowed. The young man's soul rose from his body. The Veil tore. A man of blue light stepped from the shadows as if he had been hiding on the other side of the tree, his armor resplendent, a crown forged from broken swords on his head. His Majesty brought tears to my eyes. He held out a hand to Lucas as if he were welcoming a child home. Lucas looked at his wife and child. Grief rolled from him in a palpable wave.

The hunger surged within me. I couldn't control myself. I opened my mouth and breathed. His spirit was dragged towards me like a man over the edge of a waterfall. He recognized me and scrambled to get away. "Susan, run!" I swallowed his soul.

Khyber roared in anger. He took a menacing step towards me. Time resumed and Khyber faded, but thunder boomed in a cloudless sky.

The oil fire was nearly out. The mob rallied its courage. Cassy grabbed my coat sleeve. "Come on."

A blur of motion, and instinctively I stepped in front of her. I felt a flash of pain as a knife buried itself under my jaw. Warmth rolled down my front, and my knees gave way as Cassy screamed my name. I saw her father grab her by the upper arm and pull her away, Lucas's corpse draped over his shoulders.

I gasped a breath, liquid filled my lungs, then blackness.

16

I TOOK A BREATH. Sweet and glorious. Rowan stood over me holding a bloodied dagger.

"Curious," she said, tilting her head to one side. "I felt you die, yet our link remained intact."

I pushed myself up on an elbow. My throat burned.

"The blood flows back into you. Most fascinating." The distant sound of angry voices. I tried to speak, but all that happened was a hoarse croak.

"Your soft tissue regenerates at an amazing rate. Your vocal cords were completely severed," she continued cheerily. "Most interesting. I wonder what would happen if—"

There was a blinding flash from my left eye and blackness.

FIRE COURSED DOWN EVERY NERVE. My body convulsed, vision distorted. Eventually, I was able to move my arms. I grabbed my face.

Rowan said, "Your eye appears to have fully regenerated the same pigment."

"You *stabbed* me," I raged.

"I assumed the bond would stop me, but it appears that I can wound you without ending your life. What a pleasant surprise to not have that restriction anymore."

"People are in trouble," I barked.

"Yes, I watched from over there. Very courageous, saving those humans."

"You didn't help."

"Your species is violence given flesh. why would I redirect their focus onto myself?" Rowan said.

"I thought you wanted to die?" I asked.

"Not like that, a spectacle."

I rose to my hands and knees. Shouts bounced over the fields. There may still be a chance to help get Bill and his family. I thought of Lucas and hated myself.

"You know, I've never had the opportunity to study an Arisen. I wonder what would happen if—"

"Don't you dare." My whole body went numb. The only feeling remaining was my face pressed against the earth.

"Intensely satisfying," she said, smiling like a cat with a mouse.

Blackness.

ROWAN STUDIED THE CRIMSON BLADE, turning it this way and that in the moonlight. Sensation spread down my spine. Muscles at the back of my neck were raw. I touched the open wound.

"I really hate you." Screams and yells echoed over the

farmland. I wanted to help. Rowan eyed the dagger in a way that made my eye twitch.

"Fascinating," she said. "You're reabsorbing the blood. It moves as though you exert a magnetic force upon it. You're healing at a much slower rate, and you look like a corpse, all green and waxy. I wonder if the healing process is depleting some internal reserve. Yes, the wound is healing differently. Filling with blood rather than knitting together."

"Don't you dare," I spat.

"How far away would you have to be from the blood for the draw to stop working?" she mumbled to herself. "Or if you were drained of blood? I supposed that's where the folklore about Arisen stems. Would you absorb other forms of biomass if blood wasn't available... or does blood have some intrinsic value?"

"Don't!" I took control of her, forcing her to drop the dagger.

"That's quite rude, you know." Rowan flexed her fingers as they came back under her control.

"You stabbed me in the eye." She smiled as if I'd paid her a compliment. "Just go back to the forest. It's better when you're not around."

She stood up and sighed. "Not even a thank you. You might have lain there till the sundering with that knife in your throat."

"Don't act as if this didn't make your day."

The petals of her skin reflected the pale light of the moon, giving her a glossy look. Rowan smiled mischievously and walked off into a field of wheat.

The night grew silent. The distant screams had ended. Whatever help I'd've been to Cassy and her family was irrelevant at this point.

Thirst propelled me. Repulsed by what I was doing, I fed

on the corpse of the man I'd killed. Blood flowed down my throat, the deep ache in the muscles fading. I peeled my lips from the dried husk. The taste of copper clung to my palate. I had to get away. I fingered the wound on the back of my neck. It had closed. *Khyber, save me.*

A whinny from the stables. I doubted the Harrises would need their horses. I could be in Faldaris within a month. My gaze took in the withered corpse. I'd have to skirt the villages, keep to the mountain trails. I was too dangerous to be around others.

Was this how it started for all Arisen? Some evil within pushing you to devour souls and drink the blood of friends and family. How many Arisen had fled society to save the ones they loved, only to return a monster driven mad by thirst?

I had to hold on. It was a month to Faldaris. An image of Lucas's terror-filled face as I claimed his soul flashed in my mind's eye.

I tested my leg. The skin pulled in odd ways but there was little pain. I hobbled over to the house, the sole of my boot flopping with every step. Inside the landing was an oil lamp on a side table. It appeared to be the only thing in the house that hadn't been knocked over.

Three strikes of the flint and the wick took the spark. In the entryway, I found my original boots. The trunks in the front room had been tossed. Everything was too tight and long. It took some time to find suitable clothing.

I went to the kitchen. Took a couple loaves of bread, cheese, dried fruit and a jar of cooking fat and tied it in a sheet. I stood looking at the package, disgusted at what I was doing. Avatar Wrath, the punitive arm of justice in Oppenfauld and one of the high priests of Kydaism—stealing.

I unwrapped the bundle and put the food back. I'd

weathered privation before, and my faith had kept me strong. I might be excommunicated, but I would not abandon my morals for the sake of expediency.

There were four horses in the barn, two of which came to their doors, interested in what I was doing. They were skittish from the excitement, dancing away as I approached. I got a saddle and tack and placed it on the edge of the closest stall.

"This is different. Khyber needs to know there's a traitor within the priesthood."

A convenient lie. This is a matter of national security. You think you matter at this point? Khyber will question the entire priesthood down to the lowliest scribe. He'll ferret out the traitor. You are redundant.

I hammered a fist into the saddle, silencing the voices in my head. The horses whinnied. Their fear was intoxicating. The closest shrank into the shadows of her stall. Mottled black and white. She only came up to my shoulder.

This was not a person but a beast. The thirst spiked. I undid the latch. She pressed herself farther into the corner. Soft brown eyes pleaded with me to go away. I couldn't fight this forever. The thirst was a need as primal and necessary as breathing. Better I take an animal than lose control and hurt a person. How was this any different from the roast we'd had at supper?

"No," I said out loud. "I will not eat someone's pet."

The thirst screamed at me. I fled before my resolve faltered.

I reached the road and found Molly Forester slumped in a ditch. "Help, my bastard husband broke my arm." She held it up. Hideously swollen, her arm looked ready to burst from internal bleeding. Her teeth chattered, and she glistened with sweat.

I rushed past, knowing that if I stopped, even for a moment, I'd drain her. I jumped a fence and trotted across a field. A string of profanities and curses followed me.

The night softened with the gray light of predawn. The thirst urged me to go back, to feed. I was a danger. I almost attacked the Harrises. Only Khyber's light had stopped me. I'd just fed and was nearly delirious with desire. What hope did I have of getting to Faldaris without losing control?

I needed to turn myself in. Before the thirst claimed my humanity.

I CROSSED FIELDS AND FARMS. Lamplight flickered behind a shuttered window. Strange to think that the people in these tiny homes had gotten out of bed to murder a neighbor. I was about to pass a homestead when heavy banging from inside made me sink into the shadows.

"Open in the name of the King Ascended!"

The door creaked open, and a woman spoke. "Yes, Misr."

"Religion?"

"We follow the White Flame." Four soldiers in lacquered leather armor stood on the stoop.

"Gather your possessions, come with us."

"Misr, me father's too sick to be moved."

The soldiers barged into the house. Children cried, and the woman screamed, but everyone in the family was marched out the front door in short order. The woman's father hopped like a young man with a sword prodding his back. Soldiers pressed bundles into their arms, and the lot were marched off towards the town. I waited till they were out of sight, then followed.

A well-trimmed hedge lined the road. I crept along,

hidden in its shadow. A sentry challenged the soldiers. He inspected the company, then flagged them through the archway.

From the clamor of voices, I suspected that the entire village had been rousted from their beds. A patrol marched past the archway, another family scurrying before them.

I stepped out from the shadowed hedge and walked down the middle of the lane. "Hello," I called.

The sentry raised a crossbow and took aim. I held my arms out to the sides.

"Halt, or I'll shoot." I did as commanded. "Religion?"

"Kydaism." There was a red flash of light from something around the man's neck.

"You're lying, son. Lying to an acolyte is a crime." The hedge rustled, and soldiers surrounded me.

"I'm not lying! I worship the lord of the broken sword. We're just not on good terms right now."

A spear point pressed into my ribs. "There's always one that thinks he's funny," snarled one of the soldiers behind me.

The sentry approached, crossbow leveled. "I'm going to ask you again, and if you lie to me, things will not go well for you."

"I surrender to Khyber's will." I slowly knelt down. "My name is Rodrick Corwyn, and I was once Avatar Wrath. I have returned from beyond the Veil to prove my innocence."

"Arisen!" exclaimed one of the soldiers.

Every soldier within reach grabbed me. I was shoved face-first into the road. My arms were wrenched behind my back, then tied at wrist, elbow and ankles.

"This isn't necessary. I—"

"Gag him," barked the sentry.

A handkerchief was crammed into my mouth. A spear

was threaded through my bonds, and I was lifted like a dressed stag as my joints screamed in protest.

"Right, double time to the huntsman," barked one of the soldiers.

"No," said the sentry. "The Avatar's closer. She's in the square."

The squad set off through the town. Spears were poised as if they expected me to break free at any moment. I resigned myself to the indignity. They were right to treat me like an animal.

I WAS MARCHED DOWN cobbled streets. Every house and shop had the front doors wide open and lights burning brightly. A pair of soldiers came out of a house, a terrified young man held by the scruff of his neck between them. Without a word they fell into step behind our company.

I was carried past a few of the larger homes and onto the village green. A grand maple stood at the center of a soft green lawn that sloped down to the river. It would have been the perfect spot to laze away a Sunday afternoon, except the entire space was packed with people.

A double row of soldiers hemmed in frightened villagers. The front row had locked shields, and the back had spears poised to strike. The villagers huddled together, trying to keep as much distance as they could from the forest of steel that surrounded them. All eyes fell upon me.

My gaze found a man in a green woolen vest and tooled leather traveling cloak. A sharp pain flashed behind my eyes at the direct eye contact. He shifted a fiddle on his back, then was lost amongst the sullen crowd.

I was taken along the rim of the formation, to where a

smaller group of villagers was being guarded by a second box formation. The third and largest group of civilians stood in rank and file against the hill at the base of the keep. This group was unguarded. Each held perfect military posture.

Seven people stood before a heavily armored figure in crimson and blue. Susan knelt on the ground, comforting her son, who wept uncontrollably. Bill kept fingering his neck while his wife spoke to the Avatar.

The soldiers dropped me on the ground a couple dozen feet behind the Avatar. The spear was removed, and I was rolled onto my knees. Spears pressed into my back. If I so much as sneezed, I'd receive half a dozen fatal blows.

The Avatar fixed me with an unsettling gaze. Her faceplate moved as if alive, snarling, showing the full length of its canines. The rest of the armor looked to be made of interlocking bands, giving the slight impression of a ship's prow. The seams were on a forty-five-degree angle that connected at the front and locked together over the spine. Every edge looked to be as sharp as a sword fresh from the smith's.

The Avatar raised a hand, commanding silence. Maggie choked back her words mid-sentence. The motion caused the Avatar's black half cape to spill over her shoulder. A dusky blue light rose like smoke from the joins in the metal.

She studied me for a long moment, the faceplate of her helm opening in a soundless hiss.

"Is everything in hand, Sergeant?" Her voice was soft yet sharp as a physic's scalpel.

"Yes, Avatar," the officer said. "We've captured an Arisen." There was a frightened murmur from the gathered villagers.

"Stand sure, Sergeant," the Avatar said.

"Stand sure," repeated every soldier in the square.

"Notify the huntsman."

A messenger sprinted out of the green.

The Harrises were red-eyed and ragged with grief. They looked at me in utter horror. Cassy and William stood a little to one side. She bowed her head and pressed her index finger to her forehead. The gesture was not lost on William, whose face had grown stony.

The Avatar, seeing their reaction, asked, "This creature is known to you?"

"Yes," Bill said, his voice painfully hoarse. "He brought our niece home. We tested his blood on the sword and shield, but nothing happened, so we gave him shelter."

"I watched him die," William said. "A dagger, right here." He pointed at his neck.

"You know just how lucky you are that the monster didn't strike," said the Avatar, looking each one of them in the eye. "It is good that you trust in Khyber. Do not fear. We will discover how this creature subverted the detection. Sergeant."

A spear flashed past my cheek. A single bead of blood clung to the blade. A soldier stepped from behind me, took a pendant from around his neck and touched it to the blood. A paralyzing electric shock ran through me. I struggled not to fall as thick smoke rose from the blackened spear blade.

There was a chorus of shouts and angry murmurs.

"See, we were right!"

"There was an Arisen!"

"No one could survive the swamps for that long!"

The Avatar raised a hand for silence. "Every one of you said you were there because Cassy Forester was an Arisen. Did any of you test her?"

"We're not Kydaists."

"We were right all along!" shouted someone from the middle of the group.

"No, you falsely accused an innocent girl. No matter what god you worship, each provides protection from the demons of this world. It would have been so simple, yet you chose to attack a neighbor on no more than a few impassioned words. However, in the name of Khyber's justice, I will change the charges to one count of murder and eight counts of attempted murder.

"Cassy Forester, step forward." Cassy did as commanded. The Avatar drew her sword and drove it into the ground before Cassy. A hooded judge in a long robe handed her a shield. The Avatar rested the shield against the blade, then raised her hands to the sky.

"Lord, show us if this woman is an Arisen!" the Avatar cried to the heavens. A blue light emanated from the sword and shield. The Avatar pulled a dagger, and Cassy held out her hand. Blood dripped through the light and onto the shield.

Ribbons of blue light reached out, caressing Cassy. A look of awe stole over her face, and her lips moved silently. Her blood sank into the shield, and the light went out.

"Judge Warwick," Avatar Justice said, "take a squad to the Harris farm and arrest Molly Forester. She has a lot to answer for."

A man in long blue robes bowed. The judge gestured, and a dozen soldiers fell into formation behind him.

"Cassy Forester is who she claims to be. Her soul is intact. The King Ascended has looked upon her and has seen the truth. The evidence of her trophies," the Avatar said, "is what she said, mementos from lost loved ones meant to provide closure."

❧ 18 ❧

"WHAT SENTENCE DOES the family of the victims demand?" the Avatar asked.

"Damnation," Susan hissed.

"Indentured slavery," croaked Bill.

"The state takes fifty percent," the Avatar said.

"So long as my daughter-in-law has an income, I don't care." Bill's words were half whispered, but every person in the square strained to hear them.

"And you, mother of the deceased?" The Avatar fixed Maggie with a predatory gaze.

"Damnation for the one who struck the blow, indentured slavery for the rest," Maggie said, seething with anger.

"Execution would be kinder," the Avatar said. "You would condemn their souls?"

"They didn't care about kindness." Maggie's face went beet red. "They took my eldest son and nearly killed my husband. They're lucky I didn't vote with Susan."

"Very well. Two votes of Damnation, two votes of indentured slavery." The Avatar strode towards the mob. They shied away like a flock of frightened geese, but they came up against a bristling row of spears. "Johnathan Swainson, step forward."

A young man was pushed to the front. Soldiers stepped back and created a hole for him to walk through. The muscular youth stepped forwards, quivering with fear.

"John!" cried a fat woman, catching at his hand.

"It's all right, Mama." John hugged her and stepped through the hole. His mother covered her face with her hands.

"Anything to say for yourself?" the Avatar asked.

"I'm sorry, I didn't mean to hurt him. I just—"

"Just broke your way into your neighbors' home, dragged them from their beds and clubbed a son, husband, and father over the head," the Avatar said coldly. "Prepare yourself for the afterlife. Remember, Khyber redeems those that are brave and honorable. Accept your punishment with dignity and Khyber may one day welcome you into Strothheim."

The boy nodded, though he trembled in fear. The Avatar knelt before the sword and shield. She stretched her arms out, forming the sign of the sword. John looked at his mother. The woman wailed.

Thunder cracked and a gust of wind rocked the great oak. A nimbus of blue light formed around the Avatar. Gasps of awe sounded from the civilians as Avatar Justice defied gravity.

Her form was overlaid with the king's spirit. He stood three times the height of a tall man. His plate armor was sculpted to resemble the hard body of a soldier. The pauldrons were roaring lions. His cape fluttered and snapped like a flag in a gale. Every line of him screamed of majesty, from his eagle's beak of a nose to the shards of broken swords that orbited him.

He opened his eyes, and, to the boy's credit, he didn't run. Every person there felt the power of Khyber's anger wash over them. The faithful took a knee and made the sign of the sword over their breast.

Khyber gestured, and a rent opened in the air beside John. The other side was pure black save for a distant red horizon.

John shook like a dog in a thunderstorm. A pair of glowing red eyes blinked awake and fixed upon him. The boy stumbled and fell to his rump.

"Judgment has been passed," Khyber said. His voice threatened to vibrate my teeth lose. "Will you accept the consequences of your actions?"

The red eyes stepped to the edge of the portal, illuminating a scaly snout lined with rows of jagged fangs and a pair of horns that swept along the outer edge of the jaw.

"Lord, please, it was an accident!"

"In my realm, every man owns his actions." The rumbling voice seemed to come from the stones beneath our feet. "Choose!"

Panic seized the boy. He got to his feet and ran. Khyber clenched his fist. Black iron chains shot from the portal. They tangled in John's feet and wrapped around his arms. There was a hiss, and smoke rose from where the chains bound him.

"No, I'm sorry!" Johnathan screamed. "I didn't mean—"

He was violently yanked off his feet. Chortling barks echoed from the other side of the portal. His fingers clawed furrows in the turf.

"No! Please!" He passed through the portal. A final cry of fear echoed over the green. The rift snapped closed. Johnathan's corpse lay in the green grass. His last moments contorted his face, the soul ripped from his body.

Khyber looked down at the corpse, face stern and disapproving, then over to Johnathan's wailing mother.

"All hail the king, our god!" shouted an officer.

"All hail the king, lord of the broken sword." The soldiers slammed weapons against shields while the villagers repeated the catechism. Khyber's light dimmed, and what solidity he had blew away like grains of sand in a high wind.

Justice's feet touched the ground, and the blue light vanished. She sucked in a breath as if she'd been underwater. Murmuring broke out amongst the townsfolk.

"Justice is served," the Avatar announced.

Maggie and Bill nodded their thanks. Susan stared at the corpse.

"The crown will take custody of your slaves. An income will be provided from their labor."

"But the law," Maggie protested.

"Has changed," the Avatar replied flatly.

"Yes, Avatar," Bill croaked. "Thank you." He put a restraining arm around his wife's shoulders.

"Where are you garrisoning?"

"Dun Al'veran," Bill said.

"Go to the hall of records, present yourself to the head scrivener. They will fill out the necessary paperwork for the recompense for your appropriated property. You have my condolences for your loss. Trust in our lord, speak to some of our acolytes. Lean on their strength in your time of need. I grant you dispensation to grieve in your home for a fortnight."

"Thank you," Bill said.

"But no longer. Every Kydaist is needed in the coming struggle. I strongly suggest that you make your way to Dun

Al'veran sooner rather than later. For the next time your door is kicked in, it will be enemy soldiers."

They murmured their thanks and moved to walk away, but the Avatar stayed them with a hand. "Cassy Forester, you worship Lyr'eris and her frozen fire."

"I do," Cassy replied shakily.

The Avatar nodded to a soldier. "Oppenfauld is only for those that follow Kydaism. Put her with the others," instructed the Avatar. The acolyte took Cassy's upper arm and led her to the group penned near the old oak.

"Avatar, please," William said. "I only just got her back. She's all I have left."

The Avatar placed a gauntleted hand on William's shoulder. "What you must have gone through. I know this is hard, but she can't be forced. Our country is in jeopardy, and the time of Khyber's tolerance is at an end. Those that will not side with Khyber heart and soul are no longer welcome in his house."

William's shoulders drooped, and he scrubbed at his beard.

"I see strength and courage within you. The kind that can only be gained by weathering life's storm. Come, let us pray. Allow Khyber's light to set your heart at ease."

The Avatar and William knelt before the sword and shield. Heads bowed, praying silently, after a few minutes they looked up.

"You felt him?"

William nodded.

"Khyber asked me to tell you that he stood guard at your door every night she left you with the children to sleep with another man. That every time she struck you, your restraint made him swell with pride. Our lord has seen your strength, William. You have stood alone for too long." The Avatar took her shield from the ground and presented it to William. "Come, brother. Join our ranks and stand shield to shield with your brothers and sisters, and never again face the storm alone."

William hugged the shield to his chest, tears streaming down his face. "I will."

"Rise, acolyte." The Avatar helped him to his feet.

"My daughter?" William asked, looking up hopefully.

"We each own our own choices, and your daughter is not a child. She will be welcomed into the fold. But only if she chooses." The Avatar's voice rose so all could hear. "That goes for all. Cast aside your false gods and put your faith in the god that has protected you, educated you. Speak to those among you that have emigrated. They will be the first to tell you that for the first time in their lives, they have freedom and hope for their children. But as of today, the free lunch ends. If you are not willing to give your soul to Khyber, then he will no longer protect your flesh." The Avatar's speech ended, and she waved over a couple of officers.

"Make sure each prisoner has basic kit. I want them moving by noon. There's a long way to go. Urge the citizens to move towards their designated garrison by nightfall. And discourage the troops from looting. Let us avoid another incident like Haradon's Ford."

The officers bowed, then barked orders to their squads.

The Avatar fixed her unsettling gaze upon me. She came over and crouched down, grasped my chin and studied my face. She traced the scars on my scalp. The jaws of her helm opened as if to bite.

19

"Take him to Melcor." Justice's tone was cold as a winter's gale. "This is the one we've been looking for. Triple his guard. Do not let the huntsman start the interrogation without me."

"Yes, Avatar." Acolytes saluted.

"Fourth and fifth squad, with me."

Soldiers ringed me, drawing steel. My bonds were checked. The gag tightened. I was hoisted to their shoulders. Dangling from the spear shaft, all I saw was cobblestones and spear points as I bounced from the square. They trotted me through the town and up the switchbacks to the keep.

I hadn't noticed the warmth of the sunlight until we passed into the keep's shadow. The courtyard bustled with soldiers working. They were loading some kind of long metal crate into a wagon. Six acolytes strained under its weight. Long and rectangular with the glint of polished steel. That wasn't a crate, it was a coffin.

The huntsman leaned against the inner wall. He adjusted his war mask. Its horns added a couple of feet to his already towering bulk. The grotesque thing wore a tortured expression, as though hot pokers had burned its eyes out just moments before.

A lance of pain shattered through my skull. I grunted, closed my eyes and shook my head. It faded quickly, but I'd made the soldiers nervous. Their weapons were poised to strike. Sweat beaded on brows.

The Norven stepped from a shadowed nook. Chains ground together with every step. His great sword, as wide and tall as a man, seemed a rapier in his hand. He towered over my guards, the tallest coming up to the huntsman's sternum. He bared his fangs in a cruel grin.

"Another one? We only just sealed the lid on the last. How'd you capture it?"

"It surrendered."

"Young, then."

"Avatar Justice says he's the one."

He barked out a laugh. "Did she now? Bring out the table."

"You've been instructed to wait to interrogate the prisoner until she arrives."

"Don't tell me my business, Vanyard," the huntsman snapped.

The sergeant disengaged from the ring and got right up in the Norven's face. "You'll follow orders, or I'll have you flogged."

The Norven laughed. "You think that's worse than these?" He flexed his arms, and the chains grated. He threw a punch at Vanyard. The sergeant stood his ground. Some unseen force halted Melcor. "You wouldn't last a quarter hour."

"Then I'll revoke your rations."

Melcor exposed his stained fangs. "You don't have the authority."

"A word to the Avatar and your cup will run dry for a month," Vanyard challenged, the crags and lines of his face hard as stone.

Melcor strained against his chains. They constricted, holding him in place. Heat shimmers rose from Melcor's great sword, and it took on a slight yellow glow. "One day, I'll be free."

"Khyber would never set a demon loose." Vanyard gestured to the wagons being rolled off to the side of the courtyard. "Now follow orders."

Melcor relaxed, the glow leaving his blade. The tension eased.

"Open ring," Vanyard ordered.

The acolytes parted in two smooth steps. The huntsman reached in, grasped the spear and carried me with ease like a bucket of water to the center of the courtyard. He palmed my head and pressed my face into the hard stone floor. The spear was cast aside, and my bonds were cut. Melcor picked me up, and I had to grab his wrist to prevent my neck from being broken. Then he slammed me onto a padded table with enough force to drive the wind from my lungs.

While I sucked in air, soldiers fastened soft wool cuffs to my arms and legs. Joints were torqued to their limit, and my head was strapped down.

"Look at you now." Melcor loomed over me. "The high and mighty Avatar Wrath. How's it feel to be lower than gutter scum?"

"Archers to the wall," commanded the sharp, clear voice of Avatar Justice. "Spear men, line the perimeter. Lower the portcullis." There was a single unified clap as the soldiers saluted, followed by a flurry of motion as they took their positions.

Melcor stepped aside. My vision was filled with the

snarling cat's helm, the lips peeled back. Wisps of red light rose like smoke from between the teeth.

"Why?" she snarled, low and dangerous. "Void take you, why?" My heart raced, and I tried to speak around the gag. Justice picked up the head of the table and shook it. The wood creaked under the stress. My brain bounced off the inside of my skull. The table slammed down. "What are you waiting for?" Justice snapped. "I want answers."

"My tools," Melcor said.

I tried to speak through the gag. A judge placed a workbench beside my table, then unrolled a leather tool case. Metal instruments clinked against one another. Melcor pulled out a thin metal rod with a hook at the end.

"Stand back."

The Avatar backed away. Melcor held the hook end in his palm and placed the rod against his sword. The tool took on the glow of heated metal.

"Gomms mamn du filw ook," I said.

Melcor held the rod painfully close to my eye. I couldn't move. He smiled and stuck it up my nose. I cried out. This was what they wanted, my screams. My punishment. Only then would they listen.

He removed the rod and heated it again. This time the hook end.

"Oh, you can't speak around the gag. Let me get that for you." The hook pressed into my lips, the sound of quenching metal. Burning, pulling, sawing. The gag came free.

Blood leaked down my face as the pressure built. The magic within my blood was going to rupture. Melcor opened his mouth. My blood flew to him. It was worse than the heated metal. Like the loss of a limb, something stolen.

"Why did you do it?" the Avatar asked.

"I didn't." My words were slurred. "I was framed. Someone tampered with the spell. I worked my whole life for that moment. I wouldn't have thrown it away."

"Liar," the Avatar said. "You oversaw the entire mission. You had complete control. So, either you're an incompetent fool, or you sold out the whole bloody world for personal gain!"

"The process was delicate, complex. We had to play it close to the chest."

"Goat dung. You didn't share or delegate responsibility with the other Avatars." She touched her chest. "At the time, we thought you were a self-serving egotistical control freak, but in retrospect, it's clear you were hiding treachery."

"What have I gained? I've been excommunicated, disgraced. My wife and children—" My throat hitched. "—have likely been tortured. Please, they're innocent. I am here. If they're still alive... let me take their place."

The Avatar's eyes narrowed, and a puzzled look passed over her helm.

"Immortality," Melcor growled. "A heavy price, but you've always spent the lives of others easily."

"I am supposed to be guarding the walls of Strothheim. Not wandering the Mortal Realm, cursed and feared by those I swore to protect."

"You never gave two figs about the people. It was always about what you could gain. Glory, land, title, political maneuverers. What was it you used to say? 'Those that grub in the dirt are worth more in Damnation than alive'?"

My jaw hung open for a moment, confused. The huntsman stuffed the gag so far back I choked. I worked to push the wadded cloth out of my throat, fighting for breath around the blood and mucus that filled my sinuses.

Melcor sliced the vein in the crook of my elbow. He

squeezed, forcing the blood out. He filled a shallow bowl, then stepped back and pulled the gag out.

"How did you tamper with the spell?" he demanded.

"I didn't."

Melcor backed away. The pressure of blood magic grew.

"How did you tamper with the spell?" Justice asked again.

"A deity intervened. It blocked the conduit back. Then there was an explosion and the secondary function failed. I don't know how it happened."

"That's impossible."

The pressure built. I opened my mouth and breathed. The blood crept to the lip of the bowl. "He's strong." Melcor stepped another foot back, and the blood fell back into the bowl. The pressure turned to pain, a fiery heat that scorched through my veins.

My breath came in short gasps. "I can't hold it. Get back."

"Huntsman?"

"His aura is large for one so young. Even so, shouldn't be more than a puff of smoke and a flash of light."

"By the broken sword, bring it back." The pain was too much. I fought my bonds. Wood groaned.

"Will that table hold?" Justice asked.

"That much iron and oak could hold a Grundstrad," Melcor replied.

"Make it stop!" I screamed.

"Shields," the Avatar commanded.

Magic ripped from me. The explosion flipped the table. There was a second flash, the sound of cracking glass. Wood fractured, and I tumbled to the ground, cold stone at my back. My ears rang, but I had my senses about me.

I'd been thrown over the shield wall. The table lay in

ruins. Melcor lay on the ground, smoke rising from him. The acolytes were disorientated from the blast. To my right lay the postern door. If I moved quickly, I could slip out. Make it to Khyber on my own.

"Where is he?" Justice commanded.

"I am here." I knelt and put my hands on the back of my head.

Rough hands grabbed me, twisting my arms behind my back. Melcor's massive blade was at my throat. Burns covered his neck and muzzle. They were healing before my eyes. He snarled, and it seemed to accentuate the anguish on his mask. Justice was over me, sword drawn, looking from me to the door.

"Why didn't you run?" she asked.

"I was the sacrifice that should have bought Khyber his Transcendence. Someone took that from all of us. They stole my glory, tarnished my name. They took my home, my family, my god! I fought my way back from death to prove my innocence. The traitor is still amongst you," I said. "Take me in chains or in a cage. I don't care. Just take me to Khyber and let him judge my soul."

"I could almost believe you," Justice said, "if I didn't know what a good liar you are."

Her sword took on a blue hue. She retreated, knelt, held it reverently before her. "My lord—" Justice cocked her head. "Please don't make me do that. As you command. I advise caution. We nearly lost everything because of him." She paused again. "At least let me put him in a coffin ... No, Lord— Yes, Lord. Thy will, my hands." She stood, sheathing her sword, then sighed out her frustration and said in a tone of disgust, "Let him up."

20

"No," Melcor growled.

"The king has spoken," Avatar Justice said.

"I'm chained like a beast and he gets to go free? The Void can have me before I let that happen."

"You are a beast," said a soldier a few ranks back.

Melcor turned his head, sniffing the air.

"Got your scent, Wilcons."

The acolyte shifted nervously.

"If I have my way, the Arisen will never taste freedom," Justice said.

"Good," Melcor said, "let's seal him up and—"

"He's to be guarded, not imprisoned."

"What? By who?"

"You."

"I can't do my job and play nursemaid."

"Then you play nursemaid. The intel that we'll extract from him will be critical."

"You still think I'm guilty," I said.

"As a fox in the henhouse, but Khyber is willing to give you the benefit of the doubt," Justice replied with distaste.

"If I don't hunt, I don't eat," Melcor said.

"This takes priority. Concessions will be made," Justice said.

The Veil tore. A rift opened in the sky. A shard of ice fell, crashing to earth with the force of a meteor. A shock wave of cold Neathereal air washed through the courtyard, unhindered by the stone walls. I looked at Melcor questioningly. Only a demon of smoke and ash stood in his place. The rift closed, and time resumed. Melcor was once again a Norven. He peeled back his lips in a hate-filled snarl.

"What in Damnation was that?" I asked.

"Be silent," Melcor ordered.

"What was what?" the Avatar asked.

"The whelp's just seen his first rising," Melcor explained.

"How far?"

Melcor crossed his arms.

"We will increase your rations."

"Double them."

"Fine."

The acolytes groaned.

"Two, maybe three miles," Melcor said.

"Too close to ignore," the Avatar said.

"We'll be on the move in a couple of hours. There's no point."

"Exactly. The faithful will be unprotected. I'm not leaving an Arisen behind to pick them off one by one."

"Seal this one in a coffin and I'll get to work."

"Khyber's orders are plain. He wants the Arisen in control of his wits when we arrive at Faldaris."

"I can't guard him and hunt at the same time. He'll knife me in the back first chance he gets."

"Fourth and fifth squad will be under your command." Angry mutters and nervous shifting came from the acolytes.

"They'll do the guarding. All you'll need to worry about is negating his blood magic."

"Easy as picking a mordrem blossom." Melcor rose menacingly.

"I've had enough of your insubordination." The Avatar began inscribing a rune into the air. A blue streamer of light followed her fingers.

"I'll follow orders." Melcor backed down. "But when he escapes or kills one of your acolytes, remember this moment."

The Avatar stopped, and the unfinished rune dissipated. "Fourth, fifth squad." A dozen acolytes snapped a salute. "You're now under the direct command of the huntsman. Work in shifts. The Arisen is never to be unguarded."

"Yes, sir." They saluted.

"The rest of you pack up and get the heathens ready to move." Melcor grabbed my shirt collar, pulled me to my feet and shoved me towards the gate. "Double-time. We have an Arisen to hunt."

Two squads formed up behind me. The portcullis rattled open, and we jogged out of the keep. The king's highway bordered the farmlands to the north and the Al'veran to the south. In-between lay a patchwork of lush green cornstalks, golden wheat and a myriad of orchards.

The Norven overtook me, his blade resting on his shoulder.

"Run, traitor," Vanyard shouted.

I held my tongue. I couldn't regain their trust with a single act. But once I found the real traitor, I'd make them eat their words.

Melcor pulled ahead, his long legs taking him three of my strides for every one of his. I picked up the pace to a point where I was barely able to keep my feet on the switch-backs. The acolytes never flagged.

"Make way!" Melcor bellowed as we careened down the main street. Soldiers stepped aside, their arms full of blankets, foodstuffs and clothing. They were coming in and out of homes, leaving the insides a ransacked mess.

"Stop gawking." Vanyard slapped me on the rump with the flat of his blade. Swallowing my pride, I pushed to keep up with the Norven.

After some time, Melcor slowed, raised a hand, and we came to a sudden halt. He cast about and sniffed the air before closing his eyes and turning full circle His head snapped to one side, and he stalked down the road. We followed, and after a few moments, I sensed what had drawn the huntsman: an oppressive chill that didn't have anything to do with the temperature. I had felt this before, this sense of malice, the lust for dominion. A twenty-foot circle of unnaturally smooth stone took up most of the road.

"Wait here," Melcor ordered as he walked the circumference of the circle, studying the ground.

"This way," he said, then set off across the field. The prints were easy to follow in the soft earth. Four or five sets running off towards a distant farmhouse.

Shrill cries echoed over the fields. "Stephen, Stephen!" called a woman, nearly unhinged with panic.

She shrieked as Melcor stepped around the barn then sighed in relief as she saw the Fauldic soldiers. "Thank Khyber. My husband? Stephen! Stephen!"

"Silence your bleating," Melcor snarled.

"Go back inside, Ma'am," Sergeant Vanyard said, shooting Melcor an ugly look. "It's not safe. Pray. Reaffirm the threshold."

The woman nodded and slammed the door.

The barn doors had been thrown open. In the middle of the alley lay a corpse. Dry as a corn husk, completely drained of blood. The stalls had been broken open. Whatever had killed the man broke through the walls rather than open the door. Inside, dozens of dead pigs, drained.

An acolyte knelt over the corpse, making the sign of the sword, and said his last rites.

"Tracks lead this way," Melcor pointed out. Erratic prints circled the home. The windows had been smashed, and red-fletched arrows were embedded in the window frame. But not a single footprint lay within a foot of the home.

The tracks led back to the road, to a small familiar thicket, down a hill to the river.

Four savage-looking men with pale milky skin and a young blond girl were getting into the Myi'eshan canoe. My heart skipped a beat. What was Cassy doing? The girl bellowed like a madwoman, raised a crudely hammered cleaver above her head and charged.

"Myi'eshans!" Sergeant Vanyard yelled. "Fire at will."

The girl took a bolt through the sternum. It took her from her feet, pebbles spraying as she hit the beach. Bolts sprouted from one of the men in the canoe. He toppled face-first into the water.

Melcor thundered forwards. One of the Myi'eshans jumped out of the boat, picked up the blond girl and threw her limp body into the canoe. He yelled something I couldn't understand and spun to face Melcor. He bared filed teeth and threw a spear. Fetishes and charms tied into his dreadlocks tinkled as he released. The other two set paddle to water.

Melcor twisted, but he was a big target. The spear caught him in the shoulder.

The Myi'eshan's body rippled, distorting the black

tattoos that laced his skin. Bones snapped as he changed shape. His arms elongated. Hooked claws grew from his fingers. Muscles sprouted on top of muscles. His head became bestial with a short snout filled with jagged teeth.

Crossbows fired. Bolts buried themselves in the creature's flesh. It barely seemed to notice. It leapt at Melcor, running on all fours. The huntsman swung his blade and met nothing but air. Claws raked Melcor's flank, chain links parting and blood spraying.

Melcor drove the pommel into the creature's shoulder. An audible snap of a bone sounded. The beast tackled Melcor, raking him with its hind claws and knocking the spear from his shoulder, fangs snapping at his face.

Acolytes rushed forwards, swords and spears at the ready. "Guard the prisoner!" Sergeant Vanyard commanded.

"For Khyber's sake, kill that thing," I urged.

The acolytes ignored me, taking up their positions.

Melcor's blade suddenly became red hot. The Myi'e-shan's flesh sizzled. It pulled away. Melcor slashed, and purple ribbons of viscera spilled to the shore.

Melcor grabbed the creature's head, twisted it to the side and sank his teeth into its neck. The Myi'eshan struggled, but its claws vanished. Within three heartbeats, it reverted to its human form. He was a man for no more than a second. Then its eyes sank into its skull, its flesh took on the hue of rotten meat.

Melcor pulled away from the creature, shuddering in ecstasy. He dropped the Myi'eshan to the ground.

The Arisen sucked at the air as if it fought for breath. It rose, and those sunken pits for eyes latched onto me. It felt like shards of glass shot through my skull. It shambled towards me, making that horrible sucking sound. Something pulled at me.

Melcor lazily swung his sword, taking the creature's head. The Veil tore, and the Myi'eshan's soul rose from the corpse. The soul was the beast it had turned into, only rimed with ice. Melcor breathed as if picked up by a hurricane wind. The soul flew to him. The draw was so powerful I felt as if I had to cling to my flesh.

A rift opened, a black land with a red horizon. The Myi'eshan's soul diverted from Melcor and was pulled into Damnation. The Veil closed, and time resumed. The corpse disintegrated into dust and ash before it hit the ground.

Melcor smiled at the soldiers, reveling in their disgust.

The huntsman turned to watch the canoe as it sped away down the Al'veran. The speed of the current made them little more than a distant shadow.

"Back to the keep," Melcor said.

"Orders were to catch or kill them," Vanyard said.

"We're done. The rest will flee back to the frozen north."

Vanyard stepped in front of Melcor, pointing a finger at his chest. "What if they double back?"

"They're gone."

"You're certain of this?"

"Trust me, they have what they came for."

MAIN STREET WAS PACKED cheek to jowl with disgruntled villagers. Each held a meager bundle, which for some was no more than supplies tied in a sheet. A defensive line of soldiers ringed the heathens. Shields raised and spears poised seemed to be the only thing keeping the villagers from a full revolt. My guards and I came up to the back of the line as it started moving its way up the switchbacks and through the keep's town side gate.

"I don't care about your *orders*. My crops are about to flower."

"Sir. This is not a negotiation," said an officer. "Renounce your false gods and go home or leave the king's lands. Those are your only choices."

"It's only my respect for king and country that stops me from driving my foot through your teeth, ye little shit!" shouted the farmer.

"No, Goodman, it's the thirty spears at my back. Now, do as I say and fall back in line."

"I've worked that land my whole life. I've paid my taxes, sworn the oaths, and you're gonna toss my whole family out on our ears. This country owes me." The farmer jabbed a finger at the officer.

Spears flashed. The officer raised his hand. Foot-long spear blades stopped.

"I am of the fifth heightening," the farmer said, looking at the spears in disdain. "I'd take those thirty men, and you know it."

"So, you care nothing for the safety of your fellows," the officer said, pointing to the knot of people at the farmer's back. "There'll be innocents caught in the crossfire, and what of my men? Each of them has bled to protect you and yours. While you're safe at home practicing the arts of Zenos, they bled and died."

"You're throwing me out of my home," argued the farmer, his voice thick with emotion.

"You're the one choosing to leave. Look me in the face and name another god that wouldn't have demanded your fealty years ago. Surely you know what the Norven do to their own that don't swear to Zenos?"

The farmer threw up his hands and melted into the crowd. The angry mutters continued, but no one seemed ready to defy that much steel.

Eventually the back of the line moved. I passed the vacant houses of Raider's Watch. The place already had the feel of a ghost town.

The Avatar stood atop the battlements watching the procession as it passed through the keep's courtyard and on through the east gate. Her hand rested on the pommel of her sword, shield upon her back. She watched my every step as I passed through the keep.

The east gate exited onto an arch bridge that spanned one of the Al'veran's tributaries. The midpoint was no more than two stones thick. It seemed impossible for that much rock to stay suspended.

The bridge was continuous with the king's highway. The distance to the closest city was carved into the crenellations, 212 miles to Dun Al'veran. All those miles, untamed.

The view atop the highway was magnificent. The Sovereign Guard Mountains dominated the horizon. Their peaks, perpetually covered in snow, seemed to stretch all the way to the Ethereal Battle. Deep greens of pine, fir and cedar covered the lower half.

Ahead, the highway wound through the foothills, a stark gray line that divided the land. As high as a fortress wall and wide enough for four wagons to roll abreast. The individual stones fitted together so smoothly that even the most skilled of climbers would have trouble finding a toehold.

A halt wasn't called till the sun glowed red in the west. I sat hemmed by stony faced soldiers, fingering the burns on my nose and lips as I looked out over the foothills. Tall grasses swayed hypnotically in the evening breeze. The sliver of civilization that was Raider's Watch may as well be in Illuvand it seemed so far away.

The huntsman sat upon a crenellation, his legs dangling absently over the edge, face angled so no one could see. He polished his mask, working some resin into the scorch marks. His tufted ears swiveled to catch any sound. Despite his brooding bulk, he looked somehow diminished without the horns.

I lay upon the cold stone, watching the dancing lights of the Ethereal Battle play across the night's sky. Perhaps a trick of the mind, but I was convinced I could see the different realms advancing and retreating. A section of ice blue and deep forest green clashed, overwhelming a section of burnt orange. Had I just witnessed the death of a realm? The death of a god? I took in the expanse of shifting colors.

Too many for the mind to comprehend. Gods, what did I matter in all that?

My eyes drifted to the dark expanse that occupied the bottom half of the sky. The Void advanced, almost imperceptibly, but after touching it, there was no doubt in my mind. One day it would consume the Ethereal Battle in its entirety.

A BOOT to the knee started me awake. "Get up." I clutched my leg as the pain radiated to my abdomen.

"I said get up, traitor." Melcor's steel-shod boot connected with my hip.

"Leave him alone." Cassy was being restrained by a couple of soldiers.

"He must be deaf."

I thought I was ready, but Norvens had the muscle mass of a Clydesdale.

"For the gods' sake, stop him!" Cassy shouted.

"Shut it. He's got a hundredfold waiting for him," said one of the soldiers holding her.

"Pack your things, heathen," said his female counterpart, shoving Cassy back into the crowd. "We move out in ten."

I sucked in air, fighting the urge to retch.

"I said GET UP."

I tucked, taking the blow on the shoulder instead of the face. My skull bounced off the stone, stars reeled. I had to move. I was vulnerable lying there. I got to my hands and knees. Someone stood between Melcor and me.

"You're agitating the prisoners," Vanyard whispered. "Save it for the interrogation room. We don't want them getting spooked."

Melcor's look promised pain. His gaze took in the growing mass of onlookers. He spun on his heel and strode off into the darkness with heavy steps.

"The prisoner will rise," Vanyard said. Cassy peered from the crowd. I gave her a grateful nod, and she smiled shakily. I staggered to my feet. Vanyard spat in my face.

"Forward march." The call to move was repeated down from the front. A weary protest echoed down the line.

Vanyard straightened my shirt collar. "Once we're behind closed doors, it'll be my boot up your ass." His squad chuckled. "Now move."

THE MARCH DIDN'T END till long after darkness had fallen. It'd given me the chance to walk off the stiffness and then make the limp ten times worse. Acolytes scooped thick stew from bubbling cook pots. They diced and jibed as soldiers will on campaign, while the heathens nibbled stale bread ends and bits of hard cheese.

I ignored the smell of stew and laughter. None would be shared with an Arisen. Melcor watched me from the shadows as I stretched out the bruises, his stare challenging. My thirst snarled like a beast in a leg trap. I shuddered, the desire rising.

I closed my eyes. "Khyber give me strength." There was no response.

I felt someone watching me. A bare-chested man stood on a hill. The moon reflected off milky skin. Pain pierced my skull, and thirst lashed through me. The urge to attack was as intense as a drowning man's need for air.

"Don't get any ideas." Melcor studied the distant figure, sword resting on his shoulder.

"I don't know what you're talking about." I turned my back to the figure on the hill.

"Good, denial is good," Melcor said with a nod. "We'll both pretend you weren't about to rush headlong off the forty-foot drop for a chance to tear that thing's throat out."

"Shut up."

"This is so much more fun than locking you in a box."

I knelt, making the sign of the sword. "Though I stand alone, my lord is with me."

"He's not listening," Melcor replied.

"His strength suffuses me. His will guides me through the darkness." My body trembled from the effort of restraint.

"It's only a matter of time. The thirst will take you. Bring out the demon for everyone to see."

"Though shield may shatter, and sword lay broken. I will fight on, I will stand sure, for the lord is with me and I am never alone."

A blue tracer hung in the air before me. The sign of the sword drawn by one of my guards. I reached out a hand and the blue light turned red. The heat of it scalded and drove the thirst back into the shadows of my soul.

I clutched my hand to my chest and looked up at the acolyte who had drawn the symbol. Sergeant Hilstrad stared at me as though I'd climbed out of a midden heap.

"Thank you, Lord." I flexed my hand. It didn't appear to be burned, but it still hurt.

"I want a quarter rotation every two hours," Melcor said. "After that bit of drama, he may do something in his sleep."

The squads looked to Sergeant Vanyard, who took another mouthful of stew.

"What ya'll lookin' at him for?" Sergeant Hilstrad asked. "Nox, Jenkins, Wilcons. Chow's over."

The soldiers around the campfire groaned, donned their gear and stowed their bowls.

In the distance, the moonlit figure got down on all fours and loped away.

I SAT bolt upright at the sound of grating chains. Melcor stormed towards me, winding up for a kick. I braced for impact but too slowly. I blunted the blow with my forearm, but his foot connected with my ribs.

"On your feet." He didn't give me the chance to move before he grabbed my shirt collar and lifted me from the ground. The fabric tore, buttons popped. I threw an elbow. It knocked his mask askew. Melcor's fist hammered me to the stone. I bumped up against a line of acolytes blocking the heathen's view. The thirst roared and I was on my feet, ready to smash his teeth in.

"There you are, finally come out to play." Melcor held his blade between us. "Show us the demon lurking inside."

I controlled my breathing, the bloodlust driving me to reckless abandon. I lowered my fists. "I'll not let you goad me into a foolish mistake."

"Huntsman," the Avatar snapped, "what's going on?"

"Just keeping the Arisen in line."

"It's looking worse for wear."

"Fledglings only understand one thing."

"Your orders were to keep him sound. If you repeatedly beat a dog, it goes feral. After we expel the heathens, we'll make for Faldaris. None of us like it, but be patient."

"Perhaps there's something he doesn't want Khyber to find out."

Melcor shook a forearm at me, his chains clinking. "I can't hide from him, and soon neither will you."

"I'll not have you spreading dissent amongst my soldiers," Justice said. "Keep that forked tongue behind your teeth or I will take the huntsman's advice and lock you in a box."

"I understand," I said stiffly.

"Good," Justice said. "Melcor, with me."

The two left the protective ring of soldiers and walked to the edge of the wall. Justice handed the huntsman a plain steel goblet. He put it to his lips and downed the contents. A fine mist of red rose from the goblet and down his throat.

My pulse quickened, and I broke out in a cold sweat. Hot jealous need pushed me. I put my back to them. Gods, I wanted it so bad. The soldiers shifted nervously. I looked from face to face. Each of them had what I wanted. Walking wineskins, ripe for uncorking.

"Avatar?" Sergeant Vanyard called.

Justice approached, a goblet in hand. I could smell it. My whole body vibrated with anticipation.

"Don't come any closer," I said, backing away. A spear point stopped me.

"I'll not have you losing control," the Avatar said. "You'll get the same ration as the huntsman."

I held out a hand to fend her off. "If I open that door, I fear I won't be able to stop." The Avatar looked to Melcor.

"Put it down. He'll feed," the huntsman said.

"No, take it away." I pinched the burns on my lip. The pain held the thirst at bay. "Please."

"What will happen if I respect his wishes?"

"He'll wither into a shambling corpse. The man you want to preserve will be lost, driven only by the need for blood. He'll attack anything that moves."

"Is that what you want?" Avatar Justice asked.

I shook my head. "But neither will I resign myself to becoming like him." Melcor laughed cruelly.

"The safety of my soldiers trumps your existential dilemma. Drink." The Avatar handed me the cup.

I reached for it with a shaking hand. The siren song of the blood nearly blotted out the world. I held my breath and threw the goblet over the edge of the highway.

"Wyrm spawn!" Melcor cursed. The back of his hand sent me to the stone. He strode to the edge, breathing in the spilled blood.

"Hilstrad, Vanyard."

"Avatar Justice." The sergeants saluted.

"If he makes a single aggressive move, put a bolt through his skull."

EVERY STEP WAS A STRUGGLE. My muscles burned with fatigue, and my wounds refused to heal. Yet every limping stride brought me closer to Khyber. To Anastasia and our children.

Birds sang merrily from a cluster of scraggly trees. They flitted from branch to branch before bursting out over the highway towards the Sovereign Guards. The mountains loomed, a wall of jagged fangs trying to lacerate the sky. Sharp light glinted off the snowy peaks, and I lowered my eyes from the glare. Even squinting against the light drained the willpower I needed to keep myself in check.

Ahead, a three-towered Fauld crouched over a cross-road. The procession marched through its westerly gate and out the east. My eyes followed the northern highway as it skirted the mountains, vanishing over the horizon.

"Still alive, Vanyard?" called a man from the battlements.

"Pike," Vanyard said. "Tucked safely behind your wall, Eh."

"And every night I sleep in a bed."

"Sounds blasted horrible," said Vanyard.

"You would say that, you sour old goat," Pike laughed, then disappeared from the top of the wall.

We passed through the portcullis, the very last through the gate. Melcor shoved me forward, and I caught myself before sprawling to the ground.

Pike came out from one of the towers and handed Vanyard a tankard. The two raised their glasses.

"Ram me, but you can brew," Vanyard wiped the foam from his lips. "How's the leg?" he asked.

Pike lifted his pant leg, revealing a gleaming rod attached to a metal boot. "Khyber made it. He came all the way down to the hospital to give it to me." Pike's eyes filled with tears of pride as he wiggled his foot.

"Good, good," Vanyard replied distantly.

"None of that now. I's can hold the wall. If I's ever see an Arachnid again, I's can meet it on my feet."

We were almost through the second gate and back to marching. "Good to see you, Pike. Thanks for the drink," Vanyard said, handing him back the mug.

"You all right, Vanyard? You don't quite seem yourself," he asked, concern crumpling his brow.

"Fighting hasn't started yet. I'm bloody bored is all." The two veterans laughed.

"Stand sure, old friend," Pike replied, clapping him on the shoulder.

"Stand sure," Vanyard said, clasping forearms with the man.

CLOUDS SMOTHERED THE MOON. Without the torches, the night would be as black as a mine shaft. The heathens huddled together in nervous clusters. This was probably the most time they'd spent out of doors after nightfall, the darkness too much like an eclipse.

The acolytes felt it too. Although they showed it by being alert. Two-thirds of them were on guard. Patrols moved in opposing directions, and vigilant eyes scanned the dark. Hard faces cowing any that made eye contact. Those who slept did so fully armored and with weapons close to hand.

I knelt within my protective circle, afraid to sleep. Afraid of what would happen if I let my mental guard down. My eyes kept drifting to the heathens as they ate around their cook fires. Warming cold fingers, breath rising in clouds of steam. Every action whispered of the blood that flowed within their veins.

One of the heathens waved at me. My eyes fixed on her throat. I could almost see the rhythm of her pulse. I dragged my gaze to her face. Cassy smiled. The people who shared her fire skirted away from her, save for the man in a green vest who sat beside her.

"Pretty little thing," Melcor said. "Human young are always easy prey. So certain that they know everything, confident the world is full of wonder and kindness."

"She's been through more than most."

"Still naive enough to give two bullocks about you." He absently ran a finger over his mask.

My gaze drifted back to Cassy. Her eyes flicked between Melcor and me. The girl had formed some kind of attachment to me. It was nice to have a person who didn't treat me like a dangerous animal. The only problem was I was more dangerous than any animal. The man beside her turned his back and slipped an instrument case over his shoulder.

"You!" Melcor erupted from the shadows, knocking a

hole in the ranks of soldiers. The man in green darted into the mass of humanity. "After him!"

"Huntsman!" Vanyard called after him.

The hairs on the back of my neck prickled. Something moved beyond the firelight. Pain fractured through my skull.

"Vanyard." I pointed into the darkness. All eyes followed Melcor as he scattered the heathens like frightened quail.

"Don't you ramming move," ordered Wilcons. He stood between me and the darkness.

"Behind you."

"I wasn't born yesterday. Sit." He raised his spear. Bare feet padded on stone, and something massive leapt from the darkness. He turned his head, a curse forming on his lips. I grabbed for the spear shaft, trying to trip him. But his reflexes were honed. He drove the spear into my gut.

Something the size of a bear landed on Wilcons, forcing him to the stone with a sickening crunch. The creature's arm swept out, knocking me flying. A foot of shaft and the spear blade protruded from my belly.

The Arisen was startlingly similar to the one I'd seen in Raider's Watch. Long arms and short legs that ended in six-inch claws. Too many teeth in its short muzzle. But the differences were grotesque. Its joints rotated in ways that defied the laws of physiology. Dark projections dappled its milky skin, like nubs of horn trying to push through.

Its mouth engulfed Wilcons shoulder. Jaws snapped. Wilcons's cries cut off. His body shriveled, and the Veil tore. His soul punched and kicked as the Arisen choked it down like a gull with a fish. Time resumed. The Arisen moaned in ecstasy.

I pulled the spear from my gut. Blood flowed. The Arisen swiped. I twisted, narrowly avoiding its claw. The hefty chunk of crossbows filled the night. The Arisen yelped, its hind leg coiled up to extract a bolt. I charged.

Soldiers rushed past, spears darting and swords slashing. The Arisen swept their legs out from under them and pounced. I jammed the spear under its jaw. Blood sprayed. We crashed to the stone in a heap.

Screams and a sound like water on hot coals filled the air. I barely heard it. The thirst took me. I pulled the spear from the Arisen and bit into the wound.

The Arisen howled and thrashed. Its jaws snapped, claws raked my back. The smell, the feel of it pouring down my throat, blotted out the world. I drank what felt like a waterfall. The Arisen shifted. Its raking claws changed to fingers. Its roar became a man's cry of pain.

"Rodrick," said a woman's voice, "stop." Blue light filled my vision. The sign of the sword shone like a light house beacon, breaking through the bloodlust. I pulled away.

Cassy stood just outside a ring of soldiers. "Do it again!" she said.

Hilstrad drew the sign of the sword once more. The painfully brilliant light allowed me to recover my senses. Three acolytes were down, writhing in pain. A judge stood over them, an exorcism half complete.

The Arisen smiled, revealing filed teeth and twisting his facial tattoos into something demonic. "Lyr'eris, Ja ved Caloth hon Hyi." His teeth came for my neck. I stabbed him in the chest. Hot blood soaked me. The three acolytes howled like the damned. Unbridled agony covered the Arisen's face, and his blood suddenly became ice cold.

"Shields!" I yelled. "Blood magic." I clutched the Arisen to my chest. He twisted, trying to expose his wound to the soldiers. His blood erupted. I was lifted into the air. The

Arisen was torn from my grip. Ice shrapnel whizzed about me. Soldiers screamed, shield imbuements lit up.

I couldn't move. Couldn't breathe. Ice encased me. A sharp blow broke my head and neck free. Filed teeth snapped wildly at my face. The Myi'eshan weaved back and forth like a snake. He struck but was just out of reach.

The Myi'eshan hung like a scarecrow from half a hundred icicles. He twisted, breaking himself free, heedless of the damage done to his body. His teeth inched closer to my face. I was trapped, unable to fight. Filed points scored my nose.

"Strothheim beckons!" Hilstrad shouted, plunging her spear into the Arisen.

"Strothheim beckons," the war cry was taken up by a dozen others. Weapons struck, coming away crimson. The Arisen spasmed with every blow, yet he struggled to sink his teeth into me.

The Arisen's head jerked to the side, and Melcor sank his fangs into its neck. The Myi'eshan shriveled, becoming a walking corpse.

A coffin crashed to the stone. The Arisen flailed with animalistic violence. Melcor forced him inside. Three soldiers struggled to slide the lid into place. Still, the Arisen fought on, the heavy lid bouncing. Melcor put a boot on the lid. Three twitching fingers fell to the highway.

"Where's that imbued torch?" Vanyard yelled.

"Here!" Judge Warwick knelt beside the coffin. He flipped the visor down on a face mask, and blue orange sparks streaked around him. Only after Warwick had sealed the lid did Melcor remove his weight. A heavy silence fell, save for the muffled struggles of the thing within the coffin.

My HEAD SWAM, blackness settling over me.

"Still with us?" Melcor asked, his tongue lolling in amusement.

"Ram you," I stammered through chattering teeth.

He smiled wickedly. He brought his sword above his head. "I can't tell you how long I've wanted to do this." The flat of the blade struck. Ice shattered. I collapsed to the ground, ice raining around me.

"Rodrick," Cassy called. "Are you all right?"

I curled around the hole in my gut.

"Vanyard," Avatar Justice said. "Have Miss Forester escorted to the front of the column."

"Yes, Avatar," Vanyard replied. "Jenkins." Their booted feet rang on the stone.

"Warwick?"

"They'll be fine. I was able to complete the exorcism. Bad dreams and some other side effects. Nothing a little prayer won't be able to fix," Judge Warwick said. "All four of us would be dead if he hadn't shielded us from the blood magic."

"No," Justice said, "he does not get to earn your respect. Do you understand me?"

"Yes, Avatar,"

"This *Arisen* is responsible for putting every life in this country in mortal peril. He is the reason we've had to round up friends and family. If it weren't for him, we'd all be safe at home."

The world dimmed, and I sank into darkness.

Fresh blood splashed my lips. Ecstasy washed away the world until the flow ended. I needed more. My hands and legs were bound. I could smell it, hear their hearts thundering. Piercing blue light stung my eyes, and the thirst fled into the recesses of my soul.

"Why?" I asked.

"We need to hurry. You'd have held us back." A second goblet was handed to her by Judge Warwick.

"You have no right."

"By Khyber." Justice shook her head. "If I had any doubts. You're still as condescendingly self-righteous as you always were. How she put..." She stilled her tongue and poured the goblet onto the stones beside my face. I fought to hold myself in check. But this was as primal as my need for air. I breathed it in. The stream of liquid changed direction midair, angling into my mouth. Reason and care ebbed away in a tide of satisfaction.

That ramming blue light wouldn't stop me this time. I wriggled towards the closest heartbeat, pulling for any stray droplet. A second, then a third blue sword hung in the air. I came back to myself.

"Get him up. We move out once the pyre's lit," Avatar Justice ordered, marching off.

"On your feet, swine," Melcor spat with a self-satisfied smirk.

"Huntsman. A word," Justice said. Melcor followed the Avatar into the gray light of predawn.

Hilstrad stepped forwards, drawing a dagger from her belt.

The thirst rose within me. "Stay back. I'm not in control."

Hilstrad knelt down and whispered in my ear, "Stand sure." She cut the cords and met my eye, then took her position.

I set my jaw, and I got to my feet. The twinge in my hip was gone. The hole in my belly, bruises on my ribs, burns on my face, all had healed.

Justice's angry voice carried on the morning breeze. "If

you ever abandon your post again, I'll make sure you end up in one of those coffins."

"He's a spy."

"And you scared him off."

"We're at war. I thought—"

"Don't think. Do as you're told, demon."

"Yes, Avatar."

Justice stalked past, barking orders. The line started moving.

"COME ON, Nox, this is Dun Al'veran,"

"Yep," Nox replied.

"Gor, I can't wait. You come with me, lad, and I'll show you the best this city has to offer."

"Erm."

"The Darting Coy, there's this Myi'eshan. Skin as white as bleached silk and hair as dark as coal. Does things with her mouth that'll—"

"I've had me fill of Myi'ehsans, Jenkins," Nox interrupted.

"I bet you have after last night. But trust me, the teeth make it all the more exciting." Jenkins slapped Nox on the back. "Fine, don't like 'em northerners, scary bunch anyway. The Coy has a Mirvish priestess. The very image of Enris. Golden hair down to her ankles, skin like toasted honey." Jenkins rubbed his hands together in anticipation.

Nox sighed uncomfortably.

"Girl back home got your fancy?" Jenkins nudged Nox in the ribs. "Trust me, she'll never know."

"Leave off," Hilstrad chided.

"Man nearly died. Ram me, but half his face looks like a boiled lobster. No offense there, Nox."

"More like a tomato," Nox said haughtily. The company chuckled in response.

"Come on, it'll be good for the soul," Jenkins urged.

"No, don't want my first time to be with a whore. Besides, my dah says they've this disease. Makes your manhood burst open like a sausage that's been on the griddle too long."

"Ya, ya, no need to recount the details." Jenkins sheepishly adjusted his groin.

"Quiet down, keep your minds on your duties," Vanyard snapped. "'Sides, you all know there's no leave."

"Come on, Sarge, just twenty minutes."

"Seal it. I know you're the hardest working grunts Oppenfauld has. There's a shit job to do, we do it." The acolytes thumped their shields. "Slap and nibble will have to wait till Faldaris."

My breath steamed against the cool mountain air. The sun shone in a blue sky, but I'd yet to enjoy its warmth. For hours we'd huddled outside Dun Al'veran's towering walls. The city seemed perpetually within the shadow of one mountain or another. Situated in a deep valley, it hugged the base of a cliff, with the Al'veran on its eastern edge.

So, within the shadow of the wall, within the shadow of a mountain, I wiggled my toes and rubbed my arms. My threadbare shirt provided laughable protection from the icy chill that rattled my bones. But if I did more than shuffle, my guards got nervous. I'd rather be cold and listen to their banter than be the focus of silent hostility.

The gates opened abruptly. Wide enough for thirty men to walk abreast and gilded with runes of strength. The acolytes, along the right side, made a corridor for a runner to approach.

"Huntsman, the Avatar requires your presence." The girl couldn't have been more than ten, yet she wore full military gear, complete with sword and shield made to her size.

"Lead on." Melcor made a shooing motion.

"Yes, sir." She saluted.

"Vanyard, Hilstrad. With me."

They herded me past the heathens and on through the gate. The chill lessened within the passageway. Multiple gates barred the way, and we had to wait as the one behind us lowered before the next would open. Laughter echoed through the murder holes that lined the ceiling.

Townsfolk packed the main thoroughfare. A sea of humanity, hemmed by acolytes. Skin and eye color everywhere from pale to midnight. The city's heathens awaiting their expulsion.

"The White Flame redeems," said an elder in white robes. He swung a thurible, wafting its white smoke over the people who knelt before him. "Feed the Flame your fear, your anger, your resentment. Divest yourself of this place you once called home, for it is cursed. This is a blessing from the White Flame. A sign. We must pilgrimage to the Flame Lands and leave this demon-plagued city behind."

Farther down the way, a group dressed in furs practiced one of the Norvish heightenings. "Duality is the bane of all sentient life," said a strapping man, guiding them through the moves. "Do not allow this injustice to poison your spirit. Remember, the body and spirit are intertwined only for the present. Control your mind and the spirit will command the flesh. Many of us have spoken of starting our own clan. Well, I say now is the time. Let us travel to the plains of

Fangmar and tell the Norven we're the thirteenth clan. I have the will. Do you?"

The mass of heathens was lost as the runner led us down back alleys. What shops we passed were closed. The streets were all but empty. A wrinkled hand pulled a child away from a window. The shutters closed with exaggerated care.

Stone streets gave way to wooden planks as we entered the port. The messenger led us all the way to the back corner of Dun Al'veran, to a pub that all but caressed the cliff. The sign read 'Hinsker's Fjord' and showed a man merrily drowning in a foaming tankard.

The Avatar stood examining the cliff. A drained corpse lay on the planks behind her. Despite the state of the body, it was obvious what had killed him. His throat had been ripped out.

"Ah, here you are," the Avatar said. "Melcor, can we expect this one to return?"

Melcor knelt over the corpse, looking into its eyes. "No, this one's been claimed."

She turned to an aide. "You may release the remains to the family for burning." The aide bowed, and two burly guardsmen put the body on a stretcher and carried it away with ease.

Vanyard ran a finger over an abrasion in the moss that covered the cliff. "Arachnids. In Dun Al'veran," he exclaimed, drawing his sword.

"They're gone now," the Avatar told him.

"No. They're waiting for dark." Vanyard checked the sun's position. "Seven hours, not enough time."

"Sergeant," Justice said.

"Get every Kydaist to the walls, break out the garrison's oil stores." His voice was on the verge of hysteria.

"Sergeant Vanyard," barked the Avatar.

"Blockade the intersections, create fire traps." He looked around as if expecting the Arachnids to rappel down the cliff face at any moment. "The short spears were useless against them. We need pikes, halberds, and crossbows with armor piercing bodkins."

The Avatar gripped Vanyard by the shoulder and made the sign of the sword over Vanyard's brow. "Warrior, come back." The blue tracer sank into his skin. He shuddered, and the mania died away.

"Better?"

"Much. Forgive me the old battle fatigue. I—"

The Avatar raised a hand to silence him. "The way of the sword and shield holds many dangers. Our lord is with you. Let us give thanks."

The Avatar led Vanyard in prayer, their heads bowed, a blue glow emanating from every sword and shield save Melcor's. I prayed. It was like being alone in a dark room.

"I will deal with the Arachnids," Justice said.

"The swarm will tear you apart," Vanyard growled. "I told you they couldn't be—"

The Avatar raised a hand. "Have faith."

Melcor spoke from the shadows. "It's foolish to go by yourself."

"I am never alone." The acolytes bowed their heads, but Vanyard shook his in disgust. "The people of this city need to remember their lord protects them while I deal with our new allies." I felt like someone had just sucker punched me. Since when did we ally with those man-eating beasts? "You have one job." The Avatar pointed at me. "Do it well."

JUSTICE LED the way back to the main gate. I cast into my memories, trying to decipher why I was so uneasy... so betrayed. But the majority of my life was just gone. Chalk wiped from the slate.

These streets made me feel as if I'd embraced an old friend, yet all of it was foreign. We cut across a campus close to the heart of the city. Young men and women wore uniforms that I'd never seen before, but the buttons on the collar denoted year and rank. The medals on the sash signified the areas of distinction. There an artillery engineer walked arm in arm with a heavy weapons specialist.

I couldn't trust myself. My judgment had no facts backing it up. I was so certain I was innocent. What if Justice was right, and I had cast aside king and kin for immortality? The only way to tell was to get my memories back. If I did, would that change me? All the more reason to let my faith guide me.

We exited the campus and passed through a square. A statue had recently been demolished. All that remained was the pedestal and the toe of a boot. Melcor broke out laughing, pointing at the ruins with his sword.

Justice spun, drawing a rune in the air. Red lightning shot out, dropping Melcor to his knees.

"Does my disgrace amuse you?" She didn't give him the chance to answer. She pressed her palm to the rune, and lightning arced. Smoke rose from the huntsman.

The demolished statue twisted my insides.

"I warn you for the very last time, demon. Hold your tongue." She let the rune dissipate. "Vanyard."

"Avatar Justice."

"Wait for the huntsman to recover, then escort the prisoner to the highway. I want him away from all these people."

"As you command." But the Avatar was already half a block away.

The smell of burnt hair filled the square. Melcor groaned. He fixed me with a hate-filled glare, as if I'd been the one to cook him.

The Avatar rounded a corner and disappeared from sight. What could have driven Khyber to make a deal with the Arachnids? I should have faith in Khyber and his Avatars. We... they were his will. But this felt wrong.

An idea struck me. I reached into an almost forgotten part of my mind and found Rowan. She was close, perhaps five miles from the city, at the very end range of where the tether would allow.

"Rowan."

"Master, when will you answer my prayers and die?" her voice rang in my head.

"Not today, I think. But you never know you might get lucky."

"I prefer to make my own luck."

"I'm sure the opportunity to stab me in the eye will present itself sooner or later."

"That's the nicest thing you've ever said to me."

"Yes, well, pleasantries aside, I need you to do something."

"I've no choice, remember?"

"I command you to follow the Avatar. Do not be seen or heard. She's going to parlay with the Arachnids. Watch from a distance and report to me what happens."

"Mother, save me." Her thoughts dripped with sarcasm. "I long for death, but not at the fangs of those things. At the very least, I'll get a show when they pull her legs off."

"What are you looking at?" Melcor snarled. He levered himself up with his sword. "You heard her. Lead the way."

Rowan came closer at first, circling the city. She started

moving again as we passed through the eighth gate. Rowan must have found the Avatar's trail, for all at once, she sped away. The farther she got, the greater the mental strain. It was much like trying to remember a series of numbers, only every few moments a new number would be added. My guards led me half a mile down the highway before sitting down to wait.

"*Master.*" Rowan's thoughts were a whisper.

"*What do you see?*"

"*An ocean of spiders, small as teacups and as big as wagons. They surround the Avatar. She's just standing there. It seems like she's waiting for something. Now there's a man in a black cloak. The spiders are making way. They're speaking, Master, you son of a bitch, that's Eericas. Gods, I'll be years in dying if he finds me. He's laughing at her. It's too far away for me to hear.*"

"*That's fine, just do your best.*"

"*The spiders are getting agitated, clawing at her. Justice is glowing, taking on a new shape.*" Her mental voice quivered with rage. "*She's taken the form of Khyber. I can hear what they're saying.*" I focused and was able to hear through her.

"This is a direct violation of our agreement," Khyber said.

"I haven't been paid," said a voice like sandpaper. That had to be Eericas.

"It's coming, and you know it," Khyber said. "You do not come into my land and take what you want. They are mine."

"If you can't protect them, then they are hardly yours." Eericas laughed. "And if you can't even protect your flock, I am beginning to have second thoughts about our arrangement."

"*The spiders are getting agitated again,*" Rowan thought. "*They're circling Khyber. Oh no.*"

"*What? What's happening?*"

"At least twenty of the spiders dropped from a cliff. Some protective barrier shredded them. I thought they had her. Root and stem. Khyber's threatening."

"Shut up. Let me listen."

"Don't test me, Eericas. I will eradicate every one of your children."

"You've been trying for decades, and I'm stronger than ever."

"Eericas's body is changing." I sensed her revulsion through the bond. *"He's turned into a spider, nearly the size of a human dwelling."*

"I know you've spent your power on those toys your soldiers carry. I'm willing to bet this little display cost you greatly. I think you have nothing left to defend yourself. Why else would you seek an alliance with the likes of me? You're weak and need me to do all the heavy lifting."

"Do I now?" Khyber's voice rang in my head.

All around me, acolytes turning to the east. One and all they made the sign of the sword. Blue streamers pulsed with a vibrant intensity. In the distance, red lightning rained from a clear blue sky.

"Rowan, are you all right?"

"Sadly. Would have been quick."

"What are they saying?"

"I can't make it out over the falling rocks. Eericas looks shaken. But none of the Arachnids were killed. No, wait, I can hear him now."

"You have no concept of what true power is. You have no home, nowhere to physically manifest your realm. But I can give that to you. We've discussed all this. There is so much to gain for both of us, and all you need to do is what you do best. Harry their supply lines, pick off their scouts, take the healthy, leave them burdened with injured. Make them fear the shadows, show them what it is to be hunted," Khyber said.

"And in exchange?" Eericas asked.

"You get the sum we agreed upon. Unless the deal is off?"

"I want more," Eericas hissed.

"Twenty-seven."

"Twenty-seven barrels isn't enough."

Lightning rained from the sky once more.

"Ho my, the largest Arachnids were just struck," Rowan thought.

"It's the number you stole from me," Khyber said.

"Eericas looks as if he's about to attack."

"One-thirty-second of all the blood in my realm and not a drop more."

My stomach clenched in horror, I looked up at the villagers lined before the gate.

"And I will cede you the Mother Vale," Khyber said. "That is the deal. Take it, or leave it."

"My children, my beauties. Their strands are gone forever. This insult—"

"Reciprocity is the price of treachery," Khyber cut in sharply. "Don't let it happen again."

"One-thirty-second," Eericas grumbled. "As agreed."

"Rowan. You had better slip away before the meeting ends."

"Just a few moments more."

"No, go now. Get to safety."

"All I have to do is rustle the bushes and it's all over. I can be free."

"No, Rowan. I command you don't get caught. Stay safe. That is an order."

"Just let me go."

I didn't reply, relaxing my mental hold over her. She

began to close the distance. I stared at the acolytes and saw their cold, detached efficiency in a new light. These men and women were about to commit a second genocide. They were driving the heathens like cattle to the abattoir.

I remembered the piping screams of the Spriggans as they fell to their deaths. I thought of Rowan and how her loss had stolen the joy from her life. All my fault. My plan. Had the ends really justified the means? If Khyber had transcended, the Ascendancy War would have continued. Strothheim would have been one more pretty light in the nightmare of the afterlife.

One-thirty-second of all the blood in Oppenfauld. To purchase an alliance that may even the odds in the coming war. Could I sit quietly by and let three percent of my countrymen be slaughtered? Three percent, and not a single soldier. The math made sense. Nonetheless, it left me feeling sick.

A CHEER ERUPTED from the soldiers and civilians alike, as the Avatar burst out of the trees. Her speed was unbelievable. She crossed the killing field faster than a horse could gallop, wildflower petals swirling in her wake. She leapt, catching the edge of the highway. Her armor made a whirring sound, and she effortlessly pulled herself over the crenellation.

"Decided not to stay for dinner?" Hilstrad asked.

"They didn't like what was on the menu." Justice waved to those on the walls. Flags were brandished, and cheers rose from within the city. The Avatar turned to Vanyard and Hilstrad. "Signal for the exodus to begin." An acolyte stepped forwards and did as commanded.

"Did Khyber finally kill the bastard?"

"No, he brought him to heel."

"Wyrm spawn!" Vanyard threw his spear to the ground. "That demon cannot be trusted."

"Sergeant!" the Avatar said as softly as a blade parting silk. "Are you finished?"

He nodded stiffly. "Yes, Avatar. My deepest apologies."

"I should think so. Have a little faith."

"Yes, Avatar. Won't happen again."

"Good."

The city gates opened, and the heathens were brought out. There were so many people that the far end blurred into a mass of colors.

The Avatar raised a hand, and all fell silent. "Each of you has turned your back on king and country. Yet still the king would extend his hand to you. Accept Khyber as your one true god, pledge him your soul. Vow to guard Oppenfauld from invaders, and you may return to your homes."

Angry mutters skittered through the crowd. An arm reached skyward, waving a checkered handkerchief.

"Make way!" shouted an officer. A woman, babe in arms and two more hanging from her skirts, stepped through the protective ring. She exchanged words with a judge. He drew the sign of the sword, blessing her and the children. She cast her white shawl to the pavement. Curses followed her as she reentered the city.

A few more accepted the offer. Some men and women of fighting age, but mostly families with small children. Perhaps a hundred at most forsook their gods, a mere fraction of those gathered before the gates.

"Is there no one else?" the Avatar's voice cut through the outraged babble. A stone flew out of the heathens and struck the Avatar. It bounced off her breastplate with a metallic clank. A red-haired youth ducked hastily back into the crowd. The acolytes moved as one, shields locked, spears raised. Heathens screamed in fear.

"Hold!" the Avatar yelled, her voice carrying over the cacophony. She whispered something to an acolyte, and she signaled the wall. The gates closed. "Khyber is not without mercy. As most of you know, a demon has invaded these lands."

Whispered voices all said the same. "Arachnids, Eericas."

"Yes, the Spider has returned. It would go against all that Kydaism stands for to cast you out while such a threat looms."

"We can go home?" someone called.

"You've made your choice," the Avatar said sharply. "But we will take you to a place of safety until the Arachnids have been pushed back."

Their relief was palpable.

"We are not there yet. If we push through the night, by this time tomorrow there will be sanctuary."

A grateful cry went up. The Avatar waved a hand, and the procession advanced. I looked away, unable to stand the hope that shone across their faces.

THE HIGHWAY THREADED through the mountains. At first, running along the valley's floor, past a lake with sprawling hunting lodges along the far bank. But by midafternoon the topography changed and the bowl-like valleys gave way to canyons so steep the bottom was lost in shadow.

The highway clung to the sheer cliffs like a fly on a wall. The heathens all but hugged the stone. Those who would have dared a glance over the edge were sent on their way with a hard look and a reminder that spiders can climb anything.

We came to the first bridge as night fell. A biting wind guttered torches and reefed at the cloaks on men's backs. A double row of acolytes braced against the wind with their shields, and the heathens scurried across in their lee.

Melcor stood on the edge of the bridge, leaning into the

wind, his tongue lolling. He roared into the darkness, a reckless smile on his face.

I shivered in my torn shirt and gauged the distance to the other side. Melcor jumped down from the crenellation and searched the distant line of flickering torches. When he looked back, he had the air of a coiled spring.

"Forward!" Vanyard stepped between us, his voice all but stolen by the wind.

A shield pushed me, and I stepped out onto the bridge. I put my shoulder to the wind and kept one eye on Melcor. He stalked behind, one hand holding his mask, the other in a white-knuckled grip on his great sword.

Snow fell just after midnight, dusting the stones with a white sheet. A numbness had crept up my legs, so every step felt like I was walking on stilts. The rear of the train had been flagging, and with every bridge crossing, the line strung out more.

"She's eighty, by the flame," said a woman sheltering her mother in the crook of her arm. "She can't keep up this pace. None of the elders can."

The officer herded them before her. "You know how fast an Arachnid can move? They could be from Dun Al'veran to here in under an hour."

"She can't move any faster. If we could just rest and warm up."

"By Khyber, you flame worshipers are so soft. Keep up or be left behind. If you're lucky, you'll die from their venom. If not..."

A half an hour later, the old woman collapsed to the highway. Weeping and blue lipped, she struggled to rise, but she hadn't the strength. Her daughter knelt by her side and wrapped a white shawl about them. Melcor hung back, eying them hungrily.

"Keep moving." Jenkins prodded me forwards with the butt of his spear.

"We can't just leave them," I protested.

"Vanyard?" Hilstrad said. "Fall back in line."

Vanyard ignored her and knelt down to pick up the elderly woman.

"Thank you. Thank you," wept her daughter.

"Sergeant?" The Avatar stepped from the shadows. "Return to your post."

Vanyard clutched the old lady to his chest and glared at Justice. "You promised things would change under your command."

"And they have." She flicked her wrist, and an acolyte stepped forwards, taking the old lady from Vanyard. "Every last one of them shall reach sanctuary."

Vanyard saluted and retook his place in my protective ring. His face remained as impassive as a boulder, but something about the set of his shoulders spoke of a weight being lifted. As the hours passed, more and more of the elderly collapsed. Each was carried by an acolyte. Still in full kit, pack and weapons, they toiled under the added weight without a word of protest.

The sun rose, but it brought no warmth. By midmorning we came to a crossroads. A three-towered Fauld sat in a craggy cleft. A road jutted from either side of the battlements to wrap around the mountain. We crossed a bridge that spanned a frothing river. Heavy ironbound doors slammed behind me. Gears ground as locking mechanisms fastened it shut.

The heathens had been herded through a tunnel at the rear of the keep. It sloped gently downwards. Oily torch smoke slithered up the roof, clawing at my throat and stinging my eyes. Melcor had to crouch lest the horns of his mask grated against the ceiling, but the smoke didn't seem to bother him in the slightest.

When the tunnel finally ended, it came as a blessed surprise. My senses had acclimatized to the echoing of thousands of feet and strobing shadows. To suddenly come out into open air, blue sky, the green of pine and fir, and a relief from the white noise was overwhelming for a few moments.

Ahead, the jagged peaks of the Sovereign Guards were blunted, and a lush valley stretched before me. Save for a singular mountain that dwarfed all others that came before. A doe studied our train as we limped past. Her jaw worked in slow circles as she cropped wildflowers that grew amid the killing field.

Through the afternoon and into the evening, the acolytes pressed the heathens towards the mountain that all but clove the sky. It was late when we reached the foot of that towering peak. A castle was built into its side, its walls higher and thicker than those of Dun Al'veran. Perhaps it was the hour, but to me it seemed every stone shouted it had been crafted for a single purpose—to withstand the might of a god.

The train picked up speed now that the destination was in sight. A drawbridge of solid stone lowered, sending a thundering boom that reverberated throughout the valley. Blueish light spilled from the archway as the first set of gates opened. Far ahead the Avatar stood in the archway addressing the people.

"I know you are exhausted. Inside you'll find beds and a hot meal. Before you accept Khyber's hospitality, I will ask one final time. Abandon your gods, take up the sword and shield, and defend Oppenfauld." There was a resounding silence. "If you change your mind, speak to one of our acolytes. The scriveners at the desks will take your names and show you to a room. From there you may go to the mess hall. Do not push. There is enough for all. Remember, you are guests, and this is a military facility. Do not touch the red doors. If you do, the consequences will be severe."

Blue flames burned in sconces along the passageway through the wall. Multiple gates closed behind me and my guards, each stouter than the last. Within the courtyard, rows of tables had been arranged, and scriveners in their clean-cut uniforms handed the heathens keys and led them away.

"This building is our agricultural facility. Its ground floor is the kitchen and dining rooms. Keep up please, your dormitory is this way."

I was taken through the courtyard, past the rows of disheveled heathens. The Avatar stood in front of a red metal wall set into the side of the mountain. She made the sign of the sword before it. There was a hiss like steam under pressure, and the entire section slid forwards out of the mountain and glided to one side.

The opening was large enough to sail a three-masted galleon through. The grinding of machinery and the clang of hammers on metal echoed up the long hallway.

"What's in there?" I asked.

"The chance to prove your innocence," Justice replied.

❧ 25 ❧

THE BLUE LIGHT was hard to look at. It glinted harshly off the Avatar's armor and stung as it passed through the wafts of steam that escaped through the joins in the metal. Melcor felt it too, keeping his eyes on his feet.

Doors on either side of the corridor stood open, bustling with personnel. Judges in their long robes set up surgical instruments. A cold stone formed in my stomach at the sight of rows of hospital cots. *One-thirty-second* rang in my mind.

"Double time," the Avatar ordered. The military personnel made way, saluting the Avatar as we passed. Red doors lined the main hallway, none as large as the one I'd come through but still imposing. Only a few stood open. I caught a glimpse of cubicles full of scriveners working. Another was an artillery warehouse with men stowing scorpion bolts.

After twenty or so minutes, we came to the source of the noise. Heat from a manufactory spilled into the hallway. I'd expected them to be forging weapons, but they were constructing coffins. Hundreds of metal coffins. The workshop across the hall held stacks of ceramic amphoras fresh from the kiln.

A red door capped this end of the hall. The Avatar made the sign of the sword and it slid open. Fresh air washed over me in a cold gust. I stepped out onto a ramp that spiraled deep into the heart of the mountain and high above to the night sky.

Something far below glowed like the embers of a dying fire. Hundreds of stories extended below. My legs were rubber, but the Avatar set a brisk pace, and I'd show no weakness.

A clattering of hooves echoed behind us, and a horse-drawn cart exited the main hallway and descended the spiral.

The red glow grew stronger with each floor. Every few floors stood another red door. The mountain must have been hollowed like a pine tree filled with branching passages off this central stem.

Thirst gnawed at me. Not for water or wine. I needed blood, I felt it in my bones. Without it I would lose control, and soon. Not now, when I was so close to redeeming myself.

It came as a surprise when the jagged point of a holy broken sword came into view. It hung in midair within the center of the mountain's core, rotating freely, suspended by some unseen force. Red lightning arced from the blade and coursed along the inner rim of the stairs. When it ceased, the blade separated into shards that tumbled through the air before reforming into the blade. I gave up on trying to calculate how large the sword was at the fiftieth floor.

The walls opened into a vast cavern of natural uncut stone. Directly below the hovering blade was the rune. The weapon I'd used to slay a goddess and murder her people. It was set into the stone floor. Jagged veins of iron ore spiderwebbed from it. The weapon was to scale with the blade above. The circumference could have been a racetrack. It was beautiful, a mastery of the runic arts and the skill of craftsmen. Save for a warping of the metal in the exact spot where the explosion had occurred.

Judges were hard at work cutting away the malformed piece. It looked as though the metal had heated and started pouring down a drain. As we descended the final few ramps, the judges finished and melded chains to it. Horses whinnied and strained against their yokes. The twisted rune rose on the end of a long boom and pulley system.

I was led past the line of workhorses and through the cavern. We followed one of the iron veins. The metal all but bled from the ore, black and glistening as if fresh from the forge.

Lightning arced from the sword, coursing along the iron vein and off into the cavern. A figure stood in the dark recesses on the verge of the sconce light, the brief flash illuminating a red-armored figure with a sword on either hip.

Hilstrad lit a torch. The floor became pocked with fissures, and I had to dance to keep my footing. This Avatar was taller and slighter than Justice. The armor had a different aesthetic from Justice's interlocking bands. Flexible scales clung to the sinuous body of the Avatar. Every line spoke of speed and agility.

"You have it?" Justice asked.

A forked tongue flicked out from the viper's faceplate. The Avatar handed Justice a slip of folded white silk. "Is that the traitor?" demanded a man's voice, coated with as much venom as a cobra's fangs.

Justice peeled away the silk to reveal something that looked like a cinnamon stick made of polished mahogany.

"Ram me, but he looks just like the portrait in the hall of lords."

Justice drew her sword. "He claims he was framed."

The viper snorted.

"Hold out your hand, demon," Justice commanded.

I bit my tongue and did as ordered. Justice drew the blade across my forearm. The cut was deep, and blood should have flowed from the wound, but no more than a trickle came. Instantly, the prickling pain of blood magic built.

Justice smeared my blood on the stick, and it lit up with a green-blue phosphorescence. Sudden weakness stole the strength from my legs, and I collapsed.

"Quickly," said the viper.

Justice handed him the stick. He knelt over the iron vein. Drew a complicated rune in the air, chanting under his breath. He pressed the stick to the iron, and as if it were as soft as clay, the stick sank. Green light pulsed along the vein. Mushrooms and other lichen sprouted where iron met stone. Lightning surged, and when it connected with the stick, green light pulsed. Mosses sprouted from the bare stone. A ring of life expanded with each surge of electricity.

The viper stood, arms raised to the sky. "Praise Khyber, we're saved."

"Mercy." Justice's voice was dangerously calm. "Fetch the other cores."

Mercy's demeanor changed from elated relief to the coiled tension of a headsman. With alarming speed, he took off running.

"How did you do it?" Justice asked.

"Do what?"

Justice gestured at the growing ring of life. "Steal the Mother Tree's soul."

I felt as though the floor had just dropped out from under me. "I didn't steal anything."

"Of course," she said like a patronizing parent who'd caught their child in a lie.

"I am and have always been Khyber's servant," I stated, adrenaline adding a sharp edge to my tone.

"Then you'd be willing to show me what went wrong." She motioned to the runes at the base of the blade.

"I want nothing more than to find out how this happened to me."

Justice brushed past. "Bring him."

Melcor grabbed me by the upper arm and pulled me up. I stumbled along in a daze, my mind racing down the branching paths of consequence. This was damning, nearly irrefutable evidence I had betrayed Khyber. If another deity had interfered with the ritual, they would have taken the Mother Tree's power for their own. Yet her soul resided within me.

Khyber would want his prize. This was a death sentence. They'd take me to Faldaris, and Khyber would take my head and devour my soul. Isn't that what I wanted? To allow Khyber to Transcend, to secure Strothheim's place in the Ethereal Battle? No matter the evidence, I knew I was innocent. But there was no hope of redemption now. I'd die a traitor and my family would be punished in my place.

The boom swung and a replacement rune was set in place. Judges crawled like ants over it, sparks flying as they joined the metal.

"Get your men clear!" Justice called.

"But, Avatar, we still need to file the—" the foreman called back.

"It's functional the way it is."

"As you say, but we haven't found what's causing the warping."

"That's what this diagnostic is for."

The judge bowed and ordered his workers to clear out.

We climbed the ramp to a half bridge hung over the rune. Justice gestured over the edge. "Here it is. Your promised salvation. An advanced weapon that would usher Oppenfauld into a new era of prosperity."

I gazed over the rune. Polished steel that rose nine feet above the stone and varied in width from a single inch to six feet. The runes coiled from node to node in a hypnotic tangle.

"Melcor, we'll need a test subject."

"An Awakened?"

"No need to waste. An Arisen should suffice." The huntsman sullenly stomped off down the gangway. "Ingenious," Justice said. "Discovering how to connect the mortal and spiritual realms. No wonder you were so secretive. If this method of runic layering got out, this would change the way wars are fought."

"Yes, there's at least three patterns overlaid atop one another." I traced the outline of the sword and shield carefully with my finger.

"There's five. We deciphered your notes. It's the back door we can't find."

"Back door?"

"The hidden rune." Avatar Justice held out her hand, and Judge Warwick placed a leather document tube in it. She flipped through the sheets, passing them over one at a time.

The first was a map of Oppenfauld. The bottom corner was distorted as if the ink had lifted from the paper and been spun like yarn. "Avatar Might is scouring the highways between Dun Al'veran and Dun Ungolith. He'll pull up every stone to find any concealed runes." She handed me two more sheets, a spherical shield of jagged electric lines and the broken sword, re-forged. "I suspect you wrote something into the function runes. It's the only way you could have hidden it until the weapon fired at full capacity.

"Khyber believes the interference is coming from Damnation or Strothheim. But even he can't figure out how a mortal could have tampered with his spiritual realms."

I examined the final two pages. Sunbursts coiled around a castle's battlements and what looked like the open maw of some creature with too many teeth.

A heavy thud caught my attention. Below, Melcor had returned with one of the coffins. A judge cut it open. Melcor threw the lid back and snatched a thrashing corpse from inside. The Arisen clawed Melcor and sucked desperately at the air. Melcor had it by the throat and drove a meat hook under its collarbone. The judge fused the chain to the floor. Melcor dropped the Arisen and backed away. The Arisen got up and ran at the judge. The chain went taut. Still, the Arisen lunged for the judge with a savage fury.

"So, Rodrick, where's the back door?"

"I'll find it. All I need is time."

"And give you the chance to further hide your trail? I think not." The Avatar gestured, and my arms were wrenched behind my back.

"Dammit, Justice, I am cooperating. I have no idea how this happened."

"Liar." She drew her sword and knelt before it. "My lord.

206

He is withholding the information." Blue light pulsed from the blade.

"I'm not Khyber. Please listen to me."

"I understand," the Avatar said sadly. "Tell him I tried. Tell him I love him." The light winked out. "This is your last chance, if you want to save your son."

"My son?"

"Khyber is on the way to the dungeons to cast him into Damnation as we speak."

"No! He's just a child, please!"

Rage flashed across Justice's face. Her fist drove the wind from me. "Perform the ritual! Show me where you hid it."

"Anything, just stop Khyber," I begged.

Justice signaled someone below, and captives were pulled from the wagon that had followed us down the spiral. The two old women and a young man with red hair were marched up the gangway at sword point. I recognized them: the young man who had thrown the stone, and the mother and daughter from the highway.

"What's this?" Vanyard asked. "You said we'd give them sanctuary."

"How else did you expect me to get them to cooperate?" Justice pulled a small glass vial from her belt pouch.

"You said things would go back to the way they used to be. When we were protectors of the people."

"Those days are over." Justice pointed at me. "He saw to that. Now, we protect our own, and the freeloading heathens will repay Oppenfauld for all the sacrifices we've made on their behalf."

Vanyard looked as if his teeth would splinter. The two women began to cry.

Justice handed me a dagger. "Enough words. Prove your loyalty. Save your son."

The elderly woman was grabbed under the arms and dragged to the edge of the gangway. Justice popped the cork and poured the blood of Khyber onto the rune.

I stepped behind her and covered her eyes with my hand. The waddle under her chin stretched as I pulled her head back. One sharp tug and I'd save my son. Prove my conviction, if not my innocence, that I hadn't intended any of this. My hand shook, and a tear leaked down the woman's cheek.

"I love you, Sasha."

"I love you too, Mama."

"Hurry, damn you," Justice snarled.

Memories assaulted me. The Void recognizing me as a kindred spirit. The witches, the blade descending towards my chest. How casually I'd had the Spiral's priestess murdered to activate a weapon that caused a genocide. I'd been so confident I was in the right. How many were dead because of what I had wrought? If I killed this woman, no matter how I justified it, I'd be one step closer to becoming that man again.

I dropped the knife. "This is wrong. Punish me instead. Spare my son."

"I knew it." Justice's sword flashed, and the woman's body tumbled off the end of the gangway. Before I could stop myself, I breathed, drinking the blood. Nothing happened. Melcor's hand wrapped around my shoulder and pulled me away from the edge. Her head spun from my one-handed grip.

The other two were wrestled to the edge. Their cries cut off with two quick slashes. Blood spilled to the rune below.

Their blood coursed along the runes, activating the various nodes. Red lightning surged, coalescing in the space between the rune and the sword. A churning ball of electricity, crackling and undulating. Justice formed the sign of the sword with her arms and stepped off the gangway.

With all that steel, she should have dropped like a boulder. Yet she floated towards the ball of lightning. It reached for her, embraced her, and ran through her. She reached the focal point and screamed her hatred, pain and loss. A blast of raw energy, red as blood, hit the Arisen, burning it to ash.

The secondary function activated as the Veil tore. A rift to Damnation opened below Justice, a red horizon and a dark landscape. Suddenly, I was struggling against a current, fighting to hold on to my flesh. The soul of the Arisen was pulled towards that rift, helpless as a leaf going over a waterfall. But something happened. Another rift opened, smaller but infinitely more powerful. The Arisen was snatched from Damnation and pulled into the smaller rift.

The Veil closed, and Justice expelled the rest of the energy into the broken blade. Thunder clapped and a bolt a hundred times stronger cannoned out of the top of the mountain. Justice hovered back down to the gangway. Heat spilled off her armor in waves.

"Did you see what happened?" Justice asked.

"Same as the last ten times." Melcor pointed at the freshly installed rune, now a misshapen hunk of slag.

"Bind his hands."

"Wait, Avatar. Please, my son."

"He's dead."

I didn't see the blow, only stars, and the next thing I knew, I was at the bottom of the gangway. My arms wrenched behind my back, a fist in my hair fully extending my neck. I was dangling over a chest full of Spriggan cores.

"What was your plan? To let the people starve, then swoop in as the new god of harvest, a savior? Hearts and minds can be swayed by a simple loaf of bread. I never thought you actually listened to any of Mother's speeches."

I looked up sharply, meeting her cat eyes. "Doesn't matter what I say, you've made your decision."

"You're right." Avatar Justice drew her blade across my throat. The cores sparkled to life as they drank in my blood. "And they say the Spiral has no justice."

A BLACK DOOR lay open before me, the mouth of a crude shaft that sank into the earth, candlelight glimmering within. Movement from the doorframe made me step back. A cliff of tentacles writhed and twisted, groping for something, anything, to pull into the Void.

A moan came from a small lake with an island at its center. I stepped out of the cliff's shadow. The sky burned with white fire. The flames roiled and rolled like the surf in an uncharted ocean.

For a hundred feet in every direction, this strange dream spanned, then suddenly cut off, as though shaved with a carpenter's plane. Beyond was an ocean of blackness. Not the malicious hunger of the Void, rather an empty space waiting to be filled.

A tree stood amid that emptiness, so big my mind had trouble gaining perspective. It was like looking at the moon.

I took a step towards the edge, but my feet were stuck. Unnaturally smooth stone had frozen the soles of my feet in place.

Sparks woke me from my strange dream. They spat,

burning me wherever they landed. I sat up but hit my head. I could barely bend my knees or flex my arms. I was trapped inside a coffin. Smoke filled the confined space. I needed out, needed air. Above all, I needed blood.

A molten line ran the circumference of my prison. I pushed on the lid, fear giving me strength. It slid to the side. A man stood over me. He had what I wanted. I pulled, trying to rip the blood from his veins with the sheer force of my need.

There was a heavy chunk, and the world around me succumbed to darkness.

———

PAIN BLOSSOMED THROUGH MY SKULL. Thirst was everything, the need. Suddenly I was bathed in blood. I drank this gift from the gods. It sloshed onto my chest, and I breathed in ecstasy. So much that it filled all the empty spaces within.

I blinked. A dark shape stood over me. He tipped an amphora off the coffin's rim. Liquid sloshed within.

"Easy now, or I'll shoot." I thought I recognized the voice, but it was hoarse and watery, as though he had been crying.

"William?" I asked.

"Keep your voice down. Just cuz they're off duty doesn't mean they're not watching."

My vision resolved, and I saw Cassy's father before me. He stepped back, training a crossbow at me. My coffin was in a wagon, Rows of amphoras stood neatly to either side of a long aisle. I leveraged myself up. William braced his shoulder against the stock, sweat dripping from his brow.

"Mind relaxing your finger on that trigger?"

"You would have torn me to pieces a second ago."

"I'm in control now."

"Ram it! But I've no other options. If I'm gone much longer, they'll come looking," William said agitatedly.

The low murmur of voices echoed up the hall. The facility seemed on the verge of sleep. "Then you'd better get back to your post. It's better if you don't know where I went."

I tipped the amphora into the coffin. The heavy ceramic broke, and blood spilled amongst the fragments. I drank, pulling it in rivulets up my body and into my mouth.

"This was a mistake," William said.

I tossed the wax seal in as well. "Then why let me out? You must know Khyber wants me?"

"When they find out what I did..."

"They'll hurt you, hurt your family. No amount of gratitude is worth that."

"You saved my daughter once. I need you to do it again."

"And all the other prisoners? I won't let Khyber have them."

"They're not going anywhere."

"You're a man of faith, William, but if I don't get those people out of here, they're going to be slaughtered."

William lowered his crossbow and sat down heavily, eyes filling with tears. "It's worse." His gaze fell in-wards, and he shut his eyes as if to block out the vision. "They drugged their food that first night. I helped carry them. They're on the other side of that wall. They took this long pin and hammered it up through the eye socket and stirred. Hundreds of people reduced to infants. Tubes down their throats for feeding, needles in their arms to provide a constant stream of—" His voice caught, and he gestured to the amphoras.

"All of them?"

"Yes, all of them!" He glanced at the door to see if anyone

had heard his outburst. "Except Cassy, but it's only a matter of time before—" He took a steadying breath. "—they finish taking the inventory, like they're goods on a shelf."

"Gods, William, I... Anyone you knew?"

He set his jaw, anger burying the pain. "I lived in Raider's Watch my whole life. What do you think?"

"Help me with the lid." He put down the crossbow, and we slid the top back on. "Where is she?"

"Second-tier armory, third door on your left." He reached into his pocket. "You'll need this to get through the lock. No one should be about." He passed me a badge, a shield with a sword emblazoned upon it.

He dropped it in my palm. Searing pain like I'd put my hand on a stove. The badge clattered to the stone floor. "What in the Void am I doing trusting an Arisen?" He scooped up the badge and wrapped it in a handkerchief.

The flesh was red and bubbled. I pressed my palm to the cold steel of the coffin. "Damn good question. You don't need me. With the time you spent freeing me, you could have snuck Cassy out."

"I swore an oath."

"As did I, but Khyber's proved he's not worth your loyalty."

"That's not it. After my wife, I promised myself I'd never let a vow stop me from doing what was right. But Kydaism isn't what it used to be. The Avatar made me swear a blood pact with Khyber. I'm trapped. If I flee, they'll find me. They'll find her."

"I'll get her out, but after that, she's on her own. I'm not safe to be around, and I have my own family to think about." *And a score to settle.*

The relief was plain on his face, although he hesitated. "I overheard Mercy and Justice arguing about the results from some diagnostic. Mercy said just bringing you within the proximity of the weapon should have made it function exactly the same as last time."

"But it didn't." My mind raced. The Arisen's soul was taken, yet the Mother Tree had been forced into me.

"Justice flew into a rage. But Mercy said that no amount of layering can defy the laws of nature. Or whatever that means."

"It means they know I'm innocent."

"But that defies the core tenets of Kydaism. Every man owns his actions. The virtuous and the wretched reap what they sow. For an Avatar to willingly condemn you for a crime you didn't commit is sacrilege."

"Maybe the tenets have changed. Khyber certainly has."

Booted feet rang in the hall. We crouched down in the wagon, breathing a sigh of relief when they passed.

"Well, after that, Justice got scary quiet. She said that nothing had changed. That there was no going back. Oppenfauld was in bed with our new ally, and sacrifices had to be made. She said that once Khyber transcended, they'd crush the Norven, Ivory Elves and Mirvish. That Khyber would exterminate the Arachnid and Myi'eshan, then claim the Flame Lands before finally putting an end to Wyrm. That by the time the sundering came, the Fauldic would forge a shard out of the whole world."

And it all hinged on Khyber claiming my soul. He'd soak the land in blood, subjugate those he didn't just annihilate. I felt something tear inside. I couldn't go to Faldaris. I was abandoning Anastasia and our children. But if my suspicions were right, they didn't want me. Justice hated me. This need for answers, need for redemption, was all to resurrect a man who deserved the death beyond death. The only right thing to do was run. And hope that Enris, Zenos and Glyodrin would put an end to Khyber while he still had a shred of honor left.

I took the handkerchief. The heat of the sigil through the cloth hurt but didn't sear. I slipped it into my pocket.

"Third door on the left."

"Hold the sigil before the door and make the sign of the sword."

"Goodbye, William."

"Rodrick, stand sure." His face twisted as though he'd tasted something bitter.

"Just because Khyber and his priesthood have lost their way doesn't mean you should forsake your values." I saluted him. "Stand sure."

I STOLE a glance up the hall. All was deathly silent, save for the hiss of William's torch as it resealed the coffin. I slipped off my boots and padded towards the armory. The next door over lay open. Carefully, I peeked round the corner.

White linen sheets, all with perfect mitered corners, shrouded row upon row of hospital beds. It was as William had said. Thousands of sightless eyes stared at the ceiling. Tubes ran from under the blankets, carrying their lifeblood to an amphora at the head of each bed. Attendants walked up and down the aisles. None looked in my direction.

I crossed the doorway, moving smoothly. No cry was raised, and I breathed easier. The first Kydaist who saw me in my tattered pants and torn shirt would sound the alarm. I picked up the pace and quickly came to the third door on the left. I fished the sigil from my pocket, careful not to let it touch my skin, and made the sign of the sword.

The door hissed and slid to the side.

"Cassy," I said softly.

"Father, you cam—" Her blond head popped up. "Rodrick, you scared the life out of me."

She'd met me halfway and embraced me. The softness of her pressed against me made my spine stiffen. This was more than familiar. I patted her on the shoulder blade.

"Those Fauldic bastards. Last thing I remember was having a bowl of stew, and then I woke up here with Father's note telling me I'd been drugged and that if I was found they'd kill me. Without the sun, I can't even tell how long it's been."

I took her by the shoulders and pushed her away. "He's right, we have to get out of here."

"Where is my father?"

"He swore a blood pact, Cassy. There isn't anywhere they couldn't find him. He said if he came, it'd cost both of you your lives."

"Don't know why I'm surprised," Cassy said, hurt. "He's never really been there for me."

"It might not seem like it now, but this is his way of protecting you."

"Fine," she said distantly. "Let's go."

"You know how to use any of these weapons?" I asked.

"The crossbow, but I doubt I could reload one with this heavy a gauge."

"I saw ones with a crank near the front."

"There's armor in the back." She stepped back to show me her lacquered armor.

"Meet you back here in five."

I ROUNDED the corner and came face-to-face with a cross-bow. "Sorry, Rodrick. Gods, you look the part."

"It's the only way we stand a chance of getting out of here." Cassy bit her lip and looked at her feet. "Don't do that. You break eye contact and we're caught."

"Right. Be confident."

I buckled a sword to my belt. "We're just doing our jobs."

"I'm no child," she snapped.

"Perfect. Use that face and you'll have any squad we meet fall in at your back."

She laughed, releasing some nervous tension. I shouldered a pack and a shield. "Have you seen any rope?" I asked.

"We've already got a lot to contend with," she replied.

"I don't fancy jumping off the highway, Do you?"

"I saw some over here."

"THE FRONT GATE'S THAT WAY," Cassy told me.

"We won't make it through the courtyard, let alone over the wall. Too many eyes."

"I hope you know where you're going."

We marched down the center of the hallway. And be it dumb luck, divine intervention or fate, there wasn't another living soul.

The red door slid aside, and a cool breeze washed over us. Cassy looked up and down the central column.

"Please tell me the way out is down." I walked past her up the spiral. "Khyber's a real prick."

"I... CAN'T... " Cassy panted.

"You must!" I called back to her. "Light can't be far off, and we have to be out of here before this facility wakes."

She pulled her canteen and took a drink. The artery in her throat hammered. I looked away and the thirst passed. There was no slaking it. I must have drunk the blood of three men and still it pushed me.

"I need a rest. Just a fe—"

Alarms sounded, high-pitched and loud enough to wake the dead. Cassy scrambled away from the red door she'd leaned against. It tore down the middle and seemed to burn away like parchment.

A black landscape framed by a distant red horizon stood on the other side. Some bird of prey wheeled in the distance, outlined in red. Two glowing eyes the size of my fists blinked awake. It gave a chortling bark and charged.

Cassy scrambled back but only made it a couple of feet before the thing rammed into a shimmering barrier where the door had just been.

A head twice the size of a bull's gored the barrier. Its horns came down the lateral side of its jaw. I ran forwards and pulled the sigil from my belt pouch. The barrier tore, fluttering like gossamer in the wind. Cassy fired. The bolt glanced off the bridge of its scaly nose and flew into Damnation.

I held the sigil before me and made the sign of the sword. The edges of the red door reformed, slowly closing. The beast pushed its head through. It snapped at my arm. I darted back. Its shoulder came through and then a leg. I readied a spear. The beast spasmed, biting at its hindquarters. The door closed, cutting it in half. Then its body crumbled to ash.

Why didn't the Veil tear?

"Come on," I said, helping Cassy to her feet. "We need to be long gone before they find this."

———

SHOUTS ECHOED FROM FAR BELOW. "You can do it. There's only three more flights."

Cassy sucked down the last of my canteen. "They must have found the remains."

"And there's only one direction we could have gone."

"I'm going as fast as I can."

"Just make it to that gate. If the guards see you flagging, they'll know something's wrong." Cassy set her jaw and looked as though she was about to put a bolt through me. "Good. Use your anger."

"When we get out of here, you owe me a drink." Boots echoed up the stairs.

———

A GUARDHOUSE SAT at the top of the ramp. A slot in the door slid aside, and a surly looking man stood on the other side. "What's your business?" demanded the soldier.

"Escaped Arisen. Doing a sweep of the facility," I said as casually as I could.

"Enris's shining rump. I heard the alarm, but I didn't think it was that bad."

"Open up. We need to take a look."

The man's eyes narrowed in suspicion, and he folded his arms. "Who's your commanding officer?"

"Vanyard," I said immediately. "We're under direct orders from the Avatar."

"Where's the rest of your squad?"

"They're coming up behind us," I said. There was another shout from above.

"Someone's sprinting up the stair, Sarge, and fast."

"Gods," Cassy said, real fear and alarm in her voice. "That's him! Let us in or we're dead."

The old soldier must have had a chivalrous streak. He took a long look at Cassy and caved. He slammed the door behind us and dropped the bar as something with the weight of a battering ram crashed into it. Melcor's mask filled the peephole.

"You!" he bellowed.

"Strothheim beckons!" cried the doorman, drawing his blade.

"Open the ramming door, you fool!" Melcor yelled. The wood cracked as he threw his shoulder into it. Cassy and I backed away. "I'm the huntsman!"

The guard turned, his face going pale. He drew the sign of the sword. The blue light became an angry red. He backed away, reaching for the bar. Melcor's blade punched through the top corner, slicing the guard from collarbone to groin.

"Frozen fire." Cassy ran down the hall, hammering on a second door. The thirst drew me like a moth to flame. I drank the fine mist that hung steadily in the air.

The door was ripped from its hinges and flung over the edge of the stair. Melcor filled the doorway, the other Arisen negating my ability to feed and taking the blood for his own. The doorman was leached in an eye blink.

Time stopped as the Veil tore. Melcor changed. A creature of fire and smoke stood holding a blade of molten metal. It bared its fangs and flexed wings of smoke and ash. The guard's soul rose from his corpse. The demon opened its mouth and pulled. Unseen winds threatened to take me from my feet. Screaming, the soul lost its desperate grip on its flesh and sailed towards Melcor's open maw. Yet, at the last second, a rift opened, and the soul veered into Damnation. The Veil knitted back together, and time resumed.

Melcor bellowed in frustration, locking a hate-filled gaze upon me. "Wyrm, take it. An Ascendant's soul should break these chains."

His blade shimmered with heat. I raised my shield and backed away.

"Fire!" Cassy cried as dozens of bolts flew over my shoulder, piercing Melcor's chest. He staggered, then came on, barely seeming to notice.

Melcor thrust, and I deflected it with my shield. Rock chips sprayed from the wall, his blade scoring a deep furrow in the stone. The imbuement on my shield failed in a shower of white light. I slashed but was too far away.

Four black holes opened in the air around Melcor. His chains snapped with a metallic clank. "No!" Melcor strained against the bonds, arms and legs pulled taut. His anger turned to fear. "No, Lord, I have him!" With sickening pops, his joints dislocated. His blade clattered to the floor. He bellowed as his chains tightened further.

"I know your intent." Khyber's voice seemed to rattle the very stones. "He's mine!"

"Rodrick!" Cassy grabbed my arm and pulled hard towards the back door. We blundered through and slammed it shut quickly. A double row of soldiers barred our path.

"Don't just stand there," barked an officer. The shield wall parted, and we stepped through. "Well done. Standing toe to toe with that ramming thing."

"Thank you, sir," I said.

"Catch your breath, and you can take point." The rest of

the squad laughed. "Looks like we're all feasting in Stroth-heim tonight."

"Stand sure," I said. We made our way past, through the rear postern and onto the mountain top.

A snowy path led to a lookout where a figure turned from warming themselves at a brazier. "Where in Damnation do you think you're going?" she asked, raising a crossbow.

"Perimeter sweep," I replied.

"Not with all this bloody commotion, you're not!"

Cassy nervously looked over her shoulder, and the lookout fired. Cassy grunted, a bolt sprouting from her gut, the lacquered armor fracturing like chipped pottery.

The lookout loaded another bolt, reefing on the crank. Her unseen partner began ringing a bell, and shouts echoed up the path.

I charged. There was another chunk. The bolt deflected off my left greave. My shield bashed the scout with the crossbow, knocking her into the brazier. Sparks leapt skyward. Her partner came out of the shadows, swinging a two-handed mace. My shield shattered in a spray of wood, and I let the momentum carry me through, taking his leg off at the knee.

The thirst took me, and I fell upon him like a savage beast. My teeth sank into the open wound, and I drank. The soldier screamed, kicking, his blows becoming more and more feeble.

A shield knocked me off, followed by a sword thrust. But she'd overextended. I grabbed her wrist and turned the blade. She fell, her body weight driving the blade through her sternum. I drank, the Veil tore, and I claimed her soul. At that moment, the bloodlust burst like a pricked bubble.

I pushed the dried husk off and looked into Cassy's

horrified face. The man was convulsing, his breath coming in short gasps. I pulled the belt from the corpse of the woman and made a tourniquet around his leg.

"Rodrick, we have to go." She touched my shoulder.

"Get back. I'm not safe." Shame washed over me.

A crimson blur skidded to a halt. Justice took in her fallen soldiers. Her faceplate contorted with loathing.

"Run," I said.

"Rod—"

"Go, now." I started her with a push.

Justice attacked. I caught her sword on the remains of my shield, deflected a thrust and a disemboweling slash. But a kick to the knee sent me to the ground, and a second cart-wheeled me through the air.

"We'll find your accomplice. In fact, this narrows our search significantly."

"Another scapegoat. Someone to help you justify geno-cide. With what I've seen, I'm ashamed to say that I'm not the real traitor."

"Does the slaughter of hundreds of people offend you?" She raised the visor of her helm. Her beautiful face was twisted in rage. A tuft of auburn hair peeked out above her eyebrow. Her lips were peeled back, and true hatred shone in her every line. "Because it fills me with rage! You led Khyber down this path, and then you have the audacity to moralize after the damage is done. You make me sick."

Her blade slid between my ribs, the metal colder than ice. She twisted, and blackness took me.

THE WORLD SPUN, and I shook my head. But it wasn't the world spinning. I dangled by my ankles, arms bound behind my back. An amphora directly below my head.

The Avatar stood over me, her beautiful face unreadable. All the hate hid behind a mask of professionalism.

"Will this harm Khyber's prize?"

"Not in the short term." Melcor kept his eyes on his feet.

Justice grabbed my hair and twisted my head to the side. Her blade cut deep. Choking, I pulled, desperately trying to retrieve my essence. But Melcor's proximity stopped me.

"That's enough."

Melcor stepped back.

Justice capped the amphora, and the pressure vanished. The runes inscribed in the lid glowed with a harsh blue light. Melcor cut me down and threw me into a coffin. With a sullen sneer, he slid the lid closed.

THE BLACK DOOR stood before me. Screams of torment came from its depths.

"Master, welcome," Breathy said from the bottom of the stairway.

"Come to join the feast?" cackled Raspy. "After all, it was you that laid the table." They laughed, and the screams redoubled. I slammed the door, running a trembling hand over my scalp.

Weeping came from behind me. A young man lay naked on the island. His body was arched backwards, draped over a thornbush.

"Lucas?" I took an uncertain step towards him. Thorns pierced his flesh, burrowing deep and spreading like cobwebs. The water was solid ice. I stepped onto it and something rammed the underside. I fell to my knees. Huge buggy eyes glared before disappearing back into the dark depths.

"Help me," Lucas pleaded, struggling against the thorns to turn his head. He screamed in pure terror. "No, you... you did this to me! Khyber, save me!"

I fled, my heart pounding and stomach roiling as I went. A dozen steps and I tripped. Unnaturally smooth stone froze the soles of my feet in place. I tore free, letting the ground keep a layer of skin. But there was nowhere to run.

FLASH BURNS RAINED upon my naked form. The lid to my prison opened. I squinted against the light of the moon, blinding even filtered through the canvas that covered the wagon.

Melcor's yellowed fangs filled my vision. Thirst took me. But I was bound and gagged. Nevertheless, the need drove me. He looked around to see if someone was watching, then pulled a dagger. He palmed my head and went for my throat. His chains grated, halting his arm.

"Wyrm spawn," he swore in impotent fury. He stole another glance, then picked up something from outside of my field of vision. A half-rotten corpse landed atop me. It raised its head, looking deep into my eyes. Pain blossomed within my skull.

Need. Red-hot and furious. We both pulled, tried to draw the blood from the other's veins. The dagger flashed, and the Arisen's head came clean off. The Veil tore, and I claimed it. This was no mortal soul; this was something far greater. It flowed like a river of light, knocking down a wall within me. Filling me with... power.

The Veil closed, and my body responded instantly. The wound in my neck sealed. My mind cleared. I felt whole and complete as I never had before.

Melcor leaned over me, his jealousy plain. "There's more than one way to skin a Grundstrad," he said, easing the lid closed.

I AWOKE WITHIN THE NIGHTMARE. Once more before the door set within the wall of tentacles. They groped for me, writhing like agitated snakes. I backed away from it as I would have a wild animal.

A stone archway stood at the edge of the world. I placed a hand on its weathered surface and looked through. A dark wood lay upon the other side. Twisted trees, skinned of bark, clawed the sky as if begging for help.

"MINE!" Something swooped from above. I darted back. A ghostly woman slammed into a barrier. Unable to pass, she raked at it, the ends of her fingers extending to make fleshy claws. She floated, hair and tattered dress billowing out as if underwater. "MINE!" she shrieked and streaked away, clothing snapping behind her.

THE LID OPENED, sending a cloud of ash swirling as cool night air washed over me. Melcor wasted no time. A trussed body flumped into the coffin next to me. A pale husk that shone like polished bone. A flash of pain as I recognized an Arisen. Melcor's dagger flashed, and I claimed its soul. Feet marched in lockstep, and Melcor's fist rocked my head back. The lid slid to.

"Where's Jenkins?" Hilstrad's voice resonated through a gap between lid and base.

"The latrine," Melcor said.

"He knows better," Nox added.

"Take it up with him."

"You are dismissed, huntsman," Hilstrad said. "We'll have to keep a closer eye on him. He's up to something."

The wagon swayed side to side as someone climbed in. Someone grunted, pressing against the lid. "That's not going anywhere, Sergeant," Nox told him.

"Yes, sir."

"I told you when no one's around to call me Catherine."

"Ahm, you told me that if I used your name in front of the squad, you'd—"

"And you've been a perfect gentleman." There was a soft groan of passion. "There's no one around," Hilstrad said playfully. "Why don't we kill a few hours?"

"Yes, sir. I mean Catherine." Armor clattered to the stone.

I struggled against my bonds, but the wool cuffs had been crafted to prevent escape and the use of blood magic. If I could bend my elbows, I might be able to slip free, but I couldn't while being in the confines of the coffin.

"Such sweet despair." Rowan's voice rang in my head. *"I never knew that you rodents could have such an emotional range."* She made no sound as she lifted the lid. *"Makes me regret not leaving you here."* She rolled me over and nimbly undid the cuffs around my ankles and wrists.

I pulled the gag out. *"I've never been so happy to be insulted. Help me up."*

"Pathetic fleshling." She scooped me up like an infant and carried me from the wagon. *"You're not wearing any garments,"* Rowan thought.

"Hadn't noticed."

She set me down, and I rubbed the feeling back into my numb legs. As she replaced the coffin's lid, she stepped down and, as bold as brass, made her way to the shadow of a canvas command tent.

I crabbed over like a hundred-year-old man. Every muscle in my body was cramped and weak. Rows of tents lined the highway. Braziers burned at regular intervals within the camp and below, amid the killing field. Everywhere, dark shapes moved, patrolling the night.

A cough came from the far side of the tent. Rowan held up the bottom of the canvas, motioning me to slip under.

I came face-to-face with a corpse. His neck had been twisted all the way around. I bit into him. Thick blood flowed. My weakness abated.

"He is about your size," Rowan thought, slipping in behind me. Hilstrad and Nox giggled to each other a few feet away. *"Hurry up."*

I undid the laces on the chest piece and a cot creaked as

someone shifted their weight. I groaned inwardly. *"There's no way to get a dead man out of his armor quietly."*

"Give me thirty seconds." She moved towards the cot.

"Where are you going?"

"To kill every human in the vicinity."

"Don't!"

"Fine." She irritably pushed me aside, and I fell on my backside.

The tent flap opened, spilling brazier light into the pavilion. A guard poked his head in and looked around. A table sat in the middle, and its shadow hid us. A moan of pleasure came from just outside.

"What was that?" asked the guard's partner.

"Don't know. I'll have a look." The flap closed.

Rowan tapped me on the shoulder and passed me a pair of pants and greaves. I lay down and squeezed myself into the pants. The guard walked around the outside of the tent. He hurried back to his partner.

"Jim!" the guard whispered excitedly. "Come look at this!"

"Damn it, Carl, our post. If the Avatar wakes..."

"Your loss." Cautious footsteps went round the side of the tent.

"Damn it," Carl whispered, then followed his partner.

Rowan handed me a cuirass and undershirt. Gods, she had made less noise than I had by simply breathing.

"Coorr!" Carl said.

"That lass getting the ride of her life," Jim said.

"That a chest," said Carl.

"Mmm, those muscles."

"Lucky woman."

"Ey," said Carl. The two men began breathing heavily.

Leather creaked, and things dropped to the ground with muffled thuds.

Rowan passed me the rest of the dead man's kit and I dressed. Then she crept across the tent and peeked out. Moonlight fell on the cot, auburn hair and full red lips. Justice slept under a thin sheet. She wasn't Anastasia, but the resemblance was uncanny. This was my daughter.

Her armor stood at the foot of her bed. It was a single piece that opened at the back and looked as though it was made to just step in.

Shadows played across her face. She'd been so quick to condemn me, so convinced I was the traitor. What had I done to instill such a depth of hatred? I wasn't sure I wanted to know, but at the same time, if I didn't find out, it would eat at me forever.

Rowan's fist whipped out. I halted her with my mind. A livid bruise blossomed on Justice's forehead. I felt for her pulse, steady. If I hadn't reacted when I did, Rowan would have split her head open as easy as she would a melon.

"What was that for?" I relaxed my hold on her. Rowan rolled her hazel eyes and flipped back the cover. A stiletto rolled from Justice's unconscious grip. I pinched the bridge of my nose. "What a fool I am."

Rowan stood suddenly. Shock and fear seeped through the bond. She hurried to the table and hesitantly picked up a white silk package. She unfolded the cloth, revealing a slender stick of polished wood.

Rowan inhaled, her lips quivered, amber tears welling in her eyes. "Shamoshta," she whispered. "How I will miss your laughter, little one." She pulled another. "Que'twoa, our debates were the highlight of my yearly pilgrimage."

The keen sting of shame made me look away. "Is there a

burial rite we could perform? Something to honor their remains?"

"These are the equivalent of a human brain stem." She inhaled deeply. "Their bodies must have been mutilated to extract—" The petals down her front started to peel back. "I want to kill them all."

"Do you want justice for your people or vengeance for yourself?" I asked.

"They are one and the same." She brandished the cores as if they were a blade.

"Then you become the thing you hate. It's Khyber that needs to be stopped. Without him, none of this would have happened in the first place."

"And how do you propose we slay a god when you can't even kill one of your captors?" She gestured to Justice.

"We join the allies and help Zenos, Glyodrin and Enris take him down."

"You sentimental fool. If I kill these soldiers now, it will make the allies' invasion easier."

"You kill them now and it's murder. There are good people in this army that see the corruption. I think, given the chance, many of them would rebel. They can't if they're dead."

"Fhaa." She threw up her hands and vanished through the tent flap.

I took one last look at Justice and stepped into the night.

Rowan moved fast and silent. My heart hammering in my chest, I struggled to keep up and remain stealthy. I nearly bumped into her. She stood so still, blending with the shadows. A patrol passed. Rowan took me by the upper arm and pulled me along behind her, somehow keeping us out of their line of sight.

A lone soldier scraped the remains of supper from a pot,

and Rowan carelessly strolled behind him. The man didn't have a clue. She wove through tents, skirted braziers, and then suddenly we were at the edge of the camp, striding into the darkness.

I shimmied down a rope and pressed my back to the highway. "I'm down." Rowan untied the knot and let it fall. Then she stepped off the edge, landing with no more sound than a rustle of leaves.

"I saved you because Cassy asked. I will never do so again. This clears my debt to her. If you have a shred of the compassion for me that you do for your own species, then you'll release my bond. Let me be at peace."

"There's no peace in the afterlife."

"I don't care."

"You're the last of your kind. I can't."

"You selfish bastard." She stalked away, cold fury billowing from our bond.

28

"I NEED A REST," Cassy panted.

Rowan stalked a little ways ahead. "I didn't save your life just so you could simply throw it away by being lazy."

"We've been walking all night," Cassy argued. "Have a little mercy."

Rowan spun. "You think those murderers will show any?" She shook the Spriggan cores at Cassy. "You have any idea what has to be done to a Spriggan to remove one of these?"

"They killed my people too!" Cassy yelled back.

"Then don't be so weak," Rowan snapped.

"That's enough, Rowan," I interrupted.

"Sow!" Cassy yelled.

"That's the best you can do, resort to name-calling? Pathetic."

"Rowan. Take a walk," I demanded, pointing up the trail.

"At once, Master." She laced every word with contempt, giving a sneering bow.

I waited a few moments, then turned to Cassy. "You all right?"

234

"I'm fine!" She scrubbed at her eyes. "She's right. We have to keep going." She followed Rowan down the trail.

I caught her hand. "A short break will save us time."

She sagged under the weight of her pack. "Ten minutes won't hurt."

We rested against a pine. A sparrow chirped in the branches overhead. Cassy fumbled with her pack and pulled out a loaf of bread.

"Here," she said, tearing off a chunk.

Rowan stood staring at the trees despondently. She placed a hand on it, then jerked it back as though she had been burned. Amber tears leaked down her face. She folded in on herself in sudden grief. I went to her, keeping my distance, but there should she need.

"They're dying." She covered her ears. "Can't you hear them screaming?"

"No."

She rounded on me. "Deaf, dumb and blind to the world around you. Burn the lot of you, root and stem." She looked into its bows and clutched the Spriggan cores to her breast.

Cassy had fallen asleep, her head lolled to one side, bread untouched in her grip.

The rumble of wagon wheels bounced through the trees. I followed the deer trail to a crest, and the trees opened. A highway dominated the valley floor, running northeast. I pulled the map. If I was right, that was the highway from Dun Roth'eim to the connector to Dun Al'veran. And judging by the mountains, on the other side was the East March. I'd have to travel through the wilderness, but it'd be easy going compared to continuing on through the Sovereign Guards.

It'd be nearly impossible to get to Mir'eve without using the highways. The mountains to the northeast were cruel, and the distance was unrealistic. There were too many villages, keeps and Duns. With the Fauldic rounding up those who didn't follow Kydaism, I'd be caught for sure.

Illuvand was in the Far East, beyond Mir'eve and the Plains of Fangmar, and that ruled that out. That only left one option. It would be a long road, but if I hopped the wall somewhere west of Dun Roth'eim, I could follow the Al'veran East through Mother's Veil to the Plains of Fangmar. From there it'd be a straight shot to Zenos in his mountaintop temple of Car'uk Voll.

An ox lowed. The wagon train toiled along the highway, loaded with blocks of stone, huge beams of steel, coal, forges, and foodstuffs. I traced the line from where I was, through Dun Al'veran, then west to Raider's Watch and north to where the ink coiled in on itself. I fingered the blemish on the map.

Runic layering that connected the mortal and spiritual realms. What happened at the Mother Tree had affected every copy of that rune. I looked back to the train. Perhaps it even damaged the king's highway?

Justice said I'd hidden something in the functions within the master rune. She'd also said that Avatar Might was pulling up every stone. My gut told me it'd be a fruitless search. Surely, they'd checked the focus rune where this had all started.

My path to the allies would take me through Ellodrin, I could look for myself. I studied the map once more before heading back.

"Cassy," I said gently.

"Hm, what?" she murmured sleepily.

"Time to go."

She sat up, rubbing her neck. "I was dreaming of my aunt's trifle."

"Must have been a good dream."

"Ya," she said sadly. I helped her to her feet.

Rowan stared sightlessly.

"Rowan?" I waved my hand in-front of her eyes. "Rowan," I said a little louder. No response. I looked into her mind. She was there, only curled into a ball.

"Is she pretending?" Cassy asked.

"I think she's in shock."

"Rowan." Cassy softly touched her shoulder. "Wake up. We have to go." The Spriggan turned her head slowly, her face slack, expressionless. "Take my hand."

The Spriggan hesitantly extended an arm. The other clutched the cores to her chest.

The train rumbled in the distance. "I think it's safe." We darted across the killing field to the base of the highway. I made a noose with one end of the rope, but no matter how many times I tried, it didn't have the weight to travel the thirty vertical feet I needed it to.

I ran back to the tree line and cut a young pine, trimmed the branches into a rough spear, tied the rope to that, and lobbed it onto the road. It caught on the crenellations. "Up you go," I said.

"Rowan, you first," Cassy said. The Spriggan blinked stupidly at her. "Come on. There's a good girl."

I scurried up behind them.

It rang like thunder, silencing every bird. Booted feet on stone, every step in unison. I scrambled up, dropped the rope to the other side. "Go, go." The wagon train squeezed to the side and a column of soldiers ran in our direction, a red-and-blue figure at their head.

"I need this to end," Rowan said. "The whole world's screaming."

"Come on, Rowan. The world's not screaming. You're in shock," I said gently.

"I have nothing left without my family."

"Then live for them. If you throw away your life, you spit on their memory."

Rowan looked down at the cores in her hand. "There's only one thing left for me in this world."

"Today's not that day. We'll come back for Khyber," I replied.

She looked at me grimly, nodded, and then gestured at the woods. Cassy and I scrambled down. Rowan ignored the rope completely.

"Stay low. Don't make sudden movements that'll draw the eye." I took off my helm and handed it to Rowan. "Put that on."

She looked at it in disgust. "I'm not putting that piece of dead swine on my head."

"Your head is bright red."

Growling, she did as I asked. We crouched down below the level of the shrubs and crawled across the field.

By the time we reached the tree line, the army was in plain view. We stole into the trees and broke into a run.

29

"COME ON, come on. I'm hungry," Cassy said.

I shuddered. I was hungry too. I bit my lip. The pain helped ease the craving. Cassy raised the crossbow and fired. There was a squeak. "Ha ha." she said triumphantly. "Rabbit tonight."

Cassy hurried over to her kill. I hung back as far away from the smell of blood as I could.

"Barbaric." Rowan frowned after Cassy.

"She has to eat," I argued.

"I am well aware of the nutrients that little beast will provide. It's just disgusting to watch."

Cassy came over, holding up her prize. I smiled appreciatively. We crossed a meadow to our camp on the shore of a small lake. I gathered wood and started a fire while Cassy dressed and skinned the rabbit.

Rowan glared at the fire. Perhaps we were burning a cousin. She turned and melted into the trees. Cassy skewered the rabbit and placed it over the fire.

"It's so peaceful here," Cassy said, dreamily watching dragonflies skim over the water. "Wouldn't it be wonderful to live here, away from the people, the gods and their rules, away from everything?"

"You could build a home, right there on the lake's edge. Fish, plant raspberries and hazelnuts," I suggested.

"I hate hazelnuts," Cassy said, sticking out her tongue.

"How can you hate hazelnuts?" I asked.

"They make my mouth itchy, and I get all red in the face. It's embarrassing."

"No hazelnuts, then. How about figs?"

"Figs would be lovely." Cassy reached out, taking my hand. "And you?" She smiled hesitantly. I looked into her blue eyes and felt something stir—excitement, anticipation, thirst. She brushed her hair back over her ear.

I pulled away. "You know what I am."

"Yes, I've seen the man you are."

"The monster."

"No, the person you are in here." She touched her chest.

"Cassy, you can't understand the struggle. There's this demon inside, forever pushing me to kill, trying to take control. Everyone else is terrified of Arisen. How can you possibly be interested in me after—" I strode to the other side of the fire, running a hand over the stubble of my scalp. "You saw what I did to those soldiers."

"You're not the first Arisen I've known." She stared into the embers, emotions warring on her face. "His name was —" She wiped away a tear. "Well, he saved my life when he had every reason not to. He was kind and selfless. He healed me with this golden light, and there was nothing demonic about it."

"Was?"

A flush crept up her neck, and she absently rubbed her arm as if remembering an old wound. "I believe the only way your dark side will win is if you give it the power to."

Fat sizzled and popped. Flames leapt up and engulfed the rabbit. Cassy snatched the skewer. "Damnation."

"Thank you, Cassy," I said. "Knowing there're others that have resisted gives me hope."

We sat by the lake and ate our meal, tossing the charred bits to the fish. The sun dipped below the horizon. It had been a week of travel, and fatigue rolled over me with a full belly. We set our blankets side by side and stretched out. I fell asleep, the Ethereal Battle flickering above.

FISHING BOATS SCUTTLED across the lake. From the hilltop they looked little more than toys. Orchards surrounded the village in a patchwork that spanned the countryside. Even the keep had a merry light about it. Apples and pears grew right up to its walls and along the highway.

Cassy dug through her coin purse with a melancholy air. "That bad?"

"No." She pulled out two gold coins. "I've never held gold in all my life, and Dah slips three years' wages into the bottom of my bag. He never intended to say goodbye."

"He probably didn't know how to."

She clenched the coins in a fist. "I can't change this."

"Hide them away. I've got a few coppers and a silver."

"Rowan, we'll meet you on the far side of the lake once we've gotten some supplies," I said.

"As you command, Master," Rowan replied.

The scent of apple blossoms hung so thick I could nearly taste them. I reached up and plucked one from a branch.

"Why, thank you." She threaded it through her hair.

A goose girl goaded her flock down a nearby aisle. Her

spindly arm shot into the air, and a gap-toothed smile sprouted on her face. Cassy and I waved back. "One day I'll be an acolyte, with a real sword." She flourished her goad.

I did my best to keep the sadness from my smile. "Work hard and we'll stand shoulder to shoulder one day."

The girl nearly bounced out of her shoes. "I will. Stand sure."

A gnarled farmer sat on the back of a wagon at the end of the main street, fruits and vegetables on display beside him. He tipped his hat. "See anything you like? The apples may be a bit wrinkled from winter, but you can trust old Jean. You won't find better."

Cassy picked through his wares, and I looked over the shops. A butcher, baker, chandler, and fletcher were the closest, and a hammer rang on an anvil down the way. The streets were full of people going about their daily business.

"Ay, lass. The finest tavern in the whole of Oppenfauld. Blossom's Tankard."

My gaze was drawn to a couple. A woman in a blue dress whispered something in her man's ear that made his eyes bulge. "Not while you're touring in the East March. No, you'll want the cider." Her head snapped round, and a sharp pain shot through my skull. "Call me a creeper if I steer ya wrong."

"Something hot would go down nicely," Cassy said eagerly. The woman in blue smiled wickedly, and she pulled the young man away down a side street.

"Then the pigeon pie and a glass of the rum, aged scrumpy."

She was going to kill that boy.

"If you don't dance outta the Blossom and give old Jean a kiss, well, I'll eat me hat."

"Cassy, would you excuse me." I handed her my coin purse. "I'll meet you at the pub."

"Ya, sure," she replied.

I followed the couple round the butcher's and past a few rows of houses. A flash of blue nearly swallowed by the orchard.

"Hey, stop." Still a couple hundred feet ahead. The young man pushed out his chest and reached for his sword. She playfully pulled the boy behind a tree and out of sight. I drew my sword and broke into a run.

He was slumped against the tree, dry as old boot leather. The boy's face stretched in a rictus of terror.

"You came to poach my kill," said a sweet voice from the branches above me.

"I came to stop you from killing that innocent boy."

"Ho, that's cute. You must be young to care so much for a mortal you've never met."

"What does my age have to do with anything?"

"It means you don't have any perspective," she taunted.

"I don't care how jaded you've become. You can't justify murder."

"But I can. This boy was a rapist. I could see his desire, his lust to hurt, to ruin me for the simple thrill of dominance. So, I culled him from the herd and the world is a safer place. Sooner or later you'll learn that no one is innocent. And we have to feed."

I caught a flash of movement. The thirst stirred.

"Do you want to know what I see in you? I know the desire that lies in your heart. The resentment, the fear, the hunger. There is no difference between what I just did and what you intend to do to me."

"You're right," I said, backing away. "I just assumed... All the other Arisen I've encountered were—"

"Demons?" She finished for me.

I nodded. "Yes."

"The path of descendancy is so easy. Even killing for the right reasons can corrupt the soul."

"How do you do it?"

"Do what?" she asked curiously.

I hesitated, then said, "Stay... human."

"You don't. We're as different from humans as they are from dogs." She sighed sadly, "This your first time facing another Arisen?"

"Yes," I said breathlessly.

She dropped from the tree. "Then I'll give you fair warning. Only one of us will be leaving here alive."

"What, why?"

"That's how this sick game works. The War of Ascendancy." She produced a dagger and put it to her wrist. "We fight. The winner takes the other's realm."

"Realm?" I said. "Look, I'll go. There's no need for this."

She shook her head sadly. "Sorry, handsome. The first few decades are the most dangerous."

I dropped my pack and sank into a mid-guard. "This is your final warning. Back off."

"If it's any consolation, after your soul is mine, I'll awaken." She slashed her wrist, the veins discolored as her blood pooled on the ground. "You'll be a part of something meaningful." Her puddle bubbled, and a wolf rose from the blood. The last droplets condensed to form its tail. "Better you fall to me than to some demonic horror."

The beast bounded forwards, jaws snapping. I slashed, took off its ear. It disintegrated, fluttering away in an ethereal wind before it hit the ground. The wolf, unperturbed, went for my groin. I blocked it, but the damn thing bit the blade, holding it with incredible strength.

Something bit my leg, knocking me forwards, impaling the beast. A second wolf worried at my calf. I pulled my sword free and severed its head. It crumbled into a pile of ash.

The girl took me from behind. My armor saved me from a dagger in the kidney. The first wolf stood and tangled my legs. She forced me to the ground. I fell atop the wolf and the wolf atop my sword. I brought an elbow into her nose with a satisfying crunch. The Arisen reeled. I knelt on the wolf's jaw and pulled sharply, finishing it off.

Teeth bit into my gorget, metal screeched, and my air cut off. I spun the blade round and slid it up under her ribs. I tore at the clasp and the leather strap broke, half severed by teeth.

She looked at the blade in disbelief. Something huge began to climb from the blood pooling at her feet. I closed the distance. A giant pincer like that of a scorpion reached up. I grabbed the hilt of my sword, ripped it free.

Her head rolled to the ground. The pincer lost its solidity and sloshed back into liquid. The Veil tore, and light rose from the headless body, cascading into me, charging every nerve with raw power.

I tottered like a newborn calf, a stranger in my own skin. Her remains disintegrated, leaving no more than an ash-stained dress.

I looked around. No one had seen, I hoped. I grabbed my pack, then checked my leg. The armor had saved me, though fissures ran through the lacquer from where the wolf had savaged my calf.

I hurried to the tavern. A three-story affair, freshly whitewashed. The sign showed a bushel of apples and a frothing mug. I ducked through the doorway and hit an invisible wall. I staggered back. The symbol of the sword and shield was engraved above the door, an ominous red light pulsing from it.

No one seemed to have noticed, the patrons inside focused on some musician. But old Jean studied me with a scowl. Heat at my hip, the sigil from the Facility. I took it out, holding it carefully within the handkerchief. I bowed my head and made the sign of the sword. The red light dimmed. I stepped towards the doorway with a sideways glance at Jean. The old chap was watching me intently. The threshold resisted my entry. I held the sigil before me and the resistance parted, allowing me through.

A bearded man sat on the edge of a stage playing a merry tune on his fiddle. Cassy spun from partner to partner, red faced and smiling.

I whispered in her ear. "Time to go."

"Come on," she protested. "We've only just arrived."

"I had a bit of trouble and want to get back on the road."

"There's pot pie," she pleaded, "and the cider. Stuff's bloody strong."

The fiddler finished his song and packed up his instrument to the protests of every young maid on the dance floor. "Fear not, friends. I will return to put a spring in your step once this humble hymnal has refreshed himself." He made his way over to us.

I met his eye, and it felt like a corkscrew drove through the back of my skull.

"Rodrick." She gestured to the bard. "This is Hymnal of the Golden Strings." She nodded significantly. "We met on the road to Dun Avard."

"Sweet lass, that is the name my adoring fans gave me." He flourished an imaginary cape. "We hymnals are humble purveyors of song and myth. Granted, I am one of the order's more acclaimed members. We wander the land spreading Crystal Lady's joy. And friends"—he held out his hand—"may call me Hector."

I took a step back. "I don't want any trouble... friend."

"Neither do I." He waved to an empty table. "Just some wholesome conversation."

A serving girl flagged Cassy to the bar. She pointed at the table. "You should hear about the places this man has played." She put her hand on my rump and pushed me towards the table.

I shot her a sharp look. She grinned, squeezed and plopped herself down in front of her meal. "Mam always said I was too fat to have a cream-filled dish like this, but the hag is dead, ha. So, I ordered two." She scooped out the middle of the closest pie and shoveled it into her mouth.

"My condolences," Hector said.

"For what?" Cassy said around a steaming mouthful.

"I must say I'm surprised to see you again. Both of you." Hector ran a finger around the rim of his cup. "A pair of acolytes, so far from Raider's Watch." No one else would have heard the sarcasm in his tone, but we both knew I was no acolyte. "I'd love to hear the tale of how you found yourselves in Glen Clealen."

"Forgive me, friend, but the last time I saw you, you were running for your life." Hector's face grew dark. "And I've learned to be wary of those with our... disposition."

Cassy wiped the pastry from her chin and shot me a questioning glance. I nodded, and her eyes widened.

"A prudent choice, but all I want is polite conversation."

"All the same, we'll be on our way."

Raised voices came from the street.

"You owe me a pot pie, and a whole keg of cider." She sullenly pushed away her plate and downed the rest of her drink.

Hector stood, took Cassy's hand and brushed his lips across the back. "You are aware of the nature of your traveling companion?"

"I am," she said cautiously.

"Then I will not interfere," he replied flatly. "May we meet again?"

I hurried Cassy from the pub. A crowd had gathered around old Jean's wagon. The old man's hat waved above their heads. Snippets of "Murder" and "Arisen" pricked my ears. We went down the next side street and out into the orchards.

"What was that about?" Cassy's cheeks were flushed and her gate uneven.

"If we stayed, I don't think I'd have lasted the night."

"I don't think Hector would."

"He's an Arisen, Cassy, and I think once he got whatever answers he was looking for, he'd have taken my head."

We reached the top of the next hill. The garrison issued from the keep and spilled into the town. A wagon with a steel coffin in their wake.

"What kind of trouble did you get in?" Cassy asked.

"I didn't mind my own damn business."

💥 30 💥

"WHO'S THERE?" I called into the night. Cassy slept by the fire. Rowan was in the other direction, and she was utterly silent in the forest.

My eyes scanned the darkness. Pain flashed through my skull. *"Rowan, come guard Cassy."*

"At once, Master," she thought bitterly.

"Show yourself." I pointed my blade at where the pain had come from.

"I had to step lively to keep my skin thanks to you." Hector stepped out from behind a tree.

"Keep on going. There's nothing for you here."

"On the contrary, this gives us a chance to talk."

"Every other Arisen I've met has let their blade do the talking."

"It's hard to have a conversation with a person when they could be your next meal. I give you my word, all I want to do is talk."

"About?"

"How you escaped?"

"I ran, same as you."

"You were trussed up like a deer on a spit." Hector reached behind his back. "All the way to that mountain."

"Stop!" I yelled. Cassy snorted awake, covering her chest with the blankets.

The fiddler froze. "It's only a bottle of wine, mate."

"You've been following us this whole time?"

"Yes."

"Why?"

"Come now, after Raider's Watch? The notorious Rodrick Corwyn, betrayer of kings. The one who slew the four high priests all by himself. They're telling the tale far and wide. How could I pass up such an opportunity?"

I shook my head. "I don't believe you."

Hector's face hardened. "There's only one way the Fauldic would let an Arisen walk free. You've sworn yourself to Khyber, become his vassal. I did the same once, though to a different master."

"When I first returned, I wanted nothing more than a place at Khyber's side, but no more."

"There's no need to play coy. Look at you, Fauldic regalia and weapons. Heading straight for the mustering of Khyber's former allies. You're a scout, so let's cut through the hog pen and make a trade," Hector said.

"I am a simple fugitive," I said, raising my blade. "Be on your way."

Hectors face darkened. His arm lashed out and a light uncoiled from his hand. I caught his whip with my sword. A shock jolted through me. Muscles seized, and stars danced across my vision.

Hector flicked his wrist, and my sword was snatched from my grip. "Do not lie to me again or things will turn ugly. Miss, please throw that crossbow aside." There was a rustle as the crossbow was dropped in the bush.

"Wonderful," Hector said, wrapping up his whip and tucking it behind his back. "What do you say to that glass of wine?"

I flexed the pins and needles from my arm.

"Have a seat." Hector pointed to the ground beside Cassy. Rowan's amusement at my humiliation rolled off her like the purring of a cat.

Hector produced a bottle of wine. "Have any glasses?" he asked, popping the cork. When we didn't reply, he shrugged, took a swig, then handed it to Cassy. He took a casual stance, but his hand was near his whip.

Cassy took a drink and handed it to me. I shook my head. She looked down at the bottle and looked a little sick, no doubt thinking there may be something in the wine. She passed it back to Hector, who took another drink.

"So, what do you want to hear? Because it's certainly not the truth," I said.

"I want to know your orders," Hector replied.

"I don't have any," I said, frustration sharpening my words. "I'm an escaped prisoner."

"We both are," Cassy added.

"Prisoners don't escape the Fauldic."

"We did," Cassy said.

"How?" Hector frowned.

"With help and a lot of luck," I said.

"Don't be so vague," Hector insisted.

"Cassy's father snuck us out of the mountain."

"He's being modest," Cassy said, gripping my forearm. "Rodrick fought the Avatar, giving me a chance to escape. He was so brave, but I couldn't get him out, so I convinced Rowan to. Honestly, I think she did it just to spit in Khyber's face."

"Who's Rowan?" Hector asked.

"Our third companion," Cassy said.

With a flick of his wrist, Hector uncoiled his whip. Charged sparks danced down the length, causing the ground to smoke and smolder. "Show yourself," he called.

Rowan stepped into the firelight.

"Good gods," Hector said in shock. "My lady, we thought your kind extinct. It's a miracle to see you alive, but how?"

"I am a slave. Bonded to this Arisen," she said, pointing at me.

"What?" Hector roared, rounding on me, expression filled with fury.

Rowan shot me a self-satisfied smile. "He refuses to release me." She cradled the cores to her chest.

Hector drew a long knife. "Release her. Now!"

"I can't. If I do—"

Rowan cut in, "You see, I am held against my will. Slay him and free me."

"Rowan," Cassy said in disbelief. "You know he's only keeping it for your own good."

"You have five seconds to release the Spriggan." The whip lashed out with a crack, slashing through a nearby log. The two halves fell to either side, cut as if by a miller's saw. "Four."

"She'll die without it."

"He lies," Rowan said, a manic light entering her eyes. "Set me free."

Hector looked from Rowan to me, something in her tone giving him pause.

"I'll pass the bond. I'd love nothing more than to be shot of this lunatic," I said.

"Release her," Hector said.

I closed my eyes and felt the bundle of sensations in the back of my head. I constricted the flow of energy between us. If he didn't believe me, I'd bloody well show him.

"Look." Cassy pointed. Rowan's petals were turning brown.

"Stop!" Hector said.

"No," Rowan snapped. "I just want it all to end! Kill me."

Hector took a swig from the bottle. He looked at it and then at the three of us. He handed me the bottle. I reasserted my control of the bond.

"How long has she been this way?" Hector asked.

"As long as I've known her," I said. "She's the last of her kind. I couldn't let her die when I could stop it."

Rowan laughed. "Cut the altruistic act. I feel your guilt every time you look at me. There's something you're not saying." She stalked towards me.

Cassy got between us. "You've gotten worse since you've found those. We're going to the Mother Tree to try to give you some closure. We'll have a funeral. Then maybe the screaming in your head will stop."

Rowan shook her head emphatically. "You don't understand. There's no closure, no healing. I'm already dead, same as every other plant in the whole world. Their death throes stopped days ago." She hugged the cores closer to her chest. "You're forcing me to march through a graveyard, stacked with the corpses of everything I've ever loved!"

Hector reached for the bottle, and the thirst inside me snarled. I pushed it down and handed it over. Cassy looked as though she'd been slapped.

"All dead, everything, everywhere, except you scurrying fleshlings." She backed into the night. "Set me free!" she roared and sprinted into the darkness.

"What's in the silk?" Hector asked.

"Spriggan cores," I replied somberly.

"Merciful lady," Hector said, making a fist. "Why am I surprised that they would sink so low?"

"It's not just the Spriggans." Cassy took a deep breath. "They're sacrificing their own citizens."

Hector looked up sharply.

"I'm the only survivor of hundreds of people. They're taking anyone who won't convert to Kydaism to their facility in the mountains. Rodrick won't tell me what happened to them." Her voice was monotone, disconnected. "But they're dead, I know it."

Hector handed her the wine. She gave a stoic smile and took a long drink. "So, you were traveling to the Mother Tree to help the Spriggan?"

I nodded. "In part," I said. "I was planning to travel to Fangmar."

"We," Cassy cut in, "were planning on joining the allies and helping them overthrow Khyber."

"If it truly is your intent to join the allies, I can take you to them."

"Safety in numbers," I said dryly. This was playing right into his hand. He'd have his intel from us sooner or later. Especially if he kept plying Cassy with liquor. And if he didn't, he'd be delivering me to his masters. In their eyes I wouldn't be arriving of my own accord.

"Exactly." He pulled the fiddle from its case and polished the frets with a thumb.

"You're a spy," I said.

"The very best you'll ever meet." He handed the wine to Cassy with a flourish.

"Forgive me if that doesn't instill confidence."

Hector smiled impishly, as if to say he didn't give a goat bollocks what I thought. "I am sworn to the Crystal Lady. She may not be the strongest of the allies," Hector said, "but in my opinion, she's the best of them. Zenos's duality leaves little leeway for a man to be a man. Too much shame, no understanding of simple folk. Glyodrin and his elves are forever gazing at the moon and stars, worshiping forces that humans can't even tell are there.

"But Enris is a deity worthy of trust. Her realm is music, dance, wine, and lovemaking. She wants, above all else, to preserve life from the horrors of war. With the right information, she'd strike surgically, cause the least collateral damage to the people of Oppenfauld. She'd end this war before Khyber has a chance to finish whatever he's planning." He passed me the bottle.

"The kind of information that the betrayer of kings might possess."

Hector smiled and struck a chord. "Precisely."

31

"WHAT'S IN IT FOR ME?" I asked. Cassy's eyes nearly bulged out of her skull.

"Saving lives isn't enough?" Hector's fingers danced along the strings. "I promise, Enris isn't stingy when it comes to gratitude. If you need reminding, I can play 'Her Lady's Favor' for you."

"I'm not talking about Enris. If you want me to trust you, I want answers."

"About?"

"Arisen, blood magic, the thirst. The lot of it."

Hector put his bow to the fiddle and played a soft melody. Cassy yawned. "I think the wine's gone to my head." She shoved the bottle into my hand and stumbled to her blankets, asleep before her head even had the chance to hit the pillow.

"What did you do?"

"Nothing that will harm the girl." He leant over and took the wine. "Trust me, mortals are the most powerful force on the planet. It's in everyone's best interest to keep them ignorant."

"Cassy's trustworthy."

"How do you think she'd react if the change took you?" Hector challenged. I covered her with a blanket. "I can see it in your face. You know she'd run screaming."

"Is there a way to stop it?" I asked.

"You walk the path of ascendancy."

"That doesn't tell me anything. Ascendant, Descendant, what does it mean?"

"It boils down to morality. The choices you make will push you down one path or the other. Make evil selfish choices and you will descend. Your flesh will take on a demonic aspect. The thirst will consume you till there is nothing left of the man she knows.

"However, if you seek to make the world a better place, by sharing all the wonder this life has to offer, like Enris, or by upholding what is right and just like Khyber used to, then you'll ascend. In time, you'll have no need for blood to sustain you or to fuel your magic. There lies true power in giving." He tipped back the bottle and polished it off.

"I don't mean to make it sound so black and white. Most Arisen are just trying to survive in a world where it's eat or be eaten. Those that endure the centuries are the ones that grow in strength. And regardless of the path you walk, the only way to stay alive is to claim the realm of other Arisen."

"You mean the soul?"

"Sorry to break it to you mate, but Arisen don't have souls, at least in the conventional sense. We return with a piece of the Ethereal Battle within us. Our own personal afterlife to mould in our image."

I absently poked at the fire. "I've been having these nightmares. They feel so real."

"That's it. You've found your nexus. The seed of your realm."

"I fought an Arisen. She said that claiming my realm would make her awaken."

"A threshold of power, one of many. And the crux of what drives our kind to feed on one another. There are Arisen that are consumed by the lust for power. Our mutual acquaintance was one until Khyber took him as a vassal."

"Melcor?"

"The day that demon was chained was a mighty blow against evil."

We sat looking into the fire for long moments while I digested what he told me. "I don't understand how it all fits together."

"What I've told you already takes most Arisen decades to figure out." He slipped the empty bottle back into his bag. "When you use blood magic, you're summoning an echo of the dead from your realm into the mortal world. Once something has passed through the Veil, it leaves its substance behind. Your blood allows it to take shape in this world. Be very careful, for once something has been summoned from your realm, it is gone, forever. That is why it hurts. You're tearing off a piece of yourself and casting it back into the Spiral."

"Every time I've used blood magic it's been random."

"Right now, you're a toddler with an alchemy bag. Snatching the first thing that comes to hand without knowing how to read the label. You need to spend time within your realm, meditate, and practice. For it is your weapon. One you carry with you at all times, but like a sword, it can cut both ways."

"How so?" I pressed.

"If you don't take control of your realm, it will in time rule you and the urge to feed it will consume you."

"And I'll become like Melcor," I said, overwhelmed by the immensity of what I'd become.

"I hope this proves my goodwill. Many lives are at stake. I fear for my lady. For when gods go to war, both mortal and immortal fall like wheat to the scythe. The information a former Avatar might have"—Hector stood—"could save millions of souls."

"I've lost my memory." I watched his face for a reaction.

"They're in there. You wouldn't have been able to return otherwise. Good night."

Hector walked off into the night.

"Don't you want a place by the fire?" I called after him.

"No offense, but you have to earn my trust as well. And I'd rather wake up with my head still attached."

I doused the fire, found my blankets and allowed sleep to swallow me.

I awoke before the door. The cliff loomed over me. Hector said that I could shape this place. I reached out a hand to banish this darkness. The tentacles struck like adders. I snatched my hand away. The whole wall groped the air, straining to pull me in. I rubbed my wrist, retreating.

A pain-filled moan came from the island. Lucas was arched over the thornbush. Its stem pierced the small of his back, and new shoots sprouted from him every which way.

I crossed the lake. The shrimp slammed into the underside. "Be still," I commanded. The creature bucked again, fracturing the ice.

I stepped on to the island tentatively. "Lucas?"

His head turned ever so slowly, wood creaking. Branches grew from his eyes, mouth, everywhere. I reached out to snap a branch protruding from his chest. His shriek of pain made me fall backwards. It went on and on, never stopping for breath. I made to comfort the boy, but that only made his screams more frantic.

Hector said that blood magic would summon the things within this place. I grabbed the thorns, spilling blood onto the ground. I concentrated on the bush, imagining it separate from Lucas's flesh.

A thousand needles dragged along the insides of my veins. Simultaneously, the thornbush blew away like sand in the wind. I pushed harder, the branches now level with his skin. The bush took shape at my feet, growing from my blood. Something ruptured internally, and Lucas fell to the earth with a thud.

My knees buckled, and my arm was weak and unresponsive. Lucas was whole, but his eyes stared blankly. His unending scream rattling my teeth, I shook him, trying to wake him from this hysteria. I put him over my shoulder and carried him off the island.

"Lucas!" I had to yell to hear my own voice over his screams. "Lucas!"

The scream died away, his lungs finally having run out of air. His mouth opened and his neck muscles strained as he screamed silently. Gods, this was all too much. I looked around. There was a tall pine, its bows giving a natural shelter. I made him as comfortable as possible and returned to the lake's edge.

I chipped off a couple of chunks of ice with a rock and brought them back to Lucas. "Here, let them melt in your mouth," I said.

The ice touched his lips and he finally relaxed. I fed him the ice, not knowing what else to do. I'd known that torment, thousands of slivers burrowing into every soft place, along every nerve. Had I inadvertently done that to him?

I stared at the Mother Tree. Whoever took my realm would gain her power as well. If I could only harness it, maybe I'd be able to defend myself. As spotty as my memory was, I knew for certain Khyber was coming for me.

I walked to the edge of my realm. The expanse between me and the Mother Tree was insurmountable. How in Damnation could I hope to wield the power of a goddess if I couldn't even control this place? Even using blood magic, when I wasn't bleeding real blood, had taken me out at the knees.

If I had time to learn. But Hector had implied it would take decades. I was rammed, pure and simple. If I ever found out who did this to me, I'd rutting kill them.

The memory of Anastasia on the swing came to my mind, and her laughter seemed full of mockery.

32

"RODRICK." A cool hand rested on my cheek.

"Anna."

"Rodrick, wake up."

"Just a little longer love."

"Who's Anna?"

My eyes snapped open. Cassy leaned over me. Her blond hair blocked out the rest of the world. "My wife."

"Right." Cassy sat up, crossing her arms.

"I have these fragments of memory from someone else's life. And they're a poor—"

She clamped a hand over my mouth and raised the other hand to her ear. The quiet sound of people talking, the rasp of a shield as it brushed against armor. But one thing stood out: the grating of chains.

We blurred into motion, stuffing our things into the packs. There was no time to conceal the remnants of the fire. We abandoned the main path and set off down a deer trail. Rowan was in that direction.

Rowan had guided us faithfully, despite her ambition to see me dead. She always found hidden trails through the untamed East March. How had Melcor managed to track us? Because I'd lit a beacon fire for him in Glen Clealen.

We came to a ravine. The bank was sheer but not too deep. "Give me your hand." I lowered Cassy over the edge, wincing at the clatter of stones as she landed.

I dropped in after her, and we made our way to a switchback on the other bank. We emerged onto a wide trail. Ahead, the trees parted, and the trail ran along the edge of a cliff.

"Here!" an acolyte called into the forest. A squad rounded the corner. Avatar Justice fixed me with a gaze that promised retribution.

"Run," I said, reaching for my shield.

"Bring them down!" Justice bellowed.

Crossbows fired. Cassy sat down hard. Blood soaked her front. She grabbed at the bolt protruding from her belly. I covered us with the shield as bolts bounced off the barrier. I glanced at her wound. The bolt struck close to where she'd been shot last time and was buried nearly up to the fletchings. My throat was suddenly parched.

"Take the traitor!" the Avatar yelled. Infantry rushed forwards. A judge followed close behind, bearing a standard with Khyber's holy symbol fastened to the top. A soft blue light emitted from it.

"Leave me," Cassy croaked.

"I won't."

"They don't care about me." She wiped a hand across her forehead, leaving a smear of blood. "Just go."

"Shut up." I passed her the shield and grabbed her by the collar. She huffed against the pain but managed to hold it steady.

The Avatar leapt the ravine, drawing her sword midair. "Surrender." She landed with little more than a puff of dust.

"Prove there's a shadow of the man you once were hiding in that worthless shell."

"And give Khyber the power he needs to enslave the world? I think not."

"That is what you strived for your whole life. You cast everything else aside for that goal. It's within your grasp. Please, Father, sacrifice yourself for the good of your people. Think of the lives you'd save."

"The people of Oppenfauld may prosper, but at the expense of everyone else. I saw what you did to those that didn't convert, and there's nothing that can excuse that. Kydaism has been corrupted."

"We found him, your accomplice. He said much the same thing until I peeled the hide from him."

"No! Dah," Cassy said.

"Yes, Miss Forester. His soul writhes in endless torment. It's hopeless to defy the will of Khyber. Surrender and I will spare her the same fate."

Cassy pulled the trigger. The bolt struck Justice in the faceplate. Her head snapped to the side. Cold laughter rolled from the Avatar. The cat's face snarled. The bolt hadn't even left a scratch.

I sliced my palm, for the first time looking within. Ice, fire, the strength of the forest and something dark, writhing and malicious.

"I'll never surrender, for if I do, it'll cost Oppenfauld her soul. I fight for my people, for all people. This sword is not yet broken."

I needed something that would stop her, something that would at least damage her armor. I summoned the Void. Shadows spilled from my veins, and a black pearl formed above my palm. It warped the light, twisting reality.

The Avatar flinched, raising her sword, holding the

blade in the sign of the sword.

"Shields!" she yelled.

I threw the Void towards the Avatar. She made the sign of the sword, and a protective barrier of blue light sprang up before her. The Void bolt glanced off her ward. It flew with a mind of its own, homing in on the unprotected soldiers behind her.

There was a whomp so low I felt the vibration in my chest. Then the world fractured like a chipped window. Spiderwebs of nothingness erupted in a six-foot sphere. The soldiers caught in the blast went limp. The black filaments cut through them, and what hit the ground was little more than chunked beef.

The Veil tore, and black filaments came to life. They snaked around their souls and dragged them into the Void. I stared on in horror at what I'd just done. I'd condemned those souls to death beyond the afterlife.

The Veil closed. Justice stared at the bloody mess. I used her hesitation, drew a new line of blood, and hurled a ball of white fire. It caught her in the ribs. The explosion cart-wheeled her into the ravine.

A wave of light-headedness hit me. My arm was pale and sickly looking. I didn't have much more to spare. The Arisen's soul had satisfied, but I hadn't fed on blood in weeks. If I didn't do something, they'd be on us in moments.

I cut once more, but nothing came out. More soldiers were approaching the ravine, readying crossbows. My eyes fell to the remains of the soldiers I'd killed. I dashed forwards.

Blood flowed along the ground in a thousand rivulets, filling me with the fuel I needed. I swooned in ecstasy. A bolt whizzed past my ear and I came back to the moment. I bled across the path, calling to the roots and trees within me. I pushed, the ground shook, and a wall of roots erupted from the earth, blocking the switchback. My arm went numb. My vision swam. This had taken nearly as much blood as I'd consumed.

"Frozen fire," Cassy sputtered. A line of her blood led towards me. I'd inadvertently fed on her. I shook myself, forcing down the lust that enticed me to finish her off. Angry voices yelled from the other side of the wall.

I hooked my arms under Cassy's and dragged her away. She cried in pain. The thirst whispered she was easy prey.

Cassy clutched at the bolt and gritted her teeth. She dropped the shield, and the crossbow bounced along by the shoulder strap. A red fist punched through my blockade.

"Just leave me. There's no point in us both dying," Cassy urged.

"Not happening," I said. I had to get her out of here, but I couldn't do it on my own. I reached out with my mind and found Rowan standing a few yards away, grinning sadistically as I struggled.

Rage slapped aside her will. "Take Cassy to safety," I commanded. Rowan crashed through the bushes. Whatever grace allowed her to move silently was utterly lost when I took control. She picked up Cassy and ran at an inhuman speed down the path.

Bolts zipped past. The Avatar had knocked down my blockade. Acolytes spilled onto the path. Justice sprinted towards me, quartering the distance in the time it took me to register she was moving.

I drew my sword across my forearm, desperate for something to aid me. I dove to the side as a sword passed through the space where my chest had been moments before. Panic made me grab hold of the first power that came to the surface. Ice coated my off hand, forming a club.

The Avatar skidded to a stop, her half cape flaring. She pounced, crossing the ten paces in a single bound. I interposed her strike, smashing the club into the side of her helm.

She twisted her hips. My cuirass splintered, and heat flared across my ribs. I retreated a step. Her blade stabbed through my left greave. I wasn't healing, though I wasn't bleeding either. My body was on the verge of regressing into a mindless corpse.

She feinted. I moved to block her blade, and she swept my feet out from under me. Her boot came down on my blade, shattering it.

"Don't quote scripture to me, you pathetic worm. Your blade is broken, and your fight ends here. There's no rising from the ashes for you. You're the one that corrupted Khyber, and in Oppenfauld, there is only one way to purge such a poison. Through war!"

Her blade streaked towards my heart. A whip coiled around her wrist, spinning her around. A thunderclap sounded, and Justice was lifted off her feet and thrown over the cliff. My heart skipped a beat as she disappeared from sight. I crawled to the edge, but the bottom was lost in mist.

My daughter. Gods, no.

"Get up," Hector said.

I couldn't tear my eyes away. Her armor was so powerful, but how could anyone survive a fall like that?

"Get the ram up. Now!"

Smoke lay like a blanket. Flames doubled in intensity every second. I took Hector's hand, dropping the remains of my sword.

"Out of my way!" Melcor bellowed, and the flames seemed to echo his rage. We turned and fled.

33

CASSY'S FRAME looked so small in Rowan's arms. I pushed a lock of her beautiful blond hair out of her face. She smiled weakly.

"Lay her here," I commanded Rowan as I spread my blanket on the path.

"What are you doing?" Hector asked. "We have to keep moving."

I shook my head. "We have to remove that bolt."

"Those flames aren't going to stop Melcor," Hector said.

"She'll die if we don't," I stammered.

"Then her soul will find peace," Hector said, gripping my shoulder. "I will see to it."

"You can't have her," I said, shaking him off.

"Fine. All I'm saying is that my realm can offer her sanctuary in her eternal rest. While yours is centuries away from being anything but a primordial battleground."

I thought of Lucas and what my realm had done to him. "Neither one of us is taking her soul today. Help me save her and I won't hold anything back. I'll submit to your queen. Let her die and you'll have nothing from me."

"She's important to you. I understand that. But mortals come and go like leaves in the autumn. They are beautiful and precious, but when their time comes..." He sighed. "If you love her, take her soul. Be together that way."

I rose to my feet, anger surging through me. Hector backed away, raising his hands.

"Don't you have some magic that can heal her?"

"My aspect lies in other areas," Hector said. "But if we can stabilize her, I know someone, an awakened who may help."

"How far is it?"

"A day and a half, maybe two," Hector said. "There is nothing she can't heal, provided you can make the payment. Her skin is cold and moist. She's gone into shock."

I looked at the wound. Cassy would go septic before we got there. There was no way her bowel wasn't perforated.

"It hurts," Cassy murmured through chattering teeth.

"Find something to elevate her legs." Hector unslung his pack from his shoulders and slid it under Cassy's knees.

I gently wiped away the blood and examined the puncture. The hole was bigger than the shaft. That was bad. "Help me roll her." Hector knelt down opposite me and lifted her as gently as possible. She groaned as I slid my hand under her. The bolt hadn't come out the other side. I plastered on a false smile. "We're going to get you some help."

"All right," she said weakly.

"But I have to take the bolt out."

Cassy nodded.

"I promise you won't feel a thing." Hector brought his fiddle to his chin.

"What the hell are you doing? You said you'd help. I need an extra set of hands."

He checked to see if his fiddle was in tune. "Hector, seriously, I—" The music stole the words from my mouth. Cassy relaxed, a contented smile spreading across her sleeping face.

"As I said, she'll feel nothing while you work."

"Good, good," I said, realizing I couldn't hear the music even though he was playing.

He must have read the question on my face. "I blocked you out." The bow moved in a slow, peaceful rhythm while his fingers caressed the strings. "Now hurry up before those soldiers catch up with us."

I brought the tip of my dagger to where the shaft protruded from her stomach.

"Stop," Rowan said, straining to be heard through my mental restraints. "You're going to butcher that girl."

"You're more likely to hurt her than I am."

"Look with those useless fisheyes of yours."

"At what?" I demanded.

"The bolt vibrates in time with her pulse, you fool. If you put any pressure on the shaft, you'll puncture her abdominal aorta."

I gingerly placed my fingertips against the bolt's shaft. Thump, thump, thump. "Gods, it was a miracle she didn't bleed out while we were putting her down."

"I'll help," Rowan said. I relaxed my hold on her. "The person I was died with the Mother, but her skills remain."

I released Rowan and she searched the ground, knelt down beside a sapling. She passed her hand over it. The plant gave a little shudder. Its leaves fell from the branches and it rose from the soil as if pulled by an invisible hand. She held it to her face. "Thank you."

"Rowan, are you *sure* you can do this?"

"Everything around me is dead when it used to sing."

She twirled the stem in between her fingers, whispering to it. Clods of dirt fell from the roots. Then the bark fell away, leaving pale filaments thinner than the finest thread.

The petals of Rowan's hand peeled back, revealing a taloned hardwood core. She slipped her hand into the branches like a glove. The sapling twined around her fingers. She flexed and there was an answering movement from the roots below.

Rowan brought the sapling parallel to the bolt's shaft. Hector swayed to his silent melody. The roots coiled about the shaft and crept into Cassy's wound.

Time passed as Rowan worked. I decided to make a stretcher. Fallen branches for the frame, supple pine boughs for the bed and strips of bark to lash them together. The work occupied my hands.

I finished the construction as the bolt's head was extracted. There was a suctioning pop as the head came free. The surgical tool encased a jagged piece of metal. Rowan held her apparatus above the wound. Roots stitched it closed.

Seconds later she lifted the tool from Cassy's belly, apparently so confident in her work she didn't even need to inspect it. She held her palm out, and the root untangled the bolt's head.

"It's inventions like these that make your species worse than any demon," Rowan said, casting it to the ground at my feet. I picked it up. Three little hinged arms unfolded, making it look like a grappling hook.

"For Arisen." Hector played the final note. "With that stuck inside you, you wouldn't be able to heal."

"The binding that holds the shaft to the head is made from Canra root," Rowan explained, giving it a sniff. "Very strong, durable, until it gets wet. Then it dissolves in a matter of minutes."

I dropped the head. "Thank you, Rowan. You saved her life."

"Her bowels were torn," Rowan said. "I repaired what damage I could. But she will not survive, and what herbs would have saved her are dead and rotting."

I rested my head in my hands, despair washing over me. "Hector, you said you knew of someone that could save her?"

"Bree'on Chae will be able to. So long as Cassy's willing to pay the price." Hector ran a cloth over his fiddle, then strapped it into its case.

"It's the only chance she's got," I said. We laid Cassy on the stretcher and bore her away as smoke filled the air.

34

FLAMES GAVE the cloud cover an angry glow. A gust of hot wind stung my eyes. Cassy stirred. She'd slept the entire day. I would have seen it as a good sign if she hadn't taken on a green hue.

"It's going to rain," Rowan said, looking up at the ceiling of clouds.

"If not, that wind's going to blow the fire right at us," Hector said from the front of the stretcher.

We walked as fast as we could in the waning light, but the later it got, the more we had to watch our footing, slowing our pace. The sky opened up, rain falling in sheets. I slipped. Cassy groaned.

Hector looked over his shoulder, judging the distance to the fire. Something in his face relaxed. "I think we should be fine to rest at least for a few hours." The forest fire dimmed. "There's a wayward pine."

The boughs were thick as thatch, reaching all the way to the ground, like a billowing dress. Rowan pulled back a limb and we slid Cassy inside. Instantly the rain and wind disappeared.

"I'll take first watch," Hector said. "Get some rest, but be ready to go at a moment's notice." He pulled a small wooden box from his pack and handed it to Rowan. "Mineral salts."

"Thank you. It's been a long time since I've had a good meal."

"You're welcome, lady." Hector wrapped his fiddle in his bedroll and rested it against the trunk. Rowan popped the lid from the box, took a pinch of salt and sighed in satisfaction.

I dabbed the water from Cassy's hair and gave her a drink. She was lovely. I missed her boldness, her laughter, our conversation. This beautiful broken flower deserved happiness. I hoped she found it one day.

———

HECTOR WOKE me sometime in the early morning. I perched in the high branches, watching the flames flicker in the distance. So much destruction from a few drops of my blood. Eventually predawn filled the world with soft light.

"Rodrick," croaked a hoarse voice from below. I clambered down, and Cassy smiled weakly. I picked up a waterskin and dribbled some into her mouth.

"Rowan removed the bolt," I said. "We're taking you to a healer."

"Good." She tried to sit up.

"Hey, what do you think you're doing?"

"Let me up," she said briskly. Hector blinked, eyes bloodshot, with pine needles in his beard.

"Get out of my way," she said, trying to rise again.

Rowan's head poked down from the branches above. Cassy had tears in her eyes.

"What's wrong? Are you in pain?" I asked.

"No. Rowan?" Cassy reached for the Spriggan. She whispered something in her ear.

Rowan rounded on Hector and me. "Get out and take your things with you." Hector and I stared at each other. "Now," Rowan barked and practically threw us from the tree. Hector clutched his fiddle to his chest, more concerned for it than himself. Our packs were tossed out after. "And bring me some Mullen leaves."

It wasn't long before Rowan came out of the tree dragging Cassy's stretcher. Hector and I walked over to her. Her eyes were red, and she refused to meet my eyes.

"You've done your hair," Hector exclaimed. "It looks lovely."

Cassy touched her golden locks. "Thank you."

"It does," I added belatedly.

She smoothed her blankets, and lines of tension left her face. "Rowan did it for me."

"A blessing to be in the presence of two beautiful flowers." Color filled her cheeks, and Hector gave me a sly wink. I nodded gratefully.

The going had been hard the day before, but the mud made it a slog. "We're leaving a clear trail," I said.

"Nothing we can do about it. Soon we'll abandon the path. Once amongst the trees, we'll be harder to track," Hector replied, marching on.

"My people always thought the forest would protect us, and look at what happened to them," Rowan said.

Every hour we rotated positions carrying the stretcher. Cassy fished a leather-bound book from her pack.

"What's that? I haven't seen you with it before," I asked.

"It's Mam's journal. Dah must have slipped it in my bag. He was planning to press charges. I never wondered why she was the way she was — until she was dead. Now that I might... Well, I just want some answers." We all fell silent while she read.

Perhaps an hour or so later, she fell asleep, the book open on her chest. I tucked it under her arm. I didn't intend to pry, but I caught a glimpse of runes. Seemed Molly had ambitions above simple Lyr'eris worship. She wanted to be a priestess.

I'd never found the right moment to tell Cassy what I'd seen. As the hours passed, she looked sicker and sicker. It would probably be for the best if she could put her child-hood behind her. Cassy was finally coming out of her shell, and if she found out that her mother had arisen, well, I doubted it would be good for her mental state.

Mid afternoon, Hector led us from the path. Tall cedars and great pines blocked out the light, killing the under-brush. We marched on through the afternoon, occasionally backtracking and taking a different direction. We passed cedars, that took ten to thirty strides to circumvent, with branches thick as most trees.

By dusk, my arms and shoulders were burning. The thirst nagged at me. The cuts on my arm and ribs stung.

Cassy mumbled and twitched in the throes of a fever dream. "Mam, don't. No, I'm sorry. Momma," she mumbled. Thankfully more than half of what she said was unintelligible. "Dah, come back." I took the book and stuffed it in her pack.

Abruptly, there was a sheer cliff rising above the old growth. Night fell like a headsman's ax. Bird song gave way to the clicking of insects. We followed the cliff. A stream babbled somewhere to my right. It filled the air with a fresh, clean scent that washed away some of my fatigue.

"Can you feel it?" Hector sighed in relief. "This place of power."

"It's wonderful. Are there many such places?"

"Yes. They're all over the world, but you'd be hard-pressed to find one that isn't claimed. Ah, here we are."

A truly gigantic tree grew against the cliff side. It must have taken up two acres, if not more, its lowest branches well above the tips of the other old growth.

"Bree'on Chae, dryad of the ancient wood. It is Hector, hymnal of the Crystal Lady. I have with me the last of the Spriggans and Rodrick Corwyn, a fledgling Arisen."

"The girl is why you have come," said a female voice that tinkled like water in a stream.

"Yes," Hector replied.

"Does she know my services aren't free?"

"Yes."

"Is one of her companions willing to bargain in her stead?"

"I am," I said.

"No, you won't," Hector replied sharply. "You made a pledge to my queen."

"I'm awake," Cassy mumbled weakly.

"Then enter."

A tunnel opened in the great tree, revealing a grove of unparalleled beauty. Fay light emanated from everywhere and nowhere. High above, the last light of the sun bounced down the hollow center. It reflected off a waterfall, making each droplet a falling gem. Yet the pool's surface was smooth as a polished mirror.

"Welcome."

I cast about for the speaker. Only when she moved did I see her. She blended perfectly with her surroundings. She was completely naked. Her skin tone was a dusky dappled olive, and her complexion gave the impression of wood grain. Lustrous green hair, thick as kelp, spilled down her back and cascaded into the pool.

"Sister." Bree'on Chae rushed to Rowan. Embracing her, tears streamed down her face. "Praise Cypress you were spared." Rowan held on, reluctant to let go.

"Sister." Their foreheads rested against one another's for a long moment. They smiled as they broke apart.

"Thank you, hymnal," Bree'on Chae said.

Hector bowed. "This is Cassy." We put down the stretcher.

"Have your prisoner step away and I'll examine her."

"I am no prisoner," I said.

"My apologies," she muttered, clearly unconvinced.

I squeezed Cassy's leg. Her face was waxy and covered in sweat.

"Let me see your wound," Bree'on Chae said, exposing Cassy's abdomen. Bree'on Chae's face hardened and shot a questioning glance at Hector.

"A Fauldic bolt."

"The beasts. Sister, surely this wasn't beyond your skill."

Rowan looked ashamed and angered at the same time. "The forest is dead."

Bree'on Chae looked sad. "Without the Mother Tree, all that is green and good is passing, save for the few of us that have aligned with Cypress. I fear my grotto will become an oasis in a world of dust."

So, the plants really were dying, and it hadn't been a figment of Rowan's broken mind. Gods, no wonder she'd become so unhinged.

"Cassy, you are near death," Bree'on Chae said. Cassy took a deep shuddering breath and nodded. "For me to heal you, there will be a price."

Cassy's hand went to her pack. "How much?"

"I've no interest in gold."

"I have nothing else."

"My price is sacrifice. I want you to understand if I do nothing, the infection will claim you by midday tomorrow, and you will meet your cold goddess. If I heal you to a lesser degree, by removing the rotting flesh and allowing your body to heal on its own, that will cost you your sight or the mobility from one of your hips. There is no guarantee that the infection wouldn't come back, and the amount of scarring would cause a lifetime of pain."

"And the other options?" Cassy asked shakily.

"I burn the infection from you and leave the flesh to heal. This would cost your hearing or the deadening of one side of your face or a hand."

Cassy looked sick.

"However, I could heal you completely and you could walk out of my grove as if nothing had happened within the hour."

"The price?" Cassy asked.

"Your youth," Bree'on Chae, said compassionately.

"What?"

"Without my aid, you will die and lose all the years of your life. What is a couple of decades compared to that?"

"*A couple of decades*, no way!"

"Seventeen years."

"How's three?"

Bree'on Chae laughed. "Ho, I like you." Smiling playfully. "Fifteen years of your youth. That would make you thirty-three. A woman in the fullness of her beauty and more than capable of having any man she sets her sights on."

Cassy shot me a quick glance.

"Ten years."

"I will go no lower than fifteen, and trust me, that's a bargain."

"Does that mean she'll die fifteen years sooner?" I asked. Hector shot me an angry glance and motioned for me to shut my mouth.

"Hector, control your—" Bree'on Chae snapped.

Cassy met my eye, and I willed her to ask the question.

"Just my youth?" Cassy asked slowly. "It will not shorten my life?"

Bree'on Chae shot an angry look at Hector. "You will make up the difference. You brought him here, it is your responsibility."

Hector glared at me and then at Cassy, clearly trying to decide if we were worth the trouble. "You have my deepest apologies for the interference in your negotiation. Reparations will be made."

Rowan said something under her breath to Bree'on Chae.

"I will take compensation from him." Bree'on Chae pointed at me, avarice in her eyes.

Hector looked at Bree'on Chae, then at the Spriggan. "And what is it you want?"

"To break my sister's bondage."

"We've tried that. Rowan will die if the bond is severed," I told her.

"You'll set her free? Not take the bond for yourself? Rodrick and I have an agreement, and I've extended him my protection. He must accompany me when I leave."

"I will break the bond. After that you do with him as you will. But my sister will make up her own mind," Bree'on Chae said firmly.

"You may as well cut her throat." I said.

"I'll find a way. Now, child, forgive the interruption. That was rude, but your friend broke a rule," Bree'on Chae said.

"Rule?" Cassy asked

"A mortal's soul is theirs to spend," Bree'on Chae explained. "And we immortals may not interfere with one another's pacts. Whatever pitfalls or bonuses they commit themselves to are entirely the mortal's responsibility. So, do we have a deal, then?"

"Twelve years," Cassy said.

"Fourteen." Bree'on Chae practically wriggled with excitement.

"Thirteen years of my youth that will not affect the length of my life."

"I have no control over nature after you leave my grotto. You have as much chance to die of disease or wound as anyone else."

"Fine. Deal," Cassy said.

Bree'on Chae took her hand and said as kindly as a mother, "Deal." Her long hair came alive, lifting the stretcher, carrying it to the water. They waded out. Phosphorescence sparkled in their wake. "Do not struggle, child, and remember to breathe." They dropped under the glassy surface, phosphorescent lights swirling around them like galaxies colliding.

"She can't breathe under there," I said, starting towards them.

"What are you doing?" Hector barred my path.

"She'll drown!" I tried to push past, and he gave me a sharp shove in the sternum. The thirst flared to life.

"No, she won't," he said scornfully. "This is the heart of Bree'on Chae's power. If you interfere again, you'll cost Cassy her life. Your friend will be fine."

The pool shone an eerie blue-green. Bree'on Chae broke

the surface and helped Cassy to the shore. She dropped to her knees and wretched out half the pond. "Let it out, child," Bree'on Chae said. Cassy took a few shuddering breaths, then felt at her stomach and laughed.

Bree'on Chae helped her to her feet. "You did well."

Cassy turned and gazed into the pool.

"Now, sister, we shall remove your bond," Bree'on Chae said grimly.

"IT'LL BE FINE," Hector said. "She gave her word."

"Then why does it feel like waiting for the headsman?"

Bree'on Chae stepped onto the surface of her pool. A single ripple sped across the surface with each footstep. She cradled Rowan in her arms and strode to the center, her long hair undulating in her wake.

"You must open yourself to take in my healing waters," Bree'on Chae said.

Rowan's petals peeled back into a bloodred crest that stood stiffly along her spine. It was as unsettling as watching the layers peeled from a man. They sank under the surface before the final layer had retracted.

There was a sharp tug on something inside me. It stole my breath, sending nauseating tingles along my ribs. Phosphorescence churned below the surface.

Cassy steadied me with a hand. "She only wants to help." She smiled and faint lines appeared at the corners of her eyes. She was healthy, strong and even more beautiful.

A violent yank on the bond sent me to my knees. The

vibrant purple cord that connected Rowan and me shimmered into being, only veins of green pulsed down its length. I could have severed the bond at any time, but something had changed. The spell was anchored to me, and it felt as though it would rip out my spine.

Something wrapped around my leg, Bree'on Chae's thick strands of kelp-like hair. Cassy yelled out as I was dragged into the water.

Greenish blue light swirled around me, no longer mysteriously inviting. Bree'on Chae drifted before me. Her face was longer, sharper. I struggled but she held me like a python.

"Cypress resides within you," Bree'on Chae said, coming inches from my face. "The life coursing through her is too intense to be anything else. It's almost as if..." She examined the cord. "Impossible." My lungs were burning. Hair coiled up my torso. I clawed at it. With a flick of her wrist, she shook me like a dog with a rat.

"With the Mother Tree's realm, I'd set this world to rights." Bree'on Chae's eyes were larger, almond shaped with vertical pupils. Fangs extended from her upper lip. "It should be mine, not squandered on a fleshling."

Her hair slithered up my body, pinning my arms. Squeezing the air from my lungs. "It will be mine!" She ran a hand over the green veins.

The bond was of the Void and the only thing that could save me. I forced that cold malice down the cord's length. Dark barbs erupted from the cord. Bree'on Chae wailed, clutching at a hand that was now missing three fingers.

The water frothed and bubbled as it was erased from existence. The bindings around my chest broke, freeing my arms. I bit into my hand.

Bree'on Chae flinched and her face contorted in panic.

The next second I was flying through the air, then sprawled in a heap on the ground, drawing in sweet air. I lay for a moment as the world spun.

"Rodrick." Cassy put a slender hand on my cheek. "Frozen fire, what was that?"

"Failure," Hector said quietly.

Rowan and Bree'on Chae walked out of the pool, hand in hand like two old ladies consoling each other over the death of a friend. "I tried. I am so sorry, sister." Bree'on Chae reached for Cassy. "Child, come away from that thing."

I pushed Cassy aside, drawing my dagger.

"Easy, mate," Hector said, his hand going to his whip.

"She tried to kill me!" I said.

Hector's jaw tightened. "She wouldn't be so foolish as to incur the wrath of the Crystal Lady."

"Come away. Both of you. He's not safe," Bree'on Chae said.

"He saved my life," Cassy protested. "Twice. He rescued Rowan as well. It's you who attacked."

"That is the most dangerous Arisen to ever return."

"We all struggled to walk the path," Hector said. "But I've watched him resist temptation while others, that should have known better, caved."

"There isn't an Ascendant upon Etherious that wouldn't have taken his power. The Mother Tree's realm resides within him," Bree'on Chae replied sharply. All joviality left Hector, and he uncoiled his whip.

"Murderer," Rowan said, rattling like a barrel of snakes, her crest starting to rise. "You killed my people."

"His crimes pale in comparison to what he brought back through the Veil. He is the harbinger of the sundering. The Void's chosen vessel."

"I didn't ask for any of this. The Mother Tree was meant

to buy Khyber his transcendence, but another deity interfered and forced her power into me. The man that attacked the Mother Tree is gone. Cypress caught me in the afterlife. She tortured me, tore me apart till there was nothing left. I have nothing in common with Rodrick Corwyn save his name. I hate him and everything he stood for. Rowan, there is nothing I can do to atone for what happened to your people. The shame..." I threw up my hands in despair.

"After I escaped Cypress, the Void took me. He poisoned me, sought to use me. I will never let that happen. I will not repeat my mistake with the Spriggans. For as long as I draw breath, I will fight the Void."

"He's proven his integrity time and time again." The crank on Cassy's crossbow clicked, and she took aim at Bree'on Chae. "I won't let you hurt him."

"Nobel sentiments," Bree'on Chae said. "But his words are wind, unless he backs them up with action."

"What do you mean?" I asked.

"The Spiral intended this to happen. Within you resides two opposing forces. The power of life and the power of annihilation. The power to save the world and destroy it at the same time. Beside me stands the last of the Mother's children. A connection has been forged between you. If you granted her the Mother's realm, then the Mother Tree would be reborn through her and the man that condemned Etherious would save it."

"If he embraces the darkness," Hector thought out loud, "then this world, and every soul within it, will be taken by the Void."

"The Ascendancy War has no merit beside the threat this Arisen poses to the world."

"And if he's killed? The Void would only spread to a new host." Hector scrubbed at his beard.

"The safest place for it is within him," Bree'on Chae said. "I fear nothing short of driving a spike through every organ, then entombing him under a mountain would prevent this calamity."

"His safety falls to you, Hymnal of the Golden Strings," she went on.

"Me?" Hector scoffed. "Zenos would be better suited."

"The Elder Ascendants may have more power, but that makes them arrogant. All they'd need do is reach out a hand and the Mother's realm would be theirs. Surely a god could contend with the Void." She displayed her missing fingers.

Hector shook his head in bewilderment. "My lady would never—"

Bree'on Chae cut him off. "Something comes. Something I haven't sensed in... Arachnids, skittering through the bows."

I groaned. "Khyber purchased their services."

"Not after the Arachnid wars!" Hector gasped, shocked.

I took Cassy's hand. "That's why he rounded up those that wouldn't convert to Kydaism. So he could harvest their blood. As payment."

Rowan rattled. Cassy choked back a sob.

"Well, it seems Khyber's set his hounds to track you down," Bree'on Chae said.

"If Eericas claims—" Hector said.

"I know. The Void at the command of that demon is unthinkable." Bree'on Chae waved her hand, and an arch formed in her tree. "We haven't much time if you are to escape the swarm."

A boat sat in the passage. "Climb in." With a second wave of her hand, a furrow was carved in the earth, and water poured from the pond. "I hope you are true to your word, Rodrick, for the fate of the world is riding on your shoulders. Now go. I will buy you what time I can."

"Come with us, sister," Rowan pleaded.

The water picked up the boat. "Farewell, sister."

36

BREE'ON CHAE RAN up the tunnel behind us as if the water was as solid as stone. The ground dropped out from under us, and we splashed into a stream. Bree'on Chae climbed her tree, bounding from crack to knot as nimbly as a squirrel. Hector handed out paddles, and we steered the boat into the current.

Hisses and clicks came from the canopy. Branches crashed and snapped. Wet impacts of heavy bodies rained from above. Cassy covered her ears. After a minute, the sounds of fighting faded into the quiet of the grave. Then rattling sounded from all around.

"Shhh," Hector chided.

"It's not me," Rowan whispered.

Branches swayed as if we were caught in a hurricane. The rattle clarified into a stampede of thousands of quiet feet. I crouched over Cassy, fearful to breathe lest it draw attention.

The sound of fighting doubled from behind. Bree'on Chae let out a battle cry. Rowan made to jump from the boat, but I held her, locking her inside her body. Hector signaled and we put paddle to water.

———

WOULD THE RAIN NEVER STOP? For two days it had soaked us. Hector had been wise in not allowing us more than short breaks. A fire was too great a risk. Everything was wet, and smoke would give us away. By night the light would.

I constructed a lean-to in the middle of the canoe. It kept the rain from pelting your face. But, inevitably, the bottom would fill and you'd wake to a cold bath. With Rowan catatonic, she took up most of the space, so we worked in shifts, with only one able to sleep at a time. How Cassy found the energy to pore over her mother's journal after a day of paddling I couldn't fathom.

"Your turn," Hector said.

"I'll be fine. Give Cassy a little more time," I replied.

"You need rest as much as any mortal. Cassy, wake up."

"Already?" She took my paddle and clapped me on the shoulder.

I lay down and closed my eyes. The black door stood open. The last time I was here I'd closed it.

"Master," called a young woman, her voice breathy with excitement.

"Please come in," a second voice chimed, this one sultry and melodic.

The sloping tunnel led to a chamber I'd hoped to forget. The cave was an exact replica of the one I'd resurrected in, only the filth was gone. The scent of roasted meat drew me farther in.

A table was set before the lake, torches burning along its

shore. The hearth crackled warmly. In place of the sacrificial altar was a pair of comfortable armchairs and a chaise.

Two women greeted me. One a raven-haired sprite with an impish smile, the other a tall, sultry redhead with eyes that smoldered. Both wore silk that hugged curves and accentuated every line.

"Welcome, Master," they said simultaneously. Their curtsies gave me quite the view, milky skin dappled with freckles, while the other was olive and smooth as porcelain.

The raven-haired girl bounced over, tucked herself under my arm. "This way," she said, a little breathy. Her hand on the small of my back guided me over to an armchair.

The redhead poured a thick red liquid into a silver goblet. The way she held herself was an open invitation to gawk. Red hair draped over one shoulder, a leg glimpsed through the slit in her dress. This was a practiced move. They were putting on a show, and a damn good one at that.

Anger churned my gut to acid. The redhead met my gaze. She faltered, her smile slipping, handing me the glass. I breathed in the aroma: fresh blood. My thirst spiked. I threw the glass into the fire. They shot each other a fearful glance.

"You've changed since the last time we met," I said coldly.

The petite one smiled meekly. "Thanks to you."

"We have grown supple in your domain, my lord." The redhead bit her lip.

"Please, Master, sit," the raven said. "We have been expecting you." She indicated the table. "We've roasted a joint. You won't make all our hard work go to waste, will you?"

I gritted my teeth, knowing I was being manipulated. I

sat down. The raven draped a napkin over my lap, ensuring that I got a good look at how little she wore under her dress. Long lashes blinked innocently.

The redhead poured me another glass. She placed it at my right hand while the raven brought out a roast.

"What are you doing here?" I asked.

"Surviving as best we can." The raven began to carve. "We are prisoners, after all."

"You claimed our souls." They shared a delicate chuckle. "Snatched from our lord's eternal embrace," the redhead said. "So, we make the best of our situation, don't we, Isabelle?"

"How do you like your meat, Master? Well done, blue?" Isabelle asked.

"I don't want anything you serve. It's likely poisoned," I said.

Isabelle's eyes filled with tears. The redhead reached out and squeezed her hand. "It's all right, Eleanor."

"My lord," Eleanor said patiently. "We are within your realm. Nothing here can truly hurt you. Nothing that happens here will affect your body in the mortal world. All this is happening within you. True, what happens here will feel real. Pain, lust, hunger and pleasure"—she leaned back and slowly uncrossed her legs. "—will be as intense as anything you've experienced in the mortal world. So yes, we could have poisoned your food and you would feel the effects until you returned to your physical body. But what would that gain us except your ire?"

"Our immortal souls are bound to your well-being," Isabelle added, placing a slice of meat on my plate. "Believe it or not, all we wish is to serve you."

I pulled at my collar and sat up straighter. "You two weren't Arisen?"

"No, Lord, just simple women daring enough to achieve what all mortals dream of," Eleanor said.

"Immortality, or the next best thing," Isabelle added, serving her sister.

"At the expense of others."

"Everything achieved in life must come at the expense of someone else. Yes, we took the lives, sacrificing them to the Void, but in return—"

"We got to live for hundreds of years," Isabelle finished, taking a seat on my other side. "The best deal we ever made." The two women raised their glasses in a toast.

"And the Spriggan?"

"Her soul was connected to the Mother Tree. So, in lean times, we'd siphon her life force," Eleanor said.

"And the Mother Tree would fill her back up. Until you," Isabelle said, scandalized. "How did we get so lucky? Handsome, ruthless, power hungry. No wonder the Void chose you."

This flirting was too much. Did they really think I was stupid enough to be taken in? "Is there a way to kill it, The Void?"

"Won't you try the roast? It took me hours to prepare, you know," Isabelle said, popping a piece of meat into her mouth, her chest heaving with exaggerated pleasure.

"Where did you get meat in a place like this? It's not like you could just pop down to the butcher's."

Isabelle and Eleanor shared a mischievous look. "My lord." Isabelle drew a finger down her neck and over her cleavage. "We don't give up our secrets so easily."

"Good day, ladies." I pushed away from the table and made for the door.

"Join us again, Master," Eleanor called after me.

"Next time we will have something more to your liking." Isabelle's voice echoed from up the corridor.

I pushed the door closed. I didn't want them causing trouble. I focused, willing the door to lock. The tentacles grew around the edges. I tried the door handle. Good.

"RODRICK," Hector said.

I blinked the sleep from my eyes and scurried from the shelter. Ivory elves lined the bank. Bone arrows were nocked and drawn to their long ears. Black eyes with no whites stared from ivory faces that were an exact copy of every other elf in the patrol.

Hector steered us to the bank. "Caloviial." He raised a hand.

The elf on point lowered his bow. "Hail, hymnal. It's been an age."

Hector gave a tight smile. "I never thought to see you out on patrol."

"I needed a change from the coliseum. Six hundred years of anything can begin to wear." Caloviial eyed our piecemeal armor. "Strange companions, aren't they?"

"We're on a mission of the utmost importance." Hector flipped back the lean-to, revealing Rowan lying in the bottom of the canoe.

"Moon's blessing, you come bearing gifts." The elves touched their foreheads, hearts, and then lips and cast it to the sky.

"But whatever is the matter with her?"

"There is no time," Hector replied. "The Arachnids and the Fauldic have joined forces and pursue us."

"Evil news. We saw signs of the creepers. But I'd hoped it was a stray."

"No stray, Captain. The swarm."

Eyes darted to the trees, and bows were raised. "Come quickly."

We stepped from the boat, stiff muscles protesting. Four elves picked up the canoe and led us hurriedly into the forest.

"Lean on me," I said to Cassy. She wrapped her arm around my shoulder, and we limped after the elves.

37

THE GIANT CEDARS acquiesced to maple, oak and elm. Despite the time of year, they were barren of leaf. Sapling to towering elder, the forest was barren and brown. Even the firs and pines were naked. Leaves covered the ground nearly hip deep. Every step was punctuated by a wet squish. Even the elves with their fabled agility were hindered as they waded through this sea.

They marched in silence, moving with the predatory grace of hunting cats. Their skin had a bone-like quality, and in the rain, it shone like glazed pottery.

They all had long faces with sharp edges that lent them a perpetually stern expression. Pointed ears stuck up above their heads, and their hoods had slots to accommodate the peculiar anatomy. They all had a slight build, by human standards, and wore a uniform of brown and green, with the moon and its shards emblazoned on the chest.

Evening fell and the elves made camp.

"We should keep moving," I said.

"You need rest," Caloviial replied. "You crash about like a

wounded stag. Every creeper in a hundred miles would come to investigate that noise."

"I do not."

"Rodrick." Cassy took my hand. "We've been pushing for days. A single night won't hurt."

"Of course." I took her pack. "Warm yourself. I'll find somewhere dry to sleep."

Two of the elves brought out a cooking stove that ran on some kind of oil canister like a lamp. Hector sat down with a sigh and checked his fiddle. The elves made Rowan a bed of leaves and sheltered her with the canoe. Supper was served. Cassy's first spoonful made her sigh with pleasure.

"Bloody amazing what they call camp rations," Hector said with a chuckle.

"I think it's the best thing I've ever put in my mouth." Cassy took another spoonful, growing sad. I put an arm around her shoulder to comfort her. "I wish Dah could taste this."

"He'd have insisted your aunt's cooking was better."

Cassy chuckled, sniffing back tears. "And he'd be right."

"Play us a song, hymnal," called one of the elves.

"The lay of Galanah and Brom."

"No one wants a mournful ballad in the rain, Ehh'alvro," Caloviial said. "A tale to lift the spirit is what's needed. Recite 'Jescsal the Cursed, and the Witches of the Broken Steps.'"

"Your taste was always morbid, Caloviial." Hector raised his fiddle to his chin.

I placed a hand on his arm. "Is that wise? The Arachnids?"

"Shall hear nothing," he replied merrily.

The food and music lifted everyone's spirits, but when

the sun went down, my bedroll called. Cassy wasn't far behind.

"Rodrick?" She draped an arm over my chest, her head on my shoulder. "I'm cold."

"You'll find no warmth here." I drew her in. My cotton shirt and breeches were hanging from a nearby tree, the remains of my armor piled underneath. She lifted the blanket and slid under. Soft bare skin pressed against me. Her hand ran across the stubble of my chin and down my chest. "Cassy, we can't."

"Says who?" She kissed my neck, and my body responded.

"I don't trust myself."

"I trust you. I want you."

The thirst awoke, and I took her shoulder, pushing her away. "I want you too," I said. "That's the problem. I care for you. And with what I am—"

"You're a man, Rodrick. And I'm a woman who has never felt this way about anyone else."

"I'm not human, Cassy. You deserve someone you can grow old with, have a family with. The only life you'd have with me is a life on the run."

"That would be enough for me. I don't need anything else."

I stood and put on my pants. "I can't give you what you want. If I do, I'll lose control and kill you."

She sucked in a breath. "You don't mean that."

"I'd never intentionally hurt you. Your friendship means the world to me, but we can't be lovers. I'm sorry." I pulled my shirt over my head. Her soft weeping chased me as I left.

I sat down beside the canoe, the only other unoccupied dry place. Rowan's sightless eyes were fixed on the inside of the boat. Hector put away his fiddle and climbed into his own bedroll.

The rain stopped, a high wind blowing away the clouds. A patch of moonlight filtered down through the dead trees. The elves gathered, removing their garments. They stood in a circle, faces turned to the moon's silvery light, their arms out, soaking it all in.

Basic shape was where the similarities between man and elf ended. Their spinal ridges stood out like the teeth of a saw. From the tip of their ears to the end of their fingers ran a serrated seam. Joints overlapped, making their hide look like shell. Cobweb-fine hair ran loosely down their backs, and as they stood soaking up the moonlight, their hair faded from jet black to pearly white. The moonbeam dissipated, and they prayed softly. Once finished, they gently touched forehead, mouth, then hearts and cast their prayers out to the moon.

The next morning was cold and dreary. A light spray misted. The elves blended with the landscape, but their luminous faces stood out. If you glimpsed one out of the corner of your eye, they looked like floating skulls. Now and then one would come by and place a hand on Rowan in a comforting fashion or to point out something beautiful to the Spriggan.

I could sense that Rowan perceived what they were doing, but rather than take comfort in their kindness, it only stoked her resentment. I blocked her emotions out. I didn't need her feeding my dour mood.

Cassy was pretending I wasn't there, walking at the front of the column or talking with Hector. It was for the best. The betrayer of kings, harbinger of the sundering, he who had condemned the world to starvation and death, didn't deserve love.

High above the treetops was a second canopy. The Mother Tree's branches dominated the sky like storm clouds. Her height dwarfed the distant mountains and raked the heavens. Leaves the size of bedsheets were draped upon the lower canopy. A wall of darkness severed the forest. Behind, the dead trees looked as welcoming as a spring day compared to the black depths that stood before us.

It felt like we were descending into a mine shaft. The air grew humid and thick with the scent of rot. I watched as the light of day became no more than a distant line on the horizon.

"Who goes there?" challenged an elvish guard.

Caloviial replied in elvish, and the sentry dropped down from the branches. Greetings were exchanged. The elves touched their forehead before embracing their comrades.

"Welcome, hymnal of the Crystal Lady. Your mistress awaits your arrival in the ruins of Ellodrin. King Glyodrin commanded us to let you pass unhindered," said the elfin sentinel.

"Excellent. Summon your finest coach. My friends and I will be on our way," Hector said with a wink.

"I'm sure Lord Taralin would be happy to accommodate you," the elf replied smoothly.

Hector stiffened. "Our feet will suffice."

The elf bowed, a smugness about the motion. "As you wish."

Odd lanterns that gave off an amber light chased away small pockets of the smothering darkness. We approached an iron-barred prisoner transport and an elf reclined in the driver's seat using the bars as a backrest. He turned the pages of a leather-bound tome with a gloved hand.

At the sound of our approach, he turned. His clothes were of a different cut than the other elves. He wore a cream-colored long jacket that tied over the hip. High boots with gold scrollwork up the sides hid under the bottom of his coat. He pointedly looked each of us in the eye. The now familiar pain of meeting a fellow Arisen shot through the back of my head like barbed wire tangling around my mind.

"Three two five seven, it's been too long."

Hector spat, "Not long enough. Still up to your old tricks?"

Taralin smiled, the plates of his cheek sliding under the plate above. "One can never be too careful with the Arisen." The scent of dried blood filled the air. I craned my neck to see. The transport appeared empty. "The fun ended a fortnight ago."

"The war getting in the way of the hunt?" Hector said.

Taralin shrugged. "The big one woke up last night. His body pushed the arrow out. So, I shot him through the eye. Silent as the grave ever since."

"I thought Glyodrin abolished the practice?" Hector asked.

"The millennia can grind on, and we all need distractions. And the ones that survive will be needed for the war," Taralin said.

"Glyodrin was always a pragmatist," Hector growled.

Taralin jumped down. "Quit your sulking. It worked out well for you in the end. One of them is worth at least two dozen infantry."

Taralin circled me. "I don't like this one's face." Cassy hissed like an angry cat. "Care to put him on the transport? There's plenty of room if we stack," Taralin said.

"He's under Enris's protection."

"Suit yourself." He ran his greedy eyes over Cassy. "Do let me know when it's dinnertime."

"Keep your hands off her," I snarled.

"Spirit. I do love men with spirit. Ask three two five seven. Captain," Taralin said, his tone formal once more.

"Yes, Lord." Caloviial saluted with index and middle fingers to his heart.

"Make sure your elves get something to eat. We move out within the hour."

"Yes, my lord."

We followed Caloviial to a cook station. Logs had been arranged around a cook pot, and a turquoise stew bubbled within.

"He thought I was food," Cassy said indignantly.

"I won't let that happen." I grabbed for a sword hilt that wasn't there.

"I don't need your protection." Cassy patted her crossbow and turned her attention to the cook pot.

Hector sat with his back against a tree, hands shaking. He reached for his fiddle. He ran the bow over the strings, every note harsh and discordant, but as he played, his anger slowly ebbed away. I leaned back and closed my eyes.

I AWOKE WITHIN MY REALM. I walked to the hollow where I'd left Lucas. He was gone. Scrape marks in the earth indicated the direction he'd been dragged. My stomach turned. The roast. There were no livestock here.

I kicked the door in and stormed down the tunnel. The witches jumped from their armchairs. "Back so soo—" Eleanor made a choking noise as I lifted her from the ground.

"Where is he?" I raged. "For that matter, what happened to all the other souls I've taken?"

"I assure you, Lord, that their consciousnesses are well."

Isabelle laid a hand on my arm, coaxing me to release Eleanor.

"Prove it," I snarled, dropping the redhead.

"Yes, Master. This way," Isabelle said.

Isabelle led me down the lakeside passage. She pushed open an iron door and gestured for me to enter.

I braced a boot against the bottom edge of the door and looked inside. Hollow figures shambled around the cramped room. Most stared sightlessly, moving perpetually. They bumped into walls, then carried on in another direction. Lucas lay on the stone floor, staring vacantly.

"What have you done to them?"

Isabelle held up her hands and backed away. I knelt over Lucas. He looked as though he'd been starving for months. He'd been in bad shape when I left him, but this. His skin hung from him, and all muscle tone had melted away. The only thing recognizable was his face, and even that was little more than a skull.

"Lucas." I placed a hand on his shoulder. He screamed, high-pitched and frantic. "Lucas, I'll get you out of here." The others took up the scream. I looked up into the faces of the men and women I'd killed. The girl from the mountaintop roared a wordless accusation. Every face held nothing but fear and hatred.

"SHHHH. My pretties. The demon will be gone soon Go back to sleep." Isabelle ushered me through the door. Screaming chased me up the hall. Only once we were back in the sitting room did the screaming die away.

"What have you done to them?" I demanded, folding my arms.

"Nothing you didn't do first," Eleanor said.

"What's that supposed to mean?" I asked.

"You murdered them, ate their souls," Eleanor said, driving a spike of shame straight through my heart.

"Don't you dare blame me for this. You were a cannibal long before you ended up here."

"In time they will be whole again. The soul cannot be destroyed," Isabelle said patiently. "We took their energy and grew strong upon it. So we could better serve you, Lord."

"You did this to help me? Come off it," I scoffed. "You did this for yourselves."

"Of course we did. We're survivors. And if we didn't, we'd all become like those we shelter."

"Shelter? You ate their spirit flesh."

"Yes, we feed on them," Isabelle said patiently. "As you do on us."

"Every time you use blood magic," Eleanor said. "You siphon the life force of the souls within your realm. And at the rate you use us, if we didn't feed, we'd all become like those hollows below."

"This way we retain our capacity for thought," Isabelle added. "You saw how they reacted to you. They see you for what you are, the Void's chosen. And they rather the numbness of oblivion than to face the horror of this afterlife."

"You have a greater well of energy than you would otherwise," Elenor piped in. "You may tap our minds, use our knowledge and experience for your own. We're able to serve you better than any other."

I raised a finger. "You are to feed on no one else. You will let those below heal and set them free. Am I understood?"

"Yes, Lord," they both said in unison.

"But as long as you continue to summon pieces of this realm, the souls that reside here will not recover," Isabelle said. "It will be you that consumes their spirit, not us."

"I want them freed," I said.

"And if they will not go?" Eleanor asked.

"Just don't hurt them anymore." I made my way to the door.

"There is a way for you to protect them, protect us."

"How could you know that? You were mortals."

"Mortals who had hundreds of years to study the mysteries of Etherious," Eleanor said.

"Let's hear it, then."

"Give in to your nature. Feed."

"The more souls you take, the stronger your magic will become, and the less of a toll there will be for us when you use it," Isabelle added.

"Drink blood, forge your body into a weapon, and in time, no enemy will be able to defy you," Eleanor said.

"At the expense of my humanity," I said, horrified.

"If you had any to begin with, the Void never would have chosen you," Isabelle replied sweetly.

"You are an Arisen. Death and destruction will follow in your wake no matter what you do," Eleanor said. "Embrace what you are. Retain your mind and control the darkness or it will drive you mad."

38

"Up and at'em." Hector kicked the sole of my boot.

I ran a hand through my hair. What I wouldn't give for a bath and a shave. "More like ten minutes than an hour."

"It was fifteen. Taralin has a twisted sense of humor."

A plow had been attached to the prison transport. It'd been intended to keep the leaves from tangling the axle, and for the most part, it did its job. However, it made the going harder on the poor elk.

Save for the creak of the wheels and the elk's strained grunts, the day passed in silence. The elves scanned the canopy, a hand never far from their quivers. They took turns carrying Rowans makeshift litter. The day passed with Cassy shooting me hurt looks, and any attempt at conversation was met with a command from Taralin.

"Quiet," he'd threaten without looking up from his book.

As the day wore on, one pale face rotated with another. I began to notice subtle differences in their facial structures. They still looked to be cast from the same mold, but no longer the same man.

Daylight became no more than a faint line on the horizon. The wagon driver brought out some kind of lantern the size of a fist. He gave it a twist. It grated like a mortar and pestle. Then, all at once, a cool blue light banished the gloom and replaced the amber one that hung from the peg on the iron cage.

Ehh'alvro pulled a pendant from his shirt and said something to it in elvish. A ball of green light shot out. It wove around the elk's antlers, laughing like a mischievous child. The elk snorted and stamped. Ehh'alvro spoke to the little light and it zipped out in front, lighting the way.

"How'd you come by a sprite?" Hector asked.

Ehh'alvro touched his lips and made a throwing motion. "Beautiful creature simply followed me home."

Caloviial scoffed. "Tis a tale to break the hardest of heart."

"Tell it and I'll break your arm," Ehh'alvro replied, eyes scanning the trees.

"Worth it just to see you squirm," Caloviial jibed.

"Come on, Ehh'alvro." Cassy pouted playfully. "I'd love to hear it."

"No, lady, you want to hear how Caloviial got that Arachnid fang he wears around his neck," Ehh'alvro said.

"Careful or I may sing the lay of Val'und Vale," Caloviial said. Ehh'alvro raised his hands in surrender.

"That would be wonderful," Cassy all but squealed in delight.

The elves exchanged a look, shaking their heads. "Humans."

"Quiet," Taralin growled.

Crashing leaves announced a pair of riders. They darted up to the transport, their elk puffing and blowing. One staggered and collapsed to its knees, bloody foam spilling from its nostrils. The elf tried to jump free, but his arm was injured, and the elk collapsed atop him. His comrades rushed forwards.

Taralin closed his book and set it on the seat. With a sigh of irritation, he climbed down. "Report?"

"The outpost. Attacked. Fauldic," panted the elf, still astride his animal.

"How many were there?" Taralin asked.

"Don't know," the elf said. "Killed half our force in the first ten minutes." He lurched forwards with a choking cry, and black blood spilled from his mouth. He fell, a bolt protruding from his back.

"Defensive line!" yelled Taralin, but Justice was already among them. The wagon driver jumped down, drawing a slender two-handed blade. Rowan's bearers all but dropped the canoe and rushed into the fray.

Hector looked inside the transport. "Get on!"

"We have to help!" I protested, fingering my dagger.

Hector uncoiled his whip. A charge rippled down its length. "Don't be a fool. They're here for you." He lashed the lock. It flew away in a shower of sparks. Cassy climbed into the driver's seat, took aim and fired. I ran to Rowan and threw her in the back of the transport. Half a dozen corpses lay at the bottom. I forced down the desire to feed and climbed into the driver's seat.

Justice's armor was covered with dents and scrapes. She'd lost some of her unnatural grace. Nevertheless, she dealt out death with frightening efficiency. She held Taralin's whirling cutlass at bay while adding to the pile of bodies strewn about her feet.

"Go!" Hector yelled and snapped his whip. The elk spooked, bounding forwards. Hector barely grabbed onto the iron cage before he was left behind.

"Cowards!" Taralin yelled.

A massive shape came out of the pitch black. Melcor's great sword ignited, leaving an orange streamer in its wake. Taralin narrowly avoided the strike, deflected a second, and then planted his blade in Melcor's gut. Melcor lowered his horns and threw himself upon the elf. Taralin gave a strangled cry as they punched through his chest.

Justice sprinted after us. She had a slight limp, but it barely slowed her.

"Merciful lady," Hector said.

He held onto the doorframe and pulled a blade from the closest Arisen. Its eyes popped open and it launched itself at Hector. He tossed it out the back of the wagon. The Avatar made to bat it aside, but the Arisen wrapped itself around her, mindlessly attacking.

Hector pulled an arrow from the eye of another. The daggers from a woman, one after the other, heaving them at our pursuer. The Avatar went down in a twisted heap of metal and flesh. The glow of Melcor's blade showed him rushing to her aid. Cassy fired one more bolt into the darkness. "Rip the sow apart!" she yelled.

Hector climbed along the iron bars to the driver's seat. He looped his whip around the plow and effortlessly cut through the pin that held it on. The wagon rocked. I flipped the reins, urging the elk to give all their speed.

39

A GUARD POST came in to view, braziers to either side of the roadway.

"Forgive my boldness, Miss Forester. But you both need to abandon your armor," Hector said. "There's no telling how the soldiers might react at the sight of a Fauldic acolyte."

"Point taken," she said with a stiff nod. "Rodrick, can you help me with the laces?"

I handed the reins to Hector and undid the knot under her arm.

"Who goes there?" shouted a guard.

Hector slowed the elk. The transport rumbled to a halt. "Hector, hymnal of the Crystal Lady."

"Well met, friend. I saw you play at the gardens last year."

"I hope to have the pleasure of your patronage again, having survived all the perils the road can throw at—"

"We were attacked by the Fauldic," I cut in. "Not twenty minutes back."

"I was getting there," Hector grumbled. "Have your

commander triple the guard. I'll make sure the generals are informed. I wouldn't put it past them to attack."

"Fetch the captain," ordered the guard. His counterpart rushed off.

"Where's Her Majesty?"

"God's pavilion, foot of the Mother Tree."

"Thanks, mate." Hector urged the transport on. "And join me for a song and an ale."

OUR WAGON BUMPED over the bridge spanning the Al'veran. Living wood had braided into an intricate latticework. Once it had shimmered with a vibrancy human varnishes couldn't hope to match. It had been an invitation to bask in the glory of the Mother Tree. Now it gave way to decay. Flowering vines had adorned arches, lawns softer than a feather bed enticed the weary to nap upon balconies overlooking the garden city. They appeared ready to crumble at the slightest touch, casting those who didn't watch their footing into the churning waters far below.

The allies' camp spanned miles, and for a moment, it seemed Ellodrin had been resurrected. But the Spriggans had never marred the night with artificial light. Three distant sections could be made out, each having cleared the debris to set up their tents.

The elves hung glow bulbs, and a few sprites zipped about, followed by patrols. The Mirvish banished the dark with braziers, and the discordant sound of a thousand throats all singing different songs filled the air, while the Norvish section was almost dark, save for a few cook fires.

The bridge exited onto a main thoroughfare, clogged

with soldiers enjoying what nightlife the camp followers could provide.

"Make way!" Hector yelled, making little difference. We trundled past a makeshift pub with no more than stacked hay bales for walls. A buxom girl in the robes of a Mirvish priestess danced on the bar, soldiers cheering with drunken abandon.

A few stalls down, a man beat his fist on a table while an artist tattooed his back. Beside that was a laundry. A Norven dropped off a bundle as big as the laundress. Across the way was an elderly woman calling, "Charms, wards, runes." Elves, men, and Norven all packed the street. They ate and drank, haggled and diced. All of it felt forced.

Hector turned down an alley, and the press of people vanished. At every other fire, the Mirvish played penny whistles, pipes or even mandolins and half a hundred more. Cassy watched with longing.

"Care to dance?" I held out my hand.

"I can't." She smoothed her sweat-stained shirt.

"Neither can he." I gestured to a soldier who pecked the air like a chicken and hopped about as if on fire.

"Another time." She took my hand.

The light dimmed, and music blended into the background. Here, the tents stood twelve feet tall. Norven sat solemnly, polishing armor or sharpening weapons. Each wore a mask similar to Melcor's with bull- or ram-like horns coming out the top, the faces worked into a visage of fear, pain or loss.

A fair few stood menacingly, exposing crooked teeth from their short muzzles. Their armor looked to be made of wooden planks interlocking horizontally. The effect made them even wider than their four feet across the chest. No guards challenged us, though a pair of warriors carrying polearms with scimitar-esque heads flanked the wagon.

We entered a wide ring that cordoned off the camp from the command area. Before each nation stood their monarch's pavilion. Beyond, nearly at the foot of the Mother Tree, rose a palisade. Sharpened stakes surrounded a timber wall made from the remains of Ellodrin.

Hector reined in the elk.

"What's your business?" barked one of the gate guards. His uniform was cream with gold vine-work around the collar. His fine attire was at odds with his blunt words and scarred face.

"One of the Crystal Lady's hymnals, here to pay his respects."

"You'll have to wait." The guard shot a suspicious eye to the prison transport. "On Her Majesty's pleasure. All suppliants have been postponed due to the war."

"As you can see, my situation is... unique."

"Listen... mate." Every word twisted his facial scar into an ugly sneer. "Priest, bard, whatever you are. Her Majesty is grateful for spreading the good word, but she has more important things to do than pat you on the head. Go to the clerk's tent in the morning, fill out the proper paperwork, and she'll see you when she's good and ready."

"I have sensitive information the goddess will want to hear immediately."

Scarface whistled, and three heavily armored infantry were at his heels. Each carried a wicked long-handled ax. While the two Norven leveled their spears, one at Hector, the other at Cassy.

"What part of 'piss off' don't you understand?" Scarface snapped.

"Move along, little human," one of the Norven said with a thick accent.

"Do as're told or cut you in half. Feed to Grundstrad," snickered the other.

Hector set his bow to the strings. A sharp piercing note cut through the din. Everyone covered their ears. The note got higher. The guards gritted their teeth, and Rowan stirred within her coma. Abruptly, the piercing note cut off.

"I fully understand. We simply must follow protocol in these uncertain times." He snapped the reins.

Scarface snorted a blood clot onto the ground. The other guards stood on wobbly knees. The Norven laughed, pointing at the blood running down each other's faces.

"Thought eyes pop like grapes," said one of the Norven.

"Come, Vanouchak, show my wife how we bleed from eyes." They left, laughing about exploding brains.

"You all right?" I asked.

"What was that about?" Cassy stared at the guards, brows drawn in a furrow.

"Stop that wagon." A woman in a cream-colored robe strode into the gateway.

"Halt!" groaned Scarface.

Hector reined in the elk with a look of innocent bewilderment.

"Hector?"

"High Priestess, what an absolute pleasure it is to see you again."

"Mmm." She crossed her arms and tapped a blue-lacquered nail.

Hector jumped down from the driver's seat, his smile widening.

"What do you want?" she asked.

"How could a man desire anything other than to bask in your radiance?"

She tossed her brown hair flecked with a few silver strands.

"Alas, duty calls, and ever the humble purveyor of tales, my friends and I come bearing one worthy of Her Majesty."

"Her Majesty and the other god-kings are indisposed. Come back in the morning." She spun.

"Perhaps you could recommend a tavern suitable for the last Spriggan," Hector called after her.

The high priestess had her face pressed to the wagon's bars. "You brought her in this filthy thing? You should be—"

"It was the best we could manage while we ran for our lives," I said.

The high priestess arched a brow.

"Guards, bear her inside and fetch me a valet."

"No," Cassy snapped. "Rodrick and I will bring her."

Her eyes widened. "You?" sneered the high priestess.

Cassy shouldered her way past the priestess. "Yes, us."

"Rowan has been our companion for months," I said. "She'd not take kindly to strange humans touching her." We eased Rowan from the wagon. She stared sightlessly.

"After you." Hector indicated to the pavilion.

The high priestess raised her nose in the air and barged past a very sullen Scarface.

The pavilion was larger than a circus tent. Three standards hung above the entryway: A crystal scepter on a backdrop of cream and gold. The moon and its orbiting shards. And finally, two Norven with identical masks locked in combat, neither with the upper hand.

Norvish guards pulled back the door flap, and we entered a plush waiting area. Cassy and I placed Rowan on a soft couch.

"It'll be all right, Rowan." Cassy squeezed her hand. "I won't let them touch you. I'm here."

Rowan's eyes drifted toward Cassy before un-focusing once more.

A valet brought refreshments. Hector took a champagne flute and a crustless sandwich before flopping into an armchair.

"It's good to be back," he sighed.

"Close your mouth when you chew," the high priestess demanded.

Hector stuffed the whole thing into his mouth and chewed loudly.

"As for the two of you, I won't allow you before Her Majesty in those scraps." She whispered something to the valet, and he scuttled off through a side door.

"Excuse me!" Cassy said dangerously.

"You'll have to forgive Deirdre," Hector said cheerfully. "Once upon a time, she was a farm girl, courageously mucking stalls and heroically feeding the pigs." His voice became monotone. "However, her promotion has seemingly gone to her head." He slurped his beverage obnoxiously.

Half a dozen priestesses swooped into the room bearing various garments. Deirdre quickly picked two sets, and before I knew what was happening, women were pulling my shirt off and unlacing my pants.

"Hey!" I wrested the laces from a doe-eyed brunette.

Deirdre sighed. "Fauldic modesty, so repressed." She clapped and the priestesses held up sheets. Green and yellow striped pantaloons, a matching coat, a frilly shirt and thigh-high stockings were placed on the table beside me.

"I'm not wearing those," I scoffed.

"Fine," Deirdre snapped. "You want to look like a vagabond, you can wait here."

A minute or so later, Cassy emerged. She stole my breath. The road dust had been washed from her, and her hair was pulled back in a tail. It wasn't even the dress, deep blue with a thread of silver, but the woman who wore it. Her eyes sparkled, and she smiled shyly. I couldn't bite back a return smile.

Angry murmurs came from the other side of the tent wall, followed by the unmistakable tone of a sharp rebuke. Deirdre clapped. "Out, all of you."

"What makes you think we agree to this?" demanded a deep male voice.

"Because it's in your best interest," replied a cold female voice.

The priestess and valets rushed from the room. "Isn't there something you can do to block that out?"

"They're gods." Hector gave a sarcastic shrug and snatched a glass from a servant before he scurried from the room.

"You think we're foolish enough to invite the wolf to dinner?" a man said in the refined way of the elves.

"You can't hope to hold all that land. My lady will take what she wants. The Myi'eshans will have the coast. This way, Khyber's forces will be cut in half, and we all get what we want."

"Watch your tongue, whelp."

"My mistress will not extend this offer again. Think hard before offending a transcendent. You have until tomorrow." The flap opened, and a slender girl stormed through the entryway. Her blond hair was bound in many braids with fetishes tied at the ends. She wore animal skins that barely covered her nether regions and nothing else.

My heart leaped into my throat as Cassy and her mother locked gazes.

"Daughter, you got fat."

Cassy flinched. "No, you're dead. They said you'd died."

"I was sent back." Molly smiled, exposing filed teeth. "Lyr'eris blessed me as one of the holy returned." She glanced from me to Hector to Rowan. Pain shot through my eye. Her eyes went completely blue, and the deep chill of winter passed over me.

Hector gripped his whip.

Molly gave a mocking laugh. "Still hiding behind others, I see. And two Arisen at that. You were always so good at manipulating men." She eyed me. "Did she ever tell you what happened to the last Arisen she brought home?"

"I'm not hiding anymore." Cassy's voice trembled.

"You're right. You're too fat and ugly to hide anywhere, anyway. I swear, the moment I leave you untended, you throw your life away." Molly pointed at her feet with a tattooed hand. "We'll put the frozen fire in your belly once and for all. Come."

"No," Cassy stammered.

"Shut your filthy hole and do as you're told."

"I renounce Lyr'eris and all her minions. Get away from me... demon," Cassy said breathlessly.

"Insolent child, I'll teach you your place." Molly advanced.

I stepped in her path.

She backhanded me with unbelievable strength. I stumbled, head swimming.

Deirdre called, "Guards!"

Cassy drew a rune in the air; it drank the light. Black and twisted, the rune writhed like mating snakes. A wall of dusk sprang up, driving Molly and Hector back. "Be gone, demon. You have no power over me." Cassy drew her shoulders up.

"You gave your soul to the enemy of life, and you have

the audacity to call *me* a demon? You are the greatest failure of my life." Molly pushed the guards aside as if they were scarecrows and stalked from the pavilion. I placed an arm around Cassy's shoulder, and she embraced me.

Deirdre watched us from the corner of the room, her haughtiness gone, replaced with the tension of a deer poised to flee.

"I hate family drama." Hector passed Cassy the rest of his drink, and she tipped it back. "There's always one who lives to ruin the party. Deirdre? Would you find Miss Forester accommodation for this evening?"

"Accommodations?"

Hector held up a warning finger. "And comfortable ones, where she won't be disturbed."

"No." Cassy wiped a tear from her eye. "I'll be fine."

"You're not, Cassy." I softly stroked her cheek. "Not after finding out the sow returned. Drink a bottle of wine and celebrate telling her off. I'll join you later."

She braced the crossbows stock on her hip, a long leg peeking through the slit in her dress. "No, I made a promise."

"I don't know what dark god you serve," Deirdre spat like an angry cat, "but I'll not allow you within a hundred miles of Her Majesty. Guards!" Two burly men flanked her.

"Easy now," Hector interjected.

"I've renounced Lyr'eris, and I'll never devote myself to another god," Cassy insisted.

"Hollow words. Its evil hangs in the air. I can feel it crawling over my skin. Until I know what taints you, you'll be in a cell."

"You'll do no such thing." Hector narrowed his eyes.

The guards shared a look suggesting Hector was about to be roasted alive.

"You don't have the authority to stop me," Deirdre said.

The guards' jaws dropped.

Hector drummed his fingers on his fiddle. "Don't I?"

Deirdre's face flushed.

"Cassy, dearest." He dipped his head. "Please accept my apologies on Mir'eve's behalf. The high priestess spoke out of turn. She forgets we are about to invade Oppenfauld, and the last thing we need is to offend the priesthood of other deities. Don't you agree, Deirdre?"

Enris's high priestess peeled back her lips in a travesty of a smile. "Quite right... *hymnal*." Scorn emphasized his title.

Hector placed a hand on Cassy's shoulder. He locked eyes with Deirdre. "I can assure you no harm will come to Her Majesty. I will take responsibility for her."

Deirdre trembled with bottled fury, and the guards took an unconscious step away.

"I'm not a priestess," Cassy said, shaking her head.

"You used rune magic. The gods only grant that power to their mortal servants." Hector's eyes flicked in my direction. "Something has a claim on your soul, whether you know it or not."

A valet slipped through the wall behind us. "The supplicants will follow me."

"No, Hector, this is beyond inappropriate. She waits here."

"I don't want to cause trouble," Cassy said, giving Deirdre an ugly look. "I'll wait here."

"Just try not to shoot her." Hector winked. Cassy snickered and slumped into a chair.

"Give me a hand," I said. Hector picked up the other end of the couch, and we went through the doorway.

"It appears we are destined to go without supper," said the refined male voice.

A chandelier hung from the ceiling, its crystals sending coruscating light over an opulence that nearly overwhelmed my senses. Friezes and tapestries were hung from purple canvas with scrollwork trim done in a thread of gold. Carpets covered the ground. A twenty-square-foot dining table was set. Three of the sides were occupied.

Enris could not be mistaken. The goddess dabbed her mouth with a delicate hand. My throat constricted at the sight of her. Beautiful was too inadequate a word. The youth and beauty of every woman who had ever lived was condensed into this one perfect specimen. Simply being in her presence was like being tossed off a ship at sea. An overwhelming desire to serve, to devote myself to this glorious creature washed over me.

She wore a gown of sea foam studded with diamonds. It seemed a shabby tasteless rag marring her perfection. Golden hair would have spilled to the floor if not imprisoned by an onyx net. Her eyes widened with amazement as she saw the Spriggan. We lowered the couch and knelt.

"One of the Mother's children still lives." Enris smiled, and the room got brighter. She laughed, opening her arms. "See. Not all is lost."

"Your Majesty, may we speak in private?" Hector asked.

"Too late," said the deeply accented voice. The Norven tossed a half-eaten ham hock to the floor. "You can't just parade her in front of us and bugger off."

"I should think not," said the largest ivory elf I'd ever seen. Glyodrin was taller, broader in the shoulders, his angles sharper than his subjects. He wore a crown of holly woven through his antlers. "Forgive us, Enris. This is too portentous to expect us to leave."

The Norven scowled at me. Something inside my head ruptured and I fell forward, my body spasming. Once the convulsions stopped, I knelt once more and kept my eyes averted.

"Of course, as a show of Mir'eve's commitment to our alliance, I invite you to stay," Enris said.

"How did you come by her, Hector?" the Norven asked.

"Forgive me, Lord Zenos, but I didn't," Hector said.

Zenos rose like a bear standing to its full height. "I've had all the insolence I'm willing to stomach."

"Peace, Zenos," said the elf. "Show some of your fabled restraint."

Zenos tossed his head, the curled horns of his mask threatening to knock the dishes from the table. "This *is* restrained."

"My lords, I found her," I said, "enslaved to a pair of witches. I slew them, and she began to wither. I couldn't let her die, so I took command of her bond."

"Commendable," Glyodrin said. "Preserving the last vestige of her race."

"Perhaps," I said, "if I hadn't been responsible for the genocide in the first place."

Zenos hammered a fist on the table, which snapped down the middle. Their fine dinner clattered into the crevasse. He stormed toward me, murder in his eyes.

"No, Lord, please let him finish." Hector threw himself at Zenos's feet.

"What say you?" Zenos turned to the other gods.

"Hear him out," Enris said. Glyodrin waved a hand in assent.

"In life, I was Avatar Wrath." Outraged gasps met my words. "I've come to atone for my part in the murder of the Mother Tree and her people."

"How so?" Enris asked.

"I have information," I said.

"Battle plans, layout of defensive structures, troop deployment?" Glyodrin asked.

I shook my head sadly. "I've lost most of my memories. But Khyber's made a pact with the Arachnids. He slaughtered everyone within his kingdom who wouldn't convert to Kydaism. He's taken their blood to pay Eericas, to harass your armies." I hesitated over the next bit. I couldn't even hint at the technique of runic layering. Better that knowledge die with Khyber. "I can show you where he keeps the weapon he used to kill the Mother Tree."

Zenos shook his head firmly. "Not good enough."

"When Khyber dies, all the weapons he's crafted will become inert," Glyodrin said.

"And if he uses it against us?" Enris asked. Both Zenos and Glyodrin got a faraway look. "The destruction of this weapon should be our first priority."

"Agreed," Zenos said.

"This is exactly the kind of trap Khyber would set," Glyodrin said. "Let me take Wrath's realm. I'll get what we need from him."

"I am no longer that man. I go by Rodrick now."

"My lady and lords," Hector interjected. "I can vouch for his earnestness. He truly wishes to make reparations."

"My vassal," Enris said, "when your opinion is wanted, I will ask for it. Otherwise, be silent."

Hector touched his head to the floor.

She turned back to Glyodrin. "That seems the most efficient way."

"What? I came to help overthrow Khyber."

"What do Fauldic say?" Zenos eyed me. "Every man owns his actions. Good does not cancel bad. Take his realm, Glyodrin, and make him die twice for every Spriggan."

Glyodrin slipped off his coat, exposing the wicked

serrated edge that ran down the length of his forearm. This was a mistake, to trust any god. I backed toward the door. Glyodrin clenched his fist, and I was crushed to the floor by an unseen force.

"Stop! He has the Void within him!" Hector called out.

The three gods gasped in shock. "You're certain?" Enris asked sharply.

"Beyond any doubt."

"Then the sundering is upon us," Glyodrin said, "and there's no point to this war."

"Look at her, Glyodrin." Enris pointed to Rowan. "You can't tell me there's no hope. Our alliance lasted because the five of us had a common purpose. This Spriggan proves that purpose still lives. The Spiral guides us. Do not give up before even trying."

"If the Void has entered Etherious, then time is short," Glyodrin said.

"This is why Khyber changed tactics." Zenos's tone was harsh. "He plans to weather the storm. I will not let this pass."

"I'm sorry, old friend, but I will not waste the lives of my elves when every one of them will be needed in the days to come," Glyodrin said.

"The traitor must be punished!" Zenos roared.

"Then leave him to the Myi'eshans," Glyodrin shot back. "I will not abandon my realm right before I have reaped my reward. I will survive the sundering and ride my shard into the ethereal battle." Glyodrin bowed. "I hope you will too. Goodbye, my friends."

"Glyodrin," Enris pleaded. "This alliance is the only reason you haven't fallen to Wyrm. Our united strength is what keeps our lands safe."

Glyodrin stopped in the doorway. "The pact is shattered.

Khyber saw to that."

"Don't you dare walk out on us," Zenos snarled.

Glyodrin turned angrily. "Then come with me. Do not walk into the trap. You know what he's like."

"Coward."

Enris stepped between the two gods. "If we fight amongst ourselves, we'll not survive the night. Our nations will fall to Lyr'eris, Wyrm or Eericas."

"And the sundering?" Glyodrin said.

"Changes nothing. We stay the course. Execute Khyber for his crimes. You both know it's only a matter of time before he comes for us. So, we take him now, on our terms and our terms alone."

"What do we do about him?" Zenos asked, pointing at me.

"We give him the opportunity he asked for. Let him aid us in Khyber's downfall."

"We'd be setting a serpent free in the nursery," Glyodrin argued.

"One of us must take him as a vassal," Enris said.

"And expose ourselves to the Void? Are you mad?" Glyodrin cried.

"We are gods," Zenos said. "I can master any evil."

"We all walk the path," Enris said. "Each of us is up to the challenge."

"I'll not be traded like a goat at market," I spat through gritted teeth.

"You're right." Enris placed a hand on Glyodrin's arm. "Let him up."

Glyodrin waved a hand, and the force lifted.

"You came of your own free will, and on behalf of Mir'eve, Illuvand and the Norvish tribes, we accept your aid."

By their expressions, my life hung by a thread. "Thank you, Your Majesties."

Enris gave the slightest tilt of her chin. "As a show of gratitude, we shall allow you to choose which of us you take as your sovereign."

"My lady"—my mind's eye filled with the grating of chains—"might I have a little time to deliberate?"

"I will not allow an unaligned Arisen amongst my army," Glyodrin said. "If he needs time, I'll take him to my kennels."

"If I may?" Hector interrupted.

Enris gave her silent assent.

"Rodrick has been with me for a couple of weeks. He hasn't once strayed from the path. Please allow me to guard him while he decides."

"Very well," Enris said. "Unless either one of you... no? Rodrick Corwyn, you have until this time tomorrow."

I nodded. "Thank you, Your Majesty."

"Now that it's settled"—Enris turned to the other two gods—"I bid you good eve." She swept from the tent.

"I'll have my specialists a stone's throw away if you need them," Glyodrin said.

"Won't be necessary," Hector replied grimly.

"Nevertheless." Glyodrin faced Zenos, cold anger radiating from him. Without a word, he left.

Zenos shook his head. He picked up a whole turkey from the rubble and took a bite, crunching through bone. Pointing at Hector, he spoke with his mouth full. "Keep him here. I don't want him amongst the tents."

"Yes, Lord," Hector said to the floor.

Zenos ducked through the door. The sound of bones grinding vanished as the curtain closed behind him.

40

Cassy hesitantly came through the doorway. "Everybody all right?"

Betrayal made the words stick in the back of my throat. Cassy knelt beside me and put an arm around my shoulders. The comfort felt like an invasion, and I shrugged her off. She drew her hand back as if burned.

Hector walked over to the remains of the dining table. He slipped a couple of gold plates from the pile and spooned something from a half-spilled tureen.

"Blood orange duck." He laughed. Slices of purple breast joined the plate. He handed Cassy and me one. "And this yellow dish, I can never remember the name, but the sauce is made from a pollen. This one dish employs an entire village for a year." He shook his head. "It's tasteless muck, though pretty. Come on, Rod. Don't look at me like that. I didn't know what they'd do. Try the duck."

"You told them."

"Of course I did. They were going to kill you," he scoffed.

"So, what happens now? Am I going to end up a chained beast like Melcor?"

COLIN J.D. CROOKS

"Not if you choose Enris. I can't say what Zenos would do, but you do not want Glyodrin as a master. And no, I won't tell you why, so don't ask."

I pushed my plate away and paced over to Rowan. "It's just as Bree'on Chae said. If they'd known I had the Mother's Realm, nothing I said would have stopped them." I sighed. "Then I have little choice." I took Rowan's hand, feeling the bond, the veins of life that pulsed from my realm to her.

"You'll have to choose—" Hector stopped mid-thought. "What are you doing?"

"Resurrecting the Mother Tree, righting the wrong I did to Rowan. This will re-forge the alliance and give them a common purpose beyond revenge."

"Rodrick, you can't," Hector said.

"It's the only way."

Hector threw his plate into the pile of dishes, and Cassy gave a frightened squeak. "I'd hoped things would have gone differently. There is no way the Void hasn't contaminated the Mother Tree. Think about it. You had her realm within you when you met the Void. It set you free, knowing his priestesses held the last Spriggan. He must have felt your desire for redemption and banked on you coming to this conclusion."

I frowned, not understanding. "What are you saying?"

"If you resurrect the Mother Tree, she'll spread the Void throughout the whole world. Every flower, every blade of grass will carry its poison. You'll kill us all."

Armor clinked on the other side of the curtain—the guards likely rotating. "She's pure, I can feel it."

"Are you willing to take the risk? I'm not." Hector scrubbed his beard.

"Gods damn it. Rammed if I do, rammed if I don't."

"Yep, sewn up right and proper. There's one thing left to do: drink your face off." Hector slid the door back. "Valet, a bott—"

A pair of mandibles wrapped around his head and pulled him into the foyer.

Cassy screamed and fumbled with the crank on her crossbow. Fast as lightning, three Arachnids scuttled through the door. They were the size of sheep, pale as milk and glossy smooth. The first leapt on Cassy and stabbed her with its stinger. I pulled my dagger and stabbed it through the eye. Froth poured from Cassy's mouth, and she fell back convulsing. The other two rushed me. I slashed and danced, but one I hadn't seen dropped from the ceiling. Something stabbed my side, and the world went fuzzy.

WHEN I CAME BACK to myself, I was upside down and thousands of feet in the air, wrapped in tight cords. Branches whipped past so fast they'd cut. I was on the underside of the Mother Tree's great branches. To either side were hundreds of Arachnids. The canopy boiled with them. There were too many to count and at least a dozen different varieties. The one carrying me was huge, its woolly coat mottled gray and black. They all moved with an eerie coordination as if controlled by a single mind.

The allies' camp was dwindling fast. I'd been taken to the far side of the Al'veran. From this vantage, I could see the hole Khyber's weapon had bored through the Mother Tree. The heat had split her down the center. The weight of her limbs had pulled one half of the great tree to the ground, crushing everything for hundreds of miles.

Suddenly, my angle changed. The Arachnid rappelled

from a strand of silk that seemed too thin to hold its considerable bulk.

What little light peeked through the canopy illuminated an all-too-familiar cliffside with the Al'veran rolling along far below. The Arachnid slowed our descent and touched down noiselessly.

I struggled to free myself. The Arachnid snapped its mandibles just above my nose, its curved fangs dripping with yellow fluid.

All around me, the silvery outlines of Arachnids landed. Rowan was placed beside me. Her eyes blazed with hatred as she struggled and spat at them. She was flipped over, her face to the earth. Her captor huddled atop her, pinning her beneath its weight.

Every spare inch of space was taken up by Arachnids. They dangled from threads perched on tree limbs. Their multifaceted eyes fixed on the thing coming from the shadows.

Eericas emerged from the trees. His spear-like limbs carried a body as large as the prison transport. His hide was the glossy black of oil on water. Virulent red markings, with veins of cesspool green, laced his bulbous thorax.

He pawed the air with his fangs. My heart hammered, and I avoided making eye contact. I had no desire to experience the kind of pain such a glance would induce.

He rushed forwards, fangs poised to strike. Arachnids threw themselves out of the way. I kicked, but a woolly forelimb held me down. I braced for a bite that never came.

Eericas gave a shuddering rasp, and it took a moment to recognize it was laughter. He coiled as if to pounce, but instead, the shadows gathered around him. And he diminished in size, limbs retracting into his abdomen, transforming him into something resembling a man—though anything could have been hidden within the depths of his cloak.

Sitting on his haunches, he stretched out a clawed hand and slashed the cords that bound me. Mandibles unfolded from the shadow of the hood. Pestilent green fluid oozed from his fangs. I tried to shy away, but the spider held me. Eericas cocked his head. A broken branch announced someone's approach.

One of the spiders made a clacking noise.

"What is it, my darling?" Eericas asked.

It darted forwards and deposited a couple of bodies wrapped in spider's silk.

"For me?" Eericas asked in a voice like rusted hinges. He cut a hole, exposing Hector's face. "An Awakened," Eericas cooed. "My favorite." He ripped open the other. Cassy's eyes stared sightlessly from a pale gray face.

"You ramming bastards!"

My guard hoisted me into the air, then violently slammed me into the earth. As I caught my breath, a company of Fauldic soldiers entered the clearing. Their torches reflected in thousands of multifaceted eyes.

Justice's faceplate snarled as she saw me, and the pit of my stomach dropped. To her left was the huntsman. Melcor took a defensive position at her flank, his sword shining with the heat of a forge. To the Avatar's other side limped Judge Warwick, his robes charred and sword arm in a sling. Vanyard's and Hilstrad's squads were close behind.

The Fauldic came onto the clifftop, and the Arachnids reluctantly made way. They pawed the air and hissed to each other.

"Avatar?" Vanyard said.

"Stand sure, Sergeant. No rash moves," Justice ordered.

"I was admiring the view." Eericas swept an arm to take

in the Mother Tree. "I never thought I'd get the chance to dance upon her corpse. Life is wondrous, don't you agree?"

"I see you have what we requested," Justice said.

"Yes, the Arisen," Eericas confirmed, caressing my face with his talons. He hooked them under my chin and craned my neck. "Why would such a pathetic little creature be of such importance?"

"We agreed upon a price for this job. The shipment will arrive tomorrow."

"I don't think I asked for enough. Look at where you are. If those three knew an Avatar was up here, they would come after you personally." He tapped a talon in mock contemplation. "Why take such a risk? What could be so valuable?"

"We'll sweeten the deal," Justice said.

"How sweet?" Eericas asked.

She flicked her wrist at Vanyard. He stepped aside, revealing a makeshift sled. Taralin lay upon it, swords and spears jutting from his body.

"An Ascendant, plus what we have already agreed upon. This is far more than reasonable," Justice said.

A light breeze rustled the branches. The Arachnids swung gently. Eericas inhaled greedily. "I accept."

I was picked up and dropped at Melcor's feet, while another came in from the side and dragged Taralin to its master.

"This has been a profitable exchange." As Eericas knelt over Taralin, his mandibles uncoiled from the hood. He bit into him with a crunch like breaking pottery.

"Then perhaps you will be amenable to another opportunity?" asked Justice.

Eericas looked up, black elf blood dripping from his fangs. "What do you have in mind?"

"Below, our enemies are gathering for war, and I can strike them down just as we did the Mother Tree."

"Interesting. What do you want from me?" Eericas asked.

"Simply to take advantage of the situation. There'll be chaos. Kill as many men, elves, and Norven as you can."

Drunken laughter bounced over the Al'veran as if to punctuate the point. The allies weren't prepared. It would be a massacre. I sat up, ready to protest. The jagged point of Melcor's blade pressed against the base of my neck. I held my tongue.

"And what will I get in return?" Eericas asked.

Vanyard made an angry noise. Justice raised a hand for silence. "Our aid in driving this force from your kingdom."

"That was part of our original deal," Eericas hissed.

"No, we said we would cede you the land, not aid you in taking it," the Avatar said, a note of triumph in her voice.

"Tricky, tricky." Eericas laughed. "What do you say, my loves? Shall we feast?" A chorus of shuddering hisses and clacking mandibles echoed through the night. "Go, then. Do not be seen. Strike from the shadows, trap them, snare them, and we shall feed for months to come."

The spiders scurried up lines and over the cliff, while others scuttled into the darkness of the forest. They all left except the two largest, the one holding me and the other crouching over Rowan.

Eericas knelt back over Taralin and began to feed once more.

41

"Quickly. Clear away the leaves," Justice said. Acolytes tossed armfuls out of the way, exposing the rune.

"Don't do this," I pleaded.

Heat scorched my shoulders and I lurched away, the harsh light of Melcor's sword momentarily reflecting off the rune.

"Stay silent," Melcor snarled.

Justice ignored our exchange. "Warwick, are you ready?"

"No, Avatar," said the judge. "Come and look at this." The vortex had expanded, and near the center of it, the metal was wire thin. A pendant shaped like a spiral was embedded at the core. "See, there's something there."

"That should not be possible," Justice said.

"Nevertheless, here is the proof. A second rune."

"We tested the possibility?" asked Justice.

"The only way interference could have happened"— Warwick dropped his voice—"was if the second rune was layered."

"On that small a scale? Bring it for study."

"It'll take but a moment. Vanyard, tools?"

The veteran didn't reply. He stood at the edge of the cliff, a spear in one hand and a shield strapped to the other. He stared at the remains of the Mother Tree.

"Vanyard?" Justice called, louder this time.

His eyes were red, his features stern. Eericas looked up from his meal and hissed at the interruption.

"Vanyard." Justice spoke as if to a spooked horse. "Where are the judge's tools?"

Vanyard kicked a pack over the cliff. "At the bottom of the Al'veran, Avatar."

The judge jumped to his feet. "What? No, you fool."

"Damn it, Vanyard, why?" Justice's disappointment was palpable. "*You* were the traitor?"

"You whoreson! You took everything fro—" Melcor's blade slid along my throat, pressing against the angle of my jaw. My pulse hammered against the edge with mix of rage and fear. A hairbreadth and I'd bleed out. I froze, watching in impotent fury.

"It was Khyber who betrayed us all. He broke every tenet of his religion. The god-king I followed would never have murdered a comrade." He gestured to the Mother Tree's corpse.

Justice shook her head. "How could you do this to your people?"

"Those gods don't want to kill the civilians. They're coming to cut the heart out of the cancer." Vanyard raised his shield.

The pressure vanished from my neck as Melcor tossed a pack at the judge's feet. "Judge Anders's pack."

"Excellent," Warwick said, flipping open the pack and pulling out a torch and replacement rune.

A crossbow chunked. Warwick cried out, grabbing at a bolt protruding from his back.

Hilstrad backpedaled, working the crank. Warwick crumpled, his blood spilling onto the rune. Melcor whirled, taking a step toward the acolytes. Everyone drew steel.

"Stand down!" barked Justice.

No one obeyed.

"What a wonderful day," Eericas said, giddy as a schoolgirl.

A muffled series of snaps made everyone turn. The other Arachnid shrieked, its limbs spasming. Its abdomen exploded. Rowan tore free, her petals dripping with gore.

Her gaze locked on the acolytes and Justice standing over the ritual circle, which had killed her entire people. Cold fury poured down the bond.

"Rowan, there's too many, and they may still have imbue—"

Her rage banished me from her mind.

A deep rattle emanated from her. The petals of her flesh peeled back into a stiff red crest along her spine. She was skeletal, every angle jagged and barbed. Her eyes were glowing pits of amber fury. A shriek, like timber under pressure, escaped a beak lined with rows of splinters.

Rowan darted forward, raking at Eericas's face. The spider god dodged deftly. Vanyard used the distraction to throw his spear. A half foot of steel burst through Eericas's ribs. Not slowing, Rowan barreled into Justice, who used her momentum and threw the Spriggan right into Melcor. He tripped, falling atop the soldiers behind. They went down in a tangle of limbs. Rowan tore into them with reckless abandon, lost in a lust for vengeance.

Blood showered me. I involuntarily tried to drink, but Melcor's presence negated my draw. I crawled towards the nearest exposed flesh. Suddenly, Justice's boot flung me into the air, and I landed hard. Justice looked between me and Warwick's bag of tools. With a bellow of frustration, she picked up the torch and began cutting.

Vanyard was desperately trying to get to Eericas, but the last remaining Arachnid was preventing him. Big as an ox, it lunged, then bounced off the shield's imbued barrier. Vanyard struck with surgical precision, and a forelimb dangled uselessly.

I crawled over to Cassy and felt for her pulse. She was cold and clammy, but at my touch she groaned. A lump formed in the back of my throat, and I wiped at the wetness on my cheeks.

"A little help?" Hector struggled within his bonds.

"We have to stop Justice before she activates the rune." I ripped at the silk. Though hard and stringy, it tore like a cotton shirt. A few feet away, Eericas sucked in a breath and clawed at the spear in his back.

"First take Eericas's head," Hector said. "If he revives, we're done for."

Eericas wrenched the haft from his back. Two quick strides and my dagger was at his throat. Though the blade bit, the flesh healed in its wake.

"Drain him," Hector pressed urgently. "It's the only way."

The thirst swelled like a tidal wave, and I finally gave in. With a crunching pop, my teeth broke through his carapace. White-hot power poured into me, burning like acid. Every fiber of my soul screamed in revulsion at this wrongness. I wanted to pull away, but the thirst had control.

Talons raked a bone-deep slash across my back. With this much blood, it healed almost instantly. The tide was unreal, as if standing under a waterfall and drinking every drop.

Eericas gathered the shadows around him and changed.

I rode a giant spider. Eericas swept a back leg across his torso, knocking me off. The world spun. I struck the ground, a chunk of carapace still clutched in my teeth. A moment later, it crumbled to ash.

Eericas chittered with rage. Though his front leg was unable to support his weight, the wound was healing. I only had a second or two to strike. I let the thirst have its way. My bones elongated, teeth became fangs. Skin suddenly tough and dry as old boot leather, my flesh writhed as if corpse worms burrowed just under the surface.

I charged. Eericas rose on his hind legs, jabbing a spear-like forelimb at me. I dodged, raking him with razor-sharp nails. Green blood flowed. Movement registered out of the corner of my eye. I leaned back, barely missing the red-hot blade that would have cleaved me from shoulder to groin. Melcor drove a shoulder into me, and I tumbled to the ground.

"I'm glad I got to see the demon behind those eyes before you die." Melcor planted a boot on my chest. He spun his blade, point down. I clawed his leg. The heat of his sword seared my face and arms. A black glossy limb collided with his midriff, and Melcor cartwheeled toward the cliff.

Eericas hissed, fangs aiming for my face. I caught them, holding him off with all my strength. It wasn't enough. A whip of light lashed Eericas across one eye. He screeched, pawing at the wound.

I rolled out from under him and caught a glimpse of the Arachnid wrapping its legs around Vanyard and crushing him to its bulk. Vanyard's shield was reduced to splinters by its powerful jaws. Vanyard raised his sword overhead and buried it in the Arachnid's skull.

Justice cut the sabotaged rune out and cast it over the

cliff, then fitted the replacement. Blue sparks flew as she joined the metal. Rowan was lost behind a wall of Fauldic soldiers, their blades rising and falling ominously.

The change left me and my burns healed, but the strength, the prowess was gone, and everything felt a second too slow.

Melcor bellowed, heat shimmering from his blade. He whirled it over his head and charged. I cast around for a weapon but came up empty-handed.

Eericas reared, wrenching Hector's whip from his grip. He pulled his fiddle from his back and ran his fingers across the strings. Eericas was pushed back as though struck a physical blow. Hector played a flurry of notes, each sending a wave of crackling energy that made Eericas smoke and sizzle.

Justice stood, her work finished. She threw the tools from the rune and darted over to the soldiers, grabbed Hilstrad by the hair, and pulled her over to the rune.

Melcor was almost on top of me. I bit my hand, drawing blood. He swept his blade in an uppercut aimed to cleave me in two. A flow of green welled up from the bite.

I needed something to defend myself. The ice spike and club encased my forearms. I forced everything I had into the summons. My body reverberated as molten metal met ice. Steam billowed and the air filled with the hiss of quenching metal. Thankfully, my weapons held.

Melcor rained blows upon me. I ducked under a decapitating strike and hammered the club into his jaw. Blood poured down his chin. He smiled, breathing out a cloud of fire. I brought my weapons into a cross guard. A barrier formed, and the flames parted around me.

Melcor's blade descended in an overhead blow. I caught

it, though it forced me to my knees. His weight bore down, and the club shattered. He snarled in triumph. A bolt sprouted from his neck, and he choked in surprise. The half second was all I needed to slip under his guard and drive the spike into his heart. With a twist, I snapped off the blade, and Melcor collapsed.

Cassy was puffing and blowing as if she'd run a mile. She smiled wearily before slumping down, the Arachnid's poison doubling her over.

Lightning arched, and Justice stepped into the ritual circle. She pulled a vial from her belt pouch and smashed it on the rune. At the same time, Eericas shot a string of webbing, coating Hector's entire body.

Eericas leaped upon Hector, wrapping him in silk. Vanyard had climbed out from under the Arachnid and pulled his blade free. He signaled to me, pincer attack from behind.

"Oy, creeper. I've been dreaming of this moment for years. You're alone, and I'm gonna kill you for what you did to my people."

Eericas turned, still wrapping Hector with his back legs. "Little fly, you'll be reunited once I've taken your soul. I can't wait to show you how I've twisted them."

I cut my forearm on Melcor's blade. Green blood flowed freely. Not good. Allowing it to pool on the forest floor, I searched through the magic within my realm. I grasped the forest, the roots that bore through stone.

I darted forwards. Eericas spun. "Tricky. Tricky little fly." I backpedaled, pushing a thousand splinters through my veins. Eericas was nearly on me when the blood magic released. Roots erupted from the earth, impaling him. His legs curled and twitched. Hector hit the ground. Putrid blood flowed, and I dove into the puddle.

Raw energy flowed into me. With this power, I could become anything, summon anything. I could stop Khyber, protect Oppenfauld. With this much, I would slay all who stood in my path. None could defy me. I would sit on high amongst the gods and make them bow. I pulled away, my body trembling with ecstasy, heart heavy with self-loathing.

A spear sailed through the air and punched into the joint above Eericas's hind leg. Vanyard laughed wildly and threw another. Eericas desperately tried to push himself off the roots, but they were slick with blood.

Hector's arm broke through. A funny twang, like a wire under tension, echoed through the night. I looked up into a sea of glittering multifaceted eyes. The rune came to life, crackling with red lightning, Justice floating in its center.

"Vanyard!" I yelled, pointing up at the spiders. He went ashen. The joy of battle melted into resignation. "Cut him loose!"

Vanyard turned from me to Hector, then jogged over to him and dragged him over to Cassy's unconscious form.

I snatched a spear from the ground and leapt onto Eericas. My weight drove him farther down the roots. I stabbed the spear into his neck, but his flailing threw me off. Leaning into the spear, I tried to do as much damage as possible.

I hit the ground. Before I could recover, the Arachnids touched down. They rushed me, and I had to retreat, but their only interest was to save their master. They climbed underneath him, hoisting him with their bodies. As more and more piled on, those at the bottom were crushed.

An ethereal wind rose, as strong as a cyclone. It threatened to rip me from my flesh. Blood flowed up the roots and closed Eericas's wounds. The Arachnids wrapped a few lines around their god and lifted him into the canopy.

The wind died away, and I breathed a sigh of relief. The angry clicks of the Arachnids faded into the distance.

Vanyard made a rude gesture. "Bloody ramming goat bullock. Twenty gods damn years, and he ramming got away. AGAIN!"

42

A BEAM OF RED LIGHTNING, wide around as a barrel, burst from Justice's chest. It streaked toward the camp. Halfway there, it split into three jagged lines that angled wildly, yet unerringly found their prey. Lightning struck, flash burning everything within its radius. Earth and debris hurtled into the air. Fires sprang up. The camp devolved into a swarming anthill of chaos. A discordant cry of agony filled the air. The intensity of it threatened to peel the flesh from my bones.

"No!" Vanyard ran to his soldiers. Four or five had fallen upon their swords, giving their life's blood to fuel the rune. But not all. Hilstrad's and Nox's throats had been slit, and Jenkins was curled around a spear, the shaft protruding from his back.

"My queen!" Hector screamed and struck a note on his fiddle. A blast of solid air assaulted Justice, nearly knocking her from the rune. Her head whipped round, smoke pouring from her eyes. Her mouth opened, and lightning slammed Hector into the earth and plowed a furrow fifty feet long.

Cassy was thrown by the impact. She rolled, dirt and

leaves tangled in her hair. I wanted nothing more than to pull her to safety, but she might already be dead. If I didn't stop Justice, three gods would be slaughtered, and countless mortals would perish in the aftermath of their loss. This was bigger than one life, no matter how it hurt to turn away.

Vanyard jumped back. "Ramming hell."

I grabbed his shoulder. "We have to break the rune. You have any munitions?"

"At the bottom of the Al'veran." He pulled a spiral pendant from around his neck. "After the damage one of these stupid pieces of tin did to my country, there's no way I'm letting you use a grenade. The Spiral's priestess said this would stop Khyber. She lied! And the Mother Tree died anyway, and the world went to shit."

I snatched the pendant from him. Pure white light engulfed my hand, illuminating black filaments coiled through my flesh. "There's nothing else to ramming try." I tossed it onto the rune.

Justice redirected her beam from Hector and melted the pendant to slag. A shock wave hit, and the lightning cascading from her chest stuttered. Justice cried in pain, and with a monumental effort, she held on. The lightning redoubled as she focused her attention on killing the allies.

"Gods damn it. You made the bloody thing! How do we stop it?" Vanyard yelled.

"Help me with this." I held out my hands, and a few pommel strikes shattered the ice. I gripped Vanyard's sword and sliced open my palms, calling on the darkness within me. Cold death answered. It crept up my arm. A pearl of inky blackness formed. "I have to destroy it."

"Not with that. You'll tear Oppenfauld apart."

"There's no other way."

"Then you're no better than Khyber."

The Void bolt undulated above my palm. I could try one other thing, and if it backfired, the world would be free of the Void. I shaped the darkness into a shield, a disk of annihilation, and stepped into the beam.

I was pressed back a dozen feet. The Void nullified the lightning and was consequently consumed by it. I had to continually reinforce my shield or be overwhelmed.

I snatched a dagger from the ground, the effort costing me another few feet. Gritting my teeth, I plunged it into my shoulder. Blood flowed, and I forced the darkness from my veins. Smoke billowed from Justice. Earth crumbled out from under my heel. A quick check showed a thousand-foot drop. I struggled to hold my ground, but between the strain of summoning and the blood loss, I was burning through my new reserves frighteningly quick. My flesh was growing pale. I had been so arrogant, so sure I could take on the world. And all my perceived strength was burned away in no more than a minute.

Suddenly, strong hands were at my back. "Stand sure!" Vanyard pressed with all his strength. "This blade is not yet broken!"

Together we took a step.

Melcor loomed out of nowhere, his sword raised, his wounds healed.

"Wait!" I yelled. "Once Khyber dies, you'll be free. If he wins, you'll be a prisoner forever."

"You're a fool to think those three can take him. And with your soul, I will be." His sword came for my head. A blast of sound so powerful it formed a translucent wall shoved Melcor over the edge.

"Damnation," Vanyard swore, watching him tumble through the open air.

Blessedly, the torrent of energy flickered, finally dying away. Justice crumpled into a smoking pile.

I released the shield and pulled the knife from my shoulder. Virulent green blood dripped horizontally, reabsorbing into the wound. My burns and cuts began to close, but the skin regrew as a dark, glossy husk. Putting it out of my mind, I ran to Justice and rolled her onto her back, ignoring the fresh burns.

"Air," Justice gasped, clawing at her throat. I fumbled at the visor. The metal was warped, and it only rose part way. Justice sucked in a breath. What little flesh I could see was horribly burned. "Did we do it?" she asked.

My jaw worked, not knowing what to say.

"Melcor, is that you?" She tried to touch my face. "I can't see. Say something."

I stared pleadingly around. Vanyard was bowed in prayer. Hector was climbing to his feet. He looked to have been roasted over an open fire. Exposed bone and charred flesh made him a nightmare.

"Be still," I said.

"No." Her armor protested, yet she forced the visor open. Her left eye was the only recognizable part of her. "Damnation take you, traitor."

"I couldn't let it happen again. Killing them would cause the death of millions," I said.

"*Not* killing them will do the same. It'll just be our people who pay the butcher's bill instead of theirs. The fools gave us no choice." She groaned. "Listen to me—I sound like my father."

"Justice, please," I pressed.

"That's not my name."

"Then tell me."

She sucked in air as if through a straw. "You may wear

my father's face, but you're not him. He'd be ridiculing you for your weakness, your sentimentality. He wouldn't be trying to make amends or reconcile his *feelings*. He'd do the hard thing, the right thing."

"Then I'm glad he's dead," I replied firmly.

"Me too." She doubled over in a bout of coughing, then fumbled at her side. With a click, something dislodged from her armor. She thrust the sigil of the sword and shield into my face. Red and blue light forced me back.

"Back, demon. You will not have my soul," Justice wheezed, her one eye holding me as surely as a lance through the gut. Her breaths grew shallower, her eye unfocused, and she simply stopped. The Veil tore, a blue hand reached through, and they locked forearms. "Welcome home, child," Khyber said.

Justice smiled, all the hardness, the weight of the struggle, sloughed off. She was a woman, beautiful and noble, lovelier than her mother.

"I am so proud of you," Khyber said.

"Thank you... Father." Spectral tears spilled down her cheeks. Khyber took her in his arms, and they passed to the other side.

43

"MAY she guard the walls of Strothheim forevermore." Vanyard made the sign of the sword. No streamer of light followed his fingers. He clenched his fist and bowed his head.

I closed Justice's eye. This had been my child. Though I felt sorrow, her rejection stung more than the loss. I had no way to make amends. Did her sister feel the same? Was she even alive?

"I hope you find peace," I said softly.

Hector sat down heavily, cradling his instrument. Miraculously, his fiddle remained undamaged, despite his own grievous wounds.

"Is there something I can do?"

He held up a hand. "Keep your distance. I'm not myself right now."

Vanyard hurried over to the bodies of his men, searching for survivors. Rowan had been savage, but once she'd been dealt with, they had turned on each other. If Khyber's priesthood was this divided, the people of Oppenfauld had no hope. Vanyard looked over the carnage. He wiped the blood from his hand and marched back straight into the trees.

I gave Hector some space and knelt over Cassy. The hair draped over her mouth fluttered as she breathed, and a knot in my chest eased. I brushed the hair out of her face and her eyes opened.

"Hey, nice shot," I said.

"I was aiming for *you*." Cassy groaned.

I laughed, running a thumb over her cheek.

The hair on the back of my neck rose. Hector crawled over to the closest body and began to feed. The thirst told me to attack this rival. My hand trembled, the nails growing. I clenched my fist and forced the change back.

"Rodrick, I'm gonna pass out now."

"Hang in there, Cassy. I'll get you some help." But she was unconscious again. I scooped her up and carried her away from Hector.

A Spriggan's hand reached through the pile of corpses. Her life force flickered like a guttering candle. I set Cassy down and pulled the bodies aside. When I grabbed a broken branch, Rowan cried in pain. It was her arm. I carefully moved the last few body parts off. Half of her face was the person I remembered; the other half was what lay at her core. A cruel hardwood skeleton.

"Master," she said, all hints of madness gone. "Soon, I'll be free of you." She smiled.

I couldn't help but smile back. "And I of you. I hope you find your family on the other side."

"It was you," she said knowingly, "who took them from me."

"I am not that man anymore," I replied.

"Tell yourself that, if it assuages your guilt. It doesn't erase the deed. End it."

I hung my head. I probed the mental connection and prepared to cut the bond. "You and I could bring her back. Restore your people, save this world."

"The world can burn for all I care," Rowan said.

"Those armies down there came to fight for you, to get vengeance for you and your people. Some of the Fauldic soldiers turned on Khyber. They gave their lives to stop this injustice from happening again," I said. "Don't let their deaths be for nothing."

"I don't care what happens to the fleshlings. However, if my life can buy a second chance for the Spriggans, then I agree."

I took hold of the bond and dipped inside my realm. The Mother Tree shone, distant and pristine. Rowan was fading. Any moment she might slip away.

"Wait," Hector said. "You'll condemn us all." His words brought me halfway back. I was in both places at once.

"If I wait any longer, the chance will be lost," In my heart, I knew what I had to do.

I took hold of Rowan and channeled the Mother Tree through the bond. The Void clawed and snatched, trying to stow away. I held it back, knowing if even the slightest ounce of darkness slipped through, I'd condemn the world to a fate worse than death.

Rowan shuddered, creaking like a bough in the wind. A look of rapture came over her. Roots burst from her broken limbs, lifting her towards the sky.

"I can hear them," she laughed.

The more of the Mother I gave away, the more insistent the Void became. For a split second, I was fully within my realm. Trees were missing. The ice that had covered the lake was gone. Scars from my usage of blood magic, yet the wall of tentacles was unfazed. I'd expelled more of the

Void than anything else, and it appeared to have gotten stronger.

This place was mine, and it would bow to my will. I funneled fire from the sky and hurled it at the Void, burning away the groping tendrils. But nothing diminished the core. I erected a wall of Lyr'eris stone around the Void, willing it to be real. The Void raged within its new confines, but the barrier held. I forced the Mother Tree's essence through the bond, and her massive form blew away, sand in the wind.

I opened my eyes to the mortal world. She stood before me, beautiful and tall as a hundred-year oak. Rowan at the pinnacle of the trunk, her back arched like a dancer's, her arms and legs sprouting into branches with green and gold leaves.

The last few wisps of the Mother flowed into her. The wood grew around her body, becoming one with her reborn Mother.

I fell to my knees, weak and wretched. The sound of wind through leaves came from the tree before me, then swept out over the land.

"Look at that," Hector said, awed. His flesh was still raw but healing.

The trees upon the hill blossomed into full leaf, green and healthy as though all the weeks of spring happened in the span of a deep breath.

"You've done it, mate." Hector whooped and clapped me on the shoulder. Our eyes met, and he stepped back, bringing his fiddle to his chin. The thirst bucked and crashed within me as it never had before. I thought I had known what a fight was, yet this sent me curling into the fetal position.

"Stay back," I said.

Hector retreated as if I were a stalking cougar. I had no

idea just how much strength the Mother had lent me. Now that she was gone, I was being swept out to sea by a riptide.

Voices loud and clear approached the clifftop. I blocked them out. The struggle to remain myself was all-encompassing. The thirst cramped my insides. I couldn't fight this for long.

Hector knelt before the gods. As if from a distance, I heard their words.

"He stood in the path of Khyber's weapon?" Enris asked in disbelief.

"Yes, my lady, to protect you and the other gods," Hector said.

Zenos grunted. "A mighty act worthy of song."

"One act of heroism doesn't erase the threat he poses," Glyodrin added. rubbing at the scorch marks that criss-crossed his chest.

"Goat shit," Zenos said. "You're dangerous and hold great darkness at bay. Look at him. *Look!*" He pointed. "He just gave up the power of a goddess, and still he fights!"

"The damage he'd do if he broke would be catastrophic," Glyodrin said.

"I'll not repay his heroism with prejudice," Enris replied. "Should the day come when he must be slain, we will. Until then, he has earned my respect."

The gods approached, and the change rippled through me.

"There's no need to hide your face," Enris said compassionately. She held out her hand, and a crystal chalice formed above her outstretched palm. It filled with golden liquid, as radiant as the sun, yet soft and fragile as starlight. "Rodrick Corwyn, I grant you a measure of my grace. To help you walk the path and stave off the shadows."

Enris passed the chalice to Zenos. "We are ever at war

with the duality. The evil within constantly seeks to drag you under. Take this and never back down." What looked like mercury poured into the cup. The two colors stayed separate.

"I gift you a portion of what you sacrificed." A deep green light flowed into the cup. "I know what it is to be drained of a specific power. Not until it's gone do we understand what we have lost. May Cypress's blessing comfort your soul."

Enris pressed the chalice to my lips. "Drink."

I expected the rush of blood. Instead the tension eased. My mind cleared, and the thirst receded. Whatever they had granted me, it brought me back to myself.

"Better?" Glyodrin asked.

"Thank you," I said, the change releasing me.

Following a groan, an ivory hand reached for the sky. "Taralin!" Glyodrin exclaimed and rushed over.

"Anything else I should know?" Enris asked.

"Yes, lady. A Fauldic defector stands just over there," Hector said.

"Without his aid, I would have failed," I told them.

"Then we shall express our gratitude."

"And my friend," I said, pointing at Cassy. "She was poisoned by one of the Arachnids."

Zenos was at her side, his thick hands ripping a hole in her dress to expose the wound. "There are no eggs. She will live. Though in the days to come, she will wish it had been otherwise."

"And what will become of me?" I asked.

"Hector has asked to take you as an apprentice, something unheard of for an Arisen. Given what's at stake..."

The bard gave me a crooked half-smile.

Glyodrin returned, supporting Taralin with a shoulder.

"Come rest under her branches, my love. She will ease your pain."

"Can't we just go home? I really need to find someone to eat," Taralin said.

"We'll find you something." Glyodrin eased Taralin down.

"As you command," Taralin replied, squeezing his hand.

Enris caressed the Mother Tree. "There is hope for this world once more," she said. "Our alliance was forged from a common purpose, to protect the Mother Tree and the life flowing from her. Khyber took that from us. Now we have a second chance, and I don't need to tell either of you how rare that is. Join me, brothers"—she held out her hands —"and unite our realms once more."

Glyodrin took her hand. "My people are one with nature, and without her, all that sprouts from the earth will wither. I bond myself and my people to the protection of the Mother Tree."

Zenos's hands engulfed the others. "I renew my vow. I failed in duty once. Never again. We were complacent and selfish. Attending to our own lands, own people, and neglecting each other. Khyber and Enris protect against Lyria. Glyodrin defends Wyrm's Bane, while I hold the border with Flame Lands. If only we had heeded Khyber's warnings. Now I see them for what they were, signs of discontent. The dishonor stains my clans, and this cannot be borne. From now on, we four act as one."

The Mother's leaves rippled although no wind stirred. Satisfaction flowed through the bond. A branch reached down. Zenos plucked a cluster of red berries. He broke it into three, passing them to the other gods. As they chewed, a deep rumble came from the earth, the sound of roots breaking boulders. A war cry of the earth itself.

"The pact is re-forged, our purpose remade," Zenos cried, raising a fist to the sky. "Now, to vengeance."

"Vengeance!" Glyodrin clapped Zenos and Enris on the shoulders.

"The traitor will reap what he has sown." Enris's words were the whisper of steel parting silk.

I kept my face neutral as dread crashed over me. It was written on their faces. Oppenfauld would drown in a tide of blood.

In the back of my mind, Rowan cackled with manic rage. Nothing less than the complete eradication of the Fauldic would satisfy the resurrected Mother Tree.

GLOSSARY

<u>Acolyte:</u> Warrior priest of Kydaism.

<u>Ascendancy War:</u> The war between gods and demons on the mortal plane. They struggle to claim each other's spiritual realms (souls).

<u>Ascendant:</u> A returned who follows a moral code and makes mortal lives better. They lose the ability to change or shift, but they gain a greater control of their realm and magic.

<u>Aspect:</u> The nature of a god's power and their abilities. The Void: annihilation and fear. White Flame: Cleansing fire and redemption. Lyr'eris: Ice and tyranny. An Ascendant's aspect governs how they will interact with (and feed upon) mortals, whether they instill love or fear, if they will dominate or enrich their lives.

<u>Arisen:</u> A sentient being who has died and come back to life. They return a monster, with a thirst for blood and a hunger for souls.

<u>Astral Eclipse:</u> A tri-yearly cycle where Etheriouses ellipsis brings the planet into the Voids shadow. The Void obscures the light of the Ethereal Battle and without it, the soul shines through the body. Arisen, demons and common mortals are seen for what they truly are. The only safety is upon sanctified ground. To be outside or without the protection of a patron during an eclipse is certain death.

Avatar: High Priests of Khyber. There are seven. Each represents one of Khyber's virtues.

Awakened: An evolutionary step along the path of ascendancy. Achieved by claiming the souls of other returned and awakening one's nexus. They lose the ability to shift but gain greater control over their inner realm and the magic it holds.

Blood magic: By spilling blood, an Arisen, demon or Descendant can summon a portion of their realm and manifest it within the mortal plane. But only for a brief time.

Change: AKA Shift: An Arisen, demon or Descendant can change their physical form. They gain great strength and agility and physical resilience but become a monster.

Damnation: Khyber's Hell. A dark place full of mysterious beasts. If one is condemned to Damnation, they can fight their way to Strothheim and claim their redemption.

Demons: An Arisen who is willing to commit any crime to slake their thirst. Their body reflects the evil they've done. This path is quick and easy, and they gain great strength but lose control over their spiritual realms.

Descendant: A demon that has reached godhood.

Eericas: God-king of the Arachnids.

Wyrm: A Descendant of pestilence, it resides in the Far East. None have ever seen it, but its minions are only held at bay by the Wyrm's Bane.

Duality: A paradox within the heightenings. All individuals have two halves. Good and evil, discipline and chaos, violence and peace. The two halves of one's self are forever at war, and the more one side is constrained, the stronger it becomes. If anger is suppressed, the easier it will be to lose control, yet if chaos is given a free rein, guilt will flog you for your weakness. Finding a balance between one's two halves is a constant, impossible struggle.

Dun: Castle City

Ethereal Battle: A physical manifestation of the afterlife and an endless war between transcendent gods.

Faldaris: Capital of Oppenfauld.

Fauld: Keep or Castle.

God-king: A mortal god who controls a Nation. Typically worshiped by a religion.

God-queen: A mortal god who controls a Nation. Typically worshiped by a religion.

Heightening: Zenos's religion. A series of self-disciplines that allow one to achieve levels of physical and mental prowess far beyond the body's natural limitations. Achieved through years of study. The heightenings are integral to the Norvish way of life.

Huntsman: A position within the Fauldic Military yet outside the priesthood. A huntsman is tasked with slaying Arisen within Oppenfauld.

Hymnal: An order of wandering missionaries that uses song to spread Enris's religion. A minstrel who is also a missionary for Enris.

Imbuement: Enchantment.

Judge: Specialists, technicians, sappers, chemists, anchor of Khyber's faith.

Kydaist: An individual who follows Kydaism.

Kydaism: Khyber's religion, the religion of the sword and shield.

Mordrem blossom: A flower, extremely poisonous.

Mortal Gods: Kings and queens of the mortal plane.

Enris: God-queen of Mir'eve. The Crystal Lady. Her aspects are music, drunken revel, art, feasting and sex.

Khyber: God-king of Oppenfauld. Lord of the sword and shield, ruler of Strothheim and Damnation.

Glyodrin: God-king of Illuvand. Lord of moon and star.

Zenos: He who leads by example. Chieftain of all, and greatest of warriors.

Mother Tree: God-queen of nature. She who gives life to all. By her grace are our bellies filled.

Nations: See map.

Lyria: Home of the Myi'eshans

Oppenfauld.

Planes of Fangmar.

Mothers Veil.

Mir'eve.

Illuvand.

Wyrm's Waste.

Flame Lands.

Node: Once a realm has been consumed, it becomes a Node. It fills one of the slots that surround the victor's Nexus. An Arisen has to fill seven slots to Awaken.

Nexus: The heart of a returned spiritual realm. A fragment of the afterlife brought back from the Neather Realms.

Neather Realms: The afterlife. Everything on the other side of the veil, not just the Ethereal Battle.

Place of power: A well spring of energies within the mortal plane. Gods and demons can tap into that power by connecting their spiritual realm to it.

Physic: Medics or doctors.

Races:

Arachnids: A race of sentient spiders created by Eericas.

Humans: Mankind.

Norven: Nine to thirteen-foot tall humanoids. Their

hides are covered with short tan fur and densely muscled. A tribal society based on honor and self-discipline.

Ivory Elves: As a species, they are as beautiful as a porcelain doll. Every individual is nearly identical in appearance, except for variations between the genders. Long ears that rise above the crown of the head and a plated exoskeleton with serrated ridges that run from joint to joint.

Spriggan: A species of sentient flowers.

Myi'eshan: Humans that live in the frozen north and have devoted their souls to Lyr'eris.

Realms: Used in multiple contexts. A spiritual or physical place owned by a returned.

Returned: Any being who has come back from the afterlife. Arisen, Demon, Ascendant, Descendant or god.

Rune: The language of faith. Holy symbols written by a priest. This allows them to cast spells specific to their deity.

Sanctified ground: A building or place that has been blessed in the name of a god or demon.

Scrivener: Scribes, administrative staff or clerk.

Shard: A piece of a broken planet.

Spiral: The galaxy, with the Ethereal Battle at the center. Its gravitational pull draws the Mortal Realms (solar systems) into its core, much like water flowing down a drain.

Spiritual Realm: The afterlife that grows within a god of the mortal plane.

Strothheim: Khyber's spiritual realm, (Heaven) a great fortress, built to withstand the Ethereal Battle.

Sundering: When a planet (Mortal Realm) reaches the Spiral's core, it is torn apart. The pieces are known as shards.

Transcend: If a returned has acquired enough power, they can ascend to the Ethereal Battle before the sundering.

The path of ascendancy: The struggle to attain greater power without being corrupted in the process.

Threshold: a barrier that surrounds a mortal's dwelling. Arisen and demons cannot pass so long as the ground is sanctified.

Transcendent: A god who has transcended to the Ethereal Battle.

Transcendent gods:

Cypress: Goddess of Nature. All that is green and good springs from her.

Lyr'eris: Goddess of winter, cruel, cold and hard. Her only rule is to survive and fight another day.

Void: A great emptiness that seeks to consume all within the Spiral.

White Flame: God of the consuming fire. He who is pure and good, he who will burn away your transgressions and welcome you into his embrace.

Tenet: The principles, morals and rules of a religion.

Veil: the curtain between life and death, between the Mortal Realm and the Neather Realms.

Wyrm's Bane: a great wall/cliff that separates Illuvand from Wyrm's waste.

PLEASE RATE AND REVIEW

Enjoy the book?
An honest review will make a big difference.

As an indie author, my success is at your fingertips.
So, if you could find the time to leave a review,
it will help me share Etherious with others.
Either way, thank you for reading.

You can find me at colinjdcrooks.com
And if you feel like reaching out, email me at
colin@colinjdcrooks.com.

I would love to hear from you.

Stand sure.

C.

Colin J.D. Crooks
P.O. Box 231
Cumberland B.C. V0R 1S0
Canada
colin@colinjdcrooks.com

First edition Cover art by Daniel Schmelling

Editing by Hot Tree Editing

Editing by Hannah Sullivan

Proofreading by Sheila L. Hutchison

Illustration by Hannah Rodgers

Pick up the exclusive prequel novella
The Shards of Etherious: Eclipse

FOR FREE at
colinjdcrooks.com
when you sign up for the mailing list.

———

If I don't find a sacrifice, I'll die. My goddess will abandon me to face the creatures that stalk the eclipse unless I pay for her protection with blood.

Mother's right. I'm useless. I can't even slaughter a chicken without hating myself. I pray for Lyr'eris to fill my soul with her Frozen Fire, but no matter how hard I try, my heart remains soft.

I have no choice. I must kill, or suffer a fate worse than death. If only I could silence the voice that tells me murder is wrong.

ABOUT THE AUTHOR

Colin was born at 12:01 a.m. Outside a blizzard howled, and his nurse dropped a chemical on the poor infant's face, dying him a dusky blue. Thankfully, there was no lasting visual damage ...

His early childhood was spent sliding down snowdrifts and adhering his tongue to frozen poles in Saskatchewan prairies. His family migrated across Canada to where he grew up in Invermere, British Columbia.

He began writing in grade four, with little plays he and his classmates inflicted upon their teacher.

Colin has always had a voracious appetite for Sci-Fi and Fantasy. He sat down and read the Lord of the Rings trilogy from cover to cover ... three times in a row. Tolkien taught him to read, and ever since he's devoured the works of Robert Jordan, David Farland, Steven Erikson, Mark Lawrence, Brandon Sanderson, and so many more.

He lives on Vancouver Island, Canada, and no matter what anyone tells you, it's not paradise. So definitely don't come, you won't like it.

Colin's other interests include Karate, gaming of any sort, theater, and music. But what really gives his life meaning is his ever-patient bombshell of a wife and two ferocious daughters.

So far he's been quick enough to keep all his fingers, but only time will tell ...